THE TWISTED ONES

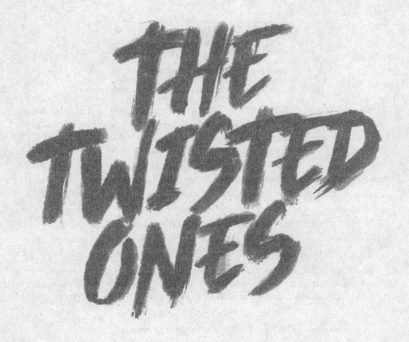

THE TWISTED ONES

T. KINGFISHER

SAGA PRESS

LONDON SYDNEY **NEW YORK** TORONTO NEW DELHI

SAGA PRESS

AN IMPRINT OF SIMON & SCHUSTER, INC.

1230 AVENUE OF THE AMERICAS, NEW YORK, NEW YORK 10020

SAGA PRESS and colophon are trademarks of Simon & Schuster, Inc.

For information about special discounts for bulk purchases, please contact Simon & Schuster Special Sales at 1-866-506-1949 or business@simonandschuster.com.

The Simon & Schuster Speakers Bureau can bring authors to your live event. For more information or to book an event, contact the Simon & Schuster Speakers Bureau at 1-866-248-3049 or visit our website at www.simonspeakers.com.

Interior design by Hilary Zarycky

The text for this book was set in Electra.

Manufactured in the United States of America

First Saga Press trade paperback edition October 2019

11 13 15 17 19 20 18 16 14 12

Library of Congress Cataloging-in-Publication Data

Names: Kingfisher, T., author.

Title: The twisted ones / T. Kingfisher.

Description: First Saga Press paperback edition. | New York : Saga Press, an imprint of Simon & Schuster, Inc., [2019]

Identifiers: LCCN 2018034136| ISBN 9781534429567 (trade pbk.) | ISBN 9781534429574 (hardcover) | ISBN 9781534429581 (ebook)

Subjects: | GSAFD: Horror fiction.

Classification: LCC PS3611.I597 T85 2019 | DDC 813/.6—dc23 LC record available at https://lccn.loc.gov/2018034136

ISBN 978-1-5344-2956-7 (pbk)
ISBN 978-1-5344-2957-4 (hardcover)
ISBN 978-1-5344-2958-1 (ebook)

For my own two daft hounds

THE TWISTED ONES

1

I am going to try to start at the beginning, even though I know you won't believe me.

It's okay. I wouldn't believe me either. Everything I have to say sounds completely barking mad. I've run it through my mind over and over, trying to find a way to turn it around so that it all sounds quite normal and sensible, and of course there isn't one.

I'm not writing this to be believed, or even to be read. You won't find me at a book festival, at a little table with a flapping tarp over it, making desperate eye contact with passersby—"Want to read a true story of alien abduction? Want to know the secrets of the universe? Would you like to find out the real truth about the transmigration of souls?" I won't shove a glossy, overpriced book with badly photoshopped cover art at you, and you won't have to suffer through my lack of a proofreader.

Truth is, I don't even know who *you* are.

Maybe you're me. Maybe I'm just writing this to get it all out of my head, so that I can stop thinking about it. That seems likely.

All right. I meant to start at the beginning, and already I started babbling about disclaimers and people writing books about crystal power and the secrets hidden in the Nazca Lines.

Let me start again.

My name's Melissa, but my friends call me Mouse. I can't remember how that started. I think I was in grade school. I'm a freelance editor. I turn decent books into decently readable books and hopeless books into hopeless books with better grammar.

It's a living.

None of that's particularly relevant. The important bit to know is that my grandfather died before I was born, and my grandmother remarried a man named Frederick Cotgrave.

Honestly, I don't know how she managed to get married once, let alone twice. My grandmother was a nasty, vicious woman. Mean as a snake, as my aunt Kate used to say, which is pretty unkind to snakes. Snakes just want to be left alone. My grandmother used to call relatives up to tell them it served them right when their dog died. She was born unkind and grad-uated to cruel early.

But I guess a lot of cruel people can pretend to be sweet when it suits them. She married Cotgrave and they lived together for twenty or thirty years, until he died. Every time I went over there, she was snipping at him—snip, snip, snip, like her tongue was pruning shears and she was slicing off bits for fun. He never said anything, just sat there and read the paper and took it.

I never did figure it out. These days, when we know a lot more about abuse, I like to think I'd speak up, say something, ask him if he was okay. But then again, people get into relationships and sometimes they stay there, and for all I know, he got something out of it that the rest of us weren't privy to.

Anyway, I was a kid for most of it, so it just seemed normal. He was my . . . stepgrandfather? Grandfather-in-law? I'm not sure which.

That bit galls me to no end. I feel like if he'd been my real grandfather, I would have . . . oh, not *deserved* what happened, maybe, but owned it a little. Even if Cotgrave and I had a relationship like a granddad and his granddaughter, I'd have said, okay, maybe I owe him this. But it's not like he ever took me fishing or taught me how to fix a car engine or whatever bullshit grandfathers are supposed to do. (I don't know. I didn't have one on the other side either. My maternal grandmother was a widow, but she didn't remarry and she spent a lot of time giving money to televangelists and telling other people about Jesus. She also believed in crystal power and aliens, come to think of it, pretty much the same way she believed in Jesus, and never saw any contradiction in the two. People are complicated.)

All I remember about Cotgrave was an old man with no hair, reading the paper and getting snipped at. My dad said he could play a really cutthroat game of cribbage. Maybe that's why my grandmother wanted to marry him, for his sexy cribbage game. Hell if I know.

The only other thing I remember about him was the sound of a typewriter. He couldn't type very fast, but I'd hear the noise from his "study," which was a back bedroom with ratty carpet. *Clack. Clack. Plonk. Clack.* Screech of carriage return. *Clack.*

I don't know when or how he died. I was in college and dead broke and nobody thought I'd come back for the funeral. We weren't big on funerals in my family. I know some families have these massive orgies of grief, where all the third cousins come back and sob over the casket, but we're not like that. Everybody gets cremated and then somebody takes the ashes, and after they've sat around on the mantelpiece long enough to get creepy, they get dumped in the ocean, and that's the end of that.

Cotgrave had a funeral, I guess, or a memorial service or something. Aunt Kate told me that a bunch of weird people showed up. "Such odd people," she said. "I think he might have been in one of those societies. You know, like the Elks or the Freemasons or whatever. They weren't rude, just odd. Your grandmother was pissed."

"Grandma's always pissed."

"Well, you aren't wrong."

Now, of course, I wish I'd known more about the odd people. But I doubt Kate knew anything. She probably talked to all of them and got their life story—she had that ability—but she would have forgotten it as soon as she heard it. Kate was a wonderful sounding board, because she had a memory like a sieve. You could tell her anything you wanted in confidence, and odds were good she wouldn't remember it an hour later. I lived with Aunt Kate after Mom died, and she really did her best to remember things like doctor visits and parent-teacher conferences, but she wasn't always great about that either.

Anyway, fast-forward a decade and some change later, and my grandmother finally died. She was a hundred and one. There's a line of poetry I always think of, though I can't remember who said it. "The good die first / and they whose hearts are dry as summer dust / burn to the socket."

Grandma burned to the socket, all right. I didn't go to that funeral, either. Actually, I don't think there was one. Dad didn't have the energy anymore. He wasn't dying or anything, but he was old—he'd been over forty when I was born, and he was eighty-one now—and he just couldn't deal with it.

"Not much point, is there?" he said on the phone. "The only reason anyone would show up was to make sure she was actually dead."

I laughed. Dad didn't have any illusions about his mother. I still remember when I was young and Mom had just died and he'd asked Grandma to babysit. I marched in that evening and crawled into his lap and informed him that she was mean and I didn't like her at all.

In another family, I might have been told that I loved my grandmother and was a naughty child. But my father only sighed and rubbed his forehead and said that yes, he knew what she was like, but he didn't have any other options. He took me to the library that weekend so that I could read in my room, and after a few months of that, I went to live with Aunt Kate.

After I'd finished laughing—not that it was funny, but it was true—I stayed on the line and listened to Dad breathe too hard. His lungs were probably going to be what killed him. They were only a little creaky right now, but you could hear it coming, a rasp down at the bottom that was going to turn into emphysema or pneumonia or just erupt one day into full-blown stage-four lung cancer, no matter how many times the doctors swore that he was clear.

"Her house has been locked up for two years," he said finally. "Mouse, I can't handle it. I hate to ask. . . . It's a shit job, and I know it. I think there's a storage unit too. Somebody's gotta clear them out."

"Sure," I said, doing frantic mental math about the projects I was working on and how soon I could wrap them up. "Okay. I'll go down."

"You sure? It'll be a mess."

"It's okay."

Dad never asked me for anything, which is why I would have done anything for him.

He sighed. "If there's anything worth keeping, keep it, or sell it and keep the money. I just want it . . . dealt with."

"Are you planning on selling the house?"

He made a short little barking sound that was a laugh or a cough or halfway between the two. "I will if it's in any condition to sell. It wasn't good when we put her in the home. It might be really bad. If you get in and it's a disaster, tell me and I'll pay for contractors to go in and strip the place down to studs."

I nodded on the other end of the line. He couldn't see me, but he could still probably guess. Dad and I had talked on the phone every week since I went to live with Aunt Kate, even in the days when that meant he was paying through the nose for long distance. To this day I think we're still more comfortable talking on the phone than in person.

Gah. I don't know why I'm telling you all these details. None of this matters, except maybe the odd people at the funeral.

I wish I knew if there was some reason to write all this down—if including every little detail will make for a better exorcism of the events from my mind, or if I'm just stalling to avoid getting to the hard parts. Like the stones.

I still don't know how I'm going to explain about the stones.

But I don't have to write about those just yet, so I'll just hope that my subconscious knows what it's doing.

One of the ironies of this situation is that I actually remember thinking, *Well, the old bat did me a favor at last.*

It was a good time for me to get out of Pittsburgh. I'd had a relationship end rather badly, and—oh, you know how it is. You're gritting your teeth when you see them together in public and insisting that you're still friends, while thinking *you cheating sonofabitch* behind your eyes and you *know* that there's a very good chance that you're going to start behaving badly.

So I put my dog in the truck and packed up a suitcase full of clothes, asked my aunt Kate to keep an eye on the house, and drove down to North Carolina.

It's a long drive. It's pretty, actually, if you go through West Virginia, but of course then you're in West Virginia. Lots of deep mountain "hollers," and I guess the etymologists are still fighting over whether the word comes from *hollow*, which would make sense, or *hollerin'*, which is a folk-art form where people yodel at one another.

I stopped regularly, both because I was drinking a lot of coffee and to take Bongo out. Bongo's a redbone coonhound, and he was named after the antelope, not the drum. They're the same color, and if you've ever seen a coonhound run, they bound like an antelope, hence, Bongo.

I have had to explain this more times than I can count.

Bongo's a rescue. I got him as an adult and he's starting to go a bit white around the muzzle now. He's not that smart, but he can detect if a squirrel passed by at any point in the last millennium. There's a tree in the backyard that he chased a possum up once, and he has visited it faithfully every day for the last two years, on the off chance that the possum has come back.

I have no idea what he'd actually do if he caught a possum— lick it to death, probably. Coonhounds usually get dumped when they turn out not to be very good hunters. Bongo is an excellent watchdog, by which I mean that he will watch very alertly as the serial killer breaks into the house and skins me.

But if the UPS guy ever tries to put one over on us, Bongo's on the case. If dogs had religion, Satan would be the UPS guy.

(Yes, I own a hound dog and a pickup truck. No, I don't have a gun rack on it. I fired a BB gun once in Girl Scouts. It went *bang* and made my hands hurt and that was the end of that.)

Anyway. It's technically a ten-hour drive, but it takes about twelve when you have a dog and an overactive bladder. We ate at drive-throughs. Bongo got a cheeseburger, which made him think that he was in heaven. (It seems very unlikely that my vet will ever read this, but just in case, this was highly unusual and I do not actually feed him scraps from the table on a regular basis.)

I stayed at a motel that night. I didn't want to face whatever might be in my grandmother's house—squatters, or hoarding, or feral cats, or whatever—after a long drive. Dad said he'd had the power turned back on. No Internet, but that's why God invented cellular data plans.

I wish I could remember what that night was like. I think it was the last one where I was standing over here, with you, on the normal side, and not over there, in that other place, with the white people and the stones and the effigies. And Cotgrave, of course.

But I don't remember it. It was just one more generic night at a motel. Bongo probably started the night on the other bed, then oozed over and flopped onto my feet, but that's more because I know what Bongo's like than because I remember it. (He's flopped over my feet right now, as I'm typing. Occasionally he looks up sadly at me. It's a lie; he's happy as long as he gets fed and people pet him. I wish I were a dog. One of the simple ones, like hounds. Border collies are too complicated. I suspect if I had owned a border collie, this story would have a very different ending, and I probably would not have been around to type it up. But I had Bongo, and he saved our lives because he is simple and made of nose.)

I'm getting ahead of myself again. I'm sorry.

The next morning, I got up and went to go see what kind of mess my grandmother had left behind.

2

"Oh shit," I said.

I said it a couple of times. There was no human around to hear me.

Then I let the screen door slam shut and turned around and sat down on the steps of the deck.

Grandma had lived about thirty minutes out of Pondsboro, which is southwest of Pittsboro, which is northwest of Goldsboro, because nobody in the late 1700s could think of an original name to save their lives.

North Carolina's a weird state, because there are all these roads that are framed by trees, and so you literally do not know how remote the area is. You're just driving through trees. The woods, once you cut them down, grow up again in a dense tangle of kudzu and buckthorn and honeysuckle and loblolly pines. You can't see through them. At any given moment, you could be surrounded by a thousand acres of uninhabited woods, or you could be thirty feet from a business park full of IT professionals. There's no way to tell.

Get out around Pondsboro, and you're more likely to be near the thousand acres of woods. There's some weird little dips in the landscape—not full hills exactly and nothing you'd call a holler, but things fold over on themselves and wrinkle up and you get weird little bluffs cut by things that are a *creek* in Pittsburgh and a *crick* down here. (I usually just call it a stream to save argument.)

Grandma's house hadn't been that remote when she'd bought it. There had been a couple of farm families nearby and a pack of hippies across the road. But people left the farm for the city, and the pastures grew up into the tangle of woods I mentioned before, and the hippies got old and most of the kids moved out. I saw a car parked over there when I drove up, but that doesn't mean anything in the South. It wasn't up on blocks, though, so maybe someone was still living there.

She'd had nothing kind to say about the hippies, but that was no surprise.

I'd passed one or two trailers on the way up, and there might be more back in the woods. For all I know, I could be surrounded by people.

Sitting on a dead woman's porch, though, I didn't much feel like it. I felt like the only other living person on earth was my dad, up north, and the world was empty except for the two of us who had to deal with what my grandmother had left behind.

Bongo was still in the truck. He stuck his head out the window and whined.

I sighed.

I haven't described the house yet, have I? I probably should.

It was a big old Southern rambler, with a red tin roof. The tin roof was in good shape and the walls were solid, but the white paint was starting to wear off. You could see bits of wood under it. The wraparound porch was weathered gray wood and the steps creaked when I walked on them. There was a carport, but no garage. Somebody had filled the back of the carport with firewood a long time ago. The whole carport had slumped like a badly made cake. I didn't even think about parking my truck in it.

The underside of the porch roof was painted pale blue. "Haint blue," they call it. The theory is that if a ghost comes up to the door, it'll look up and see the blue ceiling and think it's the sky, and drift up into it. I don't know how that's supposed to work. But I've also heard that it's supposed to fool wasps the same way, so maybe wasps and ghosts are getting muddled up there. You don't want either nesting in the porch, anyhow.

Because it's the South, there was a thin layer of green algae on all the vinyl surfaces, around the edges of the windows and whatnot. There were long squiggly lines etched through the green, where the slugs had crawled at night. There's not much you can do about either one, except scrub things off with bleach occasionally.

Nobody had been through here with bleach for a long time.

The porch was covered in all the usual yardwork detritus—a rake and a trowel and a faded bag of fertilizer granules. An old pair of gloves lay discarded on the rocker. (Of course there was a rocking chair. I told you we were in the South.) Everything was tied together with ropes of cobwebs. The rake handle was practically glued to the porch supports. It was one of the ones with a hollow metal handle, and there was a big web right around the end, which meant that there was a spider living in the handle.

I made a mental note to buy a new rake. That one belonged to the spider now.

None of this was why I'd started swearing.

I swore because when I unlocked the front door and opened up the house, the light fell on a stack of newspapers.

Behind it was another stack of newspapers. Behind that was another stack. They were tied up neatly with string, and there was a pile of magazines next to that, and another pile, and another, and *oh shit Grandma was a hoarder.*

I took a deep breath and scrubbed my face with my hands.

Maybe it wasn't as bad as I feared. Maybe it was just one room.

It's never just one room, my brain said, and of course it isn't, but maybe just this once . . .

Yeah, no. It wasn't just one room.

It wasn't . . . It wasn't *awful.* She didn't collect cats, thank God, so the house hadn't turned into one of those horrible biohazards with urine on every surface and burying beetles scuttling under the furniture. And she wasn't the sort of person who hoarded food, so there wasn't two-year-old garbage everywhere. Dad had taken the trash out when he took her to the home, and then he'd come back and emptied out the refrigerator.

He hadn't defrosted the freezer. I could tell by the dried

circle of water stains on the floor, where it had leaked out when the power was shut off. But honestly, if you have to take your ninety-nine-year-old mother out of her house and put her in a home while she's calling you every name in the book, I'll cut you some slack on remembering the freezer.

(He never said that she called him every name in the book. I'm just assuming on this one.)

Still, it could have been worse.

The newspapers were piled up and magazines were stacked five feet high, but you could still get to the living room furniture. There were places to sit. When I flipped the light on, it looked like a very cluttered room, not like an alien topography.

The place was a terrible firetrap, though. All that paper everywhere. It was a miracle Grandma hadn't burned the place down by accident.

(Oh God, if only! I don't wish even an evil old bat like her to die by fire, truly I don't, but if she could have passed peacefully in her sleep and then the house burned down a couple of hours later, that would have been fine. And I'd still be able to sleep at night.)

The hoard was somewhat organized, I'll give her that. I went from room to room, listening to the floorboards creak. There were narrow paths between the stacks. Magazines and newspapers in the living room, Tupperware and bags full of other bags in the kitchen.

It got worse as I got farther back in the house, though. The bathroom was a jumble of ancient shampoo bottles and body lotions with the caps melted on. The toilet . . . well, pray God the well pump had survived the years of inactivity without locking up.

The stairs to the second story were completely jammed with garbage bags. I prodded one with my foot. The contents moved like cloth but smelled like mice.

One of the closet doors was wedged open. The inside was a solid block of Christmas decorations, old coats, and unlabeled white jugs. The tiny bit of floor that I could see had a white crust over it where the jugs had leaked.

There were three closed doors off the hallway that probably led to bedrooms. I had originally been planning on sleeping in one of those bedrooms, but Christ only knew what was being stored in them.

The whole place stank of must and mice and silence.

Bongo barked. The noise jerked me out of my increasing despair, and I went back outside. It was an overcast day, but the sky seemed very bright.

I let Bongo out of the truck and grabbed his leash. You can't let coonhounds off the leash, not ever. They'll smell a rabbit and wind up in the next county. I owned more ropes and harnesses and tie-outs and carabiners than a dedicated bondage enthusiast.

(Okay, okay, fine, I've heard of dog owners who have hounds that are so responsive that they will heel beautifully with no lead at all. Those are smarter owners than me and smarter dogs than Bongo. But we do fine by each other, and that's the important thing.)

Bongo went sniffing and snuffling around the edge of the porch, over into the bushes, back to the porch. I let him follow his nose. I didn't have anywhere to go and I didn't want to open one of those bedroom doors before I absolutely had to.

We went over to the carport. The woodpile in the back was probably at least 80 percent spiders at this point, and shared space with a generator that dated from the Nixon administration. I looked up the side of the house, to the windows on the upper story, and I could see something pressed against them—boxes, maybe, or furniture.

Two stories' worth of *stuff*. I let out a heartfelt groan, and Bongo looked back to make sure he wasn't doing anything wrong.

"It's not you," I told him. "You're fine."

He peed on the woodpile by way of agreement and ambled around the back of the house.

The porch wrapped clear around to the back, on three sides. The back section was screened off to keep bugs out, but there were holes in the screen where something had gotten in.

Bongo went immediately on alert, which probably meant that the holes were from squirrels.

Trees pressed in on three sides of the garden: loblolly pine and pin oak and tulip tree. (Aunt Kate is a botanist. When I was growing up, she would constantly interrupt herself to reel off the names of passing plants. As a result, I can follow extremely fractured conversations and I also know common trees on sight the way most people know dog breeds.) There were some saplings making inroads around the edges, and the grass had grown high and rank in sunny spots. The shrubbery was too dense to walk through in most places, but the right-hand corner, under the oak, was nothing but dead leaves. The woods behind it hadn't been cleared recently, because I could see quite a way back there, before a stand of holly trees blocked the view.

Mostly I saw even more dead leaves and a couple of large rocks. Not exciting for anyone, except possibly Aunt Kate.

The backyard had contained a garden at some point, and bits of the deer fence were still there. The fence posts leaned drunkenly, with chicken wire bunched up between them. Mint and oregano had run riot everywhere, and every step we took kicked up a delicious smell.

I had a strong urge to pull some of the weeds, but I wasn't here to garden. Pity. I might have enjoyed putting the garden to rights. More than I would enjoy excavating the house, anyhow.

How had I not known she was a hoarder?

I'd only been a kid when I'd visited, but kids remember things. There hadn't been the piles of newspaper then. The counters in the kitchen had appliances, not stacks of Tupperware.

A memory surfaced of Grandma washing Ziploc bags and drying them with a hair dryer. Dad saying, "She grew up during the Depression, Mouse. A lot of folks who lived through that have a hard time throwing anything away."

Well. The signs had been there. And sometime in the last decade or two, she'd just . . . gone over the edge.

I pulled out my phone and looked at it, thinking of calling Dad. He could have warned me.

He did say it was a mess. And that it was bad.

Yeah, but his definition of a mess and mine are apparently a lot different!

There was no cell signal. I cursed my carrier and shoved the phone back in my pocket.

If you're thinking that she was going mad in the house alone for forty years, like Miss Havisham, don't. Dad paid for caregivers, and he went down to visit her fairly regularly when he was still able to get around. But the caregivers got harder and harder to find as she drove them off, and eventually there was just the woman who took her into town.

Maybe that's when it got bad. Maybe that woman didn't go into the house. Maybe nobody'd known the state the place was in.

Bongo wanted to go under the porch steps. "No, buddy," I said, leading him past. He looked longingly at the hollow under the stairs. There might be a possum he could lick!

"I know," I said. "I'm the worst."

We finished our circle around the house. There was a set of double doors that probably led down to a root cellar. Jesus. Who knew what I'd find down there?

Bongo's tail was wagging good-naturedly as we finished the circuit. One of his ears had flipped over along the way.

"Let me fix your ear. . . ." More wagging.

I tied him out to the railing on the front steps. He could probably find a way to twist the leash around, but I wasn't going to be more than thirty or forty feet away. And anyway, I suspected that I'd be coming out of the house frequently, just to be surrounded by clean air instead of junk.

He flumped down on the porch and looked tragically at me. I gave him a chew toy, and he began gnawing on it and making terrible canine faces of pleasure.

You know, thinking about it now, if Bongo had been scared of the house, I might have left. I was right on the edge. I could have called Dad and said it was beyond my ability, it was too full, it was a mess, and he should just hire one of those companies that deal with hoarder houses and get them to drag it all to a landfill.

But Bongo thought the place was grand. There were things to sniff! There might be squirrels! And I hadn't seen anything terrible yet, just *stuff*. Nothing I couldn't fix with a couple hundred garbage bags and directions to the county dump.

I had a pickup truck. I had a lot of irritation at my recent ex to work out, ideally with manual labor. I might as well give it a try.

Which just goes to show that my dog and I were both as sensitive to that other world as rocks, and probably that we deserve each other.

———————

I went back into town to get garbage bags and a couple pairs of sturdy gloves. Pondsboro actually has a little downtown. They'd love to be like Southern Pines, two hours away, which is so quaint it makes your teeth hurt. The rich country-club people all go there to spend money, so you can have antique stores instead of junk shops and a really good independent bookstore and little shops that sell nothing but scented candles and fancy doorknobs.

Southern Pines is in the Sandhills, though, and it's a lot easier to put a golf course there. So Pondsboro's downtown isn't nearly as ritzy, despite their best efforts. But they do have a good coffee shop and a bad diner and a hardware store that hasn't been eaten by one of the big chains. I went to that last one for garbage bags and gloves and about a dozen containers of those little bleach-soaked wipes. (And, yes, a scented candle. It didn't matter what it smelled like; it was bound to be better than the smell of musty house.)

I picked up a cheap pair of sheets, too. They were red flannel, with a Christmas-tree pattern, and since it was now late March, they were on deep, deep clearance. I felt weird enough about sleeping in a dead woman's house without sleeping on her sheets. Even if I found a clean set in a closet, they would smell like the house or (worse) like her. I'd rather have Christmas trees.

The barista at the coffee shop was a cheerful Goth woman with hair dyed black in back and hot pink in front. She skillfully extracted the reason I was in Pondsboro, how long I was staying, and who my grandmother was.

"Oh!" she said, when I said her name. "Old Mrs. Cotgrave? She's dead?"

"Hard to believe, isn't it?" I said into my latte.

"She used to come in here. She was . . . ah . . ." I could see her trying to decide whether or not to be diplomatic.

"A raging bitch, I imagine," I said. "I'm sorry."

The barista grinned. "Well, yes. And a lousy tipper."

"I'm sorry about that, too." I sighed. "It wasn't just you. She was an awful person."

"Some people are," she said sympathetically, and gave me a warm-up on the latte when I got up to leave.

I made a mental note to come back, and not just because the coffee shop had Wi-Fi.

Bongo enjoyed the drive back. He stood with his front feet on the central armrest and gazed out the front.

"If I get in an accident, you're gonna go right through the windshield, you know."

He ignored this. I looked in the rearview mirror and got a great view of the dog's forehead.

Once we got back to the house, I let him come inside with me.

He walked around, sniffing. The smell of mice was much too exciting, and I had to haul him away from the bags on the staircase.

Oh well. It's not like he can make much more of a mess. . . .

I pulled on the gloves. They were good solid work gloves, men's size medium, not the crappy little floral-print things they try to sell to women. With the gloves and the trash bags, I felt obscurely armored. Whatever horrors awaited, at least I wouldn't have to *touch* them.

I lit the scented candle. It was called "Berries and Dreams," and I am sad to say that it had been the best of the selection and the only one that did not involve patchouli in some fashion. It smelled like the lip gloss I'd worn in third grade—strawberry with notes of wax.

It was still better than mouse crap.

My first order of business was to find a bedroom. I was waiting on e-mails to be able to work on an editing job, so I wasn't losing money at the moment, but if I had to spend the whole time in a motel room, I'd start burning the bank account at both ends. Motels that allow dogs charge a lot of money for the privilege.

The door at the back of the hallway had boxes piled to knee high in front of it, so I wasn't hopeful about it, but the other two were reasonably clear. There was a rampart of plastic storage bins between the two doors, reaching to the ceiling, but you could get by them if you turned sideways.

I pulled open the first door and then slumped against the doorframe with a groan.

Christ. The doll room. I'd forgotten all about that. She'd had those awful china dolls with the painted eyes, which were bad enough, but she'd really liked the newborn dolls. The ones all made up to look like realistic babies, except that when something's that realistic, it just looks dead.

The whole damn room was full of dead babies. Most of them were still in boxes, but she'd taken a bunch out, too. Then she'd stacked the other dolls in front of them, so all you'd see were horrible hyper-realistic faces peeking out from behind the edges of boxes or piled together. It looked like a monument to infanticide, and also to the astonishing holding capacity of clear plastic bins.

On the far side of the room, over the sea of babies, was a tall built-in storage cabinet, running to the ceiling. The china dolls stood inside that, in their little shoes and little coats, their hair dusty and immaculate.

I remembered her taking me into the room—you could see the floor then—and showing me the dolls and then telling me sternly that they were *not for playing*. I can still recall feeling embarrassed and resentful about it, because I wouldn't have wanted to play with her stupid dolls anyway. I much preferred stuffed animals, and china dolls are creepy no matter what age you are.

They hadn't gotten any less creepy. They stood in the case like objects of worship, surrounded by infant sacrifices.

There is *probably* a sum of money that could have incited me to sleep in that room. I am not wealthy and I can be bought. But it would be up in the thousands. I'm easy, but not cheap.

Since no one was appearing to proffer large sums of money, I shut the door to the room again and leaned against it, shuddering.

The old woman, wandering around the house for years, buying dolls that looked like infants. For the first time I started to feel a little guilty.

Possibly you think that I should have been feeling guilty long before this. Maybe you think I'm a terrible person. My grandmother, after all, had lived alone for years and had died unloved. She was my blood kin. I should have been coming down to visit her, and . . . I don't know, reading aloud to her or something.

That seems like it would have been an excellent way to get a book thrown at my head.

You have to understand, it's just not how my family works. We don't stay where we aren't wanted. Grandma had made it clear that she wanted nothing to do with me, and if somebody wants nothing to do with you, you leave.

We are a family that divorces quietly and without contest. If someone says they are done with us, we take them at their word.

But the corollary to that, I suppose, is that we return just as quickly and with just as little fanfare. My dad and my step-mother, Sheila, were separated for nearly seven years, and then one night she called him up and said, "Please come get me." And he did, and they've been together ever since. I resented that at the time, but she takes good care of Dad, and after a while that was the only thing that mattered.

If Grandma had called me up in the middle of the night, at any time in all those years, and said, "Mouse, I need you here," I would have come. I would have gotten in the car and driven all night. I didn't like her and I didn't love her, but I would have come because she'd asked.

But she never asked.

Should I have known somehow? But I hadn't seen her since I was seven and she babysat me after my mom died, when Dad couldn't afford a sitter. That had been so sufficiently awful that I'd been relieved to go live with my mom's sister, Aunt Kate, even if it meant that I saw Dad only on weekends. I hadn't spoken to her since I was seventeen and called her to ask if she wanted to attend my high school graduation.

She had snorted at me and said that she didn't know why I was bothering to graduate. I was Catholic trash and was just going to get married and squeeze out babies for the rest of my life.

I remember that very clearly, mostly because it was so *odd*. Yes, I was Catholic, more or less, but that just meant that Aunt Kate had saint cards shoved in the edges of the bathroom mirrors and that we went to Mass on Easter. (We hadn't managed Christmas Mass in years.) I had never been confirmed, never gone to confession, couldn't say a Hail Mary if my life depended on it.

I wasn't offended. I wasn't even angry. It didn't make *sense*. Grandma might as well have yelled at me for being from Pennsylvania, or for having wavy hair, or for walking upright instead of on all fours.

I took the phone away from my ear and stared at it, baffled. I could hear her still talking, tinny and distant through the receiver. Then—this was in the days of landlines—I set it back in the cradle and shook my head.

If you think that I'm harboring some deep resentment here, I'm really not. I'd called because Aunt Kate had said, somewhat doubtfully, that I should. I hadn't thought about her in years. She didn't do holidays. She was more like a particularly unpleasant teacher remembered from my grade school years than a relative.

She'd obviously wanted nothing to do with me. So it had seemed the polite thing to do was to oblige.

I don't know. All I know is that she never asked for anything. Maybe it's genetic in my family. Dad never asked for anything, so now that he had, I'd move heaven and earth if I needed to.

And that's why I was here, in this horrible house stuffed

full of baby dolls and ancient Tupperware and mouse-stained clothes, because he'd asked.

Perhaps I am a terrible person, but give me what little credit I deserve.

I was here.

———————

The second door was not as viscerally unsettling. Not many things could be. Even a roomful of taxidermy would be less creepy, and Grandma wasn't into taxidermy.

Nevertheless, it was a sad room, and that's because it was her bedroom.

There was a road through the piles of boxes. The bed itself was covered in old clothes and newspapers, but I could see a deep hollow where she'd slept, the sheets bunched up around it. It hadn't come out, even after two years of absence. Clothes lay draped over every surface, interspersed with boxes of coat hangers. The closet had a folding door that had come off its track, but was held in place by a tower of shoe boxes.

There was a large box next to the door, unopened. The outside proclaimed it as a foolproof closet-organization method. The bottom was stained where water had soaked into it, or maybe it was mouse urine. I made a noise in my throat—I couldn't tell you whether it was a laugh or a sob—and I shut the door again.

I decided that if the third door didn't work, I'd sleep on the couch. I could have cleared off that bed, but it would have been like sleeping in my grandmother's grave. Even though she'd died hundreds of miles away, in a home, with my father checking on her all the time, I felt her presence in that room.

If she was a ghost, she would be an unquiet one.

The third door took some work to get to. I nearly abandoned the attempt—if the hallway was this clogged, the room was probably wall-to-wall boxes of Ziploc bags and commemorative plates.

I started to push the boxes out of the way but felt a stab of guilt. Moving boxes around inside the house wasn't going to help. So I picked up each one and dragged it into the living room.

One was full of coat hangers. That went in the back of the truck immediately. One was full of papers, but a quick look told me they were all coupons and PennySaver mailings turning yellow-gray with age. I riffled it briefly, but no stock certificates fell out.

Well, a woman can dream.

There was a stack of empty shoe boxes all wedged together, which went out. One of the bottom boxes had a shoe. It was not a very good shoe.

At the very bottom was a carpet steamer. Thankfully it had wheels, because I could barely lift the thing. I dropped it on my foot getting it down the porch steps, and Bongo was treated to the sound of me swearing a blue streak.

"Hrooof!" he said.

I ignored this commentary on my language and wrestled the carpet steamer into the back of the truck at great personal cost to my back.

At last the door was clear. It stuck when I tried to open it, as if it had not opened for a long time, but I wedged my foot against the bottom and pushed.

It swung inward.

Into a nearly empty room.

After my first, astonished glance, it became obvious that the room wasn't quite empty. It had a bed and a nightstand and a chair. There was a painting over the bed and a few framed photographs on the walls.

But compared to the rest of the house, it seemed absolutely bare. The hardwood floor had a thick layer of dust, but no boxes piled in it. The mice had come in, found nothing of interest, and left again.

"Oh . . . ," I said out loud. "Oh, *right*."

It was Cotgrave's room. Of course.

He had died so long ago. I suppose I had thought that she would clear it out, use it as storage. And yet it was empty. Sheets had been turned back on the bed, as if someone had just gotten up. Except for the layer of dust, it could have been abandoned only an hour before.

It hadn't occurred to me as a child that my stepgrandfather's den had been his bedroom as well. That he had not been sleeping in a bed with my grandmother when he died.

I wonder if they started that way, or if he moved out eventually.

Well. The vagaries of Grandma's second marriage were not my concern, and probably none of my business.

"But it does make my life easier," I told the absent Cotgrave. (It was easier to talk out loud. It made some sound in that house, which was much too quiet, except for mice and Bongo working on his chew toy on the porch. I really needed to buy a radio or something.) "Replace the sheets and a normal person can sleep in here."

I went to the window and opened it. The wood had swollen, but after some banging, much like the door, I managed to push it open. The screens were still intact.

Bongo sat up and came over to the window. He licked the screen and seemed puzzled that it tasted like wire.

"You're not smart," I told him. He wagged his tail and licked the screen again, on the off chance that it had become tasty.

I opened the nightstand drawer. It was full of the usual detritus that accumulate in drawers—old tweezers, broken nail clippers, the warranty for a piece of electronics that had stopped functioning years ago. There was a black book on top, with an elastic ribbon holding it closed.

I flipped the book open. It was probably just an address book, but just in case there were any hundred-dollar bills tucked between the pages . . .

There weren't. It was full of handwriting instead.

I *almost* threw it away. I had the mouth of the garbage bag open and was moving my hand toward it when a phrase jumped out at me.

She has hid the book.

I had to read it twice to make sure I was right the first time. Whoever wrote it had neat-enough handwriting, but it was tightly slanted and the s's and the *a*'s looked nearly identical.

That's wrong, I thought. *It's either* she hid the book *or* she has hidden the book. *Pick one and commit.*

Like I said, I'm a freelance editor. The *Chicago Manual of Style* is tattooed on my soul. I'm pretty lenient about these things when editing fiction—show me a character who uses "whom" correctly and I'll show you a real prat—but *she has hid the book?* No.

The next line was *I'm afraid she might have destroyed it, but there are no fresh ashes in the burn barrel. I went through the trash, but it was not there. It must be hidden. I asked her where it was, and she asked had I lost something, but there was that look in her eyes like when she hid my keys.*

I sat down on the bed. *Good God, was this Cotgrave's? And was* she *my grandmother?*

I could easily believe that Grandma would hide something and take pleasure in the other person looking for it. There's mean and then there's pathological. Once you start calling up people to laugh when their dog dies, you're way over on the pathology side of the equation.

On the other hand, Cotgrave had been getting on in years himself, and lots of old people get paranoid that other people are stealing things from them. I couldn't swear that Grandma was doing any such thing just because she was a nasty piece of work in other regards.

I flipped to the next page.

Still can't find the book. Checked all the shelves. Shades of the Purloined Letter.

> *I won't leave without it. It's the last I've got of*
> *Ambrose.*

Cotgrave was clearly a trusting soul. He'd left the journal in his nightstand, and if Grandma was hiding his stuff, you'd think he'd realize she was probably reading this. Poor guy.

I turned the page again. They were old and stuck together, so I had to tug my glove off to do it.

> *It's in my head again, like a song that keeps replay-*
> *ing. When that happens, I read it in the book, and*
> *that makes it stop, but now I can't.*
> *   This must be what going mad feels like.*
> *   I made faces like the faces on the rocks, and*
> *I twisted myself about like the twisted ones, and*
> *I lay down flat on the ground like the dead ones.*
> *   That seems to have helped. Maybe if I read it*
> *written here, it'll stop.*

At first I thought that this was the moment when it all went bad. If I had shoved the book in the garbage bag before I read that, maybe it would have come out differently. If my stupid editor brain hadn't kicked in when I had opened the journal, maybe I would have been able to walk away.

I can see myself, when I think of this: sitting on the bed, one leg tucked up under myself, the garbage bag draped over my other knee. I see myself from the outside, like a stranger—woman in her midthirties, gaining weight no matter how often she takes the dog out jogging. Wavy brown hair, with a few strands stuck to her forehead and dust smudged across her face.

And in her hand, the little black journal.

But now, writing this, I think maybe it wouldn't have mattered. I was there, and I was not going to leave until I had cleaned the place out. Maybe everything would have happened anyway, and I would have had no map to guide me — even as poor and addled a map as Cotgrave's journal proved to be.

At the time, though, I had no presentiment. I read that passage and what I thought was, *Ugh! That's kind of creepy! Twisted myself about like the twisted ones . . . yeesh.*

It was a weird thing to find written in a book by an old man who liked cribbage and read the newspaper for hours a day.

"It's in my head again, like a song that keeps replaying. . . ." Sounds like he's talking about an earworm. Poor soul.

Lord knows I'd had songs stuck in my head before. TV theme songs were particularly bad. One time I wandered around for nearly two weeks humming the theme to *Cheers*, until I had to sit down and actually watch an episode or go barking mad.

This didn't seem much like a song. Then again, I've known people who get poetry stuck in their head. My college roommate used to recite Poe's "Eldorado," and I don't think she even knew she was doing it sometimes.

Of course, she *was* an English major.

I didn't have time to keep reading a journal — I had a house to clean. I set it down on the nightstand and finished emptying the drawers.

The closet was as bare as the rest of room. A few suits of clothes. A pair of bedroom slippers and a pair of scuffed leather shoes. Three Time Life books on World War II, but that probably didn't mean anything. Books on World War II appear spontaneously in any house that contains a man over a certain age. I believe that's science.

On the far side of the top shelf was an ancient manual typewriter. I groaned. It had to weigh a ton. Just looking at it made my back hurt. I was going to have to get on a chair, lift it out at shoulder height, and probably drop it on my foot in the process.

Well, that was a concern for another day. I stuffed everything I could lift into the garbage bags, stripped the bed, and hauled the bag out to the truck.

"C'mon, Bongo. Let me show you the new digs. . . ."

Bongo seemed cautiously pleased. He got up on the bed and made putting the sheets on extremely difficult, anyway.

I resigned myself to the red Christmas-tree sheets smelling like hound. Most of my stuff does.

"For my next trick," I told him, "I'm going to see if I can't excavate a counter in the kitchen."

He accompanied me to the kitchen, discovered that I wasn't doing anything that would result in dog treats, and slumped to the linoleum with a tragic sigh. Unfortunately, there was only one bare patch of linoleum, so I was stepping over him every time I turned around.

"You're not helping."

He let out another sigh. Occasionally my dog sounds like he is deflating.

I tried to sort Tupperware for about five minutes. Then I gave up and just swept the stacks into garbage bags. Bags full of wadded-up plastic bags got the same treatment. (I can see the reason for keeping plastic bags around, but my grandmother had more than her own body weight in the things.)

I tried to think of a song to sing. I really had to get a radio for in here. The house was too quiet.

And I twisted myself around like the twisted ones. . . .

That wasn't a song.

I dismissed it and started the first song I could think of, which was one we sang at camp approximately a thousand years ago.

"I woke up Sunday morning, I looked up on the wall, the beetles and the bedbugs were having a game of ball. . . ."

Bongo let out another sigh from the bottom of his toes.

I worked my way through the vast number of verses, including the one about dying in a sewer that the counselors wouldn't let us sing, and cleared a counter back to something that was probably a toaster. Corrosion had sealed it to the countertop. There was a fork sticking out of it, which seemed like a generally bad idea. Fortunately, the electrical cord had rotted through, so the toaster was harmless. I was a little more concerned about the cord that was still sticking out of the wall socket.

There were two microwaves stacked on top of each other.

One looked to be made of plastic and one looked like it was made to withstand the atomic bomb.

Somehow I got about half the kitchen counters cleaned without electrocuting myself. The metal microwave was incredibly heavy. I made a mental note to go rent a handcart. I also uncovered a mouse nest and about twenty containers of ant poison, which sealed my resolve not to let Bongo run around loose in the house.

I opened the refrigerator. It looked very dirty, but the air inside was cold. I dithered over scrubbing it out—did it matter? It was ancient, and I was here to throw things away—but eventually decided that I didn't want my food to sit in a fridge that was covered in stains and mold.

It occurred to me, somewhat belatedly, that there's a disease you get from mold that lives in closed-up refrigerators. But I was down on my knees wielding little green scrubby pads, and whatever it was, I was probably thoroughly exposed. So, y'know. Oh well.

By the time I finished with the fridge, it was getting dark. I got back in the truck and drove into town for a drive-through meal eaten in the car. Bongo got another illicit cheeseburger. I would have to pick up groceries tomorrow, but the idea was exhausting.

We went back . . . well, *home* is the wrong word. We went back, anyway. I'd left the porch light on and most of the lights in the downstairs. From outside, it looked almost like a normal house with warm light spilling through the windows. Moths banged at the porch light.

I sat in the car so long, looking at the house, that Bongo got bored and began chewing on his nails. So I sighed and pulled the keys out of the ignition and grabbed my suitcase out of the back seat. "C'mon, boy. Let's go."

Clutter aside, the house seemed solid enough. Probably wasn't going to fall down on my head. If I could just clear the junk out, we could put it on the market. Dad had made noises about splitting the money with me, and I sure wasn't in a position to turn money down.

I told myself all this three or four times as I slogged up the steps, Bongo yanking at the leash.

3

Cotgrave's room still smelled of dust and mice. I thumped my suitcase down on the floor, dug out toiletries, considered the state of the bathroom, and decided to brush my teeth tomorrow morning with bottled water.

I lay down on the bed. The mattress had a body-shaped dent in it that I didn't like to think about much. Still, it was probably better than the couch.

Bongo leapt up on the bed and arranged himself in a neat ball. Then he farted.

"Gaaaah!"

I made yet another mental note, this time to buy even more scented candles. Perhaps incense.

Perhaps a gas mask.

I retrieved the scented candle from the kitchen. This required me to turn on every light in the hall, partly so I didn't trip over anything, partly because I didn't like the shapes the piles of boxes made in the dark.

I checked the front-door lock several times, just in case.

Since I had to keep the door to the bedroom closed, the smell hadn't dissipated. I was going to have to burn the candle and stay awake while I did it so that the whole place didn't go up in flames.

I had brought my e-reader. That would have been useful if I'd had any Wi-Fi to download books with. I'd finished my last one over lunch. For lack of anything better to do, I picked up my stepgrandfather's journal and began to read.

The pages weren't dated, so I had no idea how much time had passed between entries. He had changed pens, though, whatever that meant.

> *Still haven't found where she hid the book. Should never have married her.*

(*No shit*, I thought.)

> *She had that power, though. They didn't come around her. Needed that. Didn't realize what she was like.*

I had no idea who *they* were that didn't come around her. Probably Cotgrave's family, but really, it could have been any-body. Grandma had that effect on people.

> *Ambrose would say that as there are humans sensi-tive to the peculiar humors & wonders of the others,*

*who attract them, it must follow there are those
who are the opposite & actively drive such humors
away. But A. felt to seek out such wonders led to sin,
whereas I cannot believe that the opposite leads to
virtue. Certainly there is no virtue in her.*

*Miss Ambrose terribly. Have made a grave
error, I fear. If I can get the book back, will leave at
once, take chances with the others. Would rather
die in fear and glory than needled to death in this
wretched house.*

The sentiment was understandable, but *die in fear and
glory* was an odd way to put it. Was Cotgrave planning to join
the foreign legion?

I had no idea what to make of the bit about sin and virtue.
Apparently he'd been religious.

"Though it doesn't sound much like Sunday school. More
like Thomas Aquinas. Or maybe he was a Gnostic or something," I said to Bongo.

Bongo stretched out again. I held my breath in case that jog-
gled loose anything foul, but apparently he was done for the night.

I turned the page and grimaced.

*I made faces like the faces on the rocks, and I
twisted myself about like the twisted ones, and I
lay down flat on the ground like the dead ones.*

(Again? I thought. Cotgrave was *obsessed*.)

*Reading it here doesn't last as long as reading it
in the Green Book. Only two or three days, not
weeks. Writing it down lasts longer, though. I can
go almost two weeks if I write it down.*

It occurred to me again that Cotgrave might have been
suffering from dementia. He had been very old when he died,
hadn't he?

I had no idea how old, come to think of it. If he'd been the
same age as my grandmother, then somewhere in his eighties,
maybe? Certainly old enough for the wires to start getting crossed.

Then again, Dad was in his eighties, and he was still rather
frighteningly sane. Grandma had been too, except for the
hoarding, and the hoarding probably wasn't related to old age.

*And I twisted myself about like the twisted ones
and I lay down flat on the ground like the dead
ones. . . .*

Ugh. Well, I could see how he got that stuck in his head, I
suppose. It didn't exactly have a rhythm, but it had an intrusive
quality to it. Like when you stand on the edge of a high place
and your brain whispers to you about jumping.

*Have started going for walks just to get out of the
house. Sometimes she won't let me nap. I go into
my room, but she bangs on the door to make sure
I'm not sleeping. Don't want her in the room any
more than necessary.*

> *Took a nap in the woods yesterday. Not a good*
> *idea, probably, but was so tired.*

Poor old soul, I thought. It was painful to read. My grandmother had been such an awful person. Even knowing that
he'd died years ago and nobody was interfering with his sleep
now, I felt bad for Cotgrave.

I wondered if Dad had known about this. I had been in
college—maybe even high school—in another state. I couldn't
have prevented it. But I wish someone had called the state
about elder abuse and taken the poor man away.

Though maybe he wouldn't have wanted to leave, since he
still hadn't found his book.

> *Should probably write down everything I remem-*
> *ber of the Green Book, in case it really is lost. She*
> *keeps the living room clean for her son, but the*
> *closed rooms are a monstrous clutter. Place may*
> *burn down and the book lost.*
>
> *Would have to hide the manuscript some-*
> *where, though. If she found it, she'd hide it, too,*
> *just to spite me.*
>
> *Wish there were someone I could mail it to.*
> *Ambrose has been dead so long. Should have asked*
> *him about other students. But he sent me the book.*
>
> *I wish I'd never read any of it.*

The rest of that page was blank, except for a little "Kilroy
Was Here" doodle at the bottom.

Would you find it odd that the doodle nearly made me cry? Maybe. Maybe not. Maybe you understand how people work.

It was such a human thing to have done. The rest of the journal could have been like reading a book, albeit one in cramped handwriting, but then there was the drawing. I'd doodled that exact thing on essays and in the margins of math homework.

In fact . . .

I stared at the page, not really seeing it. Had it been Cotgrave who showed me? It seemed like I'd always known about Kilroy, but you hardly ever saw it on the Internet. I couldn't remember my father drawing one ever. And Aunt Kate had laughed when she saw one of mine and said, "Wow, that takes me back!"

If I strained, I could almost remember—or could make up the memory out of whole cloth, most likely—Cotgrave with a slip of paper, showing a little girl who wasn't his granddaughter how to draw Kilroy, in this very house, after Grandma had done something to make me upset yet again.

I couldn't remember why I had been upset. Too many things to choose from, probably. I had been close to crying, hadn't I? But just old enough that I didn't want to cry in front of my grandmother. So I had run outside, and Cotgrave had been sitting on the porch in a rocking chair and he had looked at me and said . . . said something. . . .

"Don't mind her. She's a spiteful old bitch."

The obscenity had shocked me and made me giggle all at once. I had shoved both hands over my mouth, still close to tears. "I don't like her," I whispered through my hands.

He nodded. "I don't like her very much either," he said.

I was too young to wonder why he stayed married if he didn't like her. I just nodded. When you're a kid, you're always wrong if you're mad at a grown-up. But now a grown-up had agreed with me, and that meant that maybe I was right after all.

Cotgrave had a newspaper in his hands. The "funnies," he always called them, not the comics. He folded a page over and took a pen out of his pocket. "Do you know Kilroy?" he asked.

I shook my head.

He drew a line on the margin of the comics page, next to Prince Valiant. A line with three curved shapes in it, the longest one in the middle. I watched, fascinated, and then he drew three more curves and the line became two hands and a nose. He added a curl of hair and two dots for eyes. "Kilroy," he said.

"Do it again," I said. It was like a magic trick, the way the lines turned into a person.

He drew it again and again and then taught me, patiently, how to draw it myself. "We used to draw this on things," he told me. "Mr. Chad, we called him. But the Yanks called him Kilroy, and it stuck. You'd get to a place where you'd never been and then you'd see Kilroy and you knew someone else had been there before you."

Thirty-odd years later, I looked down at the drawing of Kilroy in the journal and sighed. He'd been talking about being a soldier in the war. I hadn't known that then.

Oh, give it a rest. I was tired and sad, that was all, and the job in front of me was making me tired and sadder. Maybe I was just inventing tragic nostalgia where none should exist.

"That's enough for one night," I said. I put the journal in the desk drawer. Tomorrow I'd download a novel. A Regency romance with lots of sex and tragic misunderstandings and a happy ending like Marshmallow Fluff. Something kind and set completely apart from this awful house.

I blew out the scented candle, turned off the light, and fell asleep at once.

In the middle of the night, Bongo started whining to go out, so I got up. (This is a hindbrain function for dog owners.) I snapped on his leash and took him outside.

The moon was very bright. The trees were very dark, but the house was brightly lit and cold blue shadows lay across the ground. I'd shoved my feet into my sandals, but I wasn't wearing socks, and the cold grass soaked my bare feet. My nightgown had Eeyore on it, demanding coffee, which was adorable but not as warm as it could have been.

I don't think most people can be outdoors in a strange place and not feel a little bit of trepidation. There might have been serial killers. Or bears. I don't think I'm afraid of bears, but I'd rather not find out for sure.

Naturally Bongo needed to sniff out exactly the correct place to pee. We went around the side of the house, past the carport—"Seriously, buddy?" I muttered—and he had to stop and smell all the things.

We went out into the garden while I grumbled, and then Bongo's fur went up in spikes and he began to bark.

I wasn't afraid. I was exasperated—don't get me wrong—but not afraid. Because . . . well . . .

"It's a *rock*, genius."

Well, it was. It was a big rock, about knee high, on the edge of the cleared area, near the oak tree. It had been shaped into some kind of yard art. If I came back during daylight, I'd probably see that it had been carved into an American eagle holding the severed head of a terrorist or something. Grandma wasn't exactly a patriot, but she dearly loved having an excuse to hate a whole group of people.

I doubt she could have hated any terrorists as much as Bongo hated the rock, though. Never mind that he'd been less than thirty feet from it a few hours earlier, that rock was now making him *nuts*. He was actually snarling at it, and I didn't think he knew what a snarl was.

"Is there a possum behind it?"

I tried to lead him around the rock, but he was not having it. Bongo weighs maybe sixty-five pounds and I am probably stronger than he is, but I try not to test it in case it turns out I'm wrong and it reverses the power dynamics of our relationship. He did not want to get any closer to the rock. The rock was the enemy.

I stopped bothering with the leash and got him by the collar. This actually seemed to make him happy, although not in the way I'd expected. He stopped snarling and started barking, the look-my-packmate-is-here-and-we-are-gonna-mess-you-up bark that he uses at home when the neighbor's dog is tormenting him through the fence and I come out to take him inside.

"Come on. Come *on*, Bongo. Bongo! *Leave it!*"

He left it, reluctantly. I walked him back toward the house with my hand on his collar.

As we approached the front door, he suddenly cheered up and his tail started wagging again. He remembered that he had to pee, and I barely got my foot out of the way in time.

You may think that I'm being exceedingly dense not to think that something was wrong at this point, but in my defense, I once saw Bongo lose his shit at a garbage can. An *empty* garbage can. I've never figured out what his beef was with that can. Maybe there had been a possum in it at one point in the distant past.

What I am getting at here is that my dog is not a reliable indicator of Bad Things Going Down.

(Although hell, what do I know? Maybe that garbage can was sitting right at the nexus of where our world touches another one, and he was baying and charging at it to let me know that eldritch abominations were breaking into our reality. Who knows anymore? I sure don't.)

Once he had finished anointing the grass, he was happy to go back inside. The scary rock was forgotten. We threaded our way through the house and I shut the bedroom door behind me.

Partly it was to keep Bongo inside, but it was also because the rest of the house felt hostile, as if the clutter was going to come oozing inside on tentacles of old newspaper and baby dolls.

I kicked off my sandals and shoved my feet under Bongo's ribs. He was like a space heater, even through the blankets, and unlike my last boyfriend, he never complained about my cold feet.

I fell asleep again immediately, before I was even warm.

Just before dawn, Bongo woke me up by leaping to his feet and baying hysterically at the window.

I opened my eyes, said, "Jesus," and looked at the window. The moon had gone down, but the yard was bathed in that cold gray light that means you're either up too early or way too late.

Something pale bounded through the yard on four legs, followed by another one. Bongo lost his mind. He'd start with a bark and it would trail up at the end into a "rooooo-roOOO!" howl. Every time he bayed, he bounced on his front feet, which made the bed shake.

"It's deer, idiot!"

"*Hwuaaaaffffforrrroooo!*" he said, or words to that effect.

I groaned and flailed for my phone. The screen said that it was 5:03 a.m. I groaned again, set the phone down, and poked Bongo in the ribs with my foot. "Settle down."

"*Wuuuaaaaoorrroo-rooo!*"

"The deer are not going to come and kill us in our sleep, buddy."

Bongo seemed unconvinced. He settled down, muttering in his throat, though that was probably because the deer were gone.

"Go back to bed."

" . . . *hrwuff.*"

I could hear all the horrible noises of early morning—the birds starting up and the spring peepers. It was frog season in North Carolina, and the frogs can go all night and half the day when they're in the mood.

There was a hollow knocking sound somewhere. It sounded close to the house. Probably a woodpecker, I thought, though it was spaced out. Then again, there's a lot of different woodpeckers. The big Woody Woodpecker kind and little black-and-white ones and one that's got a head the color of a highlighter pen.

Bongo glared out the window until I fell asleep, and for all I know, he kept glaring for a long time after that.

———————

I got up around eight in the morning and poured Bongo some dog food from the bag in the car. He looked at me sadly, perhaps wishing for more cheeseburgers.

"Today, groceries," I said. "And a radio." I had exhausted most of the songs that I could sing, and while I have an extensive knowledge of the discography of Nirvana and Nine Inch Nails, neither of them lend themselves well to singing a capella.

And I twisted myself about like the twisted ones. . . .

I started singing something. I didn't even know what it was until I hit the chorus and discovered that it was the theme to *Cheers.* Bongo looked up from his food long enough to give me a disappointed look.

"Sorry."

Once he'd finished, we headed out to the truck. There was nearly a full load in the back. Maybe the nice Goth barista could tell me where to find the county dump.

As it turned out, she could, and also where to get a breakfast that wasn't watery eggs from the diner. There was a half-decent place hiding behind the gas station, as long as you weren't too picky about things like matching chairs and the existence of tablecloths.

"How bad is it?" she asked, glancing out the window to my truck.

"Bad," I said. I stared into my coffee. "She was a bit of a hoarder."

She hissed in sympathy. "I know how that goes. Ugh."

"At least she didn't have cats. It's just papers and clothes and a whole room full of dolls. . . ."

"Nothing creepy about that," she said, grinning.

"Not in the slightest." I shuddered theatrically, and we both laughed.

Back to the hardware store I went, for a radio and even more garbage bags. Then the grocery store, which was an honest-to-God Piggly Wiggly. The South is weird.

Bongo grumbled at me for leaving him in the car, even on a cool day, but when I came back with bags filled with dog treats and potato chips, he forgave me. He believes that anything that makes a plastic crinkling noise is probably for dogs. (Again, on the off chance that my vet is reading this, he got that from his previous owners. I swear.)

I checked my phone, thinking about calling my father, but the battery was nearly dead. "Dammit, I charged you last night. . . ."

I hooked it up to the truck, started the engine—sorry, environment—and drove close enough to the coffee shop to get on their Wi-Fi. The e-mail I was waiting for hadn't come through. I didn't feel like trying to call Dad and getting cut off

two minutes in. I downloaded a couple of novels and drove to
the dump instead.

The guy at the dump helped me unload the steam cleaner.
He was a grizzled old white guy in a John Deere baseball cap.
"You going to have more?"

"A lot more," I said. "I'm cleaning out my grandmother's
place. She passed away, and it's . . . well, there's a lot of junk."

"Sorry to hear that. Hang on." He went into the little office
and came back out with a sticker. "If she was a county resident,
that's good enough for me. Put this in the truck window and
you can dump for free."

"Oh God, thank you!" I hadn't even thought about the fees.
"That's really helpful."

He smiled. "Glad to help. I'm Frank."

"Melissa. Friends call me Mouse." I grinned. "As often as
I'm gonna be here for the next few weeks, you should probably
just start with Mouse."

Frank tapped the rim of his baseball cap. "Nice to meet
you. Who was your grandma, if you don't mind me asking?"

"Mrs. Cotgrave," I said. "Off Horse Bridge Road."

"Over by the commune?"

I braced myself, just in case he had opinions about hippies.
"Across the road and down a bit from it, yeah."

He nodded. "If you've got more stuff in the house you can't
lift, go over there and see if Thomas is around. He'd probably
give you a hand with it."

I am not a fan of Southern chivalry in general, particularly the sort that involves people calling me "little lady" and

charging me three times as much for car repairs, but I'll make allowances if it helps move my microwave. "Thank you."

"God bless," he said, waving as I drove away.

I checked my phone again before I got out of data range, discovered that it hadn't charged worth a damn and was also hot enough to fry an egg. "Sonofabitch . . ."

I pulled over, did a quick search online, discovered that there was a known bug in the latest operating-system release that made the phone run hot and burn battery like it was going out of style. They promised to fix it really soon.

Great.

Well, it's not like I got signal out at Grandma's place anyhow.

I switched off my nicely toasty paperweight and drove . . . Look, I'm going to call it home for now with the understanding that it was not—and never would be—home, but there's only so many clever ways I can type it out. I drove to my temporary, not-for-real home.

Bongo was extremely bitter about the fact that he hadn't gotten a cheeseburger this time and lay draped across the back seat while I unloaded the groceries. Presumably he thought if he just looked tragic enough, I would turn around and go back to the diner.

I bribed him with a dog treat and put him on a tie-out in the front yard, since I was going to have the front door open for a while. I set up the radio on the clear spot on the kitchen counter.

There wasn't a lot of signal out here. I got a country station, something called "Scripture Talk with Pastor Jonah," a salsa station, and NPR out of Chapel Hill. It was Pledge Week. It is an immutable law of the universe that whenever you listen to NPR in a strange place, it will be Pledge Week.

Pledge Week at least had human voices, even if they had the frazzled cheerfulness of people who have been begging for money for days and see no end in sight. I fiddled with the dial until I got the least fuzzy version, cracked open a bottle of water, and rolled up my sleeves.

Then I spent about two hours dragging everything else out of the kitchen.

Most of it was just the usual run-of-the-mill stuff you'd expect in a kitchen, only more of it. There were bags of flour that were probably riddled with moth eggs and jars of dried rice. I'm not actually sure if rice goes bad, but this didn't seem like the time to risk it.

I threw the glassware into a plastic bin. Some of it cracked, but I wasn't planning on reselling it anyway. There wasn't any Depression-era milk glass or whatever the ritzy stuff is supposed to be.

I suppose I could have lugged it out to Goodwill, and undoubtedly not doing so made me a terrible person, but I wanted that house *empty*.

I kept a couple of plastic tumblers for my own use, then pulled open a drawer at random. It held about two hundred chopsticks, the wooden kind you get with takeout, which had been washed and put into Ziploc bags. The ends were stained with use. I stared at them for a little while.

Yep. She was reusing disposable chopsticks.

Well. All right, then.

I took the Ziploc bags out gingerly. I was wearing gloves and I'm sure she used soap, but there was just something desperately unsanitary about the whole thing.

I got halfway to the door and Bongo started barking.

It sounded a bit like the UPS guy bark, so I hurried out to check on it.

There was a man in the front yard, and he was big.

He was at least six feet tall and extremely fat, but he had the kind of build where it goes out sideways, so he was broad as well as tall. He had sloped shoulders, but there was a lot of muscle underneath.

I hoped like hell he was friendly, because he could probably break me in half with one hand. You think things like this when you're a woman and there's nobody around to hear you scream.

"Hey!" he said, waving.

I waved back. Bongo's barks had gone from "Die, UPS scum!" to "Pet me pet me why aren't you petting me?!" His tail wagged frantically.

"Can I help you?" I said, trying not to sound unfriendly.

He shrugged. Up a bit closer, I could see he was Latino, probably in his late twenties. He had a rather sheepish grin. "Hey, just saw your truck over here and thought I'd come over." He paused and scratched at the back of his neck. "Does the old lady know you're movin' stuff out of her house?"

I relaxed a little. There wasn't a car on the road, so he'd probably come over from the commune. If I'd seen somebody cleaning out a neighbor's house, I might come check things out too. "Well, she passed away last month, so I don't think she'd mind." I tossed the chopstick bags into the rocking chair, came down the steps, and stuck out my hand. "I'm her granddaughter, Melissa."

"Ohhhh . . ." He gave a short, relieved laugh. "That's good. Not that she's dead, I mean, but it was gonna get real awkward if you were robbing her." He had a fairly pronounced accent, although I couldn't place it. Somewhere farther south, but that could cover anywhere from Miami to Mexico, with a whole lot of Texas in between.

"There's nothing in there worth stealing, I'm afraid. I wish there were."

He shook my hand and glanced over at Bongo. "Is he friendly?"

"Ridiculously so."

He crouched down in range of Bongo and stuck out a hand. Big he might be, but he didn't move like it slowed him down at all. "Hey, buddy . . ."

Bongo licked his fingers and jammed his head into the man's elbow.

"As you can see, he's a terror," I said.

The man grinned up at me. "Definitely. Hey, I live across the road at the commune."

I took a guess. "Thomas?"

"Tomas," he corrected. "How'd you know?"

"Frank at the dump."

"Ahhh, yeah." Tomas laughed. "Good guy." He stood up, to Bongo's sorrow.

There was something infectious about his grin. "He volun-
teered you, actually. But it's okay. I won't hold you to it."

Tomas groaned. "Ah, man." He ducked his head. "What for?"

"Helping me move appliances."

"Ohhh, is that all? Man, I thought you wanted me to hide
a body."

"Maybe later. I haven't gotten into the attic yet."

He laughed again. So did I, although I wasn't entirely joking.

"Sure. What do you need moved?"

"Just the microwave so far. It's one of those giant heavy
ones. I'm sure there'll be other stuff eventually."

"I'll do it right now, if you want," he said.

This was unexpected, but I wasn't going to look gift muscles
in the mouth. "Sure. Follow me."

He got in through the door and whistled.

"I know, right?"

"Didn't know it was this bad in here." He shook his head. "I
only talked to the old lady a few times, you know? Man."

"Same here, actually. I had no idea she'd been living like
this until Dad called me." I braced myself to defend my father,
but Tomas just accepted this without comment.

He had to turn sideways to get through the newspaper
stacks. I pointed to the heavier microwave. "There's the beast."

He laughed again. "No problem," he said, and picked it up
as if it weighed nothing. I felt a pang of resentment at evolution
for stiffing me on upper-body strength.

Tomas carried it out. He started to set it in the truck, then
paused. "Hey, you gonna take this to the dump?"

"That was the plan."

"Mind if I take it?" He jerked his chin over to the cluster of houses across the road. "Believe it or not, I think it's newer than the one Foxy's got."

"Foxy?" I said, a bit dubiously.

That infectious grin came out again. "Foxy. You'll know her if you see her."

I felt bad inflicting a microwave that old on anyone else and told him so. Tomas laughed.

"Foxy won't mind. She likes old stuff. Still has a landline phone and everything."

"Well, all right. The microwave's yours," I said. "I don't know if it works. If it doesn't, just bring it over and toss it in the truck and I'll haul it away. Heck, once I'm done here, if you want the other microwave, I *know* that one works."

"Sure. Thanks." He paused. "You need anything else moved, just come on over and bang on the door."

"Will do." I waited with my hand on the doorknob, ready to turn away.

He didn't leave immediately, though. He glanced upward, over the roof, and then said, "Hey, be careful, yeah?"

"Careful?" I said, a bit more sharply than I intended.

"Ah, you know. Things in the woods around here." He fiddled with the knob on the microwave.

"What kind of things?" I asked.

He was silent a little too long. I filled in the silence, which is a bad habit of mine. "Like . . . skunks or something?"

"Yeah." He seized on that as if he was relieved. "Skunks. Some of 'em got rabies."

"Bongo's had his shots."

"Good. Yeah. That's good. Thanks for the microwave."

I waved as he ambled across the street. He'd been friendly and helpful, but it had been a more awkward parting than I'd expected.

I went back inside the house and started scrubbing the spot where the microwave had been. There was a wealth of stains awaiting me.

The NPR people offered me the chance to win a trip to Paris, travel dates nonnegotiable, if I called now. The largest of the stains looked a bit like a map of France if I squinted.

I hummed and I scrubbed and I still couldn't shake the feeling that by "things in the woods" Tomas hadn't meant skunks at all.

4

I had ramen for dinner that night. I am not a cook. Bongo had dog food. He indicated that he would be more than willing to help with the ramen, but I declined.

The kitchen was not exactly under control, but I'd taken a break to clear out the bathroom. My shower situation was in danger of becoming dire.

The bathtub was an exciting range of hard water colors, and the shower curtain . . . Well, let's not dwell on the shower curtain. I'd have to pick up a new one in town. I wondered if the hardware store had a frequent-buyer discount.

I got enough space cleared that I could take something that approximated a shower. The hot water lasted roughly thirty seconds, and Bongo thought that the lack of curtain meant that it was doggy bath time. These are the trials of a dog owner's life.

The towels, on the other hand, were unused, still with little cardboard labels on them. I'd found them in the vicinity of the

linen closet. They had stiffened in the store-bought folds and
smelled like dust, but not mildew.

Finally clean, I went to bed even though it was barely nine.
I didn't feel like lugging piles of crap outside in the dark, and the
truck was nearly full anyway. I settled for pulling some of the newspaper stacks out on the porch after dinner, then called it a night.

I had downloaded a romance novel—the blurb promised
me that it was the next best thing to reading Jane Austen—but
found myself picking up Cotgrave's journal again instead.

I turned the page quickly to avoid looking at Kilroy.

The next page started with the by-now-familiar recitation:

> *I made faces like the faces on the rocks, and I*
> *twisted myself about like the twisted ones, and I*
> *lay down flat on the ground like the dead ones.*

Jeez, Cotgrave, I thought, *you really should talk to a therapist about this*. Still, it was helpful in a way. He'd said that he
could go almost two weeks if he wrote it down, so I could date
the entry to . . . oh, a week and a half, say, after Kilroy?

> *Have been sleeping in the woods again. So tired.*
> *It's the pills. But if don't take them, heart gets flut-*
> *tery. Wish she would let me sleep. Even doctors*
> *said was fine to nap, but she won't let me. Just*
> *meanness.*
>
> *Sleeping in the woods bad idea, know it,*
> *can't help it. Starting to dream about them. Not*

like nightmares, but think they're watching me.
They're close. These hills are full of them, I think.
Won't get too close to her, same way I wouldn't get
close to a dead skunk. Not scared, just don't like
it. But if I sleep outside, then they find me. They
must know. Green Book must have left a mark on
me. They're watching.

If had the book, could maybe find the signs
to keep them away, but can't remember now. Pop-
pets made of beeswax and clay? But could be what
summons them instead. So tired all the time.

I stopped reading and petted Bongo instead for a minute.
Poor Cotgrave. It read like dementia, or like the pills he was on
were making his mind wander. There was absolutely no excuse
for Grandma not letting him nap, though, the mean old bat.
That was just cruelty.

Aunt Kate had dated a guy for a little while, when I was
about nine, who was weirdly controlling about food. I went into
the kitchen to get a piece of toast for a snack and he freaked
out because he was going to cook dinner in a few hours. Like
a full-on, toddler-temper-tantrum freak-out, slamming drawers
and yelling that he didn't know why he bothered. It was nuts. I
stared at him with my mouth open, and then Aunt Kate told me
to go outside. I could still hear the yelling, but he didn't come
back around.

Being nine, I got it into my head that I'd made them break
up because I wanted toast. Kate had to sit me down and explain,

as best she could, that he'd had some *issues* (that was the word she used) around meals, because of the way he was raised, and that it wasn't my fault and no normal person would have a problem with a kid wanting a snack after school. "And thanks to you and your toast, I found out right away that I didn't want to date him!" she said, hugging me. "I could have wasted a lot of time otherwise, and life's too short for people who throw fits over little things. You did great!" And then we had toast for dinner, with butter and brown sugar and apple pie spice on it, and watched movies.

Aunt Kate was really good at that sort of thing.

I suppose it's possible that Grandma had some issues around napping like that. I could have asked Dad, but that would have been a really awkward conversation to have . . . and what would I do with the information? Feel slightly more conflicted about a dead woman?

I sighed and went back to the journal.

There was a gap of presumably about three weeks, during which he wrote nothing but his litany about the twisted ones twice, and then the narrative started up again.

> *Found my old typewriter. Had hoped that she'd put the Green Book with it, but no luck. Will write down as much as I can remember. Easier to type it out.*
>
> *Must do something. Slept in the woods yesterday and woke up and one of them was right there. Went away somehow but saw the whiteness leaving.*

"Getting creepy, Cotgrave," I said. It was even creepier because he never said what *they* were, other than a figment of an increasingly demented mind.

"I bet it's aliens," I told Bongo. "It's *always* aliens." Bongo had no opinion.

I heard the knocking sound again. It was a perfectly normal out-in-the-woods sound, but it made me jump because I wasn't expecting it.

Great. Nocturnal woodpeckers. Just what I needed.

> Should have stayed in city, but might not have worked. Woman in story in Green Book lived in town, was burned in town square, so must not have minded. Had hoped when left Wales that would not see again. No white men in this land, only red Indians, so no white people, surely?

"Don't get racist on me, Cotgrave," I warned him. "I know you were a product of your time and all, but if you start spouting white supremacist nonsense at me, I'm gonna go read my Regency."

Either his mind was wandering even farther afield than usual, or he meant something that wasn't coming through the text. Cotgrave had been getting up there in years, but he definitely didn't date from Plymouth Rock. There were plenty of white men in the land when he'd come over from Wales.

I hadn't actually known that he'd been Welsh, come to that. *Cotgrave* wasn't the sort of name I associated with Wales. Needed more *L*s and *Y*s and maybe a couple of *F*s.

The frogs were going at it again. They stopped whenever the woodpecker started, though, and took a minute to get going.

Did woodpeckers eat frogs?

I dunno. Maybe if you're a frog, it doesn't pay to stick around to find out.

It wasn't rhythmic at all. It went tap . . . tappa*tap*tap . . . tap-tap . . . tap*tap*tap . . . and sometimes it sounded like there was more than one.

It's a woodpecker, I told myself. *Or something like it. Unless it's a bug. They've got all the bugs in the world out here.* I'd already learned that if I left the lights on in the house, I'd get things on the window that were covered in legs and feelers and wiggly antennae. It made me feel like I was living on the wrong side of a terrarium.

I'd caught fireflies out here as a kid and let them go again. I'd forgotten that there were a lot of bugs that weren't nearly so charismatic.

Tap-tap . . . *tap*—tap-tap . . . tap . . .

I dredged my memory and came up with the word *katydid.* Didn't they drum or chirp or something? It wasn't quite like a cricket, was it?

The tapping held off for a while, and the frogs started in. I was going to have to get noise-canceling headphones or something. Which would allow me to sleep through Bongo whining to go out, and then I'd wake up with poop in my shoes. Hmm. Tough call.

I went back to reading.

*So many in the hills here. Crossed the ocean? Or
here originally? Can't tell. No way to find out.*

   *Folklore different here, but same too. Poppets
and dolls. Plat-eyes. Maybe the same. White creatures, not real beasts.*

   *Ambrose might know. I must send him a
letter. . . .*

I sighed. His handwriting had been degenerating over the
course of the page, and I had to work out some words by context. "Ambrose is dead, remember?"

Apparently he did, because his handwriting came back
more clearly on the next page.

*Have spoken to the doctor and changed pills.
Mind was wandering. Kept thinking that I should
write Ambrose. Would that I could!*

   *Sleeping less. Good. Too dangerous to sleep
in the woods anymore. They've got my scent now.*

   *Have begun typing. Must finish my transcrip-
tion before my mind wanders again.*

I turned the page and found nothing but the litany of the
twisted ones, written over and over again, for a half dozen pages.

"Ugh. That's enough for one night."

I flipped off the light and turned over on my side. The last
thought I remember having was to wonder what had happened
to that typewritten transcription in the end.

I got up the next morning feeling grumpy and much put-upon. Bongo hadn't needed to go out in the night, but he made up for it for taking twenty minutes to pee and losing his mind over a track in the grass. Probably deer. It crossed the yard, practically up to the steps, a dark trail in the dew-covered grass.

The dog ran back and forth along it, snuffling frantically, until his bladder finally overrode his nose. It was slightly less thrilling than I'm making it sound, but not by much.

I went into the kitchen, made instant coffee, and ate a breakfast bar that tasted like cardboard with chocolate chips in it. It tasted better than the coffee. If I was going to be here for very long, I'd have to spring for a cheap coffeemaker.

I set to work moving the largest pile of crap, which included a number of broken picture frames, assorted As Seen On TV kitchen gadgets, still in the original boxes, and a brass giraffe. Not sure about the brass giraffe. I patted its head. It was cold to the touch and had a vague, worried expression.

Moving the boxes revealed the back door. Well, I knew it had to be around there somewhere.

I opened it, found myself looking at a teetering wall of junk, and closed it again.

"Well, Bongo, ol' buddy, we'll be using the front door for a while yet."

Bongo was nose deep in his own breakfast and did not seem perturbed by this.

A few minutes later I took him out on a leash around back

and peered through the screens of the porch. In the morning sunlight, it was pretty obvious that the porch had been a dumping ground for old furniture, gardening equipment, and what looked like an ancient grill. All the corners had been filled in with more junk. It was really kind of impressive. She hadn't just hoarded; she'd made walls and ramparts out of her possessions, like she was expecting a siege.

I turned away and saw an animal on the far side of the yard.

It was only for an instant, out of the corner of my eye, but I jerked back, startled. The animal vanished.

"What the . . . ?"

Bongo was utterly unconcerned. A rabbit had been through here at some point in the last century and he was determined to track it to the end of the world. I fed out more line on the leash.

It was the rock. The big rock that Bongo had been going nuts over the other night. I'd forgotten all about it, and apparently so had he.

It was carved in a peculiar, abstract shape, with a deep swirl that went clear down to the ground, although whether the rock was partially buried or it was a deliberate choice by the carver, I couldn't tell you without getting out a shovel and digging.

I turned my head a few times, puzzled, and suddenly the animal leapt into sharp relief again. It was . . . a hare, maybe? No, a deer. The carved swirl looked a bit like the curve of hindquarters, but I couldn't tell you why it read so strongly as a living creature. There wasn't anything like front legs. The head was thrown backward so far that it lay upside down against the spine. The "eye" was two deep parallel lines. Nevertheless, when I turned my head, it seemed to move.

When I approached it, I couldn't see the deer at all anymore. The illusion worked only from a distance. Up close, it dissolved completely.

I touched the surface. It had the rough, crosshatched marks of a chisel. It was a good deal colder than the surrounding air. I shivered and wiped my fingers on my jeans, not sure if it was wet or just chilly.

"Did you see it the other night and think it was alive?" I asked Bongo. "Is that what set you off?"

Bongo strained after the scent of rabbit and didn't give the rock a glance.

As art went, it was actually pretty impressive. Much higher quality than I'd expect from my grandmother. I wondered if it was original to the place, or if Cotgrave had brought it in.

Despite the craftsmanship, I found I didn't have any desire to take it home. There was something unsettling about the lines of the eyes, as if the animal were angry. Did deer get angry?

Not the sort of thing you want at the bottom of the garden, anyhow.

"Just as well, really," I told the dog. "Staying here makes me want to go home and burn most of my stuff. I'll go all minimalist and sleep on a futon and have one perfect orchid for decor."

Bongo gave up on the rabbit and slumped against my leg, grinning hugely.

". . . and you'll probably eat the orchid, won't you? C'mon, let's go take a load to the dump and get a cup of coffee that isn't swill."

I spent a pleasant hour at the coffee shop. The Goth barista was just leaving, and I got to meet her assistant, a six-foot-plus black man with a voice that I could hear through the soles of my feet. I told him that I was reduced to instant coffee at home and he looked at me as if I had told him about a great personal tragedy.

"We sell beans," he rumbled. "I will grind them for you if you don't have a grinder. No one should have to drink that stuff."

I went to the hardware store and recklessly purchased a coffeemaker, then came back. The deep-voiced barista ground me up a pound of beans, which cost nearly as much as the coffeemaker. I could summon very little regret for this.

When the grinder had stopped grinding, he asked why I was in town, and I explained about Grandma.

"*Cotgrave*?" he said.

"Yeah?"

"My mama was the one who took her into town twice a week."

"Your mother's a saint," I said. "Seriously. A *saint*."

He grinned. "After raising my sisters and me, the old lady was nothing." He shook his head. "Sorry to hear she's gone, though."

"You're probably the only one," I said dryly. I wasn't feeling all that charitable toward Grandma now that I'd read her husband's journal. "But thank you."

"Ah, well." He bagged up the beans. "House bad?"

"Bad enough. She was starting to hoard in a big way."

He nodded. "Mama said she wouldn't let her in to see it, just waited on the front porch for her. She thought it was probably a mess in there, but she didn't keep cats and she was always dressed tidy, so no point in prying. Always wondered what happened after she went off to the home. . . ."

"She lasted nearly two years," I said.

"Tough old lady."

"That's one word for it." I smiled to soften the words—he was being much kinder than I was. "Please thank your mom for me, okay? If she hadn't been taking her into town, we'd have had to put her in the home a lot earlier, and she would have hated it."

"I will."

I waved and took my coffee with me. It smelled amazing. I might not drink it. I might just keep it around and huff the bag occasionally.

I got home, let Bongo pee on some things, and went inside. In the middle of setting up the coffeemaker, I heard a noise so loud and shocking that I nearly dropped the glass pot.

It was the phone ringing.

I hadn't heard a landline phone ring in so long that it took a minute to place it and then another minute to actually find the phone. It wasn't in the kitchen; it was over in the living room. My eyes had slid right over it—it hadn't occurred to me that it would be hooked up.

I eyed it like a snake as it rang. Should I answer? Who could be calling a dead woman?

Finally I picked it up and said, "H-hello?"

"Mouse?" The voice was tinny but clear. "Mouse, is that you?"

"Dad!" I said. "Dad, it's you!"

"I had the phone company reconnect the line," he said. "You didn't answer your cell phone."

I sighed. Dad was old enough that e-mail was a foreign land to him, and of course my phone was still barely keeping a charge. "No, we don't have cell signal out here," I said, rather than explain about software bugs.

"I'm glad I caught you. I wanted to make sure you made it there okay."

"Yeah." I blew my breath out in a huff. "It's . . . it's pretty bad."

Uncomfortable silence. I could hear him moving around on the other side of the line. Finally he said, "Yeah, it is."

I wanted to say *Why didn't you warn me?* but that sounded too accusing. Instead I said, "How long was she doing this?"

"I don't know. I knew the stairs were full of junk. You know how she couldn't throw anything away. But I hadn't gone into the rooms. I thought it was just like having a cluttered attic until I came down to take her to the home."

I leaned over and looked at the staircase. By the third step, it was impassable.

"I never stayed with her because of the dust, and she always wanted to go out. She'd been piling up newspapers, said she was going to get them recycled, but . . . I don't know." He coughed, one of the painful coughs that make me cringe. "I'm sorry, Mouse. I should have done more, but you know how hard it was to get her to do anything."

"It's okay," I said. It was surprisingly easy to forgive him. The clutter didn't feel like my father's neglect; it felt like a manifestation of my grandmother's malice. It could have turned on him as easily as on me. Would have turned on him, in fact, but I'd stepped in front of the bullet.

"It's not okay," he said wearily, "but it is what it is. Can you fix it? If it's cleared out, the place should be sellable, but you'll have to tell me if it's more trouble than its worth. Should I just get someone to tear the place down?"

A day or two ago I would have said yes. I opened my mouth to say just that.

She has hid the book.

Somewhere in the house was Cotgrave's Green Book. Whatever that was.

A day or two ago I might have just let it lie. But he'd cared about it so much, and he'd written about it, and . . .

. . . and he drew Kilroy on the page. And he taught you to draw Kilroy when you were a little kid. And your grandmother was cruel to him.

And he was obsessed with the book. The Green Book. With someone who twisted themself around like the twisted ones . . .

Oh, don't lie to yourself, Mouse. You could walk away from Kilroy and the rest without feeling too much of a qualm, but it's killing you to think there's a weird book hidden somewhere and you might not get to read it.

A bulldozer would make finding the book extremely difficult.

"No," I said, surprising myself. "Give me a while longer. I'm making headway. I can't swear that the second floor won't be a biohazard, but so far, so good."

"All right. Call me if you change your mind." He paused, and I waited. It always took him a moment to lead up to this. I don't think it came easily, but he was determined to do it anyway.

"Love you, Mouse."

"Love you, Dad."

We hung up.

———

"I'm an idiot," I told Bongo. "I could have gotten out of here. This place sucks."

Bongo thumped his tail on the floor agreeably.

"But . . . God. I think I want to find that book. As if that'll *fix* something."

Thump, thump, thump went the tail.

"I mean . . . poor old soul. I know he's not gonna care anymore. But he had to sleep in the *woods*. And the book clearly mattered to him. Why was he obsessed with this book?"

I sighed. It didn't make any sense, and I *knew* it didn't make any sense, and . . . well, here we were.

Maybe I just couldn't let a book go. Maybe it was just that I didn't want my grandmother to have *won*.

I looked around the room. It was so dark inside the house, even with every light in the place on. The kitchen looked almost like a normal kitchen and I'd shifted most of the newspapers, but there was still a corner of the living room covered in shoe boxes and old PennySavers, and the hallway was a disaster and behind every door there was more junk.

I hadn't even gotten the stairs cleared. I'd been here for *three days*.

Maybe my grandmother had won already.

If she was a ghost haunting this place, she'd be smirking at me. *Go on. Run away. I don't know why you bothered.*

I kicked a chair. It was childish, but I felt a little better. One thing I knew, though . . . I really didn't want to be here right now.

"C'mon, Bongo. Let's go for a walk. Clear my head."

I snapped Bongo's leash on him and he jumped up. We headed into the backyard and past the oak tree. He ignored the carved rock completely, focusing instead on a mourning dove that was strutting around in the leaf litter like it owned the place.

It wasn't very cold out. North Carolina weather is so erratic that it could go from blazing hot to below freezing by the end of the week, but it seemed to have settled into a springlike state. The trees had narrow green leaf buds out, but they weren't quite committing to budding yet. All the bare branches layered together like clouds of heavy gray smoke.

I gave Bongo's leash a tug, and he left the dove and walked along with me. Scary rocks notwithstanding, he usually has very good leash manners, despite his other flaws. (This is a testament to the rescue organization's training, not to my skills as a dog owner.) We kicked up dried leaves as we walked.

The open, leaf-floored woods gave way to a denser growth where the trees had been logged at some point in the past.

The pine trees were only about as tall as my head, nothing like the towering loblollies with their bare trunks. There was still a broad cut through the undergrowth, scarred by old tire tracks. Somebody might have been out in their ATVs, but not for a while.

I suppose I was technically trespassing, but it was out of deer season, and my impression was that nobody around here cared very much. I had walked in the woods when I was a kid . . . hadn't I?

I tried to summon up a memory, but couldn't. All I could remember was paved park trails. Maybe I hadn't wandered around behind Grandma's house after all, baffling as that was. I was a kid who enjoyed the outdoors, particularly compared to the cramped sniping inside the house. Wouldn't I have walked around back here?

Nothing looked familiar, or rather, it looked familiar only from trips with Aunt Kate. "Wintergreen," I muttered to myself, passing a familiar rosette of leaves. "Crane-fly orchid." That makes it sound like I'm some kind of amazing plant-identifying genius, but this one's easy. The leaves are dark purple underneath and even a botanical bystander like me can remember it. Their old name was *crippled crane-fly orchid*, but it's one of those names that's softened as people learn not to be total assholes to one another.

Bongo snuffled through the scrubby brushes, occasionally poking himself in the nose with a twig. Then he'd jerk his head back, looking offended, and snort.

I gave him a little bit more line so that he could run back

and forth. Every now and then he'd get it wrapped around me and I had to do a balletic twirl to straighten it out again.

I was in the middle of one such twirl when I looked up and saw a woman watching me.

My startle reflex was so strong that I gasped. Not that there shouldn't be people there—I mean, this probably wasn't even Grandma's property anymore—but I just hadn't expected anyone.

Bongo really wanted to go make friends. I pulled him back, just in case she didn't like dogs, and waved.

The woman looked at me for a little too long, then raised her hand in the limpest sort of greeting. She was tall and had long, pale hair. Her clothes were loose and flowing, sort of hippie-earth-mother type, only in gray and brown, which was probably why I hadn't spotted her at first.

She turned and began to walk away.

Well, then.

"Guess she doesn't want to make friends," I told Bongo quietly.

Bongo was all for running after her and forcing the issue, but then a squirrel scolded him from the trees, and by the time that encounter had come to its natural end the woman was long gone.

I heard the woodpecker tapping again, which meant that I was looking up, not down at the dog, and so of course Bongo took that moment to fling himself into a gap in the bushes.

"*Yrrrrk!*"

Bongo let out an excited bark and strained against the leash.

"Dammit, dog . . ."

It was a weird little gap, almost like a streambed. I think it had probably been a drainage ditch at some point, but it was dry now. Trees had grown up over the sides and laced together to form a crisscrossed roof overhead.

The ground was cracked clay. It was as good a direction to walk as any, and if it got too narrow, I could step up a foot or two onto the bank. And Bongo really wanted to see what was down there.

"Fine . . ." I stepped down into the ditch.

Bongo had his nose down, straining at the leash. When I came after him, he glanced back at me—*good, you're here, let's go!*—and took off at a trot.

Every now and again, somewhere in that dense skull, some relay clicks over and Bongo is suddenly competent. *I know what I'm doing. I'm a professional. Follow me.* It's amazing to watch, except for the bit where he can cover an enormous amount of ground without even noticing and then wants to be carried home.

But it's not like I had anywhere to be. I hurried after him at a trot, watching my feet in case there were any sudden holes to step in.

That'd be just awesome; step in a hole and break your ankle a mile from the house.

I'd rather be out here with a broken ankle than back in that house right now, I thought to myself, even though that was probably a bit melodramatic.

No, you wouldn't. You're wasting time. You should be back at the house clearing out the bedrooms. Those rooms full of dolls and Tupperware won't empty themselves.

Ugh. Maybe I *should* just call Dad back and tell him to hire a bulldozer.

If you were back at the house, you could be looking for the Green Book. . . .

Well, there *was* that.

The corridor of trees grew more solid. When I glanced up briefly, I had an impression that I was surrounded by wicker walls. Bongo was dappled with sunlight through the breaks in the branches. He looked a bit like photos of the antelope he was named after, bits of bright light and shadow on dark red hide.

Antelope probably did not move with that businesslike, ground-eating trot. The leash was taut but not straining.

We were going uphill, I realized. There were more rocks underfoot now, some of them half buried in the clay, some lying loosely on the surface. One turned when I stepped on it and I had to catch myself. Bongo looked back at me again—*still with me? Come on, human. We've got places to be.*

The path got darker and steeper, and Bongo started doing some of the work of pulling me up the hill. I have friends with huskies who do a type of cross-country skiing where they hook the leashes to their belts and let the huskies pull them along. Huskies are made for pulling, though. Coonhounds are mostly made to follow their nose to a tree and then bay hysterically until a hunter comes along and shoots whatever is in the tree.

Still, he got his shoulders into it and didn't complain. He was bound and determined to go up this hillside even if he had to drag me.

"Buddy, if this tunnel gets any lower, I'm sure as hell not crawling after you!"

It did not get much lower. I had to duck my head, but I was

going hunched over anyway. I couldn't believe how steep it had gotten. We talk about the hills around here, but they're not like you get up by the mountains, when you have actual honest-to-God valleys. I must have been going downhill at a gentle slope for most of the walk to have an incline like this waiting for me.

Oh well, at least it'd be downhill on the way back. . . .

I tried to say this to Bongo, but I was wheezing and he was making that raspy *whrrrff* noise that meant his collar was cutting into his neck. I couldn't go any faster, but he wasn't about to stop.

About five minutes before we both died, light bloomed around us. Bongo took three steps into grass and froze.

I took two more steps and fell to my knees on top of a mountain that shouldn't have been there.

5

I was on a bare, grassy hillside scattered with stones, and that was impossible. I could see for miles in every direction, and that, too, was impossible.

I started to laugh. It wasn't that it was funny. It was just that if I laughed, it wasn't serious. I've heard that people who get shot start laughing sometimes, that they'll tell you they're fine even when they're holding their guts in with their hands.

As it happens, I knew exactly where I was, or at least I knew what where I was *was*, if that makes any sense. It was an Appalachian bald.

I only know this because of Aunt Kate, and I'm probably getting it wrong, but as I understand it, it's a thing that happens in the southern mountains where you get the top of a hill that ought to be covered in trees, and instead it's all grass, as if someone has been lugging a lawnmower up a few thousand feet. There's no reason for it to be grass and nobody's quite sure why it's not a forest. Hence the name *bald*.

Our family vacations to the Great Smoky Mountains involved visiting a bunch of balds. I didn't really mind. After a couple of days in Pigeon Forge, home of hillbilly mini golf, hillbilly laser tag, and hillbilly bumper cars, a bare grass hillside started to seem positively restful. And it made Aunt Kate really happy. There's a bunch of plants that only grow on balds, so botanists get very excited and narrate the plant life while they wander around on their knees. "Ooh! Creeping St. John's Wort!" and so forth.

I say all this to indicate that I know an Appalachian bald when I see one—or at least a bald of some sort. I guess it's possible I wasn't in the Appalachians after all, since, as I may have mentioned earlier, this was completely impossible.

There aren't any balds near my grandmother's house. There aren't any *mountains* near my grandmother's house. There are very gentle hills, sometimes cut away into miniature river valleys. There are absolutely, positively, not the sort of hills where you stand on top and gaze over the landscape and see the horizon tinted blue-orange in the distance.

I knelt atop the bald and gazed at the blue-orange horizon.

"This is fucked up," I told Bongo.

Bongo was looking around warily. His ears were up and alert as if he was hearing something. When I spoke, his tail wagged once in acknowledgment, but he was holding it in the stiffly upright curl of a dog on the job.

White stones littered the grass. I don't know much about

rocks. If Aunt Kate had been a geologist, I could probably talk for hours about glacial remnants and thrust faults, but she wasn't, so hey, they were big white rocks.

Right. Geography lesson over. I was somewhere impossible.

I dug my knuckles into the grass and touched dirt. The world was not painted on some kind of enormous canvas designed to fool random dog walkers.

So my options were that I was dreaming, hallucinating, or that Bongo and I had just walked a few hundred miles in twenty minutes.

"Or aliens," I told Bongo. "Maybe we've had missing time. Maybe we were abducted. Did you get probed? I don't think I got probed." My nether regions did not feel any different than they normally felt. I assume you notice that sort of thing.

I stood up. Nothing much happened.

I turned in a circle, passing the leash from hand to hand. Behind me, where we had come up, stood the tunnel of trees. There were thin, scruffy bushes around the entrance. They hadn't leafed out yet, or perhaps they were dead.

The tunnel seemed very small and very steep. I had a hard time believing that I'd climbed it at all, and getting back down was going to be an experience. It seemed to go straight down, surrounded by the bare branches, which were layered densely on top of one another until they faded together like dark smoke. If I tried to go back down through the bushes instead, I was going to get flayed alive by twigs, assuming I could get through them at all.

I turned away from the tunnel and looked out across the bald. On two sides, it seemed to fall away sharply, but the third

side, opposite the tunnel, stretched out in a gentle slope, littered with stones.

Bongo was facing that direction, and when I took a step, he
strode out as if we were going for a perfectly normal walk. His
ears and tail were still up, though, and I had the impression
that he was thinking very hard about something (or more accurately, that his nose was thinking very hard about something.
Bongo's nose is far more intelligent than the rest of him, and I
believe it uses his brain primarily as a counterweight).

His nose was working now, nostrils flaring in and out.

Well. I reasoned that either one of two things was going
to happen. Either I would go down the tunnel and be in the
woods behind my grandmother's house—in which case either
my understanding of geography was completely and utterly
messed up or Something Weird Was Going On—or I would go
down the tunnel and discover myself somewhere in the Great
Smoky Mountains and have to walk to a ranger station and get
a lift to a rental car place so that I could drive home (and yes,
Something Weird Would Be Going On).

Neither of these situations seemed likely to change if I went
forward and investigated the rest of the bald for twenty minutes,
and for all I knew, there would be a sign from the Park Service
saying, "This is an amazing optical illusion and you are actually
at sea level."

We went forward.

A little breeze sighed over the grass, rippling it in fine,
straw-colored waves. When I looked into the distance, I saw
more hills. They had the same dark, smokelike quality of bare

branches as the ones around the tunnel. And the ones around my grandmother's house, for that matter.

As my heart slowed from my run up the hill, I began to think that I was being stupid.

I could still be behind my grandmother's house. It's totally possible.

I'm going to go into Pondsboro and say, "Did you know there's a bald there?" and they're going to look at me like I'm stupid and say, "Yeah, obviously, that's Moonshine Hill," or something like that. And maybe I'll just have been looking in completely the wrong place all this time and didn't notice the hill.

And then I'm gonna feel like an idiot for thinking that it was aliens.

One's own idiocy is often a cheering thought. I veered to the left, wondering if I'd be able to see my grandmother's house, which would make me feel better about the whole thing.

Bongo gave me one of his human-going-the-wrong-way looks, but allowed himself to be led to the edge of the bald. His nose stayed pointing in the original direction, though, which provided an interesting physics lesson in how a hound's body can rotate around a fixed point.

I got to the edge, such as it was—at least, the point where the slope became steep enough that I didn't feel like going any farther—and saw more bare trees, rank upon rank. No roads, not that that meant anything. The trees could be in the way. All those dark trees sinking down into a valley and rising up again into another hill and another, a whole circle of hills around this one, hung with endless colorless trees.

*I'll say, "Did you know that there's a whole bunch of hills?"
and they'll say, "Yeah, obviously, that's the Moonshine Range.
You're in hill country. What did you expect?" And I'll feel like an
even bigger idiot. . . .*

I dug my nails into my palms.

I *wasn't* in hill country. I *knew* I wasn't. But—

Well, either I was wrong or the hills were. And while I have
known people—and dated at least one—who would stubbornly
maintain that they were right in the face of geography, I am
not one of them. Which is why we're no longer dating, among
other reasons.

"Right," I said. "I'm in hill country."

Bongo strained at the leash, nose working. I let him lead
across the bald, through the gray rocks.

A shape coming out from under one rock startled me badly
for a minute, until I realized that it was a small tree, or had been
at some point in the distant past. It was the bleached gray-white
color of dead wood, and it twisted around like a snake, gnarled
by wind and weather. Aunt Kate would have been thrilled by it,
I'm sure—a tree growing on a bald, where trees were supposed
to grow but didn't.

I was less thrilled. It looked diseased.

Bongo was still going forward. His head was up, not down,
not tracking but scanning for . . . something.

Maybe a bird. I remembered birds in the last bald. Little
warbly things that buzzed, each buzz going up and up like a
question.

I couldn't hear any birds here. Not even the apparently

invisible woodpeckers that seemed to fill the woods around Grandma's house, tap-tappa-tap . . . tapping.

Well, a woodpecker wouldn't find much to eat up here, would it? That one tree wouldn't make a meal for anybody.

I glanced over my shoulder toward the tunnel—and shrieked.

Bongo yanked on the leash in surprise, then turned and cowered behind my legs. He was hoping I would protect him from whatever made me scream, but the end result was that he pulled me off-balance and I fell backward over him, and we landed in a flailing heap on the grass.

"God—shit—damn!" I said, or something like that.

We sorted ourselves out. The leash got wrapped around my thigh and I had to do some unwrapping, complicated by Bongo trying to climb in my lap to make sure that I wasn't mad at him.

I felt like an idiot for yelling. But I'd been badly startled when I turned around and saw that on this side, every one of the gray rocks was carved into a shape.

The carvings were the same sort as the deer-stone in the backyard, but bigger. They had *weight*, like . . . oh, those giant stone Olmec heads in South America, say. Some of them even looked a bit like those heads, with leering human faces on them. The style was different, don't get me wrong, but there was the same feeling of mass.

I got up and went over to one. It looked as if it went down into the ground instead of sitting on top of it.

Hell, maybe it did. There could be weird ridges of rock sticking up that someone had carved into various shapes. Rocks did that, didn't they?

I could have poked it, I suppose, but that would have involved touching one. I didn't want to touch one. It looked like it would be cold, which would be normal for stone, but some part of my brain insisted that it would be warm, maybe not like a human but like a lizard lying out in the sun, and then I'd probably have to run screaming. I kept my hands to myself.

I'm an editor. I have a vague knowledge of botany gleaned from my aunt and a highly specific knowledge of one particular breed of dog. I don't know anything about archaeology or modern art. I couldn't tell you if the carvings were ten years old or ten thousand.

I mean, probably they weren't ten thousand. Were there even humans here then? Were there still mammoths wandering around? Err . . . hmm. Probably not mammoths. Ten thousand years ago was before the pyramids, but after mammoths, wasn't it?

I was a bit hazy on the details. Normally I'd look it up on my phone, but . . .

Actually, that was a great idea. I took out my phone, turned it on—it was at about 5 percent power, no signal—and took a photo of the nearest head. It made the camera noise, then immediately shut off.

Stupid damn phone.

Bongo peed on the dead tree in a meditative fashion.

The carved face glared at me. It had bulging eyes and an almost nonexistent nose. Its lower lip was pulled down to reveal broad, flat teeth that went most of the way to the ears.

It wasn't the most pleasant thing I've ever seen.

All the carvings were like that. They weren't all faces. Some of them were animals, like the deer-stone, but even the animals were messed up. Their hind legs curled up into their bellies and over their backs, or their mouths were open like they were screaming or panting or laughing. They were elongated and earless, like snakes.

A couple had swollen bellies and long breasts that wrapped around their bodies like their legs. I put an involuntary arm across my chest. It was painful just to look at that.

As a modern art installation, it was grotesquely effective. As prehistoric art . . . Well, I'd wonder a bit about the people who made them.

Also, I'd wonder why there wasn't a park ranger standing over them to slap anybody who got out a can of spray paint. I'm pretty sure that you can't just have ancient ruins lying around without some idiot tagging the things.

I'll say, "Hey, guys, I was up on those hills that are apparently in my backyard and there's all these carved rocks," and they'll say, "Oh, yeah, that's a State Historic Site, the Moonshine Hill Stones. Didn't you see the sign?" and I'll say, "Isn't there supposed to be a ranger or something?" and they'll say, "Well, you know, budget cuts . . ." and we'll nod sadly about the way local government cuts things like this, and also education, but the police department gets an armored assault vehicle even though they mostly deal with rogue cows. . . .

I went a little farther through the stones. Bongo was getting annoyed with my frequent stops, but really, these were fascinating. Like gargoyles, only not as friendly. You got the impression that gargoyles were there to chase away evil spirits.

These things looked like they were there to chase away gargoyles.

A whole line of them lay flat on the grass in front of me, and here I could tell that they actually went underground, either partially buried or actually anchored into the hill itself.

Two were pretty clearly supposed to be humans. They lay curled up on their sides, arms over their heads, as if they were sleeping or weeping or dead.

I couldn't even begin to guess what the other ones were. I took a few steps back, hoping they'd come into focus the way the deer-stone had, but they didn't. They were just contorted masses of lines, twisting around in unpleasant, erratic ways. The carver had clearly heard of the golden ratio and wanted no truck with it.

For all their abstraction, though, you got the feeling that they were supposed to be alive, the way the snaky animals were alive. They were the creepiest of the lot.

Bongo yanked on his leash again.

"Fine, fine," I said. "Let's go see what you're after."

I felt a bit of a chill turning my back on the carved stones. The flat ones were close enough to one another that I had to walk carefully so as not to touch one. Bongo picked his way between them like a dancer.

There were more ahead of us, though. They got bigger as we followed the curve of the bald forward and down, and the carved lines contorted in the corners of my vision. It was all very creepy.

I found myself humming tunelessly to ward off the creepiness. If only there had been birds calling, or something! But there was just Bongo and me, two little creatures toiling down the grass through the forest of silent stones.

"Oh Susanna . . . ," I sang, not very well. "Don't you cry for me . . ."

I looked behind me again. We'd come far enough down the slope that the top of the bald was no longer visible. Several of the stones were outlined against the sky, dark gray on light gray.

"I've come from Alabama with a banjo on my knee. . . ."

Where on earth had I learned that song first? We sang it in grade school, but I remember knowing different lyrics and getting frustrated that the teacher sang it wrong. They sang "The sun was so hot I froze myself" and I knew it as "The sun so hot I froze to death." Arguably I was a morbid child, but I must have gotten that from somewhere.

My father used to sing it, I think. Or maybe my mother, who had died so long ago that I could hardly remember her.

Your mother's probably here under these stones right now.

It was such a weird and intrusive thought that I fumbled the chorus. "I . . . ah. Right. And if I do not find her, then I will surely die . . . and when I'm dead and buried, oh, Susanna, don't you cry . . ."

All the dead are here under the stones.

I don't want you to think that I was being mind-controlled or something. It wasn't from outside me. It was just the unpleasant little voice that pops up in the middle of the night to remind you about the stupid thing you did in high school, or to whisper that maybe there's a monster under the bed. But something about the stones and the creepiness and the isolation of this place made it louder.

Keep walking and you'll walk out of the sky and down the hill down under the ground among the stones among the dead. . . .

"The fuck?" I said out loud, which shut the voice up for a second.

Bongo glanced back to make sure I wasn't swearing at him, then kept leading me forward.

There was a tall stone ahead of us. He seemed to be headed for it. "All right," I told him. "That far, and then we go back. This place is weirding me out."

this place this place is weirding this is the weirding under the ground the weirdlings come out to play and then the sun freezes them into stones but they'll move again when your back is turned.

I started singing again to drown out the thoughts. This was like having the world's strangest anxiety attack.

"I had a dream the other night, when everything was still. . . ."

The tall stone was much taller than I had thought. The base was set in a deep depression in the ground, perfectly round like a bowl. Gray rocks stood all around the lip of the circle, facing inward, like a knee-high Stonehenge.

"I thought I saw Susannah dear, a-coming down the hill. . . ."

There may have been a seep in the depression. Mosses grew in a thick blanket around the base of the stone, shaded by tiny green ferns. I don't know my ferns. They all looked alike to me. Aunt Kate said it wasn't worth bothering unless you really wanted to get into spores. I do remember that one was called *ebony spleenwort* because I always thought the name was funny, particularly since it was a green fern and not ebony at all.

" . . . a buckwheat cake was in her mouth, a tear was in her eye . . ."

The tall—monolith? Dolmen? Big-ass rock?—was the only one that wasn't carved into some unpleasant shape. There were two lines near the top, broken in the middle, a bit like eyes. Otherwise it was smooth and white.

Bongo, having come this far, had stopped. He stared at the rock and gave the thinnest thread of a whine. Whatever he had been following, he hadn't expected it to be this.

Would the surface of the monolith feel rough, like sandpaper, or polished smooth? It didn't reflect as if it were polished. I put a hand on one of the low rocks and used it to lower myself to the ground on the lip of the bowl.

Bongo whined again, more loudly.

"Says I, I'm comin' from the South, Susannah don't you cry . . ."

The monolith was carved, I could see now. It was very faint, that was all. The lines swirled up and around and down, looking like . . . like . . . something. I couldn't quite make out what it was supposed to represent.

The bowl was steeper than it looked. I was afraid that I was going to roll down and smack into the monolith. That was one way to tell if it was smooth or rough, but I didn't want to find out with my face. I wanted to run my palms over it and feel the chisel marks on my fingers. Then I would be able to tell what the carving represented.

Then perhaps I could put my cheek against it and feel the coldness of the stone growing warm underneath my skin.

And through the stone pressing down into the other place the voorish dome under the ground the other place where the dead go

Bongo wouldn't leave the lip. He pulled back against the leash until the collar was up around his ears.

"Come on, you stupid fucking dog," I snarled, and my voice was harsh and grating and *what the hell was I doing?*

I blinked a few times.

I was standing partway down the depression in the ground. My hand felt greasy where I'd touched one of the carved rocks. The moss was too yielding underfoot, as if I were leaving bruises.

"Jesus," I said. "*Jesus.*"

I don't know what had come over me. I hauled myself out of the depression, even though I had to touch the gray stone again. I'll be honest, I was nearly expecting it to bite me. Bongo pressed so close to my thigh that I nearly fell over him again. His ears were down and his tail was tucked and he was making little champing motions with his mouth.

"Right," I said. "Right. You're my good dog. I'm sorry I yelled."

I wiped my hands on the seat of my jeans and glanced over my shoulder at the tall white monolith. It gazed eyelessly over my head. Why had I wanted to touch it?

Bongo whined again.

I knelt down right there, even though the presence of the stone made my skin crawl, and pressed my forehead against his. You have to reassure dogs right away. They don't have a good sense of time, and they don't link past behavior to the present.

Why had I yelled at my dog anyway? What had come over me?

go down the hillside out of the sky under the ground through the stone to the gray place

"You're a good dog," I said to Bongo. "A good, good dog."

He sighed and leaned into me.

"You said it. C'mon, buddy, let's get out of here."

We made our way back up the hill. The voice in my head buzzed like a gnat, growing more distant as I shoved it down, like the desire to jump fading as you stepped away from the edge.

The rocks stared at us as we passed. The flat, twisted stones pulsed like a moiré pattern.

I made faces like the faces on the rocks, and I twisted myself about like the twisted ones, and I lay down flat on the ground like the dead ones—

I inhaled sharply.

Christ, I'm stupid! This is what Cotgrave was writing about!

Probably you're thinking I'm an idiot not to have made the connection before. But Cotgrave's diary was decades old, and honestly, I'd been thinking more about its relation to my grandmother. You don't expect that ramblings of a sad old man to suddenly turn up in real life.

I felt like I'd been kicked in the chest. But that was stupid too—of course Cotgrave must have known about this place; it was practically in his own backyard, and there was the deerstone actually *in* the garden. The deer-stone had to have come from up here. He must have found a small one that wasn't buried and carried it back home.

Unless he carved them himself. That's possible, isn't it?

This was an unsettling thought. I couldn't reconcile the image of the tired old man who had sat in a chair reading the newspaper with whatever mad artist had created the field of carvings.

You couldn't possibly create something like that and then wander around like a normal person, going to the grocery store and worrying about heart medication and paying the water bill, could you?

Serial killers do it all the time.

No, that's unfair. It's not like these are actually hurting people. They're just creepy, that's all. Whoever made these is a sort of . . . Goth genius, that's all. Like H. R. Giger or that guy who does the album covers with all the super-pale people and the skulls.

Still . . .

Lying down like the dead ones, I could just about see. In order to make faces like the faces in these rocks, though, you'd have to be able to lick your own eyelids. And I don't think any person with bones could twist themselves about like the twisted ones.

"It can't be done," I told Bongo. I tried to make a face like the one on the nearest carving. Its lower jaw was distended like a snake about to swallow and its eyes bulged. "See, 'ook . . ."

I opened my eyes and mouth as wide as I could and *wider, wider, wide enough to eat the sun this is the one that puts the stars out when the shadows go over them this one's eyes can see in the gray that's left behind after even the darkness is eaten.*

Oh shit.

I tried to close my mouth and it didn't want to close.

What the hell is going on oh my God Aunt Kate always said my face would freeze like that and holy shit I think it is.

I put my hand up under my chin and shoved it up. My teeth slammed together. The hinge of my jaw ached like when you get dental work and they hold your mouth open for an hour.

"Right," I said in a high, panicky voice. "Don't taunt the evil rocks." And I bolted past the last of the stones with Bongo running beside me, and I didn't stop until I saw the tunnel of trees.

Relief hit me so strongly that I thought for a minute my knees were going to buckle. I hadn't realized how frightened I'd been that the tunnel would be gone.

Of course it isn't. This is perfectly normal. Absolutely nothing weird going on here. I'll go into town and say, "So there's this tall white stone . . ." and they'll say, "Oh, yeah, that's the Moonshine Monolith," and I'll order a coffee with a shot of Irish cream syrup and sit down and look it up on the Internet and there'll be a whole page about how the rocks were carved in the 1700s by a local mason called Zebadiah or Asa or some other old-fashioned name.

And I just had a weird spasm in that one muscle—the temperomandibularwhatsit, the one that goes out sometimes and clicks—because I was making a face at the stupid rock and not because the rock was talking in my head and trying to get me to imitate it, not at all, because that would be crazy.

I went down the tunnel of trees, half on my feet and half on my ass, and Bongo slithered and scrabbled down with me.

By the time I got to the bottom, I was pretty much willing to chalk up the incident with the stones to the power of suggestion.

It was weird and creepy and you were already on edge and

the line from the journal just set you off, that's all. And staying in that house would disorder anyone's nerves. Focus on the things that are actually real, like the fact that Cotgrave's journal talked about the carved rocks.

We hurried back through the trees. The way seemed shorter, probably because Bongo knew that dinner awaited him at the house and was suddenly all business.

I wanted nothing more than to run into the bedroom and snatch up Cotgrave's journal, but Bongo needed water (and for that matter, so did I). And I was covered in twigs and dust and my skin still felt greasy where I'd touched the stones. So I got us both water and then took a shower and scrubbed down with a bar of gritty yellow soap that Grandmother had stashed in a bathroom drawer.

I was drying off when somebody rang the doorbell, and I let out a shriek.

The door slammed open. "Jaysus!" cried a voice. "You bein' murdered? Where you at, honey? I'll get 'em!"

And that is how I met Foxy.

6

Foxy had a face that was well lived in for fifty or in good shape for seventy, and since she never told anyone her age, I couldn't say which it was. She was six feet tall and wore black leather boots with heels. She had on a denim skirt, a hot pink top, three necklaces, and a bright orange scarf. Her earrings would have reached her shoulders, but they kept getting tangled up in her scarf and then she'd free them with a practiced flick. Her nails were a brilliant turquoise.

On 99 percent of humanity, the outfit would have been a riot of mismatched color. On Foxy, it somehow all pulled together. She looked like a cross between a drag queen and a wildflower meadow.

After we sorted out the issue of whether or not I was being murdered, Bongo had to be soothed with petting and dog treats, and I had to put on something more substantial than a towel. Foxy leaned against the kitchen counter and looked around.

"Forgive the mess . . . ," I said hopelessly.

"Ain't your mess, hon," said Foxy. "We all know what the old lady was like. Tomas said you're here to clean the house out, and I wouldn't wish that job on anybody."

"Tell me about it . . ."

"Came over to thank you for the microwave." She moved restlessly, setting her jewelry clicking together. "And—shit, you ain't eating ramen for dinner, are you?"

I shuffled hurriedly in front of the ramen on the counter. "I . . . uh . . ."

"Come have dinner with us tonight," she said. It was somewhere between an offer and an imperial command. "It's just me and Tomas and Skip, but we'll do you up a damn sight better than ramen."

I was torn between a strong desire for a real meal and human company—particularly after that weird afternoon in the stones—and an equally strong desire to stay home, read the rest of Cotgrave's diary, and maybe get to the bottom of things.

"Well . . ."

"Your momma alive?" asked Foxy abruptly.

"Uh . . . no?"

"Then if she's lookin' down from heaven, she'll want to make sure somebody was feeding you, not eating ramen in this nasty old rattrap."

I bowed to a will superior to my own. "May I have an hour?" I asked humbly. "I'm still damp."

Foxy grinned. "Look at me, rushing in here and dragging you out to eat dinner with soap still in your hair. Come on over when you're ready, hon. Just across the road and up to the big house."

And with that she swept out, leaving me slightly dazed in her wake. I could hear her immense boots clack on the steps as she went out. I couldn't imagine wearing heels that size on a gravel driveway, but she didn't seem to notice.

"I guess I'm going out to dinner," I told Bongo.

But first there was something important to do. I put a towel around my shoulders to catch drips and sat on the bed with Cotgrave's diary in hand.

If I was hoping for a great revelation—"By the way, I've taken up sculpting"—I didn't get it. There were several pages about the adjustments to his medication and a few repetitions of the litany of the twisted ones. It gave me the creeps reading it, now that I'd seen what it probably referred to.

I made faces like the faces on the rocks . . .

"You did not," I muttered. "Human faces don't work that way." I deliberately did not think about what had happened on the hill. It was just me being stupid.

Then, about halfway through the book:

> *Slept in woods again. Had to. Saw one of their poppets. Just watched, didn't do anything. Don't know if they can hurt someone or just scare them. With my heart, not much difference!*

He'd underlined *difference*. The rest of the page was blank, except for another drawing of Kilroy, sideways this time.

Another few pages of nothing much. I squeezed water out of my hair.

Then:

> *Met girl in woods, near place of stones.*

I sat up straighter. "Hel*lo* . . . ," I muttered. Had Cotgrave been having an affair? No, he was old with a bad heart. Although that doesn't always stop people.

> *She knows. One of them? Doesn't seem like it. Not normal, though. Beautiful hair. Ambrose believed in changelings. No reason to think he was wrong. Younger than the ones I saw in Wales, anyway, if one of them.*

Cotgrave had seen changelings in Wales? Well, I'd never been, but it seemed like the sort of place you'd get them. Perhaps Welsh fairies stole children and confiscated their vowels.

> *Have almost finished typing up manuscript. Remember more than I thought I did, but know I'm forgetting parts. Hid it. Won't say where. Think <u>she</u> might be reading this.*
>
> *If you are, then you're an awful old biddy and I wish I'd died before I married you. Go ahead and say something about that, if you're willing to admit you've been snooping.*

"Ha!" I punched the air. Poor old Cotgrave—but he'd gotten in a blow there. Grandma would never admit to wrongdoing. If she yelled at him for calling her names, she'd be in the wrong for reading his private papers. It must have driven her up the wall not being able to call him on it.

I sighed. And she'd probably taken it out on the old man too. But it's not like she would have been sweetness and light otherwise, anyway.

> Won't say any more here. Doesn't matter anyway.
> Gonna get out one way or the other. And you'll
> finally be free of me, <u>you old bat</u>.

He'd underlined *you old bat* twice. And that was it. The last entry. The rest of the book was blank. I flipped through it, carefully at first, then increasingly annoyed.

"Dammit, Cotgrave . . . you couldn't have said something? A helpful clue for the person reading your journal? *By the way, the girl I met lived down the road, and here's her phone number if you'd like to ask her about the stones.* Gah."

Well, presumably there was more in his typed manuscript. Which quite possibly my grandmother had found and disposed of.

No, she wouldn't have disposed of it. She hadn't disposed of the diary, and it insulted her to her face. She couldn't throw away anything. It was in the house somewhere, surely, with the Green Book and a thousand old PennySavers and the corks to every bottle of wine she'd ever opened.

I sighed and shoved the journal into the desk drawer, then ran the towel over my drying hair. It was time to dress for dinner.

––––––––––––

Foxy was sitting out on the front porch. She had a mason jar in her hand, full of ice and amber, which she waved in my direction.

"It's a mint julep," she said. "Want one?"

"I don't see any mint," I said.

"Yeah, we ran out."

"Doesn't that make it just a julep?"

"No," said a gray-haired man stepping out onto the porch behind her, "because she doesn't put any simple syrup in it either."

Foxy grinned. "Aw, but mint juleps are so classy. Just straight bourbon over ice makes it sound like I'm a lush."

"I'll take one," I said. After my experience with the carved stones, getting blitzed seemed like a delightful idea.

The house was a sagging, ramshackle affair with a battered tin roof. There were a couple extra additions and a covered carport that held cobwebs and elderly machinery. I could see a single-wide trailer set at right angles to it, and another farther back on the property.

A radio played tinnily from inside the house. We sat on the front porch drinking un-juleps and watching fireflies blink on and off over the grass.

The gray-haired man was named Skip. He had a thick braid down his back and pretty much screamed *aging hippie*. He was a potter.

"Not that it's hard to be a potter around here," he said. "The clay's alive. Red clay, like blood. It wants to be useful. Practically throws itself."

I nodded politely into my un-julep. Foxy rolled her eyes behind his back.

Tomas came up with grease on his hands and launched into a diatribe about tractor engines that I didn't even begin to understand.

"Cool, cool," said Foxy. "Dinner's nearly ready, hon."

"It needs a new glorshometer with a zappulater cap," he said. (Okay, not really, but hell if I can remember what he actually said.)

"That glorshometer's been fixing to go for ages," said Foxy.

"Well, it's gone now. We'll have to get a new one."

"Ah, just thump it a few times. It'll be fine."

Tomas sighed, gave me a *you see what I have to put up with* look, and went to scrub off his hands.

We all tromped inside. It was dark in the house, with battered seventies wood paneling, but there were shockingly Day-Glo rock posters on most of the walls. Bob Marley smiled down benignly over the dinner table, holding a joint between his fingers.

Skip pulled a casserole out of the oven, baked in a broad pottery dish. Foxy refilled my un-julep to the top.

"Did you make the dishes?" I asked, as Skip slapped out generous spoonfuls into bowls.

"He did indeed," said Foxy proudly. "He sells 'em for a small fortune at a gallery in town, but we get to eat off 'em every day." Skip ducked his head, looking embarrassed.

The casserole was a fine example of what can be done with cans of cream of mushroom soup. It still beat ramen. We ate in silence, except for the radio and the sounds of silverware clinking against stoneware.

Foxy put a scoop into a bowl and set it on the floor for Bongo, who slurped it up with great enthusiasm. (I must take steps to ensure that my vet never reads this.)

Tomas had seconds and then gathered up the bowls. "You doing okay over there?" he asked. "Nothing bothering you?"

"All kinds of things are bothering me," I said, compelled to honesty by the alcohol. "I was up the bald hill behind the house. . . ."

They looked at me. I waited for someone to say, "Oh, yeah, that was just Moonshine Hill. . . ."

"A hill?" said Skip. "No real hills around here."

Tomas came to my defense, probably out of chivalry. "There's some rises back there. If you're walking, it sure seems like you're climbing."

This was what I'd feared, but I plowed ahead anyway. "No, it was a real hill. You know, the one covered with all the carved stones?"

The table went suddenly silent, except for the blare of the radio. It was playing "Lydia the Tattooed Lady."

If you are ever planning on having a serious conversation with people you barely know, about weird carvings on an impossible hill behind your house, try to get a better soundtrack.

Foxy looked at me solemnly across the table. "You seen those stones?" she said.

"Uh," I said. "Yeah? I mean, there's a hill and a whole bunch of them on top."

"That's not a good place, man," said Tomas. "My grandma, she'd say there were devils up there."

"Huh!" said Foxy. "Don't know about devils."

I noted that we had somehow skipped completely over the question of whether the hill existed. This did not make me feel better.

The radio informed us that we could learn a lot from Lydia.

"They were just carvings," I said, even though they hadn't been just carvings. But if I admitted they were more than that, I'd be opening a door to a whole lot of things. I wanted that door to stay firmly closed.

"Mostly," said Foxy. "Mostly they are. Sometimes they ain't. Like the hill. Sometimes it's there; sometimes it ain't."

"Who made them?" I asked, shoving the question of disappearing hills behind that mental door, with the rest.

Lydia, we were told, could show you the world on various parts of her anatomy.

Foxy turned her head and said, "Shut that damned thing off, will you?"

Skip leaned back in his chair and flipped off the radio. I was more relieved than I could say.

"Don't know," said Foxy. "Not sure anybody made them."

"Somebody had to make them," I said.

"Maybe they grew," said Foxy. "Ever think of that, eh?" She slammed back the rest of her un-julep.

This was a very unpleasant thought. "Couldn't it have been . . . I don't know . . . Indians or something?"

Foxy snorted. "There were people here for a thousand years before white men landed," she said, "but I doubt any of them were ever fool enough to make things like that."

She glanced at Skip. "Don't look at me," he said. "My people were all Chemawa. Whole other side of the continent, like sensible folk. If you want a wise old Indian to dispense sacred wisdom, go find somebody from around here. Me, I throw pots."

"I'd stay away from them," said Tomas, who had been listening silently the whole time. "You leave stuff like that alone, it leaves you alone. Mostly."

I wondered what counted as "leaving stuff alone." Not wandering around in fields singing to myself? Not making faces at the rocks?

No, that was just nerves. Nothing really happened. You're suggestible because the whole thing was freaky, that's all.

I licked my lips. They stung a little from the bourbon. "Did any of you know Cotgrave? My—ah—stepgrandfather?"

"Before my time," said Tomas.

"I did," said Skip, surprising me. "Decent old man. Used to ramble around the woods a bit. Rambled a bit in his head, too, I think." He sighed. "Felt bad for him, being married to—well, I shouldn't say, on account of her being your grandmother—"

"Don't worry about it," I said, taking a hard swig and nearly choking. Foxy pounded me enthusiastically on the back. "I—urk—know what she was like. It's fine."

"Cotgrave wasn't bad," said Skip. "Mostly I think he just wasn't *there* most of the time." He tapped his forehead.

"Probably the best way to get through being married to my grandmother," I said. "Did he—ah—did he ever say anything about a man named Ambrose? Or . . . ?"

I wanted to say *the twisted ones*, but I couldn't. Not that something was stopping me, but the phrase sounded suddenly stupid in my head, like a cheap slasher film. *Oooh, the twisted ones! Scary!* All we needed was a bleached blonde co-ed to scream convincingly.

Skip thought for a moment. "Ambrose . . . Sorry, no. He might have, but it was so long ago now. And I didn't know him well. He just would come by the studio sometimes on his walks. Helped me with a kiln opening a time or two."

"Ah, well," I said. "Worth a try."

"Don't go spooking yourself," Foxy suggested. "You're already in that house with all that crap. No sense making it worse."

"Thanks," I said dryly. "I've been trying to forget."

She grinned and topped up my bourbon. "Here. This'll help."

It is extremely difficult to find a book in a hoarder's house.

No, let me qualify that. It is extremely difficult to find a *specific* book.

I spent most of the next day yanking drawers open, searching for the Green Book—or Cotgrave's manuscript, I wasn't picky—tearing through boxes, even looking under the couch cushions. I accomplished nothing, except to trash the newly cleaned living room, and eventually gave up in defeat and admitted that this was not the way to find anything.

"Systematic," I told Bongo gloomily. "I have to be systematic. She could have put it *anywhere*."

Bongo opened one eye, decided that this did not sound like food, and closed it again.

Anywhere. Upstairs or on the blocked-up porch or even in a garbage bag I'd thrown out before I knew what I was looking for. Crammed under a dead baby doll or in the box of something As Seen On TV. And she was trying to hide it, which made it ten times worse.

Cotgrave's typed manuscript should be easier, shouldn't it? In theory? He wasn't a hoarder.

Assuming she didn't throw it out after he died . . .

I straightened up the living room, feeling discouraged, took Bongo out, and went to bed.

I dreamed that night about the white stone.

People in books always have such wonderfully clear dreams that show you their secret fears or reveal some key element of their tormented past or whatever. But in reality, if you try to explain a dream, you end up saying, "I was talking to Abraham Lincoln, but he was also sort of my father, and we were in the house I grew up in but the window screen kept falling out and I was trying to wedge it back in, over and over again, and I was getting really frustrated and also I wasn't wearing pants."

Well. In my dream, I was talking to Cotgrave, who was also sort of my father, and I was looking for someone, except that I kept digging through the boxes in the doll room trying to find them. We were in my first apartment, but the doll room was in it. I was getting very annoyed because Cotgrave wouldn't help me find whoever I was looking for.

Then the dream changed and I went into another room— the living room of my first apartment, with the popcorn ceiling and the bong-water-colored carpet—and the white stone was standing in the middle of the room. I was enormously relieved because that's who I had been looking for all along.

In the dream, I saw the carvings and understood what they were supposed to be.

I went up to the stone and pressed myself against it, wrapping my legs around it, trying to touch the stone as much as I could, cheek and breast and belly and thigh, and the stone was cold and no matter how closely I held it, I couldn't warm it at all.

Then something woke me up and I rolled over and discovered I'd kicked most of the blankets over Bongo. He was snoring. I hauled the blankets back over myself and went back to sleep and the dreams after that were all the usual foolishness about not being able to remember what period I had math class in.

Maybe if I'd had a terrifying nightmare about the stone, things might have gone differently and I wouldn't have stayed. Maybe I would have thrown on my clothes, told my father to have the house demolished, and driven away. But I don't know. I think by then, probably, I was already in too far.

I woke one more time that night, when Bongo launched himself off the bed at the window, baying like a lunatic.

"Gaaaah! Ack! What?!"

He smacked his nose against the window, rebounded, and the bay turned into a yelp, then back to a bay again. Bongo, as I believe I have mentioned, is not the sharpest knife in the drawer.

It was deer again. Skip had said they were everywhere out here, and here was proof. Long-legged shapes bounded across the driveway into the trees.

"Dammit, dog, you're a coonhound, not a deerhound. . . ."

Bongo scrabbled at the window, indicating his willingness to branch out.

I put my chin on top of his skull and looked out the window. His ears were pricked up as far as they could go (not very far, given the floppiness) and made two soft bumps on either side of my jaw.

Two more deer went by, and then the last of them. There was something wrong with this one's front legs. It was not exactly limping, but it held itself wrong. For a moment I thought I was looking at a person running stooped over with their arms dangling in front.

I jerked back, startled. The deer crossed the moonlit gravel drive. No, it was only a deer. It had the long neck and the tapered head. There was just something wrong with its front legs, or perhaps its back, that made it shuffle along.

It vanished into the trees. Bongo said "Hrrrwowooo-ufff!" and dropped down, sulking that I wouldn't let him eat the deer. I sighed.

I felt bad for the deer, whatever was wrong with it. I suppose I could call a wildlife rehabber or something, tell them there was an injured deer in the woods—for all the good that would do. It's not like I had it in my truck, ready to deliver. Anyway, if a deer was an adult and walking, I'd read that it was more stressful to be captured and treated then just to wander around with a broken leg.

Assuming it was a leg. It had actually looked more like a back problem. Were there hunchbacked deer?

Well, there was that dolphin at the one zoo that had scoliosis and was bent sideways. . . . Maybe it happens to deer, too.

I mean, you'd think wolves would eat it, but there hasn't been a wolf around here in a hundred years. Two hundred.

Anyway, I had enough on my plate without taking on the woes of damaged deer. Dreaming about the carved stones . . . oof.

I'd taken a photo of one, hadn't I? The phone had made the camera noise before it shut off. I turned my phone on, noted that despite more than a day on the charger, it was at 15 percent battery and sinking fast, and checked the photos.

The last one in the roll was washed out, a gray shape on a white background, badly distorted. The lines looked less like carvings and more like a badly filtered fingerprint. I sighed and turned the phone back off. It had dropped to 9 percent while I was squinting at it.

Bongo climbed onto the bed, grumbling in the back of his throat.

"Go back to sleep, nitwit." I shoved my feet beneath him.

If I dreamed at all after that, I don't remember it.

7

"**D**ad?" I asked.

"Yes?"

"What did Cotgrave die of?"

For a minute I thought he wouldn't answer, and then he let out a long, whistling sigh. "Oh, jeez, Mouse. That was a long time ago. It was exposure."

"Exposure?" Whatever answer I'd been expecting, it wasn't that.

"Well, his mind was wandering quite a bit, and my mother wasn't the best person to take care of someone like that. . . ."

We both made noises that might, under other circumstances, have been laughter. My stepmother always says that she can tell we're related because we have the same laugh. I suppose that means that we have the same not-a-laugh-but-otherwise-we'd-cry sound, too.

It had been five days since I'd started the cleaning project.

Two since I'd been up on the hill with the stones. Dad had called, as he'd promised, to check up on me. I'd been tackling a hall closet. It wasn't a bad one, by which I mean that nothing fell on me when I opened it. Mostly it was old coats and cheap windbreakers. The plastic had gone stiff and cracked around the hoods. No Green Book.

"There was some talk about putting him in a facility," said Dad. "He'd seemed to be interested in the idea—probably to get away from her, honestly—but then he changed his mind very suddenly. And of course Mother was dead set against a caregiver in the house." He sighed again. "And then one afternoon he just wandered off, and she called the police the next morning. I'm afraid it took a couple days to find him. Turned out he was in the woods behind the house. Hypothermia. It wasn't that cold, but he wasn't in good health."

"That's awful," I said, imagining Cotgrave lying at the base of a tree somewhere. Had he scraped "Kilroy Was Here" into the bark in his last moments?

Jesus, what a morbid thought. Get yourself together, Mouse!

"I think it happens more often than we think. Anyway, I've heard it's not a bad way to go, really. And at least he was out of it."

He didn't have to clarify what "out of it" meant. I was standing inside *it* as we spoke.

Some instinct prompted me to ask, "Was he . . . uh . . . ? Was his body . . . ?"

"Oh hell, Mouse." I immediately felt guilty for asking. It was morbid curiosity, nothing more. Had to be. "No," Dad continued. "No, he'd been outside too long. Closed casket."

"Christ. I'm sorry I asked. I just keep finding his stuff, and . . ." I trailed off uselessly.

"No, it's fine. How is the cleanup going?"

"Oh Lord." I looked around at the house. I suppose it was better, given that I'd gotten the kitchen mostly cleaned out and moved the stacks of newspapers. I was grimly aware of the untouched second floor above me. For a minute I felt like I was in a cave and I could feel tons and tons of weight pressing down, except that instead of stone, it was old magazines and Franklin Mint plates and boxes from the Home Shopping Network.

I looked out the kitchen window, hoping for relief, and caught a flash of movement. There was a woman walking through the woods on the far side of the yard. She glanced at the house curiously, but kept walking. I wondered if she was the same woman I'd seen while walking Bongo the other day.

"Mouse?"

"Sorry—someone out in the woods. Hiker. Just distracted me for a second. I'm making some progress. I've gotten a good chunk of the downstairs done. I haven't even started on the upstairs, or the dead baby room."

"The *what*?!"

"Ah—" I laughed again, a bit more genuinely this time. "Sorry! Did you know she collected dolls?"

"I knew she had a few." He groaned. "Oh Lord. She didn't have just a few of anything, did she?"

"'Fraid not. The room looks like a morgue for dead plastic babies. I'm starting on it tomorrow."

I could almost see him shaking his head. "If you want me to send in the bulldozers, just say the word."

"Nah," I said. "Or not yet, anyway. I really am making progress."

"You don't have to do it just because I asked, Mouse."

I paused. The correct answer was, *Yes, I know.* The true answer was, *Yes, I do.*

I waited too long, and he said, "I could un-ask, you know."

I was shocked by my own resistance to the idea. A few days ago I'd been seriously contemplating throwing in the towel. Now, having seen the carved rocks, I wanted to get to the bottom of Cotgrave's mystery. Even if they weren't his creations, he'd clearly seen them and felt strongly about them, to have written that litany in his journal over and over.

And I twisted myself around like the twisted ones. . . .

Had he found them by accident, just like I had?

If I could find his typed manuscript, maybe that would help me learn what was going on with the rocks. If I could find the Green Book, that would definitely help.

Unfortunately, the only way I was going to do that was to dig through forty-odd years of my grandmother's life.

"It's fine, Dad," I said. "I kind of want to see this finished. But if I get to the second floor and it's just an unspeakable mess, I'll let you know."

"All right. Offer's open."

"How are you doing?" I asked, changing the subject.

"Oh, you know . . ." He trailed off. I listened to him wheeze for a few minutes. "They've given me an oxygen tank. There's still nothing wrong with me, to hear the doctor tell it, except for the bit where I'm not breathing."

"Maybe the oxygen will help," I said.

"I'm sure it will," he said, and we both knew he was lying, and we both knew that I knew. But families run on optimistic lies sometimes, so neither of us called the other one out on it and we said goodbye.

———————

I went into town to drop off the contents of the closet and get coffee and Internet. The Goth barista was on a tear about a woman who had brought in her baby and tried to change it on the coffee table. "I told her no and she just kept saying it was no big deal!" she said, waving her hands in the air. "It's a big deal to me! It's incredibly unhygienic! I mean, if you want to bring a kid in here to get coffee, that's fine, whatever, but don't put their poopy diapers on my table!"

I looked at the table that I had been about to set my laptop on and took a step back.

"It's fine," she said, collapsing over the counter. "I hosed it down with bleach. I hosed *everything* down with bleach. Do you want coffee?"

"Yes, please," I said meekly, hoping that it did not come with bleach.

She filled a coffee mug and slid it across the counter. "How's the house coming?"

"Horrific," I said, feeling vaguely pleased that she had remembered who I was. Small towns. I'd forgotten what that was like. "She had a baby doll collection. There's a whole room full of these awful dolls."

"Ewwww," said the barista, which was strangely gratifying to hear. She wrinkled her nose.

"Yeah." I opened my laptop. "I had all these thoughts about donating them to needy kids or something, but I think the needy kids have probably suffered enough. I'm just going to take them to the dump."

"Probably for the best."

I passed a pleasant afternoon in the coffee shop, feeling . . . normal. I was a perfectly normal freelancer in a nice little coffee shop in a nice little town, doing my job trying to convince authors that semicolons were their friend. My problems were normal problems, like chasing invoices. Other than having to go outside and close the sunroof on the truck when it started to drizzle, everything was fine. (Bongo was napping in the back seat and did not notice that he was getting rained on.)

Eventually, though, I had to go home. The coffee shop closed at five, and there was still time to get a load of dead plastic babies ready to go to the dump. *Note to self, do not call them that when you see Frank.*

I swung by the hardware store and bought even more gloves. I got dark gray work gloves this time, with serious-looking straps and buckles and rubber guards over the knuckles. These were gloves for handling a doll collection.

The doll room itself was . . . not as bad as it could have been, honestly. I turned up the radio and began hauling out clear plastic bins. I didn't have to actually open them to see what was in them, which made it go a lot faster. A quick look through jumbled jointed limbs, no typed manuscript wedged in anybody's diaper, no green book covers, bin is done and can be shoved into the living room.

Once I had moved out all the bins, things slowed down. I had to grab loose dolls and shove them into trash bags. The gloves helped. As long as I had the gloves, I didn't have to touch them. The gloves made me invincible.

I stayed invincible right up until one of the dolls batted its eyelashes at me.

I let out a yell like I'd been shot and flung the doll across the room. Bongo leapt to his feet, baying in a panic.

The doll landed head downward, facing me. The eyelids slowly clacked back open, aided by gravity.

Oh. Oh. It's just one of those stupid dolls that open and close their eyes. Right. Okay.

I picked it up gingerly and shook it back and forth. The eyelids moved in time.

Yeah. Yeah, okay.

Bongo stood in the doorway, stiff legged, making sounds he usually reserved for the UPS guy.

"It's all right," I said. "It's okay, buddy. Just . . . a little more on edge than I should be . . ." I dropped the doll into the trash bag and cinched it closed. Let it bat its eyelashes at Frank at the dump.

I went into the kitchen and turned the radio up as loud as it could go. The announcer introduced herself as Elaine Rogers and told me about how much they depended on my support to bring them all the great programming I enjoyed.

Her cohost made a pun that would have needed a major over-haul to achieve the level of a dad joke.

If I did not want to be listening to Pledge Week for the rest of my life, I was going to have to finish clearing this goddamn house.

Bongo cocked his head and gave a last "Hrrrr-ufff," although whether it was a commentary on dolls or the radio, I couldn't say.

I had taken the precaution of buying a bottle of wine. I poured a glass—still wearing my work gloves—and went back to work.

A couple of days went by, and I'd tell you if anything interesting happened, but it really didn't. We got into a routine. I'd get up, hit the on switch on the coffeemaker, take Bongo out to sniff around and pee on things, go inside, drink the coffee, eat instant oatmeal, and drag trash out to the truck. When the truck was full, I went into town, dropped it off with Frank, and went to the coffee shop. I then had more coffee, worked on edits, responded to e-mails, and pretended I was a normal human being who wasn't spending the evening sleeping in a dead man's bed with a flatulent coonhound. I would eat lunch. I would come home, take Bongo for a walk, load up another round of trash, take it to Frank, go back home, throw junk in bags, listen to public radio, and either eat ramen or (increasingly) go across the road and eat with Foxy, who was horrified by my ramen habit.

"Your momma wouldn't let you eat that," she said. "It's deep-fried, you know."

"We're having deep-fried pickles," I said.

"Pickles is pickles. It's a vegetable. It's practically health food."

I swirled my breaded, deep-fried pickle slice in ranch dressing and did not argue the point.

I got to know the trio at the commune pretty well. Tomas was the responsible one. He did jobs, he said, helped out some farmers here and there. "Ah, you know . . . hog-cutting season, snip-snip . . ." He made vague hand gestures. I didn't ask for details.

Skip had a sly sense of humor and didn't talk much, but when he told stories, everybody listened.

He didn't come to dinner one night, and when I asked, Foxy shook her head.

"Bad brain day," she said. "Skip's got the bipolar thing. He's got meds for it and he takes 'em real good, but he still has bad days. I'll take him out a plate later."

"He does real well," said Tomas, almost defensively. "He's a real good potter, hey?"

"Relax, Tomas, she didn't say anything."

"Friend of mine in college was bipolar," I said, and watched Tomas visibly relax. "It's cool. They didn't have the good meds back then, you know? She's doing a lot better now."

"Amazing the stuff they've got these days," said Foxy, popping a fried pickle into her mouth. "But they still can't do shit about a hangover." She poured out more bourbon, possibly determined to be a viable test subject.

After dinner at the commune, I went back home. Bongo

would find something outdoors to pee on, and we'd be in bed by nine-thirty or ten.

I still hadn't found Cotgrave's typed manuscript. It had to be in the house somewhere—my grandmother would never have thrown it out—but it wasn't in the doll room or in her bedroom. I was starting to worry that it was upstairs. I couldn't handle the thought of upstairs. Every time I looked at the stairs, I just looked away again. The downstairs had been so bad—nine days of work and I was only about two-thirds done—and the idea that there was *another floor left to go* was more than I could take.

I did clean out her bedroom more easily than I'd thought. I'd worried I would be sad, but I was still angry over the way she'd treated Cotgrave, and the anger carried me a long way. I kept the radio on loudly, and every time I would look at the pitiful pile of junk and start to feel melancholy, Elaine Rogers would remind me of why I valued public radio.

Honestly, that Pledge Week had gone on so long that I no longer really believed in it. One of these days I was going to drive out to the radio station and it'd be an empty field with an old man saying "Rogers? She's been dead nigh forty years! Ain't no coffee mugs here!" and there I'd be, haunted by the most benign ghosts known to man.

Anyway, the closet in my grandmother's room was all old-lady clothes. I hauled the whole pile out and dumped it in the Goodwill donation area and drove away before they could associate me with the bags.

There was also an underwear drawer. I emptied that straight into a trash bag and tried not to think about anything. I mean, obviously my grandmother wore underwear, but I could have gone my whole life without having to *see* it.

The mattress required wrestling. I enlisted Tomas one afternoon and we dragged it out, and the bedframe and dresser too. He wouldn't take money, so I picked up a bottle of good bourbon at the liquor store and brought it over to the next dinner.

It was all fairly normal stuff. Aunt Kate e-mailed to say that the house was fine, nobody had broken into it or set it on fire or anything. My father called occasionally to see how I was getting on. Frank started greeting Bongo by name and reaching in the window to pet him behind the ears.

I tell you this so that you won't think I'm a complete idiot—or maybe so that I can convince myself that I'm not a complete idiot. Maybe after the stones and Cotgrave's journal, you think I should have been on edge. And yes, I probably should have been. Hell, I should have been yanking up topographical maps and conducting experiments to see where the hill with the bald was and where it wasn't. I should have bought a camera and taken photos of the stones with something that didn't catch fire when I turned it on.

But I didn't. My days were all normal. And they were normal in a stressful kind of way, and I needed so much mental energy to keep from freaking out about the fact that I was cleaning out this awful hoarder house for a woman I hadn't even liked. I just didn't have anything left over to think too much about the stones. It seemed like something distant that had happened a long time ago.

If I thought about it, I mostly thought, *It was just a weird*

thing. I had low blood sugar, and maybe some trick of the land-
scape made it look like a hill and valley. That's all. And the
stones were strange and I twisted myself around like the twisted
ones, but they were just stones and somebody carved them into
weird shapes.

I didn't gnaw it over like you might think. I couldn't get any
farther with it by thinking about it, so I sort of shoved the whole
experience aside and stopped worrying about it. I had so many
things on my plate that weird stones in a place I wasn't going to
walk again just didn't seem that important.

And then the next thing happened, and this time it was
something I couldn't ignore.

Bongo was restless. It had rained the day before and he'd been
stuck inside because if we went outside his feet would get wet.
He will happily stand in a puddle or chest deep in a fishpond,
but wet grass on his paws is an abomination. Dogs, man. *Dogs.*

I was spending a rare day at the house, not going into town.
It was weird to find that I was missing it. Not just getting away
from my grandmother's house, but seeing the people. I liked
the Goth barista. I liked the waitress at the diner who called me
ladybug. There are very few people who can use a pet name on
me, but Southern waitresses can get away with it every time.

Frank at the dump saw so much of me these days that I
was close to writing him into my will. Mind you, emptying two
truckloads of dead doll parts together is a bonding experience.
(There was still at least three loads left. I had to take a break.

You can only be shoulder deep in those things for so long before it starts to take an emotional toll.)

Anyway, he had stared into the bed of the truck yesterday and scratched up under his ball cap and said, "Oh my. That's . . . that's a thing right there, ain't it?"

I agreed that it was.

There was something viscerally satisfying about chucking the dolls into the trash compactor. Is that wrong? Probably that's wrong. Still, these days I was taking entertainment where I could.

I'd asked Frank if he knew of any weird stones in the woods. He scratched under his baseball cap.

"Stones? I mean, there's one shaped like a"—he remembered suddenly that he was talking to a woman young enough to be his daughter and his eyes slid away—"a real funny one out behind the Rolling Goat Farm. Kids go spray paint swears on it sometimes. Drives Madeline nuts. She's the goat farmer."

This did not seem like the sort of stones I was pretending didn't exist.

Back home, Bongo whined to let me know that he was extremely bored.

I went outside to check the shed, since the weather was nice. It contained a selection of old tools. No books and, thankfully, no dolls.

I went back inside and Bongo inserted his nose under my elbow and flipped it up to indicate that he was dying of sorrow. I gave in and put a leash on him.

"Okay," I said, "but we're not going anywhere near those creepy rocks, okay?"

Bongo cocked an ear back at me, which means that I made a noise, not that he has any idea what I've said.

We went out for a short walk. I went down the road instead of behind the house, and that seemed acceptable. Tomas was leaning over the hood of a car and waved at me. I waved back.

This was nice. It was *pleasant*. You could imagine living in Pondsboro and learning people's names and actually knowing a little bit about their lives. I didn't have that in Pittsburgh.

A semi came screaming around a bend in the road, interrupting my thoughts and reminding me suddenly of why walking by the side of the road on a country lane was best reserved for historical romance and Led Zeppelin songs. The blast of wind blew my hair back and flung grit into our faces.

I crossed the road and went back into the woods. I could still see my grandmother's backyard through the trees. We'd gotten about fifty yards away, all told.

"Fine . . . ," I said. Bongo took off happily through the soggy leaves, running back and forth on the end of his leash.

Were we on private property? Oh, probably. There weren't any signs about it, though, or fences, so usually people don't care as long as you aren't shooting things or wrecking the place. We passed a NO HUNTING sign, but deer season was over, and if we got shot, somebody would have to explain their poaching.

Also I was wearing a purple hoodie and most deer aren't purple.

I had a vague sense that the hill with the stones was off to the left. I tried to keep right, but Bongo wasn't that interested in linear directions, and then we ran into a clearing that *did* have a fence around it, and a couple of shaggy cows gazing at us with vague benevolence.

I said, "Hi, cows." I am like that. The cows did not say anything.

We walked along the fence line. I tried to stay a little inside the trees, in case there was a farmer out with the cows. It wasn't so much that I thought I was doing something wrong, but I didn't want to have to talk to somebody and have that conversation—"This here's private property; you want to go back t' the road"—and then even if they weren't mad, I'd be left feeling horribly awkward about it all.

We went along the fence until we ran out of fence and cows and pasture, then kept going. Now it was all just scruffy pine and dead leaves. Junk pine, as my aunt would say, the stuff you get a decade or so after logging. Not very botanically interesting, not much of an understory, just the occasional Christmas fern and scruffy little clumps of sedge.

"Sedges have edges," I told Bongo. He flicked an ear back at me, unimpressed with my botanical identification skills.

I listened to woodpeckers knocking on the trees. One made a high-pitched supervillain cackle. A crow called somewhere and another one replied.

Bongo bounced around, his nose working, occasionally demanding that we halt so that he could get a thorough sniff of a particularly good dead leaf. One good leaf led to another and he wrapped his leash behind my legs so I had to do a little pirouette to unwind myself, and *that's* when I saw it.

There was something hanging in the trees.

It hung by heavy ropes. My first wild thought was that it was a person—some kind of trapeze artist—and then that someone had been crucified. Or lynched.

Bongo let out a thin, frightened whine.

My eyes traveled slowly upward. It was naked and split in half and it had hooves.

It was a deer.

I felt a stab of relief—*it's only a deer it's not a person nobody's been crucified or lynched or murdered it's just a deer some hunter probably hung it up to clean it*—but the feeling vanished almost as soon as it had begun.

The deer wasn't hung up like a hunter was cleaning it. It was split open from the rib cage downward, and the hind legs gaped obscenely wide. The guts were missing.

The front legs stuck out straight to the sides, with a rope at each ankle. The hooves dangled like limp hands, and black rags fluttered from each "wrist."

It did not exactly have a head.

The deer's own head was missing. There was a skull where the head should be, some kind of large animal skull, but it was turned upside down. The skull was clean white bone. Because of the angle, it looked as if the deer had no neck, but a dreadfully misshapen head with teeth jutting from the top.

The empty eyes stared at me. Someone had run ties through the severed neck and lashed them into the sockets.

The ropes creaked as the monstrous thing swayed.

Stones were hung from the rib cage, tied with twine. They knocked together like a grisly wind chime. Two of the stones had holes in the middle.

Stones with holes are called hagstones, I thought. (That is true, incidentally. It is also possibly the most useless thing I've ever thought in a crisis.)

I stared at the thing for probably half a minute.

It wasn't that I couldn't look away. I wanted very much to look away. But I stared because if I could find something—a seam, a tag that said it was a Halloween decoration, a video camera, even a goddamn artist statement nailed to the tree— then it wasn't real.

I wanted so very much for it not to be real.

Bongo whined again, louder.

My thoughts were moving very slowly.

I think it's real.

It's really there.

Someone made this.

The slow flow of thoughts sped up.

Who could have made this?

Who would have made this?

Images stuttered through my head, none of them terribly coherent—sociopaths, serial killers, Satanic death cult, some stupid college kids, performance artists, *monsters monsters monsters*—

and I twisted myself about like the twisted ones

If someone had made this, then they had been *here*.

Where I was standing.

They might still be here.

They might be coming toward me *right now* while I stared at their grisly effigy.

My fingers closed convulsively on Bongo's collar, and I turned and ran.

8

A coonhound in good condition is a superb natural athlete. Even a lazy, elderly one who can't hunt is pretty impressive. Bongo half dragged me through the woods, for which I was grateful, because otherwise I don't know if I could have run nearly so far or so fast.

I didn't dare look over my shoulder. If I wasn't looking at the ground, I'd break my ankle on a tree root. More importantly, if I looked over my shoulder, I might see what was coming after me.

Since I didn't look, my fear filled the woods with black shapes, hunched over and shuffling after me.

If I was being chased, I couldn't hear any footsteps behind me. That wasn't a surprise, though, because I was gasping and my blood was pounding and my side stabbed with pain as if there were shards of glass in it. But I didn't dare stop running because they could be close, they could be right behind me. In another second a hand could close over my shoulder and jerk me backward, and what if it wasn't a hand? What if it was a hoof and the woods were full of dead deer with their heads on upside down and their rib cages full of clacking stones—

I believe we had gone a little more than a mile at an ambling pace to reach the effigy. I also believe that Bongo and I covered that distance back in less than six minutes. I could not have duplicated that feat for all the money in the world.

It was Bongo who got us home. I wasn't looking where I was going beyond the next step and the next. Leaves crunched under our feet, and suddenly they stopped crunching because we were bursting into the backyard. I heard the *tok-tok-tok* rapping of the woodpeckers fall silent, probably because they'd just seen a woman and a dog go running by at full speed.

I didn't even think about going into the house. If we went into the house, we were trapped. I could lock the door and drag things in front of it, but they could come in the windows, whatever *they* were

the twisted ones

so we ran around the side of the house instead.

I tore the doors of the truck open. Bongo went into the passenger seat without losing momentum. I slammed the door behind him and bolted around the front.

I couldn't help but look behind me then.

There was nothing there, but that didn't slow me at all. They could be hiding. They could be in the trees or behind the house. They could be invisible. The fear I was feeling was no longer a rational fear of other humans, but had cracked open some deep vein of childhood terror—monsters under the bed, shadows gathering under the basement stairs.

The truck started before I was thinking enough to be afraid that it wouldn't start. I blessed the engineers at Nissan and peeled out of the driveway at top speed.

If there had been a cop on the road, he would have stopped me, since I was going at least eighty, but there wasn't. Too bad. I really could have used one.

I looked in the rearview mirror, expecting to see . . . something. Black shapes on the road. A deer with its head on upside down chasing the car.

Don't even think *that.*

I slowed down as I came into Pondsboro, because there were other cars, and if I rear-ended one, my truck might stop working, and if my truck stopped working I couldn't get *away.*

For lack of anything better to do, I pulled into the parking lot of the Piggly Wiggly. I wanted to be around other people. Monsters didn't get you in broad daylight. I had to tell someone. The police? The fire department?

The whole idea of having to explain it was so overwhelming that I parked the truck, threw my arms around Bongo, and burst into tears.

Hounds are very huggable dogs. He bore this patiently, tail wagging, and licked my face occasionally. He was very calm.

Dogs are lucky to have short memories. Then again, from Bongo's point of view, he'd gone for a walk, been scared, ran away, then had a ride in the car with his person, and now his person was sad but that was okay because he was there to lick her.

Someone tapped on the window. I screamed.

"Whoa!" I heard, muffled by glass.

It didn't sound like a monster.

The Goth barista from the coffee shop was looking at me. She was carrying a gallon of milk and had a worried expression on her face.

I rolled the window down.

"Are you okay?" she asked. "You're . . . uh . . ."

"Fine," I said automatically. When people ask if you're okay, you say "fine." It's a hindbrain function.

She looked at me skeptically.

"Not fine," I corrected. I was suddenly aware that my face was covered in tears and dog slobber and possibly snot. I stank of sweat. There was hair sticking to my cheeks. "Yeah. Not fine."

"Right," she said. "Why don't you come to the shop? You can use the bathroom and I'll make you some tea."

Tea. Oh God, I could have tea. I could get a cup and drizzle honey into it and watch it sink through the liquid to the bottom. I could put my hands around the mug. Everything would be awful still, but there would be this little space that I understood.

"Tea would be good," I said. And then, "Wait. I can't leave Bongo."

"Bring him in," she said. "As long as he doesn't bite or pee on things, he's fine."

"He won't."

Somehow or other I got out of the truck. It's probably good that she'd come along when she had, because otherwise I might never have left the truck again.

Bongo put on his best manners to be introduced. He sat down very politely and gave the Goth barista his very best tragic hound look. She scratched him under the chin. "Hi, Bongo. I'm Enid. You're a good boy, aren't you?"

He put his ears down and wagged his tail to indicate that he was indeed a very good boy and also no one had ever petted him and he would like it very much if she was the first. She complied.

Enid. That was good to know.

We walked to the coffee shop. We were about two blocks away, down streets lined with houses that had been turned into offices. Enid kept up a stream of completely inconsequential chatter along the way. I looked behind me for monsters.

Bongo stayed close by my heels as we went into the coffee shop, then flopped down under the table. His nose worked, probably separating out coffee bean varieties, but the mile run, dragging my ass through the woods, had clearly exhausted him. He let out one of his deflating sighs. I put my feet under him.

Enid brought him a dish of water and then brought me a mug of tea. I put my hands around it and stared into it.

And I twisted myself around like the twisted ones. . . .

"You wanna talk about it? Should I call someone for you?"

"Yes. No. No, there's no one to call." (Really, what was I going to say to my father? *Hey, Dad, there's a monstrous effigy in the woods. Did you know about that?*) "Wait, no. The police? Maybe? I'm not sure."

She sat down at the table across from me and put her chin in her hands.

"Right." I took a drink of tea. It was too hot and burned the roof of my mouth, but it was tea and tea was good and I was in a world where there was tea, not in a world where there were monsters in the woods. Those were two separate worlds. As long as I stayed in this one, I was safe.

"I saw a thing in the woods. Someone made a thing. A deer." I tried to focus on what I was saying. My teeth wanted to chatter, even though it wasn't cold. "It was like when a hunter hangs up a deer, you know? Except it wasn't a hunter."

Enid's eyebrows were starting to climb under her hot pink bangs. "Are you sure it wasn't a hunter?"

"Yes. Very sure. It was crucified. They'd taken off the head and put a skull on it, upside down. It was sewn to the neck all through the eye sockets. And the rib cage was full of—of—like wind chimes—made of rocks. I swear I'm not on drugs."

Enid blinked. "That's too bad. Sounds like you could use some about now. Was this by your house?"

I started to nod, then shook my head. "Behind it. But not right behind it. Like a mile. We went for a walk." I reached down and rubbed Bongo's ears. He leaned against my shins.

After a minute, I said, "I kept looking for a tag. Or a camera or something. Like maybe it was art."

Enid drummed her fingers on the tabletop. "You know . . . that's not a bad guess. We've got tons of artists around here. Somebody could have hung this thing up and be taking photos of it as it rots or something."

I shuddered. "Why on earth . . . ?"

"Oh, you know." She rolled her eyes. "It's a statement about mortality, or local food, or how their last girlfriend didn't love them enough."

I laughed. It wasn't much, but it was a genuine laugh. For a few minutes that afternoon, it had seemed like I'd never laugh again.

"I don't know," I said. I remembered the blind panic I'd felt running from it—but yeah, I'd been on edge lately. Had I freaked out over nothing much?

No. Crucified deer in the woods are freaky. Even if it's art.

Enid glanced at her watch. "Tell you what. One of our local cops comes in for a red-eye around three-thirty every day. If you hang out until then, you can ask him what to do, without having to . . . you know . . . call the police station and make a big deal out of it."

"Will they believe me?" I asked. Listening to myself talk, I was having a hard time believing me, and I'd been there.

"*I* believe you," she said. "I don't know what it was you saw, but you don't seem like the type who melts down for no reason." She refilled the hot water in my tea. "Wait an hour until Officer Bob comes in, and then we'll see what he has to say."

———

I waited. After a few minutes, I even felt good enough to go and get my laptop out of the truck and do a little work. One of the e-mails that I was waiting for had come in, and I got to go through a file and see all the changes that the author had made. He was supposed to be fixing problems I'd pointed out, which he mostly had, but in a way that introduced several new problems.

Normally it might have been frustrating, but it was such a familiar problem that it was soothing. Bongo lay under the table, being very polite about the people who came in for coffee, and I slipped him bits of a day-old muffin.

Officer Bob was a tall man with big shoulders. He wasn't fat, but middle age had definitely smoothed him down a bit, and his crew cut couldn't quite hide the bald spot in back.

Enid pointed to me and said, "She needs to talk to you," and I found myself telling him the whole story.

He turned toward me with an expression that said, very briefly, *Oh Lord, now what?* but he hid it well.

At "crucified deer" his eyebrows went up, and he actually brought his coffee over and sat down at the table.

He asked a couple of questions along the way. "How far did you go? Was it on your property? Do you remember where it was? Any landmarks?"

And then, "Did you take a photo?"

I stared at him, and then touched my jeans. My phone was still in my pocket. Turned off, because of the software bug, but if I'd turned it on, surely I would have had enough juice to at least take a photo of the effigy. It might have just made a camera noise and turned off again, but at least I'd have *something*.

"I didn't even think . . . I . . . oh God, I'm *dumb*."

He grinned. "No. You had a shock, sounds like. Don't feel dumb. Everybody does that. It's just that if you took a photo, it would have GPS data on it, and we could figure out exactly where it was."

I groaned. "I take photos of particularly good *salads*. I can't believe I didn't take a shot of the thing."

He leaned back in his chair. "Well, people who put up a thing like that probably plan to leave it there for a while. We can go back and try to find it."

I blanched.

"Tell you what. I can take what's called an informational report. So we can document what you saw, and it'll be on file." (He didn't say "So we can talk about this at the station afterward," but I suspect that was implied.) "And afterward, we can go back out there and see if you can find it again."

He leaned down and scratched Bongo. "Or if this fellow can. Dead deer should bring him running."

It hadn't occurred to me that Bongo might have led me to the effigy in the first place, but of course that made sense. If it had been . . . well . . . dripping. . . .

Eww.

He glanced unobtrusively at his watch. "How about you write the whole thing down and e-mail it to me? I'd rather hear it in your own words than try to write my version and get it wrong. Then we can get it on file, and we'll have someone meet you at the house later and you can show them where you saw it."

"I can do that? E-mail you, I mean?"

"Sure," he said. He grinned briefly. "We have e-mail and everything. We even read them."

Enid snorted. I got his e-mail address and he got my physical address. "Someone will be around later. Hopefully me. And maybe Bongo here can lead us back to it." Officer Bob paused. I don't know if his sympathetic look was something cops learn to do, or if he was genuinely feeling it. It was a good look either way. "Really, it's probably just kids trying to be edgy. But we'll check it out anyway."

He waved with two fingers around his coffee cup and went out the door. I suspected he was probably going to go tell the people at the station about the crazy lady who was seeing crucified deer, but that didn't matter. If he came out, I could show him the deer.

If someone else saw it, then it was real, not a monster thing, and they could find out who'd done it and it would be their problem and not mine.

I wrote the e-mail. I don't have too many useful skills, but I can by God write an e-mail. And this was good. I sounded very calm in e-mail and not like a woman who had driven at breakneck speed down the road and burst into tears in the parking lot of the Piggly Wiggly. That woman would sound awful on a police report.

Subject gave the following statement: Holy shit there's a nasty thing hanging up in the woods. Subject appeared agitated. Subject's dog requested ear skritches, which were duly provided. . . .

I floundered for a bit trying to think of how to describe what I had seen. Eventually I wrote *effigy* and hoped that the police had access to a dictionary.

No, that was unkind. Officer Bob had seemed pretty sharp.

How do you end an e-mail to the police? You don't write *Love, Melissa.* Even *Sincerely* seemed weird. *By my hand on this twenty-third day of March* . . . No, probably not.

Eventually I just typed my name and the date underneath.

Enid brought me more hot water. I swirled the tea bag around in it, extracting the last molecules of tea. "Am I nuts?" I asked her.

"Undoubtedly," she said cheerfully. "But that doesn't mean somebody didn't hang something weird in the woods. This place is full of freaks, and I say that as one of them."

I let out a long sigh. I felt better. I had *told the police*. I was *being responsible*. Whatever happened now, it wasn't my fault.

"Thank you," I said to Enid. I was starting to feel embarrassed. I'd bought coffee from this woman like eight times now, and she'd pulled me out of a truck, sobbing. "I swear, I don't usually have breakdowns like that in the parking lot."

She snorted. "If I ran into a crucified deer, crying in the parking lot would be the least of it. Dude. I'd run screaming through the town stabbing people."

I paused. "How would that help?"

"Oh, it wouldn't, but I'd have a great excuse."

"Fair enough," I said, and took my leave.

Going back to the house was not the easiest thing I've done in my life.

Deep breaths, I told myself. *Deep breaths. It's just a weird sculpture. It didn't chase you. It wasn't alive. It was just some thing that somebody hung up. Officer Bob will show up and you'll go find it and he'll tell you that it was just some weird hunter's idea of art.*

It took me a few minutes to get out of the truck even so.

*It's fine. You're fine. You don't need to go out in the woods
alone looking for it. It's not like somebody dropped it on your
porch. It has nothing to do with you.*

and I twisted myself around like the twisted ones

Stop it.

I got out of the truck. I'll be honest, if Bongo had been
upset, I would probably have gone back into town and asked
Enid if I could drink coffee until Officer Bob was available, but
Bongo acted like nothing much was going on. So I went back
inside and turned on the radio and heard all about the great
programming that my pledge helped pay for. (I had yet to hear
any of this great programming, but hey, it had been less than
two weeks.)

Waiting for the police to show up is rather like waiting for a
package to be delivered, except that you have a vague nagging
worry that the package is going to tell you you're breaking the
law and arrest you on the spot. I tried to fill another garbage
bag with old newspapers, while jumping up and going to the
window every time a car went past on the road.

I thought about going across the street to Foxy, but it
occurred to me that between Skip's mental issue and Tomas's
not being white and Foxy being Foxy, they might not be on the
best terms with the cops. I stayed put.

About five o'clock, when I'd nearly given up on anyone
coming out at all, a black-and-white Charger pulled into the
driveway and Officer Bob got out.

He waved as I came out to meet him. Bongo remembered a
friend and demanded petting, which was duly provided.

"Living out here?" asked the cop, gazing at the porch.

"Well, for a couple days. Or weeks, I guess, until I get the house cleared out." I stifled a sigh at the thought of more weeks spent in the house, living on a steady diet of ramen and public radio.

"The old lady called us out a few times," he said, still rubbing Bongo's ears. "Wanted her neighbors arrested."

"What neighbors?"

"Place across the street." He jerked a thumb over his shoulder. "To hear her tell it, they were throwing all-night parties with drugs and rock 'n' roll."

I groaned. Something else to apologize to Foxy and crew for. "They've been so nice to me."

Officer Bob chuckled. "Yeah, they're nice folks. But you know how it is. Some people just like to complain."

"Lord, ain't that the truth!"

This pretty well hashed out the conversation. I tugged Bongo's leash. "Ready to go?"

"Lead the way."

9

We couldn't find it.

I swear that I combed every inch of ground for half a mile around, and it wasn't there. I found the cows. I found the fence. I walked to the end of it, I walked past it, and there was nothing in the trees.

"I know it was here," I said to Officer Bob. I felt a strong urge to cry, which was stupid. I should have been *glad* it wasn't there. I should have been thrilled that there wasn't a horrible monstrous art project made of dead-deer bits dangling from a tree.

Instead I would have given all the money in my bank account to find the damn thing again.

Bongo was no help. Bongo just about knows *sit* on a good day. He wandered around, snuffling at the leaves with enthusiasm.

I knew Officer Bob probably thought I was a liar or seeing things or making stuff up for attention. He was being very nice and very professional about it all, but I was sure that I was being mentally shuffled from *reported a problem* to *is a problem.*

"I swear it was here . . . ," I said, probably for the hundredth time, as we slogged back toward the house.

Bob nodded. "It's all right," he said. "It might still be. All these trees look alike if you're not used to them, and it's easy to get turned around." He waved vaguely into the woods. "If you do run into it again, take a photo. That'll help us find it again."

"But who could have put it there?"

He shrugged. "Without seeing it, I can't really say. I don't know. Kids, maybe."

Any kid who would make the thing I saw was on their way to being an avant-garde artist or a serial killer.

He was very polite and he didn't make me feel like I was wasting his time, and after he left, I went into the house and cried into Bongo's fur for twenty minutes anyway.

The rest of the evening was uneventful. Foxy came over to ask if I wanted dinner, but I told her I wasn't feeling great.

She left and came back twenty minutes later with a Tupperware container of enchiladas.

"Tomas swears by 'em," she said. "If your innards are giving you trouble, these'll blow the sick right out of you."

"High praise," I said, taking the enchiladas. "Thanks, Foxy."

She fidgeted for a moment. "You need anything, hon? Saw there was a cop here earlier. You in some kind of trouble?"

"Oh. Yeah. Him." I sighed. "No. I called him. I thought I saw something in the woods."

"Something?"

"There was a dead deer in a tree," I said.

Her hot pink lipstick skewed sideways as she frowned. "That's weird. We don't got any cougars around here. I mean, people say they see 'em, but it's always just some big house cat or a coyote they didn't get a good look at."

"No, this wasn't a cougar. . . ." I tried to explain what I'd seen, while downplaying how scared I'd been. *No, of course I didn't run away screaming and crying. Why do you ask . . . ?* "Officer Bob said it was probably just kids."

"Yeah, sure," said Foxy. "Kids always stick dead deer in trees with their heads on upside down. It's the next thing they play with after Legos." She rolled her eyes.

"*Thank you!*" I felt more vindicated than I'd like to admit. "That's what I was thinking!"

She shook her head. "Nasty things out and about," she said, half under her breath. Then, louder, "You be careful, hon. Lock your door at night."

"I always lock my door." I glanced around. "Although with this place, I'd be grateful if someone broke in and stole some stuff. . . ."

She laughed at that. "Fair enough. I'll let you alone, then. You have any problems or just get spooked, come on over. We got a spare room."

She left, and I stood over the sink, eating the enchiladas, while the radio told me how grateful they were for listeners like me.

Bongo woke me up in the middle of the night *again*, baying. I nearly jumped out of my skin.

I sat up and looked out the window, on the off chance that it was whoever was hanging freakish effigies in the woods. (*Kids*. Right.)

But no, it was deer again.

"Dammit, Bongo . . ."

"*Hrrruuuwwuuuuufff* . . ."

Two of them bounded across the yard. A third followed slowly, hugging the woods. Probably the one I'd seen before. Poor sod was lucky it hadn't been hung up in a tree. We killed the wolves and then the apex predator was cultists or artists or dangerous lunatics.

My apex predator bounced on the bed, stomping on my calves. "Go to *bed*."

He tried to pretend that he wanted to go outside, but I was fairly sure that it was in order to find a deer to bark at, so I glared at him until he flopped back down on the bed.

"You're a wretch."

" . . . *rrrfff*."

———————

"Hi, Bongo!" said Enid, when I dragged into the coffee shop the next morning, probably looking like death warmed over. And then, as something of an afterthought, "Hi, Mouse. Coffee?"

I was not offended, as of course you greet the dog first and the human later. "Yes, please."

She brought the coffee over and sat down at the table across from me. Bongo put his head in her lap and looked tragic. "So I had a thought," she said, rubbing his ears.

I gazed into the coffee. "Ah?"

"You couldn't find the thing again, right?"

I looked up from my coffee. "How'd you know?"

"Officer Bob came by this morning for coffee," she said. "So I asked—yes, you're precious, puppy dog—and he said you'd gone looking but couldn't find anything."

I sighed. It was still embarrassing. "I know it was there," I mumbled.

"Hey, no question. Either it got taken down or you got turned around. Woods are like that. Anyhow, if you go on the county's website, you can look up who owns the property behind you. That way you get an idea whose land it was on, and then you can ask them about it."

The idea of tromping up to a stranger's door and saying, *Hey, did you know there's a horrible vanishing dead-deer sculpture on your property?* was distinctly unappealing. Still, it *was* a good idea. I pulled up the county website and went to work.

It was a pretty fancy website. It had topography maps and property line maps. It also had a crappy user interface if you actually wanted to find out any real information, but that's government for you. You could click the property maps and get a reference number, and then if you dug around the website long enough, you found a place to enter your reference number and it would tell you what name the property was registered under.

There were three people who could conceivably have owned the property behind my grandmother's house, and two of them were holding companies that were, Enid told me, just waiting until Pondsboro became big enough so that they could develop exclusive housing communities and charge a million dollars an acre. No luck there. I looked up the third property, and it belonged to a neighbor whose property abutted hers. (Dad's property now, I guess. Eventually mine. What a dreadful thought.)

I stared at the topographical maps for a while. There were no hills behind the house. The hill with the white stone was not there.

Well. Of course there weren't. I'd known it at the time. I just had tried not to think about it, because thinking about it was too hard.

I went a long way, that's all. I went a long way around. The map is old. The satellite photos were taken in a different season. . . .

Even I didn't buy that one. Hills aren't like trees. They don't subside in winter and come back in spring. The National Geological Survey, or whoever does these things, had been tromping around with their little survey tools before I was born, and there hadn't been a hill there, and there still wasn't a hill there, except that I'd been on the hill.

Sometimes it's there, and sometimes it ain't, Foxy had said.

and I twisted myself around like the twisted ones

My grandma, she'd say there were devils up there. . . .

Tomas's grandma was, it was almost certain, a better person than my grandma. Mine had been wicked enough that even devils would stay clear of her.

That thought rang around in my head a lot longer than it should have.

Cotgrave had said something about that, though, hadn't he? About how they avoided her like the smell of a dead skunk?

He hadn't been talking about devils, though, had he? *Plat-eyes* and *poppets* and *them*, whatever *they* were—

Stop. This is stupid. You're working yourself into a fit because a poor old man wrote down his dementia in a journal.

The dead deer effigy hanging in the tree hadn't been dementia.

Bongo, generally as perceptive as a cinder block, flopped his muzzle over my foot and began licking my ankle. Probably he was just hoping that there was food on it, but it did make me feel better.

Don't start crazymaking. You're alone in a house in the middle of nowhere with a bunch of dolls. If there was ever a time to not start down the horror-movie road, this is it.

Besides, my grandmother's presence was still all over the house. If it had kept the . . . the twisted ones . . . away in life, I couldn't imagine it had dissipated just yet.

Enid refilled my coffee. "No luck?"

I shook my head. "I don't know. It was a good thought. Does"—I checked the name—"A. Chandler seem like the sort of person who would hang dead deer from the trees?"

Enid snorted. "She keeps cows."

I digested this. Were dangerous people who make deer effigies allowed to keep cows?

"I mean, I don't know her well, but I'm pretty sure she's not the type. She has sheep, too. And I think some kind of endangered chicken."

"Endangered chicken," I repeated. Well. Of course there would be endangered chickens. Everything's endangered these days. Why not a chicken?

"There's a lot of that around here. Rare-breed livestock stuff, you know."

I nodded glumly. Another dead end, then. I closed the topography website.

"Maybe I'm nuts," I said.

"Sure, that's possible." Enid seemed untroubled by this.

I tried to focus on work for the next few hours, for all the good it did. It was too easy to lose my place and read whole passages without absorbing any of it. I think it took me an hour to edit a single page, and it wasn't the sort of page that would normally require an hour of work, just some rogue commas and a spot where the word flow was choppy instead of smooth.

Eventually I closed my laptop and took Bongo home.

———

I woke up very slowly. There was a sound that I had been hearing for some time, and gradually I came awake, still hearing it.

It was Bongo. He lay flat at the foot of the bed, his fur standing up in spikes, and he was growling.

His growl was harsh and awful, like nothing I'd ever heard before. I could see the square of moonlight coming through the window reflected in his eyes.

It came to me, rather distantly, that Bongo was terrified.

My first instinct was to sit up, put my arms around him, ask him what was wrong. Being only half awake may have saved me.

I did not move my head. I looked over to the window, where Bongo was staring.

There was a white face in the window.

I didn't scream. That's the thing that's still the most astonishing to me about the whole terrible encounter — I didn't scream.

It was horribly misshapen. The eyes were huge and dark, it had an impossibly thin, vapid smile, and the forehead jutted upward.

It took a moment, as I lay there not screaming, to realize that it was an animal skull, upside down, and what looked like a smile was the suture between plates of bone. The jutting forehead was the skull's snout, flipped over. Teeth gleamed at the top and the eye sockets were laced with black.

It was the effigy.

I don't remember what I thought in that moment. Something that allowed me not to scream or go mad, I suppose — *it's not real. I'm dreaming, or if it's really there, it's someone trying to scare me, they've dragged that awful thing on the porch as a prank* —

It turned its head.

It moved like a living thing, like a great bird, turning the skull head on the hanging folds of neck. It turned and looked at me.

I knew it couldn't possibly see me. I was lying in the deep shadow of the wall, and my eyes were slits. Even if it could see me, it couldn't know that I was awake. It was very important, somehow, that it not know I was awake.

Because it's a monster and monsters can't get you when you're asleep and if I pull the blankets over my head it can't get me but I don't dare move because I can't get the blankets over my head fast enough and it could still get Bongo if I move it can come through the window but as long as I stay still it has to stay out there—

It turned its head again, sideways, so that one dark eye socket stared in the window. Bongo's growl was so loud that I could feel it in my teeth.

Tap. *Tap*. Tok. Tappa-tap. *Tok*.

The hollow woodpecker noise. Right outside the window.

Caused by the stones hanging from the effigy's rib cage knocking together.

The sound I'd been hearing for days now.

I stopped thinking in words. My mind was a pure white terror.

The skull tilted sideways, still birdlike, as if it saw something that interested it. Bongo's fur stood up in spikes.

And then it left.

I heard it drop to the planks of the porch, heard unsteady footsteps going away, down the steps. (Two feet or four? I couldn't tell.) Heard the *tok-tappa-tok* of the holed stones. One knocked against wood—probably the railing post—and the sound was loud, as loud as I had ever heard, *and that means it's been here before*

it's been here all along

oh God

the twisted ones are here

the twisted ones were always here

The front door was locked. The back door was probably locked, but even if it wasn't, an intruder would have to move a few hundred pounds of newspapers to get to it. The windows were all shut and had screens. If it tried to take the screens off, surely I would hear it.

What felt like a long time later, Bongo stopped growling.

I finally moved.

I rolled off the bed, pulling the blankets with me, and dragged them into the closet. I crawled to the bedroom door on hands and knees and locked it. I didn't take my eyes off the window. I had no way to barricade that, but at least I could hide.

I pulled Bongo into the closet with me and slid the closet door shut. It was one of those stupid sliding doors that are basically fiberboard panel and laminate fake wood on a little rail.

Don't think about the closet door sliding back don't think about looking up and seeing the effigy standing there with the hagstones knocking don't think it don't think it don't—

I leaned down and gripped Bongo's collar and buried my face in his ruff.

"We'll leave," I whispered. "Tomorrow morning. We'll get out of this horrible place and I'll call Dad and he can burn this awful house down and we'll go home and never, never come back again."

He licked my face. I took this as approval.

I don't know how I slept. It seems insane that I could sleep, but terror is exhausting, so somehow I did. I don't remember dreaming, or if I was dreaming, it was about sitting in a closet, so there was no real difference.

When I woke, it was morning and the thing was gone.

The door was still locked. The window was unbroken.

I looked out the window with my heart in my throat, and I

saw the porch and sunlight and nothing more. Bongo pawed at my leg, making his want-to-go-out noises.

"Yes," I said. "We'll go. We'll go for good." I could not spend another night here, of course. You didn't spend the night in a place with monstrous deer creatures staring in the windows. I didn't care about the manuscript or the book or the potential money from selling the house. I wanted *out*.

I picked up my purse and my laptop bag. I snapped Bongo's leash onto his collar. I did this all as if it were normal, as if I were packing to go to the coffee shop. I would leave my suitcase behind. The suitcase didn't matter. Clothes could be replaced. All I needed was my wallet and my phone and my computer and my dog.

Opening the front door took more courage than I have ever needed in my life.

I looked through the screen and waited for the thing to get me.

Nothing happened. The sun was shining. I heard birds singing. I wanted to scream at them, because how dare there be birds singing when the woods were full of monsters?

Bongo shoved his nose against the screen and whined.

Twenty steps to the truck. Twenty steps, put Bongo in, and then another half dozen around the front to the driver's side. Twenty-six steps. I could do this.

I opened the door and flung myself outside.

One step, two steps, three, four—shit!

On the fourth step, halfway down the porch stairs, my foot came down on something that rolled. I tried to catch myself, missed a step, and landed on my knees in the grass. The shock of the fall slammed up my wrists and into my spine.

Do you remember when you were a kid, and you fell down constantly, and it was just no big deal? Somewhere along the way, that changes and you start to realize how old folks fall down and die as a result.

I knelt in the grass, not thinking, for several seconds. Adrenaline had whited out my mind completely. "You're fine," I said aloud to myself, in the same voice I use when Bongo gets the leash wrapped around himself. "Nothing's broken." (I had no damn idea if anything was broken or not; I was just saying it in hopes that it would be true.)

The panic faded. I sat up and flexed my wrists and my ankles, and nothing did seem to be broken. Okay. Okay. A deer monster hadn't eaten me yet. I just had to get up.

My first reflexive thought was for my computer. I'm not proud that was the first thing I thought of, but there we are. Had I cracked the screen? Would it work?

It was still on my back. Okay.

My second thought, belatedly, was Bongo.

Had the sudden fall hurt him? Was he okay? I hadn't heard a yelp.

I lifted my hand and stared at it.

It was empty.

I had dropped the leash when I tried to catch myself.

Bongo was nowhere to be seen.

I looked down at his tracks in the mud, deep and clear, with the nails sharply defined. They ran around behind the house. I was on my feet before I realized it and running, discovering that I'd skinned my knees in the fall, not caring.

He wasn't behind the house. The tracks got into the grass and then into the leaves. He'd smelled *something* and while I'd been on my knees mumbling to myself like an idiot, he'd gone after it with all the single-minded intensity of a coonhound on the scent.

Hounds are almost all dumb as posts, but if their nose turns on, suddenly they are professionals on a mission. This is why you never, ever let them off the leash.

"Bongo!" I called. "Buddy! Bongo! Where are you?!"

Five minutes ago, I had been terrified to make a sound, because I thought the deer monster would get me. Now I was screaming, for all the good it did me.

I circled the house once, twice, not knowing what direction to go. What if it was the wrong way and I got too far away to find him? I was paralyzed with indecision.

"Bongo! Come back!"

I looked at the tracks again and thought *I've really got to trim his nails*, and then I burst into tears because I was already stretched past what humans should have to deal with and now my dog was gone.

I collapsed on the porch stairs and put my face in my hands.

I couldn't leave now. I couldn't leave him. He was wandering somewhere around these awful woods, probably chasing rabbits or deer or something, but what if the . . . the things got him?

What if he was scared, wherever he was? What if he wandered onto a road? He wasn't that smart. He didn't really understand roads. He'd try to make friends with a car. . . .

I cried until it became obvious that Bongo wasn't going to show up and lick my face. Eventually I stopped, because I was on the porch, and the porch wasn't safe.

Were the things still there? Had Bongo run out and chased them off? Had he saved me?

And I twisted myself around like the twisted ones. . . .

I couldn't deal with that, so I decided not to think about it anymore.

"Okay," I said. My voice was shaky, but I couldn't dissolve into a useless pile of snot. Bongo needed me. I had to do the right things. "I will get up. I will make coffee. I will find a phone book in this wreck, and I'll call every pound in the county and make sure they know he's missing."

I stood up. I felt light-headed.

Maybe you think I was stupid. Maybe you're right. Never go back for the cat, right? That's how you get eaten by aliens.

But I knew perfectly well that I couldn't leave.

My dog was out there somewhere. Until I had him back, or had proof he wasn't coming back, I was going to stay.

10

I drank coffee and then I called three different pounds on the landline. Yes, he was chipped. Yes, he'd had all his shots. Yes, he still had the collar with the rabies tag on it. No, this number didn't have voice mail. No, my cell phone wasn't working reliably, but they could leave a message. Or send an e-mail. Or they could call the coffee shop in town. I prayed Enid wouldn't mind. I didn't think she would.

It was all so normal and efficient. There was a system. I put on my pleasant doing-business-with-people voice and I answered questions, and all the time I wanted to scream, *Do you know there are monsters in the woods, and if there are monsters in the woods, then the whole world is not what we pretend it is? Do you understand?*

I did not say this, because that would have made me sound crazy, and it wouldn't have helped get Bongo back. But every time I got off the phone, I had to pace back and forth for a minute, drinking lukewarm coffee while my teeth chattered on the edge of the mug. I wasn't cold. I was jittery with knowledge and horror.

When I had called the last pound, I stared into the empty coffeepot. Apparently I'd drunk all of it.

I went to the front porch and looked down the steps.

The round thing that had turned under my feet was a bone. I know that sounds sinister, but when you have dogs, you get used to some things. I don't know what kind of bone it was, just a normal bone with a knob on one end and a gnawed-off spike on the other.

It was stained deep orange-red. You didn't need to be a geologist to know it was the color of the red clay that lay under the soil here, exposed every time someone dug a hole.

Had the effigy left it? Dropped it on the steps as it left the house, like it was shedding?

No. Get ahold of yourself. It's just a bone. For all I knew, Bongo had dug it up sometime when I wasn't looking and it had gotten kicked onto the stairs.

Should I call the police? And tell them what, exactly?

I saw a monster and then there was a bone on the stairs and my dog ran away after something.

I thought of Officer Bob. I thought of walking through the trees, looking for the effigy, and then I thought, *Oh, sweet fuck, what if it was alive when I saw it? What if it was hanging in the tree watching me? What if it was just playing possum and laughing to itself? What if it was chasing us when we ran—*

No. No. It had been daylight. Surely things like that weren't allowed to come around in daylight, were they?

Allowed by whom?

This train of thought would end with me crouched in the bathroom with a shotgun aimed at the door. This would not help Bongo and also I didn't know how to use a shotgun.

If I were a good owner, I would go out into the woods and call for him and bring treats.

I inhaled sharply at the thought.

I couldn't do it. I knew I should, I really did, but I couldn't go back out just yet. Not alone. Not even for him.

What if I go looking and I find another effigy and it's Bongo?

What if they make another one out of him and he comes to the window with his skull flipped over and his paws on the windowsill and I twisted myself around like the twisted ones—

I screamed. I actually screamed and swept everything off the counter. It was only the ramen and the oatmeal boxes and a plastic cup of water. The cup bounced.

I never do things like that. I don't throw things. I don't scream. I never understood people who lob toasters at their boyfriends. Why would you waste a perfectly good toaster?

Well, I'm under a lot of stress. Monsters are stressful. And I should probably stop drinking coffee.

I paced back and forth. I went to the bathroom. I paced back and forth some more.

I should do something. I should move boxes.

Why am I moving boxes when there are monsters in the woods?

I paced back and forth, clenching and unclenching my fists, and finally I said out loud, "Because the boxes have to get moved."

I went to the doll room. It smelled of my grandmother's malice, which was nothing compared to what had stared in the window last night. I hauled plastic bins out of the hallway, filled with dead baby dolls and plastic newborns with their eyes squeezed shut, and I felt only vague, impartial disgust.

I wrestled the bins onto the tailgate and into the bed of the truck. Somehow I'd thought there'd been more doll bins in the truck already—I vaguely remembered taking some out last night—but the bed was nearly empty, so that must have been the last load. Probably all the junk was starting to blur together.

Probably I wasn't terribly reliable at the moment.

The truck filled with dolls. I slammed another plastic crate down on the tailgate, hard enough to make the truck bounce. The lid popped off and dolls flew.

"Shit!"

"Holy Jesus," said Foxy, coming up the drive. "Was your grandma in a cult or something?"

I let out a thin laugh, choked on it, and put my face in my hands.

"Oh, honey! What's wrong?"

Before I quite knew what was happening, I was sobbing on Foxy's nonexistent bosom. She was all collarbones and necklaces.

"Bongo's gone," I choked out. "He ran off—I hope he ran off—there's things in the woods, Foxy, I saw one—I think I'm going crazy—oh God, what if they got him?"

"Easy now," said Foxy, patting my back. "Easy, hon. We'll get it sorted." She patted me for a few minutes, just long enough for me to start feeling horrified and embarrassed instead of horrified and overwhelmed, and then produced a handkerchief from somewhere in her pockets.

I wiped my eyes. "I'm sorry," I said.

"Don't be. You ain't the first to cry on me. Or the tenth. Now, let's go to my place and have some lemonade, and we can sit on the porch and you can tell me all what happened."

"You'll think I'm crazy," I whispered. My throat was raw.

"Sure, but I won't hold that against you."

Foxy led me across the road as I leaned on her arm. I felt like I was limping with both feet.

As soon as I was sitting on her porch, I felt better. Foxy had wind chimes hanging all over the porch, and some of them were stones with holes in them. But they went *click-clack-jangle* in a cheerful manner, like Foxy's bangles rattling together, not like a monster with stones in its ribs.

There were other people around. I had an idea somehow that the thing wouldn't show up in front of other people. Maybe that was a horror movie idea, that monsters only show up when you're alone, but I felt . . . safe.

Foxy went inside and came out a moment later with a pitcher of lemonade and two glasses. I took one and drank it while the condensation ran down over my fingers.

"All right," she said. She sat down beside me on the steps, and we looked out over the winding driveway in the grass. I couldn't see my grandmother's house from here. From the very slight elevation, I could see a little way over the woods behind the house.

There was no hill, and no ring of hills, and somehow that didn't surprise me.

I told her everything. I started crying again when I had to explain that Bongo was missing, and then I said out loud the thing I hadn't wanted to think, which was that the thing would get him and I should have protected him and I'd failed and he'd trusted me because I was his human, and then I burst into tears again.

"Now, stop that," said Foxy sharply. "You don't know that at all. He might come on back tonight, full of deer ticks and smelling like skunk."

I scrubbed at my face. "Do you think so?"

"Wouldn't surprise me. Dogs are smart enough to be afraid. If he ran off, I can promise it wasn't after one of *them*."

I took another gulp of lemonade. "You believe me? About the thing?"

"Believe you? Shit." The lines of her face deepened, and for a minute she looked a lot older than sixty. "Of course. Didn't realize until just now that you don't know."

"Know what?" I said blankly.

"'Bout them. The people in the hollers. Whatever you want to call 'em."

"I don't know anything!" I spread my hands. "What am I supposed to know?"

Foxy shook her head. "I messed up," she said. "I thought you had to know about them, at least a bit. Figured your granny would have told you."

"Ha!" I said, and took a slug of lemonade.

"Yeah, not the brightest thing I've ever thought. But when you said you saw the hill, I figured you *had* to know something,

'cos you got up there in the first place, and then got out again."
She glared into her lemonade.

"I don't know anything!" I repeated. "What am I supposed
to know about? Who's in the hollers? There aren't even any
hollers around here, are there?"

"Ehhh. Sometimes there are, sometimes there ain't. It
comes and goes. Most times there's no problems, you understand. Sometimes things get turned around and you end up in
country that ain't supposed to be there."

"Like hills that don't exist?"

"Yeah, like that."

"But how is that *possible*?" I flapped my hands. "Hasn't
somebody made a topographic map or taken photos or something and noticed that there was a hill that wasn't supposed to
be there?"

Foxy shook her head. "Don't think it's that easy to get there.
I only done it once myself. And you show up spouting foolishness about hills being where everybody knows there's no hills,
who's gonna believe you? They can look over and *see* there's no
hill there."

"But what . . . ? How . . . ?"

Foxy sighed. "I dunno. I mean, people say they know things
and try to look smart, but I don't think anybody knows anything
for sure. The hills're just where the holler people live. Old-
timers talk about seeing 'em now and again. Tall and skinny
and white like nobody you ever saw."

"I didn't see anybody like that," I said. I thought of the
hiker I'd seen, the one dressed like a hippie, but she hadn't

been particularly tall and pale, had she? Not unnaturally so, anyway.

"Yeah. Never seen one either. But the deer thing's one of theirs. They leave stuff around sometimes. Mostly it's piled-up stones and marks on trees. Talking to each other, like. But sometimes they make something that walks around."

I clutched my lemonade. The porch didn't seem quite so safe anymore.

"But *why*?"

Foxy shrugged. "Dunno. I only seen it twice. One was a hog, but they'd stuck a wasp's nest where its head oughta be. It was out digging up fields and a friend of my daddy's shot it. Couldn't get too close to it 'cos of the wasps, so they threw hay over it and burned it. They're uncanny, but they ain't fire-proof."

"That's a relief," I said faintly. "What about the other time?"

"Raccoon. Thought it had rabies or something. It was sort of shuffling around, but you got close enough, you could see it was all held together with cords 'n' junk."

"What did you do?"

"Ran it over with the tractor a coupla times. Had to stop using that chunk of field, of course. Daddy said the ground would be bad under it. This was over in Bynum. When we sold the place, we told 'em that bit was bad, but I doubt they listened. Still, I figure if you're growing all those weird-ass glow-in-the-dark soy beans, a little bad magic ain't gonna make things much worse."

"So it's magic, then?"

Foxy rolled her eyes. "It's makin' dead animals walk around and hills vanish. What the hell else would it be? Aliens?"

"But magic—I mean—" I flailed. Magic in my head was a mix of stage magicians in white gloves and really well-meaning people who did yoga and believed in the healing power of crystals.

I attempted to express this to Foxy, who looked at me like I was a baby bird that had fallen out of the nest and hit its head.

"I don't think the holler people are doing yoga," she said.

"But where *are* they?"

"I dunno. Little to one side of here, I think. Somewhere like this, but with hills and hollers. They come through sometimes and we go through sometimes, and sometimes the way's open and sometimes it ain't. You must've gone through when it was open. Dumb luck or something."

"It was Bongo," I said. "He found the way through."

"Yeah. A lot of dogs would've thought twice, but hounds get a smell and their brain turns off. Well, you know. But even he was smart enough to be scared of one of their walking things."

"And nobody reports this? Nobody says, 'Hey, there's a bunch of scary people around here making—making dead animals walk around?'"

She snorted. "Yeah, that'd be good for a story. 'Hillbillies Claim the Woods Are Haunted, Blame Little People.' Or, if they did find one of the walking things, it'd be 'Redneck Satanic Horror!!' We'd have reporters in the shitter and nobody'd find anything. Assuming anybody even listened in the first place."

"So nobody knows, then."

"Eh, most old-timers around here get a notion. But you talk about it and you sound crazy, so nobody talks about it much. And the cops just shrug. That sheriff fellow who was out here earlier? He knows the stories, I'll bet you, but what cop is gonna admit they believe in that kinda thing? They'd get laughed outta the station. And if you get any of them ghost hunter people, they head over to Chatham and the Devil's Tramping Ground. Though I'll tell you, I've been there, and the Devil needs to throw out them old refrigerators if he wants to do any serious tramping. Place is a dump."

"But—"

She looked at me over the rim of her jar. "Think about it, hon. You tell somebody, how you gonna start?"

I took a deep shuddering breath and drank more lemonade, trying to think of an answer. Sure, Enid and Officer Bob had believed me about the effigy hanging from a tree, but if I tried to tell them it had been in the window, that it had been *alive* . . . Officer Bob probably already half believed that I was making things up. Enid seemed like she might be more sympathetic, but what was she going to do about it? Come fight the effigy off with a thermos of decaf?

I imagined calling my father and saying, *Dad, there's monsters in the woods. Dad, I saw something horrible, and the weird woman across the road says it's the holler people, and I climbed a hill that wasn't there and there was a deer effigy hanging in the trees, but when I tried to call the cops, it was gone, and then it came back at night in my window. . . . No, I didn't dream it. . . .*

Even in my head, it sounded stupid.

The wind chimes blew back and forth in a wind that smelled like turned earth and spring, not like raccoons held together with cords and hogs with wasp nests where their heads would be.

"Like I said, I figured your granny'd have told you something," said Foxy after a while. "Didn't think about what a nasty piece of work she was."

"I don't think she knew," I said. "Cotgrave—her husband—he knew something. He had a journal and said he saw them in Wales."

Foxy nodded. "Figure you get any set of old hills, you'll have something in it. Probably holler people all over the world, if you know where to look."

I shuddered. This was not a comforting thought. "He also said he thought that things didn't come around her. That she smelled bad to them or something."

"Huh," said Foxy. She thought about that. "Suppose that makes sense. Some smells you just don't want to be around. Skip can't stand liver, won't even come in the house if I'm cooking it. Doesn't mean he's scared of liver. Don't think the holler people are scared of much, but I can see 'em giving that house a wide berth unless they had to go there."

"I think it's why he married her," I said. "He had some kind of experience with them in Wales, and then he thought she was safe because they just didn't want to be around her."

Foxy snorted. "Lord. Talk about bein' caught between the Devil and the deep blue sea!"

"Yeah. His journal's rambling, but by the end he's saying he'd rather deal with them." Cotgrave's *white people* must be the same as Foxy's *holler people*. If I could find his typed manuscript, surely it'd have something more . . . wouldn't it?

Assuming it existed. Assuming he knew anything for certain. Assuming his medication hadn't been playing tricks on him and it wasn't a letter to Ambrose.

Ambrose, I don't know who you were, but I wish I could talk to you or smack you or something!

"So what are you going to do?" asked Foxy.

"I have to stay," I said. It was easier to say out loud than I expected. "Until Bongo comes back."

Foxy nodded. "You can come stay here," she said. "I ain't saying they won't come here, but company's better than none."

I took a deep breath. "I want to," I said. "But if he comes back, he'll come to the house. He got out once back in Pittsburgh and he came back after three days of rabbit chasing." I tried not to think about what would happen if Bongo decided to go home to Pittsburgh. The noses on hounds are good enough that I won't swear he couldn't smell his way back there, while I sat in a house surrounded by deer monsters.

There comes a point where terrible things are funny. It's the point where the furnace is broken and the hot water heater is leaking and your dog comes in smelling of skunk and the check engine light has come on when you go to get tomato juice. You stop crying and you stop being frustrated because none of that will help. All you can do is start laughing hysterically because that's the only thing that's left.

Foxy let me laugh until it started to get weird, and then she slapped me on the back repeatedly, as if I were having a coughing fit. "Settle down there, hon. Get it all out. I got some stuff that might help you or might not, but it never hurts to try."

Foxy's "stuff" was a little velvet bag of herbs and a rosary with round wooden beads. "Got it at the state fair for three dollars," she said cheerfully. "The roots, though, that's from a guy down south who said he studied under Doc Buzzard."

"Doc Buzzard?" I asked.

"A hoodoo man. He was probably lying, but you never know. Anyway, it ain't gonna hurt. You know how to pray the rosary?"

"No?"

She looked faintly disappointed, but rallied anyway. "It don't matter. The holler people ain't religious. But the beads are hickory and hickory's special."

In all of Aunt Kate's botanical musings, she had never covered the specialness of hickory. I knew oak and ash and rowan, from reading fantasy novels, but not hickory. I said as much to Foxy.

"No, no," she said. "It ain't magic. It's the other way around. We got hickory over here, but I don't think they got it over there. You got hickory with you, you got a piece of the world that's normal. It's so normal it'll cancel out some of the weirdness. You follow?"

Clearly I was losing my mind, because that actually made a kind of sense. I went back to the house with a hickory rosary and a bag of dried roots draped around my neck.

Maybe it was the rosary or the talk or the lemonade. Maybe it was just guilt, or the restless, edgy feeling that I had to do *something*. But I took my courage in both hands and walked into the woods, shouting Bongo's name and listening for the knocking of hagstones in between shouts.

I scoured the woods around the house, but Bongo still wasn't there.

"All right," I said, going back into the house. "Next thing." I turned the radio on so I had something to talk to and went through the house, checking for monsters. There weren't any, or if there were, they were upstairs on the second floor.

I shut down that train of thought quickly. Elaine Rogers told me about the great programs that were only available because of my help. I was starting to wonder if this radio station ever played anything but Pledge Week spots.

If I was going to stay in the house tonight, I was not going to sleep in the bedroom with the window right there where things could look in. Bongo was loud enough when barking to wake the dead—if he showed up on the porch and started yelling to be let in and given dinner, I'd be able to hear it through a few layers of wood.

"Bathroom it is, then," I said.

I stripped Cotgrave's bed and tossed the blankets aside, then wrestled the mattress off the box spring and dragged it into the bathroom. It took up the entire floor and curled up at the edges. That was fine.

"If I have to pee, the toilet's right there. This'll be *efficient*," I told the radio.

"We have some fun gifts as a way of saying thank you," said Ms. Rogers, sounding tired. "We've got a mug, and at the hundred-dollar amount, this exclusive hoodie. . . ."

An exclusive hoodie sounded pretty awesome. Clearly I was developing radio Stockholm syndrome, on top of my other problems.

I went back to get the blankets . . . and stopped.

Spread across the box spring, where they had clearly been wedged under the mattress, lay a pile of papers. They were covered in double-spaced type. Someone had handwritten notes and corrections in ballpoint pen between the lines.

I picked up the top page.

> *I was first lent the Green Book by my friend and mentor, the philosopher Ambrose, as an example of what he referred to as "true sin." He believed that the greatest sin lay in seeking things outside the natural order, not in mere wickedness such as murder. "A passion of the lonely soul," Ambrose called it. The Green Book was a diary of one such sinner. . . .*

I had lost my dog and found, quite by accident, Cotgrave's manuscript.

11

It was not terribly long. As I scanned it, it became immediately obvious that Cotgrave was one of those people who typed better than he wrote by hand. You see that sometimes as an editor, when people are writing notes in the margins of printed pages. The difference between the voice of the manuscript and the curt, scribbled notes in the journal was striking, not just the bits where he was transcribing another book, but his interjections as well.

I made another pot of coffee and pulled a chair into the entryway. With the screen door shut and locked and the front door ready to slam, I could see Bongo if he came back, and . . . hopefully . . . I'd have warning if the deer monster returned.

I sound so calm about that, don't I? Like I'd do some kind of action-hero move and slam the door on it, or if it came through the screen, I'd beat it to death with the chair. I know perfectly well—and probably you do, too—that at that moment, I'd have peed myself and died and probably wound up as a skeletal effigy tapping on Foxy's window. Still, I couldn't think of anything better to do.

I had hours until nightfall. I had a lot of coffee. I had a manuscript to read, and hell if I was going to stop halfway through.

"All right, Cotgrave," I said aloud, settling the sheaf of papers in my lap. "Let's do this thing."

I was first lent the Green Book by my friend and mentor, the philosopher Ambrose, as an example of what he referred to as "true sin." He believed that the greatest sin lay in seeking things outside the natural order, not in mere wickedness such as murder. "A passion of the lonely soul," Ambrose called it. The Green Book was a diary of one such sinner, a sixteen-year-old girl who had been the daughter of an associate. When he died, he left it to me in his will.

I am going to try and record my memory of the Green Book as closely as I can. I have read it many times, and parts I can recite, but it was very disjointed and my memory is not what it used to be. But since my wife has hidden the book, or perhaps destroyed it, I must write down what I remember before I forget even more. In places where I cannot remember the exact words, I will make note of what I do remember.

The Green Book is what we used to call a

pocketbook, but not like they are called in America, where they mean a book for holding cheques. It was old and had gold end papers and the binding was broken in two places from rough handling by the mail when Ambrose sent it to me at the last. He said he had known the girl who wrote it, but he never told me her name.

The book starts with a description of where the girl found the blank pocketbook, in a drawer in her home. I don't think that part was important. The narrative then begins:

I have a great many other books of secrets I have written down and hidden all in a safe place, and I am going to write here many of the old secrets and some new ones, but there are some I shall not put down at all, in case someone ignorant should find it and read it. I must not write down the real names of the seasons. . . . There were other things here that she must not write down, but I do not remember them all. It was an extensive list. Languages, I think, and letters. Some of them may have been made up. I remember the word "Aklo" and "chief songs." And then that she could not write down the ways to do things, "for peculiar reasons," or "say who the Nymphs are." The Nymphs appear later, and I believe them to be some kind of spirits, perhaps the numen of a place, expressed in physical form.

"Cotgrave," I said, putting the read pages facedown on the floor, "if you were a client and came to me for editing, I'd fire you. Footnotes are your friend."

> *Narrative continues:* **These are the very most secret secrets, and I am glad that I know what they are and glad when I think of how many wonderful languages I know that others do not, but there are** *some things that I call the secrets of the secrets of the secrets of the* **secrets** *—don't remember how many times she wrote "secrets"—that I dare not think of unless I am alone.*
>
> *There was a section here I don't remember well at all. She says that she puts her hands over her eyes and says a word and the Alalaa? Alala? comes. She does this at night in her room or in the woods. She must also do a number of ceremonies, which are named after colors. She liked the Scarlet Ceremonies the best and the Yellow Ceremonies the least because it made her "feel so queer," as if she had eaten something disagreeable. There is no information about what the ceremonies are or what she does.*

"Did they have psychosis when you were young, Cotgrave?" I mused. "I mean, they must have, but did they call it that? Because this is starting to sound like the diary of a girl with some very grave issues."

I know it's wrong to try to diagnose people who aren't there, and I'm a hack armchair psychologist who hangs out on the Internet, so my opinion was worth exactly nothing, but I started wondering about the ceremonies and the rituals some people get with OCD. If she called those "ceremonies" and had to perform them when people weren't looking . . .

Well, that would be a very tidy explanation right up until we got, y'know, *horrible deer monsters looking in the window.*

Ugh.

I wondered what the Alalaa was, or if it was anything at all. The sound or maybe the shape of the word made me think of *glossolalia*—you know, speaking in tongues. I had to proof a thesis about it once, and I don't think the author spelled the word the same way twice. The thesis said it sounded nearly the same whatever the culture was, though, and had endless citations to back it up.

Maybe this kid got alone and did something and kicked off a glossolalia fit. Lots of people can do that, usually at tent revivals.

Maybe I was reaching for explanations that had no bearing on anything.

> *Ambrose believed that the ceremonies were some form of folk magic survival, most likely learned from her nurse, meant to propitiate the white people.*
>
> *In the next section she described someone talking about her, probably servants, saying that she had been a strange child saying words in the cradle. Chronology is confused, though I have*

*tried to make sense of it. . . . **I can remember things***
***before that, only it has got confused.** Says she remem-*
bered "little white faces" looking down at her and
talking to her, and a white land with white grass
and white trees when she was very young. White
faces went away and she forgot the words.

Next, a description of a short journey with
her nurse to a pond in the woods. At the pond,
the nurse leaves, and shortly after she sees the
white people again, says two of them came out of
the water and the woods to dance and sing and
play with her.

Description of the white people here, as "a
kind of creamy white, like old ivory." One was fe-
male and had dark eyes and hair. The girl likes
her, "the white lady." Says they danced and sang
and played games together until she fell asleep.
I thought this was probably a dream when I first
read it, but not now, of course. Ivory is not a bad
description, but not quite right. They're white like
bone after the flesh has been pared off.

Sitting in my chair in the entryway, I felt my eyebrows
climb toward my hairline.

Of course, he mentioned seeing white people in his journal,
so I don't know why I'm surprised. Maybe by the description of
flesh being pared off. Yikes.

I got up, closed the front door before turning my back on

it, and got a warm-up on my coffee. Elaine Rogers asked me if
I valued investigative journalism.

"I do," I told her. "I wish somebody would have done some
investigating about this. . . ."

Of course, Foxy was probably right. If a reporter went
digging around in the hills and somehow did manage to turn
something up, it'd be dismissed as hillbillies and aliens.

I looked out the screen door for a moment before sitting
back down. No dog. No monsters. No white people, other than
my pasty Caucasian self, and I was pretty sure that wasn't what
Cotgrave's girl had meant.

> When she wakes up, the nurse has returned and
> the girl thought the nurse looked like the white lady.
> Nurse cries, becomes frightened, threatens her with
> "being thrown into the black pit with the dead peo-
> ple" if she speaks of it. My nurse used to threaten to
> beat my head against the wall when I misbehaved,
> so not sure if this was anything but an idle threat
> against misbehavior, though it is strangely specific.
>
> *I was thirteen, nearly fourteen, when I had a
> very singular adventure, so strange that the day on
> which it happened is always called the White Day.*
>
> Lengthy description of walk follows, "up
> thorny thickets on the hills, and by dark woods full
> of creeping thorns." Much of the Green Book is
> descriptions of journeys. I am not sure any of them
> are relevant or just untutored storytelling.

"You're one to talk," I muttered. "And I want to know more about this nurse threatening to beat your head against the wall. Child-rearing has changed a lot."

Honestly, I wanted to know more about the girl's nurse too. Was she supposed to have been the female white person dancing around? Was she traveling in disguise? Was this like a horrible fairy godmother?

I sighed and ran my free hand through my hair. "Or maybe she was just a woman whose charge started babbling about fairies and didn't want anybody to know that she'd left her alone so she could sneak off and hook up with the hot butler."

Sixteen years old when she wrote this. But there was something strange about the way she was writing—a kind of twee *Alice in Wonderland* phrasing—that made her seem younger, or like someone's idea of what a younger girl should sound like.

Maybe Cotgrave had made the whole thing up. Or maybe that was just the way she wrote. I've read much more grating narrative voices, Lord knows.

It occurred to me, depressingly, that maybe the Green Book had nothing to do with Foxy's holler people at all. Maybe Cotgrave had just been obsessed with the book and had run afoul of the holler people and had cast his experiences in relation to the book. Maybe if he'd had different reading material, I'd be working my way through a bad rewrite of a Regency romance. Maybe I was sitting here wasting time with a useless partial transcript of a diary written a hundred years ago by a woman with severe issues and meanwhile there were monsters outside and I didn't have a gun or a chain saw or even a large brick.

> *And it was a long, long way . . . repeats this*
> *phrase. Rocky floor, dried-up stream, a "dismal*
> *thicket," climbs a hill. I went on and on through*
> *that dark place; it was a long, long way.*

Incidentally, I disbelieved in the semicolon. Getting adult authors to use semicolons is like pulling teeth. They distrust them. Teenage girls handwriting in journals do not use semicolons. How much of this was Ambrose, and how much of it was really the Green Book? How accurately was he remembering things?

Then again, it was the . . . what, Victorian era? I couldn't remember the exact dates, and without the Internet, I couldn't look it up. If Ambrose had known the daughter . . . oh Lord, but she could have died at the age of a hundred and handed him an old diary on her deathbed, and then Cotgrave got it, and if he'd died in his nineties . . . well, figure he had to have been at least twenty when he met Ambrose . . . but then again, he could have been sixty. It could have been pre-Victorian. Hell, it could actually have *been* Regency.

The math made my head ache. Also my butt was falling asleep. I squirmed in the chair, trying to carry the one, and eventually working out that I had no idea how old the book was, and for all I knew it came from an era when semicolons were routinely scattered about like flower petals.

> *And I came to a hill that I never saw before . . .*
> *there were black twisted boughs that tore me as I*

*went through them, and I cried out because I was
smarting . . . may have been stinging or hurting . . .
all over where they tore my frock, and then I went
up a long, long way until the thicket stopped and
I came out crying on top of a big bare place. There
were such ugly grey stones lying on the grass, and here
and there a little twisted tree came out from under a
stone, like a snake.*

I read that passage, and then I reread it, and then I just
stared at it as if it, too, were a snake.

*I came to a hill that I never saw before. . . . There were ugly
grey stones lying on the grass. . . .*

For some reason all I could think was that the word *grey*
was spelled *gray* in America and I would have to mark that for
changes. Which was a stupid thing to think, but most of my
brain was whimpering and blundering around inside my skull
like Bongo during a thunderstorm.

I had climbed up a hill I had never seen before, and I had
come to a place with ugly grey (or gray) stones on the grass and
there had been the little twisted trees coming out from under
the stones, like snakes. Hell even the path I took was suddenly
familiar—a dried-up stream, a dismal thicket, a long dark way.
If I hadn't been obsessed with the stupid semicolon, maybe I'd
have picked up on it sooner.

"This was in Wales," I muttered. "This was in Wales. Or
England, anyway. Over there. Cotgrave said they were over there."

Except that apparently they were over here, too.

Was it the same place? Was there was one here and one somewhere in the British Isles? Was there a way through in both places?

Foxy had said that sometimes the hills were there and sometimes they weren't and sometimes you could go through and sometimes you couldn't. Had this girl been to the same hill that I had?

Had Cotgrave been there?

> *I went up to the top a long, long way* ... *description of "big ugly stones" as coming out of the earth or being rolled? Maybe both. I think there was more here, but I can't remember it. They went on as far as I could see, a long, long way. I looked out from them and saw the country* ... *countryside? Maybe a different word here* ... *but it was strange. It was wintertime, and there were black terrible woods hanging from the hills all round; it was like seeing a room hung with black curtains, and the shape of the trees seemed different from any I had ever seen before. I was afraid, but I repeated to myself the words that Nurse had taught me before she went away and I was brave again. Then beyond the woods there were other hills round in a great ring, but I had never seen any of them before; it all looked black, and everything had a voor over it. It was all so still and sad and silent, and the sky was heavy and grey, like a wicked voorish dome in Deep Dendo.*

I am not certain what a "voor" or a "voorish dome" is, although they are referenced several times in the Green Book. At the time, I thought it was like a mist, but Ambrose thought a "voorish dome" might be the roof of a cave in the hills, where the white people survived. "Deep Dendo" sounds like a place that would have stone, but "had a voor over it" sounds like an atmospheric difference, a haze perhaps.

I have lately come to think that perhaps a voor is like a glamour, a spell of misdirection, and since the girl was obviously sensitive to such things, she might see the voor over an enchanted place, and thus a wicked voorish dome could be a place with a wicked spell over it.

This is further confused, however, by the fact that she refers later to the Kingdom of Voor, "where the light goes when it is put out," but that could as well be referring to a kingdom with many voors, or from which such spells originate.

I went on into the dreadful rocks. There were hundreds of them. Some were like horrid-grinning men; I could see their faces as if they would jump at me out of the stone, catch hold of me, and drag me with them back into the rock, so that I should always be there with them and anyone who walked this way should see me looking out, and perhaps they might not recognize me then. And there were other rocks that were like animals creeping, horrible animals, putting out their tongues and licking the grass, and others were like words that I could not say, and others like dead people lying on the grass . . . Might have been another description here, but I think I remembered them all. I have read this section so many times, parts of it pound in my head and reading it makes the pounding go away. I may have missed a few words, but I think this is mostly right.

I went among them, though they frightened me, and my heart was full of the wicked songs that they put into it which I will not write down and I wanted to make faces and twist myself about in the way they did, but I did not and I went on and on a long, long way until at last I liked the rocks, and they didn't frighten me anymore and they reminded me of secret things that I knew. I sang the songs full of words that must not be spoken or written down. Then I made faces like the faces on the rocks, and I twisted myself about like the twisted ones

I dropped the page.

I didn't mean to, but it slipped out of my fingers and fell to the floor the way that nothing other than sheets of paper fall, then slid a little way and wedged one corner under the couch. The litany of the twisted ones was pounding in my head like a song that had gotten stuck.

"Well," I said out loud. "Well. Now I know where it comes from."

My voice sounded very calm. It sounded like my aunt's voice more than mine. It sounded like a grown-up's voice and not at all like someone who was about to cry or scream or curl up in the bathroom and wait to be eaten by monsters.

I took a sip of my coffee and discovered that it was stone cold.

I nodded to myself. I picked up the sheet of paper and I put it on the pile of pages and tapped the edges together as if I knew what I was doing, and I went to reheat my coffee.

12

It was a criminal act to warm that beautiful coffee up in the microwave, but I did it anyway, because I hadn't drunk more than an inch worth. I sang something—some stupid song from the eighties; I don't even remember which one, probably about love or cocaine or driving fast cars or maybe all three and one was a euphemism for another, and then I couldn't remember the next line and so I sang "Jingle Bells" and then the coffee was hot. I had to grab the handle with my shirt because it was too hot to touch.

Probably the words that the girl said could not be written down were not about a one-horse open sleigh. It didn't seem likely.

I glanced out the window and saw that it was still light. That seemed strange somehow, like when you come out of a movie theater and are startled to see that it's still daylight. It seemed like it should be much later. It seemed like half the day should have passed and it should be past midnight.

By the clock, I think it had been about forty-five minutes. Long enough for coffee to go cold, not much longer.

I walked through the house and turned on every light. I cranked the radio up and then I ran the ice maker, not because I needed ice but because it was loud and I needed it to be loud in the house right then.

You are going to think I am entirely mad, but I proceeded to fire up my laptop and play three games of solitaire at high speed. I just needed to do something that wasn't reading, something where black cards went on red cards and nines went on tens and everything made sense. As soon as I got stuck, I restarted. It probably took about five minutes. It wasn't even long enough for the Pledge Week to break back into the radio program, which was a lengthy discussion of a coup, except that I'd missed what country it was in. I wondered who I was supposed to be rooting for, the military or the government, because both sounded pretty bad.

When Elaine Rogers came back on, sounding punchy and tired, I closed the laptop. I wondered if poor Elaine slept during Pledge Week. I would have traded places with her. She could have my grandmother's house and my stepgrandfather Cotgrave and a ring of hills in winter like dark curtains and I twisted myself around like the twisted ones—

I grabbed the coffee mug. The handle was too hot still and I swore and I drank it anyway and burned the roof of my mouth, and that was fine. A burned mouth was a thing I understood. It had nothing to do with twisted stones and songs that must not be spoken and voorish domes, whatever the hell those were.

I'm being stupid. I knew that line had to come from the Green Book. He said it did. I should have expected to see it. It just . . . startled me, that's all.

Truth was, the litany of the twisted ones had been growing in my mind since I read it days before. Not that I kept thinking it the way Cotgrave had, but I kept *seeing* it, or remembering it at odd moments and the idea of it had gone from *what is my stepgrandfather smoking, anyway?* to *poor old fellow was obsessed* to . . . to something else. Something I couldn't put words around. It was—okay, you remember *The Shining?* I felt like I was flipping through a stack of papers that said *All work and no play . . .* over and over again, but I hadn't yet turned around to see Jack Nicholson standing there grinning at me.

The radio blared. Someone was delivering a testimonial about how much community radio meant to them. Rogers told us about how grateful they were for people like the Bolanders, who really understood what a service the station provided. I wondered if the Bolanders got matching hoodies.

I picked up the page I had dropped. I forced my eyes to finish the line that they'd stopped at.

> *Then I made faces like the faces on the rocks, and I twisted myself about like the twisted ones, and I lay down flat on the ground like the dead ones, and I went up to one that was grinning, and put my arms round him and hugged him. And so I went on and on through the rocks and it was a long, long way.*

There was a gap in the text here, and it started again on the next page. Cotgrave had thoughtfully labeled each page in the corner in blue ballpoint pen, so I knew I was going in the right order. I felt a pang of sympathy for the old man, who had to stop in nearly the same place that I had.

Looking back on what I wrote out yesterday, I believe that it is mostly accurate, or at least, as close as I can come. It may be that it is tainted by my own experience of the stones. Or perhaps, since I read the Green Book long before I climbed the hill myself, my experience of the stones was tainted by reading the book. Are hers the same as the ones I saw in Wales? There is no way to tell. I knew enough to turn away, in any event. If I had gone on, perhaps I would have seen what she saw, or perhaps I would not be here to write this.

In any event, I do not remember the rest of this part so clearly. The girl went to a place in the middle of the hill and climbed a tower or a hill to a high place, I think, and looked down on the stones and saw them all arranged in patterns. She becomes dizzy and the patterns began to spin, and then she climbs down. I danced as I went in the peculiar way the rocks had danced, and I was so glad I could do it quite well, and I danced and danced along, and sang extraordinary songs that came into my head.

She continues on, possibly through another tunnel, while dancing in this fashion, and describes being stung by nettles and thorns, but they only make her tingle and she does not mind this because of the singing.

There are many stories, of course, of religious pilgrims scourging themselves and becoming insensitive to pain, swamis walking on hot coals, and so forth, so perhaps it is something like that. I remember when Ambrose and I first spoke, fire-walking was considered a baffling mystical art. And yet I saw a television program on fire-walking last month that explained how it was done with physics.

Perhaps someday even things like the Green Book will be explained by physics, and there will be no more of Ambrose's passions of the lonely soul. If fire-walking is in the natural order after all, as it seems, then what more may we yet learn? Perhaps a day will come when all things can be fit somehow in the natural order, and then Ambrose's definition of sin will be of no more use to us.

Then again, as isolated as I am now, perhaps we have explained many things already. The fire-walking program may be only one. She thought it was interesting and left it on. I think she was hoping someone would burn themselves, but no one did.

I snorted out loud at that last bit. It had been a margin note in blue pen. Cotgrave had no more illusions about his wife than any of the rest of us did, apparently.

Ambrose spoke often of how terrifying it would be if flowers began to sing to us, or a dog to speak, in violation of the natural order. He spoke of such violation as the true form of sin. And yet now there are theme parks where you can go and mechanical flowers will sing, movies where dogs will talk. Have we thus all begun to sin, or have our senses become numbed so that we will no longer recognize true sin when we see it?

To continue, much of the rest of the "White Day" is an account of travel. There are thickets and valleys and ferns. She drinks from a stream which "gives her a kiss" and believes that there is a Nymph within it. She comes to a wall of moss and believes that it is the end of the world, after which is only the Kingdom of Voor, where the light goes when it is put out, and the water goes when the sun takes it away.

I wondered how I should get home again, if I could ever find the way, and if my home was there anymore, or if it were turned and everybody in it into grey rocks, as in The Arabian Nights. I sat down on the grass and thought what I should do next. I was tired, and my feet were hot with walking.

She finds a well nearby, the bottom covered in red sand that is constantly stirring, and puts her feet into it to soak. Climbing the wall, she sees "the queerest country" full of "hills and hollows" and two large mounds like beehives. *It was so strange and solemn and lonely, like a hollow temple of dead heathen gods.*

She then recounts a lengthy story told by her nurse, of a hollow that was a "bad place" where people did not dare to go. A poor girl goes in. She claims the hollow is full of grass and stones and flowers and is later seen wearing extravagant jewelry. When asked, she says the emeralds are grass, the rubies and diamonds only stones. She goes to the court of the king and queen, wearing a crown of "pure angel-gold" which she claims is only yellow flowers in her hair. The king's son marries her, but on his wedding night, there is a tall black man with "a dreadful face" standing outside the door, saying: *"Venture not upon your life/This is my own wedded wife."* (May have been "mine own" or some other construction.) The bedroom is full of screaming and shrieking and crying. They cut the door open with hatchets and find only black smoke and the remains of flowers and stones.

After recounting this story, the girl says a charm that her nurse taught her, to ward off the black man and keep bad things away.

Still not sure now who or what the nurse was.
At first I thought she was one of the white people
herself, but now I wonder if she may have been one
of their servants, or what my mother used to call
"cunning folk." Or perhaps the nurse was both, or
a half-breed of sorts. Ambrose suggested once that
the girl may have been a changeling, that perhaps
the white people breed with humans and then
send their servants to train them until they are old
enough to take their place among their elders.

I rubbed my hands over my face. My eyes were swimming from reading, especially from reading Cotgrave's cramped margin notes in ballpoint pen.

Well. The story of the poor girl and the stones was a fairly straightforward pact with the Devil, with a little old-fashioned racism thrown in. By itself it wasn't proof of anything, except that the nurse had strange ideas about bedtime stories.

To continue the narrative: She travels on even
farther, finding a certain wood, which is too secret
to be described, and nobody knows of the passage
into it, which I found out in a very curious man-
ner, by seeing some little animal run into the wood.
After this there is very little concrete written, only
that she sees "the most wonderful sight." She does
not describe it at any point, but runs away back
home. She lies in bed attempting to remember

*this wonderful sight, but cannot see it clearly. It
is referred to afterward as "the wonderful secret"
which she knows and others do not.*

*The girl herself begins to wonder if her nurse
was one of the "beautiful white people."*

*After this point the chronology of the Green
Book becomes even more jumbled, or perhaps my
memory of it is worse than I thought. She refers to
several stories told to her by her nurse, which begin
"In the time of the fairies." One is about a young
man who chases a white stag until he enters a fairy
mound and meets the Queen of Fairies. She gives
him wine to drink from a golden cup (shades of
Parsifal?) and when he awakens, he will not drink
wine or kiss another woman for the rest of his life.*

*Ambrose was most interested in a tale "about
a hill where people used to meet at night long ago,
and they used to play all sorts of strange games
and do queer things that Nurse told me of." I only
remember one stretch of it well, but there was a
great deal to it, much of it repetitive.*

*And the song was in an old, old language that
nobody knows now, and the tune was queer. Nurse
said her great-grandmother had known someone
who remembered a little of it, when she was quite
a little girl, and Nurse tried to sing some of it to
me, and it was so strange a tune that I turned all
cold and my flesh crept as if I had put my hand on*

something dead. Sometimes it was a man that sang
and sometimes it was a woman, and sometimes the
one who sang it did it so well that two or three of
the people who were there fell to the ground shriek-
ing and tearing . . . (Can't remember much more
of this. Not tearing their hair, but can't remember
what it was.)

Ambrose believed that this section—and perhaps all the Green Book—represented a survival
of folk ritual, perhaps to appease the white folk,
or to harness their power for the user. He used to
say that many dark things were cloaked in simple
stories of fairies and humble rural superstition.

I rolled my eyes a bit at that one. *Humble rural superstition.*
Ambrose sounded like a bit of a jerk. The sort of person who'd
stand by the maypole at the Renaissance Festival and tell you that
actually it was a fertility rite, like you didn't bloody well know—

"Hey, you eaten lunch?" asked Foxy.

I let out a squawk and lurched backward, nearly knocking
the chair over. Papers went everywhere.

"Sorry," said Foxy. She leaned against the screen door and
waited for me to unlatch it. "You got that radio up so loud I
could walk a brass band past the door."

"Yeah," I said, picking up papers hurriedly. "Yeah, it's . . . I
needed noise."

She nodded. I let her into the house and she handed me a
Tupperware container with a sandwich in it. "Skip made tuna

salad. I figured you were probably workin' yourself into a state, so I came over."

"Thank Skip for me." I wolfed down the sandwich and realized I could have eaten about ten more. "I've been drinking coffee all this time. I didn't realize it was lunchtime."

"It ain't," said Foxy. "It's closing in on supper. It'll be dark soon, and I figured I'd come sit up with you tonight."

I looked at her blankly.

"In the house," she said patiently. "Tonight. In case your monster comes back."

"You'd do that?"

"Well, of course!" Her bangles clacked together as she flailed her hands in the air. "You don't let your neighbors get et by monsters alone. Tomas'd do it, but he's a boy, so it wouldn't be respectable. And I ain't sure how much he knows about the holler people. They got different stuff going on where he's from, or maybe the same stuff walkin' around in different skins."

I shuddered at the mental image, vague though it was. "You mean in Mexico?"

"No. I mean Arizona. Tomas's from Phoenix."

Annnnnd I'm a racist ass. And here I was just yelling at Cotgrave about that. . . .

"Never been out that way myself," Foxy continued, "but he says they got a whole tribe way back when who built big cliff houses and then vanished off the face of the earth." She pointed a finger at me. "Mind you, we got that out here, too. That Lost Colony they do the play about."

"I'm pretty sure that colony went off and lived with the

local tribes," I said weakly. "Apparently that happened a lot back then."

Foxy dismissed the weight of decades of archaeology with a wave of her hand. "Well, maybe. But I ain't convinced, and there ain't any of those local tribes around talking about it, are there?"

I opened my mouth to launch into a diatribe about *why* there were no local tribes, then thought better of it. While I am generally willing to rant at people about smallpox and colonialism, this did not seem like an opportune time. If I lived through the night, I could find Foxy a book on the topic.

At the moment I had something else for her to read. "Foxy? I'm in the middle of reading this manuscript my stepgrandfather wrote. Would you mind reading it too?"

She raised one painted-on eyebrow. "A manuscript? What sorta thing?"

"I think it's about the holler people."

Her other eyebrow went up. "Oh," she said. "All right, then. Let's see what the old man had to say."

Foxy wanted to head back home before it got dark and bring over a sleeping bag. I dragged the cushions off the couch and set them up in the kitchen for her. The wraparound porch didn't run under the kitchen window, and I didn't think the deer monster would be tall enough to look through it unless it could run up the walls like a spider. *Stop, stop. Don't think about that—*

I played another game of solitaire to settle my brain.

Then I went to the stairs and the wall of junk. Had I seen a tea kettle in there earlier? I could swear I had. . . .

Aha!

The kettle was lurking under a grid of wire coat hangers and a dish drying rack with a broken hinge. It took some wiggling and there was a dent in the side, but I managed to haul it free. I scrubbed it out and was heating water for tea by the time Foxy returned.

"I brought more sandwiches," she said, holding up more Tupperware.

"I'll make coffee," I said. "Or tea." The tea bags in the cupboard were about a thousand years old, but Lipton doesn't go bad, does it? "Err . . . do you drink tea?"

"I'll drink just about anything, hon." She patted her purse. "Brought something to put in it, too."

"Is it a good idea to be drunk if there are . . . uh . . . things out there?"

Foxy snorted. "You kidding? It's the *best* idea."

We settled back down. I took my chair again, and Foxy sat in an armchair that I'd managed to liberate from the newspapers. I passed the pages over as I finished them. The radio droned pleasantly in the background. It could almost have been cozy, if things weren't so deeply bizarre. Together we settled down to read.

> *There is a story of a young man happening on the secret rites, but it follows the ordinary sort of cautionary tale, where a man looks on forbidden knowledge. (I think this is a different young man from the one who visited the Queen of Fairies, but I fear it has been too long to be sure. There were*

too many young men in the stories, and they have all blurred together in my head.) He is bound up by some invisible force and wakes the next morning. When he tries to tell the villagers what he has seen, those who go to the rites already know but will not speak of it. The rites are largely unspecific, except for "making a sound like thunder," which is probably the use of a bull-roarer or other primitive instrument. Supposedly this sound is answered from far away. Bread and wine are passed around and "secret things" brought out. Ambrose pointed out the connections here to the Eleusinian Mysteries, but I have always considered this tenuous at best. One could describe a High Mass nearly the same way, with bread and wine and smoke and singing.

Somewhere in these descriptions, the nurse takes her to make a clay doll, keeping it hidden, doing "queer things with it." She describes the nurse as making "such funny red faces" while she kneads the clay, singing the entire time, while her face gets redder and redder. The nurse impresses the importance of secrecy on her, with more threats of being thrown in the black pit.

It was long after I came here, and after Ambrose died, that I learned of the hoodoo men in the South who claim to make dolls, or poppets, and can use them to cast sickness on a person. Voo-

doo dolls have become a silly toy on television pro-
grams now, like fire-walking. If there is some grain
of truth to these stories, I would not be surprised
if it is related to the clay doll in the Green Book.

They perform strange rites with the doll, "pay-
ing their respects." The narrator does as the nurse
does, calling it an "odd game" that they are play-
ing, but agrees to do what the nurse does because
she likes her. She gives no details. She says that
the nurse looks at this time like the white lady
from the wood.

I'll be honest, if I heard this from a modern narrator, I would
have Child Protective Services on the line so fast it would make
your head spin. All this stuff about odd games that have to be
kept secret set off *serious* warning bells.

But . . . well . . . different era. Different language. Maybe this
wasn't as creepy as it seemed. Or maybe it was, but I couldn't
very well call the cops on a book.

I was a bit surprised that neither Ambrose nor Cotgrave
commented on that, but then again, they were also from a far
older time when I suppose you just didn't talk about that sort
of thing.

On the other hand, if you were summoning up people from
another world and making—I dunno, the English equivalent
of voodoo dolls—you'd probably want to keep that secret too.
Maybe it was just perfectly innocent devil worship.

I rubbed my forehead.

"You're thinking awfully hard," said Foxy, turning a page.

"There's a lot to think about," I said. "How far have you gotten?"

"She's going a long, long, long, long, long, long way," said Foxy. "I'm getting the impression it was a bit of a walk."

"Do you think her white people are the holler people?"

"If they aren't, they're at least kissing cousins." Foxy rubbed her forearms, setting her bracelets clicking. "I dunno. She's a strange one, isn't she?"

"Yes!" I said, more strongly than I meant to. "Or Cotgrave's writing her strange. I don't know. I . . . I don't *like* her."

"Well, she's been dead a good long while," Foxy pointed out. "So I don't think that's gonna hurt her none."

I exhaled. I had been feeling a strange sort of guilt about it. A bright young girl caught up with a clearly bizarre nurse, in peculiar circumstances . . . I should have felt sorry for her.

Instead . . .

I edited a manuscript once that wasn't terrible. Most of it was pretty good. But they'd tried to do a point-of-view thing with a feral child, and that bit had been completely dreadful. It had read pretty much exactly like a reasonably smart man trying to write like he thought a naive innocent would write, and it had come off like Norman Mailer trying to write virginity, only with more eating bugs in the woods. This wasn't that bad, but it was, as Foxy would say, kissing cousins.

I mean, it might have been Cotgrave. Maybe he was transcribing it wrong. But there was something strange about the girl in this book. I couldn't put my finger on any one thing.

I didn't trust her, or her stupid semicolons.

"Maybe Cotgrave's just leaving out the sympathetic parts," I said, struggling to be fair.

"Could be," agreed Foxy. "Anyway, I'll tell you in a bit. She's still going the long, long, long way around."

"I thought the stones sounded like the ones on the hill," I said.

Foxy grunted. "Only seen 'em once," she admitted. "Years ago. And I turned right the hell around and left again. Those things weren't right."

"There's one in the backyard," I said.

She looked over the edge of the paper at me. "Didn't know that."

"Should we do something with it?" I asked. "Like . . . um . . . bury it or smash it or something?"

Foxy dropped the paper in her lap and waved her hands. "How the hell should I know? I'd say burn the thing, but I don't know if you can burn rocks."

"You can if you get them hot enough," I said. "I guess we could find a volcano. . . ." I had a mad image of Foxy and me, two unlikely hobbits lugging a two-hundred-pound rock to Mount Doom.

"Not a lot of volcanoes in this neck of the woods," she said. She took out a silver flask and poured several healthy glugs into her mug of tea. "Let me finish reading this thing, and then we can go take a look at your evil rock."

"Technically I think it was my grandmother's evil rock, not mine. . . ."

She grinned down at the paper.

> There is a story of a poppet like this one,
> owned by a beautiful woman "of the high gentry"
> who lived in a great castle. And she was so beau-
> tiful that all the gentlemen wanted to marry her,
> because she was the loveliest lady that anybody had
> ever seen, and she was kind to everybody, and every-
> body thought she was very good.
>
> The lady puts her suitors off for a year and a
> day, but one disguises himself as a girl to hide in
> the castle and befriend one of the maids. It is a
> plot worthy of the Bard, but the lady is more akin
> to one of Macbeth's witches.
>
> She knew more of the secret things than anyone
> else, and more than anyone knew before or after,
> because she would not tell anybody the most secret
> secrets. She knew how to do all the awful things,
> how to destroy young men, and how to put a curse on
> people, and other things. . . . There may have been
> another awful thing here, but I cannot remember
> it. . . . And the dancing people called her Cassap,
> which meant somebody very wise, in the old lan-
> guage. And she was whiter than any of them and
> taller, and her eyes shone in the dark like burning
> rubies; and she could sing songs that none of the oth-
> ers could sing, and when she sang they all fell down
> on their faces and worshipped her. And she could

do what they called shib-show, which was a very
wonderful enchantment. . . .

Neither Ambrose nor my later research turned
up anything on either the title Cassap or shib-
show. Shib-show, as described in the text, is a kind
of taming of serpents. The serpents leave her a gift
called a glame stone, which is presumably derived
from the same root as "glamour." Her description
as being whiter and taller than others, with eyes
like burning rubies, would indicate that she was
one of the white people herself. A changeling?
One trapped on this side, or simply amusing herself among humankind?

At any rate, the lady has a poppet made of
beeswax, which the narrator compares to the one
her nurse made out of clay. She feeds it and bathes
it in wine and it becomes a man, who kisses her.
It becomes clear that the poppet is her true husband,
although unlike the story of the Black Man, this one
appears to be subservient to her. She makes more wax
dolls and assigns them each the name of one of her
suitors, then ritually kills them off one by one, drown-
ing, burning, and strangling them with violet cords.
When only the disguised young man is left alive, he
goes to the bishop and reveals everything.

It is worth noting that there are multiple
suitors, and after two or three had been killed,
he might easily have gone to the bishop and thus

saved several of his rivals, but the author of the
Green Book never comments on this.

The Lady Cassap is burned alive, with her
wax husband hung around her neck, and the poppet is said to scream when it burns.

*And I thought of this story again and again as I
was lying awake in my bed, and I imagined the lady
in the marketplace, with the yellow flames eating
up her beautiful white body. And I thought of it so
much that I seemed to get into the story myself, and
I fancied I was the lady, and that they were coming
to take me to be burnt with fire, with all the people
in the town looking at me. And I wondered whether
she cared, after all the strange things she had done,
and whether it hurt very much to be burned at the
stake.*

Much of the rest of the Green Book is of no
great account. The girl writes rambling comments
about whether anything she has learned is really true, about stories in her head, which she does
not explain, and ruminates on the wonderful secret that she knows, but she never reveals it. She
mentions a few things that her nurse has taught
her. *Nurse said she would show me something funny
that would make me laugh, and then she showed
me how one could turn a whole house upside down,
and the pots and pans would jump about and the
china would be broken.* She reveals that her nurse

*went away some years before and no one knows
where she had gone, and that her father had been
angry when she spoke of the stories the nurse had
told. She also mentions an old game called "Troy
Town" where one dances a pattern and then must
answer questions truthfully . . . or was that earlier? I can't remember. It might have been when
she talked about the rituals and the bull-roarers.
There is no organization to the book, and it has
been so long since I read it.*

*Troy towns are, of course, our common laby-
rinths, though they do not call them that much
over here. Americans seem uninterested in laby-
rinths and mazes. Probably they require too much
mental effort.*

Thanks, Cotgrave. Nobody deserved to marry my grandmother,
but apparently some people didn't deserve it less than others.

I glanced over at Foxy. She had nearly caught up to me,
only a page or two behind.

She must have sensed me looking at her and glanced up.
"They say people used to go up in the hills and do devil things
here, too, in the old days," she said. "But it was mostly moonshiners, and I expect they put the stories about to keep people
off their stills. And the Klan of course." She made a gesture as if
to spit and then remembered she was indoors. "They're dumb
enough to mess around with the hollers, I expect, but too dumb
to live through it."

I snorted. Moonshiners and white supremacists. Lovely. If that was what Cotgrave was seeing up in the hills, I could see how he'd gone sarcastic about Americans.

"It surprises me, though," I said. "I mean, I wandered onto that hill. You'd think more drunk kids would do the same thing." I could picture two frat boys wandering around the hill, trying to knock over stones and refusing to admit to each other that things had gone strange.

"I doubt it happens much," she said. "You followed your dog, didn't you?"

I nodded.

"I'm only guessing, you understand, but I think there's probably different ways to the hills. Animals know ways through stuff that we don't. That one time I saw the stones, you know? Been out deer hunting and only clipped 'im. Well, you don't let a deer bleed out and leave it lying—it ain't right—so I went after, and next thing I knew I was more'n halfway up that hill and saw the stones. Only time I've ever let a deer fall and not brought it back, but I wasn't chasing anything into that country."

She took another slug of tea and bourbon. "I never could find my way back on my own, but I ain't saying I tried very hard, either."

I let out a long sigh. It didn't mean that I'd get Bongo back, but the idea that I might not be driving down the road and suddenly slip into a terrible different dimension relieved a fear I hadn't realized that I'd been harboring. The idea that you could just be walking and one minute you were in the world and the next everything changed and was full of gray stones and white people and effigies. . . .

I said as much to Foxy, or tried to.

"Nah, not so much. Oh, I expect that now and again there's ways people go through on accident, but not often. And they either get out or they go missing."

"Or get eaten by deer monsters," I said.

"There's always that, sure."

> An example of the ramblings in this section that I remember: *But I shall always remember those days if I live to be quite old, because all the time I felt so strange, wondering and doubting, and feeling quite sure at one time, and making up my mind, and then I would feel quite sure that such things couldn't happen really . . .* (more such here, cannot remember exact words). *But I took great care not to do certain things that might be very dangerous. So I waited and wondered for a long time, and though I was not sure at all, I never dared to try to find out. But one day I became sure that all that nurse said was quite true, and I was all alone when I found it out.*
>
> The cause of the narrator's moment of revelation is obscured. Ambrose believed it might be caused by the menarche, traditionally a highly dangerous time in the spiritual life of women.

Oh, gag me, I thought. *Your first period's not dangerous unless you plan on wearing white pants. Freaks you the hell out, sure, particularly if nobody bothered to explain it.*

Foxy was a fast reader. She got to that section a few minutes after I did. I could tell by the explosive snort.

"Just like men," she muttered. "Periods scare the crap out of 'em, so they assume the whole damn world's scared of it too."

"*Thank you!*" I said, with feeling.

"Although I s'pose this nurse could have told her she'd start bleedin' and she took it as proof of everything else, too," Foxy added. I grunted.

> *Then she decides to repeat her journey to the grey stones to see the secret again. She makes a poppet of her own, a much finer image than the one her nurse had made; and when it was finished I did everything that I could imagine and much more than she did, because it was the likeness of something far better.*
>
> *She makes no further mention of the poppet or what it is used for.*
>
> *And a few days later, when I had done my lessons early, I went for the second time by the way of the little brook that had led me into a strange country, a long, long way.*
>
> *At one point she turns and sees the country-side behind her resolve into two figures and re-members a story in which the two figures are called Adam and Eve. She blindfolds herself with a red silk handkerchief.*
>
> *Then I began to go on, step by step, very slowly.*

My heart beat faster and faster, and something rose in my throat that choked me and made me want to cry . . . something else here, not sure *. . . Boughs caught in my hair as I went, and great thorns tore me; but I went on to the end of the path. Then I stopped, and held out my arms and bowed, and I went around the first time, feeling with my hands, and there was nothing. I went round the second time, feeling with my hands, and there was nothing. Then I went round the third time, feeling with my hands, and the story was all true, and I wished that the years were gone by, and that I had not so long a time to wait before I was happy for ever and ever.*

Neither Ambrose nor I were ever entirely clear about this section, but it seems likely that the narrator realized that she herself was a changeling or descendant of the white people, and that she will at some point return to her own people. She looks in the water and remembers the white lady that she saw before, presumably comparing her reflection to that figure and believing that the lady must be her mother.

The Green Book cuts off abruptly shortly after this. She remembers about Nymphs, which she must look for everywhere, and some are dark and some are bright, and resolves to go and call them up. The last words are *The dark Nymph, Alanna, came, and she turned the pool of water into a pool of fire . . . .*

*Ambrose believed that the nymphs were refer-
ences to certain alchemical processes, couched by
the narrator in somewhat childish terms. This then
would indicate that the narrator has learned to
control some of those processes, perhaps in the form
of prayers to "Nymphs." In a more mature mind,
Ambrose speculated, we might see them as a recitation of the formulas required for a certain result,
perhaps somewhat like a mathematical equation.
The ancient alchemists undoubtedly knew such
formulas, but they cast them in mystical terms too,
like Virgin's Milk and the Philosopher's Stone.*

*The Green Book was not very long and the
narrator had reached the end of it, with the last
line written on the endpaper itself.*

*Ambrose did tell me of what he called "the se-
quel" to the Green Book, a story only, in which the
girl was found dead before a white stone statue in
the woods, perhaps a year after the writing of the
Green Book.*

So much for dying in bed at a hundred years old, I thought.
Well, if she was in her late teens and Ambrose was old enough
to be a friend of her father . . . Oh hell, I couldn't make sense
of the chronology. Late 1800s, maybe, assuming Ambrose had
been holding on to the Green Book for a while. Maybe a little
later. I still didn't know if Cotgrave had met Ambrose before or
after the war.

It didn't matter now, I supposed. Everyone was dead, except the holler people and me and, please God, my dog.

> *I pressed him on the subject, and he at last relented enough to say that the girl's father had called him in and the statue, which he had seen, was an image of copulating beings. He said that he would be hard-pressed to describe those beings, being a representation of things belonging to heaven or hell, not to earth, but that they were of two different kinds, and the offspring of such a union would be most terrible. He went on to say that the statue was known to have been incorporated into the mythology of the Witches' Sabbat.*
>
> *I wish now that I had asked where he knew that last bit from, but Ambrose enjoyed his secrets, particularly if they had a questionable bibliography behind them.*
>
> *The girl, he suggested, had seen the statue once by chance and then had blindfolded herself to avoid seeing it again. It is likely that one day the blindfold slipped, or perhaps she took it off deliberately, and then perhaps she became impregnated by the forces of the statue through a sympathetic process, though Ambrose hastened to say that her virtue was intact and she was blameless in the conventional sense, even if she had, quite by accident, stormed the gates of heaven.*

*In any event, the servants had noted her com-
ings and goings and the changes associated with
pregnancy and so jumped to conclusions. When
she was found dead, Ambrose was called in and
he had the statue destroyed. The nurse could not
be found.*

I scowled over the pages. I'd been thinking that this *statue*
was the same as the white stone I had seen, but clearly it must
not have been, because the stone was intact.

Unless it was a different stone. Unless there was more
than one.

*Well, why wouldn't there be more than one? If Ambrose's
stone was in Wales, the holler people could have another one
over here. It'd be pretty inconvenient to cross the Atlantic whenever you needed to get a confused teenager knocked up by a
rock.*

The fact that I even had to think this sentence was probably
proof that things had gotten badly out of hand.

*The pregnancy killed her in the end. "Poisoned by
knowledge beyond her understanding," Ambrose
said. He did not say, at the time, whether she
had borne what she carried, or whether her body
had proved too frail to contain the forces within.
It seems unlikely, in that time, that her father
would have consented to an autopsy, particularly
as Ambrose was not a medical doctor. But the*

stone itself was in the woods, not terribly far from human haunts.

I wish that I had never learned that. It is not pleasant to think that there may be such forces in the world lying in wait for the unsuspecting to stumble over.

It is even less pleasant now that I have discovered what lies behind the house. The hill of stones is there. I saw it once, but I knew to look away. The second time, though, I sought the stones out like a fool. I was close to falling into Ambrose's sin, I know. Now I wish that I had never gone and never seen them. I got away from them in Wales, but blood calls blood and I climbed the hill at last. If I had stayed away the second time . . . but there is no point now in wishing.

If Ambrose were alive, I would ask him about those twisted stones, but he is not, so I must make my own guesses. The white people carved them. Of that there is no doubt. Perhaps one of them might derive information from such a stone, like a man reading a signpost. Perhaps the hill of stones is a vast library of knowledge, which I am too blind and mortal to comprehend.

And I twisted myself about like the twisted ones.

And I twisted myself about like the twisted ones.

This phrase rings in my head, but I no longer believe it was meant for me. The writer of the

Green Book knew many things and she knew there were things she should not write down, but she was young and untrained. It is not surprising that perhaps a phrase bled over imperfectly, and I find myself saying these words like an incantation against the darkness in my mind.

There is a girl in the woods that I see sometimes now, and I have tried to warn her away, but what can I say? I am an old man who is not allowed to rest and I sound mad if I say, "Don't look at the stones on the hill or you will be a mother of monsters."

If I had the strength, I should go and find the white stone and hammer it down, as Ambrose did, but I do not know, in practical terms, if I am strong enough to wield the hammer.

If Ambrose were alive, perhaps he would have some idea what to do. But it has been a long time since we had those conversations. I don't even know if I am remembering them right myself.

If Ambrose were alive . . . If I were stronger . . . I have become an old man, obsessed with the tasks I can no longer finish.

I have done my best. It seems unlikely that my mind will ever be clearer than it is now. I have written the Green Book down as best as I can recall. I thought I would remember more than I did. I certify that all that I have written is accurate, to the best

of my recollection, and if parts are blurred or forgot-
ten, it is a failure of memory and not of will.
 Frederick Cotgrave
 United States of America
 but once of Wales
 March 1998

13

I stared at the signature for a while. The parts about impregnation were getting dangerously *Rosemary's Baby*–esque to me. Was I supposed to believe that the Green Book narrator had been pregnant with a monster from looking at a statue of monsters doing it?

It seemed far more likely that in the year after the book was written, she'd discovered boys. After all, the whole world is full of boys and really short on statues that knock you up.

On the other hand . . .

"She's screwing the clay doll, right?" Foxy broke in. "'I did everything that I could imagine and much more besides.' And the bit about the nurse's face getting red. That's the takeaway here, right?"

"Oh God. I didn't want to say it, and maybe it's the language difference, but that's the impression I got too," I said glumly, setting the last page aside. "I mean, I think she was seventeen at the time, so it was . . . errr . . . legal, I guess?"

"Also the bit where it's made out of, you know, *clay*."

I groaned. "Yeah. I don't know. I mean, do you think she got that from the nurse? Is this a story about abuse? Should we call someone?"

"Bit late for that, I'd say, since everybody's dead." Foxy turned the page.

If she was actually running around with human boys and trying to cover it up by blaming a statue in the woods—not, arguably, the most normal thing to blame it on—then why would she have written it in a book she never intended anyone to read? The Green Book was a diary of sorts, wasn't it? Would she had invented some elaborate code about clay dolls to stand in for boys so that no one would know?

It seemed bizarrely far-fetched.

Yes, that's certainly much more far-fetched than a teenager getting pregnant by looking twice at a rock.

Of course, if she'd been doing things with the clay statue, maybe that had opened the way somehow for—uh—monstrous impregnation—

Oh, don't be stupid. This is insane. There's horrible magic things in the woods, okay. There's a weird-ass hill that's sometimes there and sometimes not there, fine. But you're reading a book that's badly remembered, by a man with creeping dementia, written by a dead teenage girl who is clearly imaginative, weird, and probably abused, and trying to make it fit with the horrible things in the woods, and they probably don't go together at all.

I dug my fingers into my scalp as if I could pry the ideas out and make sense of them.

The only thing that kept me from pitching the book aside as a waste of time was the description of the stones. I *knew* those stones. There was one behind the house, for Christ's sake!

Cotgrave hadn't mentioned it specifically. I wondered if the deer-stone had turned up later, if it was a signpost as he said. Maybe to warn other holler people that my grandmother lived there. Heh.

And the white monolith . . . the monolith with the carvings I couldn't make out, the one I had wanted to press myself against until it grew warm . . . I couldn't even blame that one on the power of suggestion, because I'd seen it and had the dream before I read the transcript of the Green Book.

Oh Jesus, the monolith. Did this mean I was about to get horrible monster babies?

Joke's on you, holler people. I got an IUD in there. Let's see your monolith get past that!

I wondered briefly about the girl in the woods he'd tried to warn. He'd mentioned her in the journal too, hadn't he? But that was twenty years ago, and she was long gone by now, or at least she wasn't a girl anymore. She'd have to be my age or older. Was that too old to get impregnated by evil monoliths?

Why was I even having to think things like this? My face felt hot. Maybe I had a fever, or there was black mold in the walls and I was hallucinating all of this. Maybe Bongo was still here and I was curled up on the floor giggling while he waited for dinner.

In the next room, Elaine Rogers reminded me why we valued public radio. It was a valuable resource in our lives. She seemed to lose the thread for a second and said "valuable" three or four times before her cohost cut in.

And that clinched it really. If I was hallucinating all of this, I could have probably cooked up the effigy and maybe Foxy and definitely Kilroy, but I don't think I could have come up with the world's most exhausted public radio manager. Black mold could only go so far.

"Well, that was some weird shit," said Foxy, finishing the manuscript up.

I started laughing—a real laugh, although I won't swear it didn't have hysterical edges. Yes. Yes, that was some weird shit, all right. The whole world was teetering on a thin skin over the top of horrific realization. *Definitely* weird shit.

Foxy poured me a slug of whiskey in a teacup. I had actually finished the tea sometime earlier, but that was fine. Better, anyway.

"You okay?" she asked.

"I am so far from okay that I cannot see okay from here. Other than that, I'm fine." I looked out the door, and somehow it wasn't dark yet, which seemed almost as unnatural as everything else. "Do you think that was real?"

"What, the story?" She made a complicated shrug that was mostly collarbones and chin. Her bracelets rattled. "I expect it was really written by some girl that got mixed up with the holler people. Or whose daddy did, and then they got her in the end."

"Can they *do* that?"

"Shit, I dunno. They can make a hog walk around with a wasp nest for a head; you'd think sleeping with a fellow was no big deal. I tell you, though, I haven't heard much about that out here. Plat-eyes—they got them down south a bit, the big things that look like white animals. And there's stories about the Devil's daughter coming to a dance, and when it rains while the sun's out, some folks say it's the Devil's daughter getting married." She snorted. "'Course, I always heard that was the Devil beating his wife, but whichever. But it's not like back in Ireland or whatever, when it was all changelings and fairy folk and whatnot going around and knocking people up with fairy babies."

"Maybe they're different over there," I said. "If they're even the same thing."

Foxy tipped her hand back and forth. "Eh, maybe? You got me. We got monsters, sure, but I don't think they're all the holler people. There's more than one thing in the world, and just 'cos some stories are true doesn't mean they *all* are."

"Did I show you the bone?" I asked abruptly.

Foxy raised a painted-on eyebrow.

I dug out my phone and turned it on. I swear I could actually watch the battery drain. I had taken it out earlier to take a photo of the bone on the steps and then I picked up the bone with gloves and put it in a trash bag and put that in another trash bag and then I buried it in boxes of things-as-seen-on-TV, which were the least dangerous things I could think of, and threw the whole mess out by the road, where the trash pickup supposedly came once a week.

I'm not saying that I thought it would do anything. I'm just saying that if something out in the woods is making shit get up and walk around, out of bones all tied together with cords, you're real careful with weird bones after that.

I wasn't gonna let it anywhere near the baby dolls, for one thing.

I handed the picture of the bone to Foxy. The phone was already starting to get warm.

"Huh!" she said, looking at it. "That's a bone, all right."

"Do you recognize it? It was on the front steps this morning. I tripped over it, and that's how I let go of Bongo's leash."

"I mean, it's a bone. You want to know what it's from, I can't tell you. Probably not a deer—looks too thick." She handed the phone back, and I switched it off before it decided to catch fire.

I thought about Foxy's hog with the wasp-nest head. "Did you ever hear about one of these things coming up and banging on somebody's window?"

Foxy shook her head. "No, but that don't mean anything. Like I said, I ain't an expert. There used to be people around who might know what it was, and you'd prob'ly be better off with one of them. Problem is . . . well . . . you know. People move away or they die. Their kids go off to get a job and the farms get chopped up and sold. And half the old-timers are just old men bullshittin' and tryin' to act like they know things." She shook her head. "Believe me, if I had somebody I could call and say, 'Hey, bad shit goin' down,' I'd have done it as soon as you told me 'bout the deer. But I guess I'm what we got."

I had been afraid of that. On some level, I'd hoped that Foxy had people she could call, reinforcements who'd come charging in like the Ghostbusters and handle this whole mess for me. I could have stepped back and said, "So sorry, above my pay grade," and it would be somebody else's problem.

Until I get Bongo back, it's still my problem.

Shit.

We went into the kitchen and ate more sandwiches, because it seemed like a good idea. I was maybe a little woozy from the bourbon, and there is something very nonthreatening about a tuna-salad sandwich. If I'd had the chance, I suspect I would have eaten a couple dozen of them, just because they were real and they made me feel like I was real too.

Foxy eyed the staircase. "Yikes. You been up there yet?"

"Haven't had a chance to get the stairs clear," I admitted.

"Doesn't look too bad. Two-man job, maybe. Or two-woman in this case." She pushed the sleeves of her denim jacket up, revealing tanned forearms.

"You want to move stuff? Right now?"

"I ain't got anything else to do right now," said Foxy. "Why, you got a hot date?"

"Well, no . . ." Honestly, I wasn't going to argue with an offer of help. I needed to do something while the things in Cotgrave's manuscript settled into my head, and clearing the way to the second floor would be more useful than playing endless games of solitaire. I got out my gloves and passed her a pair.

It wasn't bad. It was easier with two people. I'd lift a box and carry it to my staging area in the living room, and by the time I got back, Foxy would have shoved most of the contents of a step into a trash bag. It took only an hour to break a gap in the wall, and then I pushed my head and shoulders through the resulting hole and saw the upstairs for the first time.

There were three doors on the left-hand side of the hall, presumably leading to the bedrooms that made up most of the upstairs. A line of windows on the right-hand side of the hall let in the faded denim-colored light of late afternoon.

It was . . . empty.

Not *completely* empty, of course. There was an old clothes hamper in the hallway, with the lid open and an ancient towel dangling from it. There were a few boxes, with the by-now-familiar cargo of old wire coat hangers sticking out haphazardly. But compared to the downstairs, the hall looked as empty as a minimalist photo.

My knees got shaky for a minute, and I had to grab the banister.

"You okay?" asked Foxy from below. "The air bad up there?"

"No," I said. "No, I'm fine. It just . . . it's not bad. I expected it to be terrible, and it isn't." I felt as if I'd been braced for a blow that hadn't come.

"Well, that's good." She poked her head up alongside me. "Oh. Huh. Cleaner than my place. Looks like she kept putting stuff on the stairs to take up here, until she couldn't get up the stairs anymore. Well, that's a relief, ain't it?"

"Let's see if the bedrooms are bad. . . ."

The first one wasn't bad. It wasn't great, mind you, but it wasn't anything like the doll room or my grandmother's bedroom. There was a sort of semicircle of junk around the door, as if she would open the door, plop something down, and then leave. When the semicircle filled up, she'd set things out as far as she could reach, but she hadn't systematically packed things up the way she had downstairs.

The bathroom was in a pretty bad state. The cupboard under the sink was overflowing with boxes of soap and bulk packs of ancient toothpaste, and the tub was full of clothes in garment bags hanging on the shower rod.

The last door was at the end of the hall. I opened it and let out a groan.

She'd started here, apparently. The far wall was stacked with boxes like ramparts. The wire coat hangers were snaggled together like metal macramé. There was, I kid you not, a freakin' *stuffed moose head* in the corner. A sea of knee-high bags and boxes obscured the floor, and while I'm nearly sure there was a window on the other side of the room, you couldn't see it from here.

"Give you five bucks for the moose head," said Foxy.

"If you can get to it, it's yours."

It's not like I expected to find anything good up there. I really didn't. It wasn't like my grandmother was hoarding gold bars or anything useful. I didn't really expect to see the Green Book on a reading stand in the middle of the hall. I was just hoping for . . . oh, I don't know.

No, I do know. In a story, if you go through a big, miserable trial and you don't complain . . . much . . . you get a reward at the end, right? You get the happy ending or you marry the prince or you get a pot of gold. And this was a big miserable trial and it even had monsters, and my job was to know the shape of stories and help other people hammer them into place, and I guess I thought on some level that when I got to the last room, there'd be some kind of reward for it.

I picked up a bag and looked in it. There was a roll of paper towels that had gone yellow with age, three cans of Spam, some Christmas lights still in the box, a pile of coupons, and a couple of cassette tapes.

Some reward.

"Well, come on," said Foxy. "We can get a couple more loads out before we lose the light, I bet."

I leaned against the doorframe wearily. "What's the point? God, I mean . . . why even bother?" I couldn't believe how depressed I was over this. Then again, I couldn't believe I was still cleaning the place out. "I can't sell this place."

As soon as I said it, a weight seemed to descend on the top of my head. My chest was already squeezed tight over Bongo, but this was like having a cinder block lowered onto my skull.

Because I *couldn't* sell it, could I? How awful would I have to be to just hand the keys over to someone to live next to a hill full of nightmare stones, with the effigy roaming around in the dark?

This wasn't like claiming that the dishwasher ran great or that those stains had been there for years. You couldn't even warn people about it.

I told myself I wasn't upset about the money, but dammit, I could have really used the money too.

I felt like I would have been fighting back tears, but I couldn't even get up the energy.

"Here, now, hon, let's not do that." Foxy put an arm around my shoulders and led me back downstairs. She made a cup of tea—real tea, not bourbon—and shoved it into my hands, and eventually I calmed down or came up for air or something. A couple tears leaked out and she didn't say anything about it and neither did I.

"Come on," she said again. "Sell it or not, it's gotta be shifted. Even if you decide to burn the place down, I want that moose head first."

And I nodded and I stood up and I carried out that stupid bag with the can of Spam and the cassette tapes and then another bag and another one, and eventually we got the moose head downstairs just before it got dark.

It's a bit awkward figuring out how to go to sleep when there might be monsters outside. Do you sleep? Do you stay up all night and risk seeing them? Do you turn the lights on to scare it away or turn the lights off so that it thinks no one's home?

I would have liked to stay up, frankly, but I was exhausted. At the same time, I was jittery with nerves and my stomach was rebelling after the pots of coffee I had poured into it. I had to go to the bathroom about once every half hour.

"You're nodding off right here at the table," said Foxy accusingly.

"I am not," I said, sitting up.

"Then what were we talking about?"

"About . . . about . . ." I tried to remember. "A boyfriend you had, wasn't it?"

"That was an hour ago. Go to bed."

"I'm too scared to sleep," I said.

"Like hell you are. Heck, I'm a little afraid you'll fall asleep on the pot like this, but I suppose you'll just fall on the mattress."

I yielded to the inevitable and went to bed.

I think I fell asleep instantly, but I'm not sure for how long. I hadn't thought to plug in a clock in the bathroom, and anyway, the outlets weren't looking all that trustworthy. Without a working phone, I couldn't tell if it was nearer to midnight or dawn.

I was not deeply asleep but not quite awake, drifting aimlessly from thought to thought, when an arm came through the crack in the door.

I would have screamed, but it was accompanied by Foxy's voice hissing, "You awake?"

"No!" I whispered.

"Well, you better wake up damn quick because there's something in the road out front!"

I woke up damn quick.

"Stay low," Foxy ordered. "Follow me."

I crawled after her on my hands and knees. She was wearing a bathrobe with either flowers or a giant squid on the butt.

I couldn't *not* look at the windows. I didn't want to look at them, but I did anyway, in case there was something there.

There wasn't.

We got into the kitchen and stood up. "Sorry," said Foxy. "It was in the road, but I was afraid it'd come in closer. Up the stairs, quick. You can see it out the window."

She led the way up, the stairs creaking under her bony feet. "Went upstairs to use the pot," she said.

"You could have used the downstairs one," I said, somewhat inanely under the circumstances.

"Didn't want to step on your head. Also, we ain't so good of friends yet that I'm gonna pee in front of you. Anyway, I got a look at it out the little window there. You can see it better out the one in the bedroom, though."

I didn't much want to see it, but what was I going to do? I followed her into the bedroom—the mostly empty one, which was emptier now that we'd cleared it out—and over to the window. We stood on either side of the frame, peeking around the edges.

Moonlight blazed over the empty road. There was nothing there.

"Shit," said Foxy, disgusted. "It must have moved."

"What was it?" I said, although I had a pretty good idea already.

"Dunno. Weird thing. On all fours, and then it stood up a few times. Not a person. It was right on the edge of the driveway, like it didn't want to cross the road."

Someone else had seen it too. It probably wasn't black mold. I wasn't crazy, or if I was, it was catching.

Oddly, this was not as comforting as one might wish.

We waited for five or ten minutes. Foxy adjusted her bathrobe like she was buckling on armor. In the reflected light, I could see that the robe did in fact have giant flowers on it, not squid. This was vaguely disappointing.

I wiped my palms on my jeans. I'd taken off my bra but slept in my clothes otherwise. It just seemed easier.

"I guess it's gone . . . ," Foxy began, and then deer burst from the woods.

Three of them, as always. The first two running, with their tails flagged high, and then after them came the hunched-over one, the damaged one, *and oh shit, how stupid am I?*

It was mostly a deer. I hadn't exactly been wrong. But now that I was really looking, not just yawning at blurry deer charging through the yard, it came into focus.

The dark eye sockets. The front legs that didn't quite touch the ground.

It wasn't really on four legs. It was running bowed over with its arms dangling, chasing after the deer. Was it chasing them? Were they a herd of deer, or was the effigy herding the deer, running them through the yard night after night, for its own obscure purposes?

If it caught one, would it make another effigy like itself?

It was not as fast as a running deer, but not slow. It finished crossing the yard and vanished into the trees. The moonlight beat down on my truck and the road and the carport.

It hadn't touched my truck. That seemed very important. If it had touched my truck, then how could I ever drive it again?

"That was the thing in the window," I whispered. I sounded very calm to myself.

Foxy nodded. "One of them things," she said. "Like the hog and the raccoon. They make 'em for some reason, but damned if I know what it is."

"Do you think it's dangerous?" I asked. Which was also stupid, because Jesus Christ, *of course* it was dangerous. You just had to look at it to know that.

"I think it'd try," said Foxy. "I dunno how much it could do. Mebbe no more than a dog would, but dogs kill people sometimes." She rubbed the back of her neck. "Fire stops 'em," she offered. "But enough fire stops damn near everything, so I don't know as that's much help."

I swallowed. "Do you think if we burn that one, it'll be over?"

Foxy looked up at me. The shadows hid her eyes, but I didn't really need to see them.

"It's possible, hon," she said very gently, "but I gotta tell you, I don't think it's likely. Not with the stones up there on the hill and one in the yard and everything. I think there's something goin' on here."

I nodded. I wasn't surprised.

Foxy reached out, underneath the level of the windowsill, and squeezed my hand.

We came down the stairs slowly, moving like we'd just come out of a bar and weren't quite sure if we were sober enough to get home. I wasn't tired. I couldn't have had more than a couple hours of sleep, but I was wide-awake again.

"Tea?" I said.

"Yeah. Can't hurt to—"

Something banged against the screen door.

I nearly leapt out of my skin. Foxy slapped a hand over her heart and muttered, "Kee-*rist!*"

"What is it?" I whispered. As if Foxy would have any more idea than I would.

As if we didn't both know what it was.

The screen clattered as whatever was out there hit it again.

We stared toward the door. It was locked and bolted. I knew it was. But there was a window right next to it, looking into the living room, and what if the thing moved six feet to the left? It could come right in through the glass. . . .

I took a deep breath and stepped forward.

"Don't open it!" hissed Foxy.

"I'm not going to! But what if it's Bongo?"

"I don't care if it's Elvis and the Blessed Virgin. Don't go opening that door!"

"I won't!" Which was partly a lie, because if it was Bongo, I was going to open the door, and if it was something dressed up in Bongo's skin—

don't think it don't think it don't think it

—then I guess it'd get me too, and maybe we'd be a couple of skins wandering around the woods together.

The ten feet from the kitchen to the front door was the longest walk I have ever made in my life.

The screen door banged again.

I was about to look through the peephole. I knew it was

going to be the deer effigy. I knew it, and I was still going to put my eye to this ridiculous little piece of glass and squint out at it like it might actually be the UPS guy delivering at three in the morning. What else could I *do*?

I looked out the peephole.

The deer skull grinned at me, upside down, and I jerked back just before it slammed its hooves into the door again.

I fell over on my ass. Probably it hurt, but I didn't feel it. I just scrabbled backward on my hands to the kitchen.

"Is it—" Foxy started to say.

"Well, obviously!" I snapped. I was mad because I'd known perfectly well what it had to have been and I went and looked anyway.

Foxy didn't hold it against me. She and I crouched down behind the counter in the kitchen, looking over the top at the front wall of the house.

Bam! The screen door crashed again.

"Why isn't it coming through the window?" I whispered. "Is it just trying to scare us?"

"Shit, what am I, the monster whisperer?"

I looked around the kitchen for a weapon. A cleaver, maybe? Would a cleaver be any use? No, it was mostly bone. I needed a baseball bat or something like that. Was there a baseball bat in the house?

Well, I suppose I could try to fend it off with the stuffed moose head. . . .

I put my forehead against the silverware drawer and made a noise that wasn't a laugh.

"Stay with me, hon. If you crack up, who's gonna appreciate my jokes?"

There was a loud, final bang, as if the screen was being torn completely off its hinges, and then silence.

We waited.

A shadow prowled in front of the window, back and forth. It was too dark to see anything but a humped outline with a jagged face.

Foxy had her fingers locked on my forearm. We watched, not breathing, not moving, two small animals crouched motionless while the shadow of the hawk passed overhead.

The deer effigy stopped in front of the window for a long time. I heard the tap of bone against glass.

And then it dropped to the porch and went away again, but neither of us moved from the kitchen until dawn.

14

I slept most of the day at Foxy's house. She made some kind of stroganoff thing. I ate it dutifully.

"Should we stay here tonight?" I asked miserably. Not willing to leave completely, but it wouldn't do Bongo any good if I stayed in my grandmother's house and was eaten by walking deer bones.

Tomas and Skip looked at Foxy. Foxy scowled.

"Hate to say it," she said slowly, "but this place has three times the windows and twice the doors of yours. And . . ."

She stopped. She looked embarrassed, which was not an expression that one usually saw on Foxy's face.

"You don't want them coming to your house," I finished for her.

"Shit, hon, you say it like that and I sound like a real asshole."

"No." I shook my head. "I wouldn't either. You came and stayed with me. That was more than enough."

"I'm staying with you again tonight," she informed me. "In case that thing comes back with reinforcements."

"But . . ."

"Not just her," said Tomas.

"What?"

"Skip and I'll come too," he said.

"But . . . but you . . . Wait, you believe me?"

Tomas rolled his eyes. "Hey, everybody knows there's things in the woods here."

I remembered when we'd first met, when Tomas had come up the drive to move the microwave. That's what he'd said, wasn't it? *Things in the woods.*

"Could be you're both crazy," said Skip, as if making an observation about the weather. "But doesn't hurt to have other people around for that. Believe me, I know."

I flailed. Foxy had been an unexpected gift, but I felt terrible about putting her into danger. Two more people, though?

"I don't have enough beds!" I said, falling back on possibly the least useful argument I could make.

"Hon," said Foxy gently, "I don't think we're going to be doing much sleeping."

Well, when she put it like that . . .

A little before twilight, we all tromped over there. Skip hadn't seen the inside of the house before. He looked around, then gave me a sympathetic look.

"I'd apologize," I said wearily, "but it wasn't my mess."

"I hear you."

Foxy made tea. We all sat around, waiting for the monsters to come.

"Skip, you doin' okay?" asked Foxy.

He looked up from the magazine he was reading. I got the

feeling he was actually thinking about the answer. Finally he said, "Well enough. The timing's not great, but at least I'm on the way down, not up."

It occurred to me that they were talking about Skip's bipolar disorder, and I looked away, feeling like I was observing something that was none of my business. Skip must've caught my expression, though.

"It's all right," he said. "Not a big secret. Down is better than up for this kind of thing. Down, I have a hard time getting out of bed, but up, I get weird."

"I'm sorry," I said, which was useless, but there aren't a lot of social conventions for this sort of thing.

"Don't be. I got stuff that mellows most of it out. When I was younger, it was hard." He considered. "Had ups back then where I'd be throwing the door open here and yelling at your monsters to fight me."

"I'd be right behind you," said Tomas cheerfully.

"Yeah, and you'd both get et," said Foxy. "Last thing we need is you two running out and gettin' in a dick-waving contest with a deer skeleton."

There was a brief silence while we all tried to recover from Foxy's metaphor.

"That was . . . a thing you just said. Yes," I said.

Skip shook his head. "It's fine," he said to me. "Just don't expect a lot of small talk."

"I think Foxy's got that covered for all of us," I said.

Foxy crowed with delight. "You better believe it! Oh, that reminds me, put down that magazine, though. You guys should read this book her granddaddy left. It is some grade-A weird shit."

"I been trying to avoid weird shit," said Tomas, a bit plaintively. "My grandma always said if you leave it alone, it mostly leaves you alone."

"Yeah, but here you are," said Foxy.

"Hey, once they start banging on doors, all bets are off."

Foxy got out Cotgrave's manuscript and handed it over. Skip began to read it. Tomas tried, then eventually put it down.

"Look, I can't even watch reruns of *Alien*," he said. "This is too much. Maybe when it's daylight."

"Hon, you realize we're sitting here waiting for a thing made out of bones to show up, right?"

"Yeah, but I been trying to pretend you're both crazy."

"Oh God!" I said, louder than I meant to. "I wish!"

There's that awkward moment when you've just talked too loudly and nobody says anything to fill the silence. I started to flush, and then bone cracked against the front door.

I cannot say that I was grateful for the reprieve.

We all looked at the door.

"Is there somebody there?" said Tomas.

"It came to the door quicker than usual . . . ," I whispered.

"Maybe it thought you were throwing a party, hon."

I swallowed a braying laugh that would have come out even louder than the "I wish!" had.

Skip stood up and went to the door. He looked out the peephole, just as I had done yesterday.

Crack!

He stood there for a long moment, and then he stepped back.

"Tomas," he said quietly. "They're not crazy."

"Shit," said Tomas, with feeling. He got to his feet and went to the door.

Crack!

He lasted maybe two seconds, jumped back, and turned around, shaking his head. Strangely enough, he was laughing.

I understood the impulse. *Look how much I'm not freaking out. Look how calmly I'm taking this.*

"Shit," he said again, and then he let out a long string of what I think was profanity in Spanish, although it might have been prayer. It ended with "Shit, shit, shit."

"I know, right?" said Foxy.

The living room filled with the absolute silence of four people who have absolutely no idea what to say next.

Crack!

Tomas took out his phone and shoved the camera up to the peephole, muttering to himself.

"You're never gonna get a good shot like that," said Foxy.

"I sure as hell ain't opening that door! I've seen horror movies!"

"You just said you can't watch scary movies."

"How do you think I found out I couldn't?!"

We had moved on very rapidly from the potential dick-waving contest with the deer skeleton. I was glad of this.

Skip looked at the big window, nodded once to himself, and said, "We gotta block the windows."

Tomas stopped trying to film the effigy and grabbed one

end of the couch. Skip took the other. They turned it so the
back was against the glass. Foxy and I hurried to turn the regular chairs to hold it more or less in place.

"It didn't try to get in the windows before," I said, almost to
myself.

"Let 'em do whatever makes them feel better, hon. I don't
think that sofa's worth much anyway."

Skip and Tomas stepped back and looked at their handi-
work. The hammering against the door had stopped.

We heard the sound of footsteps on the porch, walking sideways, and then it began to tap against the glass.

"Do you think it knows we're in here?" asked Tomas.

"I think the sofa suddenly appearing in the window might
have given it a clue, hon."

Tap . . . tap . . . tap . . .

"Nobody should go out there," said Skip, quite unnecessar-
ily. "Is there another window?"

"Cotgrave's room," I said, pointing.

He and Tomas vanished down the hall. I tried to remember
if the doll room had any windows, but no, that one was walled
up with boxes and doll containers.

Tap . . . tap . . .

Foxy and I moved away from the door and into the kitchen.

"So," said Foxy. "How about this weather we're having?"

"Foxy . . ."

"Don't mind me, hon, I get sarcastic when I'm scared to
the tits."

A thudding noise made me nearly jump out of my skin, but

it was only Tomas and Skip upending the bedframe to wedge in front of the window.

They reemerged. "Anything else?"

"All covered by boxes," I said. "Except the kitchen window here, and it's too high up. I think."

Skip looked at the window and nodded.

Tap . . . Tap . . .

"Now what?" said Tomas.

"I don't know," I said. "Wait until . . . wait until morning, I guess. It doesn't stay in daylight. I don't know if it has to hang up in a tree or if it just leaves or what."

The words coming out of my mouth sounded absolutely bizarre, and the fact that Tomas and Skip were both looking at me and nodding as if I was making sense was the worst bit about it.

We stood in the kitchen, the way people do during a party. Tomas sat down on the steps going up to the second floor.

After a while I realized the tapping had stopped. I didn't want to go look and see where it had gone.

"Right," said Foxy finally. "We got tea and I got a deck of cards. What do you want to do next?"

"You're suggesting we play cards," said Skip. "With a monster out there."

"You got any better ideas?"

Skip rubbed his forehead and said nothing.

"We should make plans," said Tomas. "Figure out what to do tomorrow, after that thing's gone. Assuming it's gone."

"It's always gone away in the middle of the night before . . .

I think . . . but it's not like I went looking," I admitted. I had a strong feeling that it shouldn't be *allowed* to be out during the day, but that was more like believing that monsters couldn't get me if I was under the covers.

"Don't think I want to test that, eh?" Tomas nudged my arm, which might have been encouraging or warning or both. "So in the morning. What then?"

All three of them looked at me, as if I had any idea what I was doing.

"I don't know!" I said. "I've got to get Bongo back—*if* he's coming back—I can't stay here, but I also can't leave. . . ."

"Does it do anything other than knock on the door and tap on the windows?" asked Skip.

"Not that I know of. I still don't know why it doesn't just break the windows. . . ."

"Some things can't cross boundaries very well," said Foxy. "You know. Running water and vampires and having to be invited in."

"Don't think this is a vampire," said Tomas.

"Damn shame. I could use a sexy man hanging off my neck about now."

Skip and Tomas exchanged looks but did not comment. I raked my fingers through my hair.

"We could tell somebody . . . ," Tomas began.

"Yeah, that'll go over well," said Foxy, with heavy contempt. "They'll think you're high. And what's adding more people gonna do? You gonna make a cop spend the night here with us?" Tomas grimaced at the word *cop*.

"We'll take it in shifts," said Tomas. "We won't let you stay here alone. At least for a couple days, until we're sure . . ."

He trailed off, but I knew perfectly well what he meant. *Until we're sure Bongo's not coming back. Until we're sure there's no point in anyone staying.*

"I just want my dog back," I said, and my voice cracked and I didn't even care.

15

Bongo came back the next day.

I had been braced for the worst. You do that, when pets run off. You hope and hope and hope, but a little nagging voice whispers to you about cars and highways and dogfighting rings and then one day you wake up and a few weeks have passed and you know that little voice was right. You're no longer a person with a dog who's missing. You're a person who had a dog once. You cry and stomp around and then you grieve and move on.

It's easier with hounds in some ways. They'll run for miles on a scent. You can at least tell yourself that they ended up six states over and some nice family adopted them and gives them treats and belly rubs.

All this assumes that you do not live somewhere with monsters lurking in the woods, pretending to be deer. I don't know if you can grieve and move on after that. I was dreading finding out.

When there was a scrape at the front door, I about leapt out of my skin. It was broad daylight, but what if the thing had gotten bolder? Foxy's wasp-nest-headed hog had gone about during the day. I didn't have any proof that the deer effigy went around only at night, except that I'd only seen it at night so far.

Does it hang itself up on a tree to sleep, like a bat? Did I surprise it taking a nap?

I heard that woodpecker noise during the day before, didn't I?

The scraping came again. I picked up the tea kettle because it was metal and heavy and, God help me, I should have bought a machete. I should have bought one days ago. What was *wrong* with me that I didn't have anything better . . . ?

I looked out the peephole of the front door and saw nothing. The scraping sound was at knee level, against the door-frame. And it was a scrape, not a bang. It sounded like Bongo did when he wanted to be let out.

I took a deep breath, thought, *It's either Bongo or I'm about to have the worst moment of my life*, and opened the door.

Bongo looked up at me, tongue lolling, and pawed at the screen frame again. He wanted in. Why was I, designated opener of doors, not seeing to it at once?

I let out a sob, flung the tea kettle aside, and threw the screen door open.

What followed was a lot of sobbing on my part and a lot of puzzled but enthusiastic licking on his part. I buried my face in his fur and drank in the strong, oily scent of damp hound, which is not normally a smell that one is glad to encounter.

Bongo endured this for several minutes, then finally rolled to his feet and went into the kitchen to paw at his food dish.

"The prodigal son has priorities, I guess," I said. I made sure the door was shut again and went to pour out some dog food. He tore into it like he was starving, but that didn't really mean anything, because he believed that he was starving unless he was actually in the act of chewing.

He didn't look hurt. There were some dead leaves in his fur and a couple of burs. The nice thing about coonhounds is that they're such a short-furred breed that you can see any injury instantly, and I wasn't seeing any.

There was a stick shoved through the buckle on his collar. It took me a moment to figure out what it was, because there was a piece of paper wrapped tightly around it.

Working the stick loose was difficult, partly because Bongo was eager to lick my face and partly because it had been jammed through one of the holes in the collar where the tongue of the buckle fits. I had to pin my dog in a headlock and put my chin on top of his skull while I pried it loose. (He enjoyed this enormously. Bongo has always been a very huggable dog.)

When I finally got it loose, the paper was somewhat worse for wear. It was about the size of a fortune cookie fortune and the edges were badly scuffed.

It didn't need to be large, though. There were only two things on it.

One was the word HELP.

And on the back, torn but still recognizable, a drawing. A

straight line interrupted by semicircles, two eyes, and a curl of hair.

Kilroy was here.

I stared at the scrap of paper for quite a long time.

Understanding came very slowly, not a splash of cold water but a slow chill.

HELP

Kilroy.

Someone had written this note and attached it to Bongo's collar, hoping that someone would find it.

Help. Kilroy.

Cotgrave had drawn Kilroy.

Cotgrave was dead.

He can't need help. The dead don't need help.

Who wrote this note?

Bongo huffed and sprawled across my lap. I dug my fingers into his ruff.

Deep breaths, I thought. *He taught me to draw Kilroy. He could easily have taught someone else. There could be someone in the woods back here who learned it from him.*

Or learned it from someone else, for that matter. It's not like Kilroy wasn't all over Europe. You couldn't kick a rock in World War II that didn't have Kilroy scribbled on it.

While this was true, I couldn't quite believe it. Of all the things to attach to a note that was attached to my dog, Kilroy seemed too specific. Cotgrave had drawn it in his book and again at the end of his typewritten notes, and here it was again. And why would you take up valuable space on your tiny piece of paper with a silly drawing like Kilroy if you were sending a note for help, unless it was important?

I was forced to believe in some impossible things these last few days, but believing that this was a coincidence seemed to be going entirely too far.

It felt like a message.

A message to me? Or to Cotgrave? Do they know he's dead, whoever they are?

I did not dare think too long about the alternative, that Cotgrave wasn't dead, that he was out there in the woods somewhere, desperately trying to get someone to help him.

No. It can't be. He'd be at least a hundred years old. It's not possible.

It was not possible that deer bones walked with stones knocking together in their ribs. It was not possible that you could go through a tunnel of trees and come out in hills that were found on no map.

He's dead. They buried him.

And still the nagging voice in my head said, *But did you see the body?*

No, it wasn't possible. This assumed that my grandmother would have been involved somehow in faking a funeral, and that wasn't in her nature. She'd have been thrilled if he'd vanished. She'd have decided that he ran away to spite her, probably with another woman. She'd have milked that so hard that she'd have lived another thirty years on pure hate.

It couldn't be Cotgrave. But someone out there was sending a message. Someone Cotgrave had known.

Unless . . .

*They can't know that Cotgrave taught me to draw Kilroy.
Surely they can't.*

I closed my hand over Foxy's talisman. If the holler people
were able to . . . what? Read my mind well enough to pluck the
memory of Kilroy out? . . . then there was probably no hope at
all. They could tell what I had for breakfast. They could tell
which direction I was going to drive when I leapt in my truck
and drove away screaming.

For some odd reason, I did not seem to be leaping into my
truck and driving away screaming.

HELP

I had Bongo back. There was no reason at all that I
couldn't bundle him up, hit the gas, and tell Dad to bull-
doze this place to the ground. I could put all this behind me.
I could sleep in my own bed, leaving the lights burning all
night, and eventually I'd probably stop screaming when I
heard woodpeckers. I could get back to my life. I could blame
it all on black mold.

HELP

Kilroy was here.

Someone had asked for help.

It didn't matter that they might not have been asking me
specifically, that it might have been the equivalent of a note in
a bottle, where the bottle was a large, good-natured doofus of a
dog. They'd *asked.*

"This could all be a trick," I whispered into Bongo's fur.
"They could be trying to get me to go out in the woods."

Bongo's tongue lolled. He had been in the woods and apparently taken no damage from it at all.

Underneath all the fear, there was still a vast well of relief that my dog was alive.

Well. If Bongo could survive the things in the woods, surely anyone with two brain cells to rub together could do so as well.

"I hope so," I said, and I put my face down into his fur and cried for a little bit, just in case I was going to die.

———————

There were three things I had to do before I went looking for whoever had written that note.

The first was to tell Foxy. I went across the road with Bongo on his leash. She opened the door, looking tired, and then saw him at my heels.

"He made it!" she said, and looked ten years younger. She went down to her knees and hugged him. Bongo flattened his ears and wagged his tail. He was getting a lot of attention this morning, and he was fine with that.

"He came back just a few hours ago," I said. "He was hungry, but not starved."

She nodded, rubbing his ears, and looked up at me. "You gonna be leaving now, then?"

I shook my head and held out the note.

She read it, turned it over, frowned.

"It was on his collar," I said. "Somebody's out there. They sent him back to call for help."

"Could be a trick," she said, turning it over again.

"Yeah, it could."

I explained about Kilroy. It sounded nuts when I said it out loud, but what didn't these days?

Foxy listened and didn't tell me that was crazy.

"You think it's your granddaddy?"

"No," I said. "Yes. Maybe. I don't know. It can't be, can it? He'd be nearly a hundred years old. Someone he knew maybe."

"Maybe."

"Listen," I said, "I'm going in to town to get Internet. I want to see if I can find out about Cotgrave. He had to at least have an obituary or something. And then I guess I'm gonna go into the woods and see if Bongo can find that hill again and find . . . them." *Them* was easier. *Them* was a word that didn't mean I was looking for a dead man.

She just looked at me that time.

"I know," I said. "I know. He might not find it and I'll probably die if he does. It's stupid. But I can't very well bring the cops, can I? So—well—look, he got back once on his own. If we go and I don't come back and he does, this is my aunt Kate's number, okay?" I had written it down on a scrap of paper. "Just . . . can you make sure she gets Bongo? She'll take care of him. She's got a stupid Irish setter that he loves. He'll be happy." Was I babbling? Maybe I was babbling. I put my hand on my forehead.

"Come inside," said Foxy. "You can't tell me you slept worth a damn last night, and I know I didn't. I got a couch in the den. You and he can have a nap, and if you still want to do this when you wake up, fine."

"But—it's been hours. What if they were in trouble? I mean, obviously they were in trouble—" I already felt guilty about having planned to take the time to look Cotgrave up on the Internet, but I had to be absolutely sure it wasn't him out there in those woods.

I'm not saying I wouldn't have gone out after him. I still would have. But I wanted something like a coroner's report or at least his obituary that said he'd died and there was or wasn't a body. I just . . . didn't want to be surprised.

(I realize this sounds bizarre, like it was going to be any better if Cotgrave was still alive or undead or whatever, but I don't know that I was thinking all that clearly. Somebody had sent for help and I had to help them. Because the note had come to me, and that made it my job because *that's what my family does*.)

Foxy rolled her eyes. "If they were dangling off a cliff, they probably wouldn't have time to write a note. You aren't gonna help anybody haring off half exhausted. Take a *nap*, hon."

"But . . ." I said that to her shoulder blades. I appeared to be following her inside. I appeared, in fact, to be taking off my shoes and climbing onto the couch.

Bongo hopped up next to me, delighted, and settled across my legs with a happy groan.

Foxy flipped off the lights and said, "When you get up, we'll have lunch, and then we'll see what happens next."

———

I slept for probably three hours. It was nearly noon when I woke up, and Foxy handed me a ham sandwich when I came out of the back room, and then another one down to Bongo.

He was delighted to have another meal. I should probably have objected, but really, I was about to drag him to God knows where, so it seemed like a stupid time to argue about eating people food.

There was mayonnaise on the sandwich. Maybe when we met the holler people, Bongo's gas would knock them out.

I went to the coffee shop, fired up my laptop, and deleted 90 percent of the e-mails, which seemed deeply unimportant now that I was probably going to die. Did I want to get involved in a fight about e-books? I did not.

There was an e-mail in there from a name that looked very familiar. I couldn't place it until I clicked it, whereupon I realized it was from the ex-boyfriend I'd left town to avoid. He was apparently sending me a cautious it-is-possible-he-could-have-handled-that-better overture.

Jesus, of all the things I no longer cared about in the slightest . . .

Well, I suppose there's nothing like stark blazing terror and the upending of your entire worldview to cure a broken heart. I deleted it. If I died, let them not find that in my in-box.

The only really important e-mails were the ones to my authors. I'd gotten another delay on the one project, and that was good enough for me. I had done my due diligence. I'd waited patiently for more than three months at this point. I'd sent reminders. Now it was her fault for not delivering before I was killed by holler people.

The other one . . . that was the one I felt guilty about. He'd paid the whole thing up front and it was almost good enough and I owed him a final pass. So I finished it off, at breakneck speed, and sent a note saying I thought it was good to go as it was, I was going to be out for a bit on some family stuff, and not to wait on me if he was ready to publish. He was a nice client and he was terribly insecure about his work—occasionally with good reason—and I didn't want to leave that loose end dangling.

When that was done, I searched for Cotgrave's obituary.

I should probably have done this days ago, but it simply hadn't occurred to me. He was dead, after all, and if he wasn't, it wasn't as if a newspaper clipping would say COTGRAVE'S FUNERAL FAKED TODAY.

I punched in his name and the town, and there it was, three lines down. Nineteen years ago, give or take a few months. His first name had been Frederick, which I vaguely remembered from his signature on the manuscript. He was a World War II veteran.

Well, of course he was.

Had he been Freddy when he was young? Drawing Kilroy on things, along with his fellow soldiers? Freddy Cotgrave, who saw all the horrors of war and still wasn't done with horror, who married one enemy to get away from another one . . .

Poor sod.

There was no cause of death, but there often isn't in an obituary. He'd died at home, it read. Granted, that made one think of dying in one's bedroom, not outside on a cold night, but still, he'd been on his own property. Close enough.

If I'd had a lot more time, I could have tried to find a coroner's report, check the cause of death or whether there had been an inquest. There weren't any newspaper clippings from the day of or the day after that seemed to have any bearing on the matter. Even way out here in Pondsboro, an old man wandering away from the house and sitting down and dying wasn't much of a story, I guess.

And that was it. Nothing much to show for a life.

On a whim, I typed "Frederick Cotgrave death" into the search engine and waited.

Nothing.

Almost nothing.

On the second page of search results, after the obituary and an archive of the exact same thing and a bunch of websites that promised me they could find hidden records on anyone, I turned up a single link.

The Society of the Embers of Dawn wrote that they were saddened to hear of the passing of their brother Frederick Cotgrave, who had been a member many years ago.

I looked up the Society of the Embers of Dawn and sighed.

"What's up?" asked Enid.

"Why does every secret society have a crappy webpage?"

"Immutable law of the universe," said Enid. "I've thought of joining one sometime just to fix their website, but I'm not really interested in knowing the secrets of the cosmos if it means I have to make web pages."

I poked around the website, but it was a dead end. Literally. Half the links didn't work. It looked to have gone defunct not too long after the funeral, and I couldn't make heads or tails of what they actually were. Their website was doing a pretty good job of keeping things secret, anyhow.

Odd people at the funeral, Aunt Katie had said. *Well, maybe that was it. Maybe that's how he met Ambrose or maybe he just joined for the dental plan.*

There was contact information on the bottom of the website, including a phone number, God help us all. *A website old enough that people still leave their phone numbers lying around on it.* On something slightly less than a whim, I turned on my phone and punched in the number.

It rang five times and then somebody picked up. I nearly jumped out of my skin. I'd expected it to be as defunct as the website.

"Hello?" said a man's voice on the other end of the line.

I didn't have a name or anything else. I blurted out, "Did you know Frederick Cotgrave?"

Silence.

"Is this a prank call?" asked the man, sounding less angry than tired.

"No! I'm his granddaughter. His stepgranddaughter. Please, I think it's important."

A longer silence. Then, "I don't know what could be so important. He's been gone for a long, long time."

"Please," I said. "It's about the holler people. Uh, the white people. The—the ones in the hills—" I got up and went outside the coffee shop so that Enid didn't think I'd cracked up completely.

A sharply indrawn breath on the other end of the line was the only acknowledgment.

"Please," I said again. "I need to know—" What did I need to know? God, stupid question. I needed to know a thousand things, probably, and I didn't even know what questions to ask. "He's dead, isn't he? Really dead?"

"He's really dead." The voice at the other end was grave. "They buried as much of him as they could find."

"*What?!*"

I remembered Dad saying that Cotgrave had been outside too long and that the funeral had been closed casket, but this was something else again.

"I know he died of exposure. . . ." The damn phone was already starting to heat up and I switched it from one ear to the other.

The man sighed. "Probably. No reason to think he didn't. But the scavengers were at him while he was out there. A lot went missing. I believe they identified him by his dental records and his wedding ring. I was at the funeral. We looked. I wish we hadn't."

Odd people at the funeral, Aunt Kate had said.

"It's just . . . I got a message. I mean, it had Kilroy . . . Kilroy was here . . . you know?"

The voice gave a choked laugh. "Mr. Chad. Yes. I remember. . . ." And just like that, I was pretty certain that the man on the other end of the line had been no stranger to World War II and Freddy Cotgrave.

"Can you tell me anything about the people in the hills?" I

asked desperately. The phone was starting to cook my ear, and I swapped it again.

"I can tell you to stay away," he said, and then my phone beeped twice and went dead.

And that was the end of that.

There was one task left that I had been putting off. Now it seemed that I was out of time.

I went back inside, pulled up a file on the computer, and wrote down all the important information I could think of—the vet Bongo went to and the name it was under and my aunt Kate's contact information and the password to my e-mail. I didn't have a will. I didn't have enough stuff to really need a will. The bank would probably take my house back shortly, once I stopped paying the mortgage, and Aunt Kate had keys so she could get in and get anything she wanted before it all got cleared out. The truck was paid off, so I made a note where the title was in the house.

I sat back and took a slug of coffee and stared at the list. My life in a nutshell, and mostly it was my dog.

Should I say something to Kate and Dad? Something that would make sense of it all?

What could I possibly say?

I thought for another minute or two and then I typed, "I'm going into the woods to try to find someone. I'm afraid they might be in danger and need help. If something goes wrong, here is all the information for everything. Give Aunt Kate and my dad my love, and make sure someone takes care of Bongo."

I saved everything, put the file on the desktop, and named it PLEASE READ THIS.

Give Aunt Kate and my dad my love. It felt like the coward's way out, but I didn't even know where to begin otherwise.

I shut down the laptop and stared at my coffee. And then I felt a pang of guilt and started it back up, so I could add a note at the bottom that I hadn't finished the project for the one author and to please refund her three-hundred-dollar down payment, because if I wound up dangling from a tree with wind chimes hanging off my ribs, I didn't want my last thoughts to be that I owed her, even if she was three months late.

"You doing okay?" asked Enid.

I looked up at her and thought that if we'd had more time, and if everything hadn't been so insane, we could probably have been friends. I *wanted* to say, *I'm about to do something stupid, and incidentally, the world is totally different than we think it is.*

"I'm tired," I said instead. "Just . . . everything. Tired."

"Any more things in the trees?" she asked.

I shook my head. "No," I said. "Not in the trees."

Her gaze got a little too sharp at that, and I thought of all the things I'd have to explain to get around to the effigy in the window. Did she know about the holler people? No. She wasn't from around here, was she? At one point she'd mentioned being from New Hampshire. Did they have holler people in New Hampshire? I looked down at my coffee cup instead.

"Let me get you a refill," she said.

"I'm about done," I said, putting my laptop away.

"Then I'll get it for you for the road."

I left the shop with a hot cup of coffee in my hand and hoped it wasn't the last one I'd ever drink.

Just past the coffee shop was an empty gravel lot. The edges had grown up into the unruly hedgerow you get when nobody bothers to weed for a couple of years.

The hickory tree wasn't even as tall as I was. It had been cut to the ground a couple times and was sending up suckers with unkillable enthusiasm.

I crouched down and snapped off a couple of dead twigs at the base and stuffed them in my pocket. Then I looked around to see if anybody had seen me, stealing bits of wood with coffee in one hand. Nobody had.

I went to the truck, feeling invisible, and as far as I know, nobody saw me go.

16

Foxy was waiting for me at her house. She handed me another Tupperware container full of sandwiches. "You'll want these, I imagine. And have some food."

"This is insane, isn't it?" I said.

"Oh, you're completely out of your head," said Foxy agreeably, heating up meat loaf in my grandmother's ancient microwave. She pushed it toward me.

Tomas came in. I wasn't sure how much he knew, but he looked at me and said, "It's a bad idea," so I figured he knew enough.

"I know," I said. "But I have to." Saying it out loud made it sound even more fragile. Did I? Why? Because somebody had drawn Kilroy on a scrap of paper? "Somebody sent me a note asking for help."

Tomas nodded. He went into the back of the house, and I heard a door open and close.

I was dragging the last forkful of meat loaf through the gravy when he returned. He was wearing a battered leather jacket and hiking boots. "I'm coming with you," he said.

I stared at him, blinking stupidly. "What?"

"Look, my momma would beat me senseless if I let you and Foxy go off without me."

"Don't be stupid," said Foxy sharply. "You gotta stay here and take care of the place. We can't *both* go."

"I'm half your age!" said Tomas.

"So you got more to live for!"

"You're both nuts!" I said, rising out of my chair. "You can't come with me! I'm going to get killed!"

"Better to do it in company, then," said Foxy. "I ain't scared. Tomas, you're staying here, and that's final." She folded her arms. "It's your name on the deed. *And* the power bill."

This was not a line of argument I expected her to take. We both stared at Foxy.

"So?" said Tomas.

"So you ain't got a will, so iffen you die, they're gonna take the whole place and throw Skip out on his ear. And shut off the power. So you gotta live, and maybe that'll teach you not to die intestate like a damn fool."

Tomas's mouth opened and closed. He looked at me, but there was absolutely nothing I could say to this, and also I was still dealing with the fact that Foxy was coming with me.

"But, Foxy—"

"Don't argue. I got a will all made out. *And* notarized."

I looked at her. She was wearing ripped jeans over black

fishnets and the sort of spiked boots that you'd wear to a punk show. Her lipstick was a particularly savage shade of pink.

She was perhaps the most unlikely bodyguard I could imagine, but the alternative was going alone with my dog.

"Notarized?" I said weakly.

"Yeah, and I had to pay five dollars to have that done, so I don't want to hear any more about it."

I finished my meat loaf in defeat.

I tried one more time before we left, standing in the doorway. "Are you sure? I mean . . . this is way past being neighborly. . . ."

"Ain't paid you for the moose head or the microwave," said Foxy. "And if we all come back, I ain't going to."

I just looked at her.

Astonishingly, a little bit of a flush started to creep up her sharp old face. "Look," she growled, "you're doin' a dumb thing for a good reason, and maybe I'm not that different from Tomas. If I let you go off in the woods and get et by holler people, or whatever it is they do, I wouldn't be able to look myself in the mirror anymore." She rallied a bit. "And I gotta look in the mirror. Makeup this good doesn't happen blind."

"Thanks," I said.

She snorted. "Don't thank me too hard. I'd be lying if I said I wasn't a little bit curious about what's on the other side of those stones."

"Yeah, well . . ." I held the door open for her. "I was pretty scared."

She went out past me, hefting her backpack strap over her shoulder. "Oh, don't worry. You still oughta be."

There were still a few hours of light left as we set off into the woods. Bongo bounced around on the end of his leash, in enormous good spirits. I hoped this was a good sign. If he had been terribly traumatized by visiting the place where someone had put a note in his collar, he didn't show any sign of it.

"Probably should start out in the morning," said Foxy, "but I ain't looking forward to another night waitin' for monsters to come in the windows."

"You and me both."

Leaves crunched underfoot as we walked. The house vanished behind us.

"I don't know where we're going," I confessed. "I figured we'd start at the stones. I think sort of . . . this way-ish? But Bongo led the way the first time."

"Think he can find it again?"

We both looked at Bongo. He was peeing meditatively against a tree stump.

"I don't think there's any way to ask him," I confessed. "He's . . . uh . . . kind of an idiot."

Foxy grinned. "Well, I got there by shooting a deer, and deer are about the dumbest animals in creation, so maybe we'll get lucky."

In retrospect, if we'd been really lucky, we probably would have wandered around in circles for a bit and then gone home for more meat loaf. I still probably wouldn't sleep well at night,

but I'd have managed. I could have convinced myself it was all
an elaborate hoax and some weird neighbor had dressed up in
a deer outfit to scare the crap out of me.

But we weren't lucky like that.

Bongo picked up a smell that was probably a vole under the
leaves and dragged me after it, huffing on the end of his leash.
When he reached the invisible spot he was after, he scuffed at
the ground for a minute, then, disappointed, he straightened up.

I watched his nostrils working. His ears were lifted, alert,
and then he struck out south and east. He wasn't quite running,
but moving with the concentration of a dog on a mission.

"It doesn't mean anything," I muttered, to myself or to Foxy
or both. "He does this for squirrels, too."

It wasn't a squirrel. It was something else. He began to
move faster and faster, into a ground-eating lope, tail up like
a flag.

I glanced beside me. Foxy was keeping up despite the heels
on her boots. "Don't mind me," she panted.

"There's a lot of holes. . . ."

"Hon, I been living in these woods my whole life. You just
watch your own feet."

"Yes, Foxy."

We veered more south than I remembered. I was starting
to wonder if maybe we were chasing a squirrel after all, when
there was the dry streambed.

Despite the recent rains, the leaves were dry and crackling
instead of slimy. Small blessings, I suppose.

In what seemed like no time at all, we reached the wicker-like tunnel. It was still dry and dead-looking, and the afternoon shadows were starting to lengthen under it. I ducked down into it while Bongo sniffed along the leaves.

"Whew," said Foxy. "Not the way I came last time. Or maybe it was, and stuff grew up around it."

We went forward. Pretty soon we were almost jogging along. There was a sense of urgency that I can't explain. Part of it was the desire to get to the stones before the sun went down, but there was something else, too. As if a door was closing, and we had to reach it before it shut.

No, not like that. As if a door was opening, and we had to be out of the room before whatever was on the other side came through.

Foxy hooked her hand under the strap of my backpack. I glanced back, surprised.

"I ain't slowing down," she said, although she was breathing hard. "But feelin' weird."

"Your heart?" I said, panicky. "Are you—"

"No, not my heart! Don't make me slap you upside the head! My heart's fine!" She rolled her eyes. "I mean it feels like you're goin' on ahead of me and it's gettin' harder to follow. I'm thinkin' something doesn't want me along." She tightened her grip on my pack. "Ain't gonna give it the satisfaction."

I nodded. Bongo was hauling on his leash now, whining at our slowness.

The tunnel tilted upward. I had to hunch over, feeling Foxy's knuckles still hard against my shoulder blade. We had to hurry. The door was opening, and if we weren't quick . . .

There was a single hollow *tok!* on the other side of the wicker, and my heart lurched.

If it had stopped there, I could have convinced myself it was a woodpecker. Maybe. But it didn't stop there. The noise came again and again, louder, until it was directly beside me. If the wall had not been in the way, I could have reached out and touched it.

Tok! Tok! Tok!

The sounds of stones in a hollow chest of bones.

Bongo began to run.

It was there.

Tok! Tok! Tok!

I could hear the stones rattling and the sound of its feet hitting the ground, and a strange scraping noise, like scissors opening and closing.

Is that what it sounds like when bones run?

All that stood between us and the effigy were thin dead branches and dry vines woven between them. I could see flashes of light and shadow through the gaps and I thought, inanely, *I knew it could go out in the day. I knew it. It could have been there all this time, watching me—*

Bongo heaved forward against the leash, and I ran after him, trying to remember if there were gaps in the tunnel, if there was a place where the effigy could come through. Please no, God no . . .

I remember very little of that flight up the hillside. I don't know how long it took. It must have been much lighter than I remember it being, because it was only late afternoon, but in my memory it is a dark, closing tunnel. I could not see my feet. Occasionally I would catch a flash of brightness from the metal rings on Bongo's collar. I ran blind and Foxy ran behind me and, outside the tunnel, the effigy kept pace.

Was it on the left? The right? I didn't want to look because if I looked, maybe I'd see it, and if I saw it, I was afraid I'd fall down and curl into a ball until it ate me.

Tok! Tok! Tok!

Oh God, was there more than one? It seemed to come from both sides. *Oh God, let that be echoes let it not be two of them I can't handle two of them I can't even handle* one *of them oh God*

Something struck the wicker tunnel. The precarious root-and-vine frame bowed sideways, and fragments of bark and dried leaf rained down on us. The walls shook wildly as whatever it was—*shut up, you know what it is*—slammed against the side and the *tok! tok! tok!* was no longer a woodpecker knock but a staccato like gunfire.

Foxy never faltered. I must have paused, because she shouted in my ear, "Keep moving!" and I lunged forward, while Bongo heaved upward at the end of the leash.

Foxy was in better shape than I was, for all that she was close to twice my age. When my backpack began to slide down, she wedged it back up on my shoulder, and pretty soon she was pushing me forward and Bongo was pulling, and the effigy rattled the hagstones in its ribs and I dragged air into my chest that stabbed like knives and not suddenly, not suddenly at all, not anywhere close to suddenly, an eternity later—

—we fell out of the wicker tunnel and into the field of twisted stones.

17

I couldn't have leapt to my feet if my life depended on it. Foxy was crouched over me, and Bongo was trying to stand over me protectively and also to hide underneath me in terror.

When a minute or two had passed and my heart was slowing and I still wasn't dead, I whispered, "Is it gone?"

"Think so," said Foxy. "If there was ever anything there, which I ain't entirely sure of."

I looked up at her silently. She snorted and looked back down the tunnel. "Fine, okay," she said. "Yeah, it's gone."

I breathed for a few minutes. The sky was gray. Bare trees hung on the hills like—yes, like curtains in a dark room. Bongo hunched down and fit himself under my knees as best he could.

"I kept thinking it was a woodpecker, before," I said finally.

"Can see why."

I didn't say, "Do you think there were two of them?" because I didn't think I could handle it if she said "Yes."

"Do you think it was trying to keep us from getting here?" I asked instead.

"Something was," said Foxy. She held out her left hand.

There was a raw red stripe across her fingers and palm, as if something had taken the top layer of skin off. Blood beaded at the edges.

"Foxy!"

"It's fine," she said. "I mean, it hurts like the devil, but it's not deep. It was where I had your backpack. Toward the end there, it felt like a handful of nettles."

I grabbed my backpack strap as if expecting it to be made of sandpaper, but it just felt like normal nylon.

"Expect it was meant for me, not you," said Foxy matter-of-factly. "I felt it before, too. I'm not supposed to come along."

"Why would it want that?"

"Who knows what the holler people want?" She grinned sourly. "Maybe they figure my ratty old bones won't look good on their mantelpiece."

"And mine will?"

"Hey, maybe you got cute bones."

I started laughing, half high on adrenaline, and stood up. Bongo, reassured that everything was all right again, licked the back of my hand.

I dug my fingers in behind his ears as I looked around the hillside.

The sky was the same shade of gray as before. If sunset was coming on, there was no sign of it. It was gray, gray, gray.

A *wicked voorish dome.*

Under the sky, the hills. Same as before. And the trees that hung like curtains on the hillsides were still bare. I wondered if they ever leafed out at all. Were there even seasons in this place?

"Shit," said Foxy, looking around. And then, more quietly, "*Shit.*"

"Eloquent," I said. "Is it like you remember?"

"Yeah. Pretty much. Only"—she waved her hand—"more."

I nodded. It had been only—what, ten days? Eleven?—but my memory had whittled down some of the edges of the place. It wasn't that I didn't remember it. It was just that the reality was indeed *more.*

The tree slithering out from under the stones was more like a snake. The leering carvings were stranger and sharper, and the animals twisted themselves more grotesquely in pain or in ecstasy. As if my mind hadn't quite been able to hold everything.

No, wait, the girl in the Green Book had described the trees like snakes. Maybe that had gotten into my head somehow too.

"Which way?" said Foxy.

"I have no idea." I hefted my backpack. "I still don't even know if Bongo was here when he got the note. We might be in completely the wrong place."

"Never stopped me before," said Foxy.

"The white stone's this way," I said. *The white stone, yes, the white stone, the tall one, the one that's carved with something that you need to see again . . .*

My voice sounded totally normal, and the fact that I sud-

denly had a weird itchy desire to see the white stone again
didn't seem to impact it.

I could touch it. I could figure out the carvings this time.
Would it be warm or cold? Smooth or rough? In my dream, it had
been cold and I tried to warm it. . . .

"Good a place to start as any."

Of course she couldn't know that I wanted to see it. I
shouldn't tell her. It would make me sound weird or controlled
by holler people, when the fact was that . . . was that . . .

The fact was that . . .

Oh, it doesn't matter. Stop worrying and start walking.

Past the carvings, the scowling ones and the ones like animals and the ones that lay down like dead things . . .

And I twisted myself around like—

Shut up. Just shut up. Get to the white stone.

"Ugly little bastards," muttered Foxy, eyeing the scowling
stones.

"Don't try to imitate them," I said. "They don't like that. Or
they like it a lot. I don't know which."

Foxy gave me a sharp look. "You okay?"

"Yeah, I—sorry, it's this place." I rubbed my forehead.
"Brain fog. But the stones, yeah. I tried to make a face like
one the last time, and I shouldn't have. I was almost able to. I
thought I was going to dislocate my jaw."

Foxy raised her eyebrows. "Huh!"

"Yeah, I . . . I sort of forgot about that." I tried not to make
eye contact with the grinning faces in the rocks. "It seemed so
crazy and it's all crazy and I was afraid I was *going* crazy, so I

figured it was just my mind playing tricks and maybe I had a muscle spasm or something. But now I think it was probably real."

"Probably." Foxy shook her head. "These things . . . If Skip was here, he could tell us what kind of carving it is. He went to some fancy art school out west, and every now and again he'll come out with 'That's postmodern pre-Raphaelitism,' or something like that."

"I dunno if they covered things like this in art history class." The stones that lay down like the dead ones were curled in the grass in front of us. "I guess we could take a photo for him. . . ."

Foxy snorted. "I didn't bring a camera. Kinda doubt things would come out real well even if I had."

I remembered the way that my one photo had come out overexposed, looking like a bad photoshop of somebody's fingerprint. "Probably."

Bongo gave the dead ones a wide berth. He didn't seem frightened of them, but he definitely didn't want to get too near them, as if they were a hole in the ground he was afraid to fall into.

Maybe they're a hole in the world, and if you look too long you'll fall through. . . . The lines seemed to swim in front of me as if they were breathing. I felt dizzy and hot.

It's just like being seasick. The horizon's wrong. Go find the white stone, use it as an anchor, and everything will settle down again.

"The white stone's past these," I said, careful to keep my eagerness out of my voice. My hands appeared to be shaking.

That was very odd. It wouldn't do to let Foxy see that. She'd get the wrong idea. I shoved them in my jacket pockets as well as I could while holding Bongo's leash.

Something jabbed me in the knuckles. My head seemed to clear abruptly.

Wait, what?

"Foxy . . ."

"Eh?"

"Um. This is odd. I want to see that white stone again."

She looked over at me, faintly puzzled. "We're going there, ain't we?"

"No, I mean I suddenly *really* wanted to and I didn't want to tell you about it, and I think that's weird and suspicious."

Her gaze sharpened. "Now, *that's* interestin'. Good on you for fighting it."

"I don't think I was fighting it," I admitted. I dug around in my jacket pocket for what had jabbed me and pulled out a twig. "I poked myself with this."

"Is that hickory?"

"Yeah. From outside the coffee shop."

Foxy nodded. "Hickory'll help. I'm wearing, like, a pound of it myself. You still got that rosary?"

"In my backpack."

"Well, put it on, then! You think evil's gonna sit around and wait while you get dressed?"

Chastened, I pulled out the string of hickory beads and dropped it over my head.

The air seemed to lighten. The twisted carvings still moved

when I looked at them, but they moved less, more like a bad moiré pattern than like breathing.

I thought of the white stone carefully, as if I were probing a sore spot with my tongue.

Big white rock. Some weird stuff going on with that rock. How we feelin' about that rock?

I had no particular opinion about the rock, other than that it was another creepy thing on the pile of increasingly creepy things. I was pretty sure that it was another rock like the one in the Green Book, and thus there was a slim chance it might try to get me pregnant, and that I was a bit miffed at it for apparently trying to get into my head. I reported this to Foxy.

"Complicated old world, isn't it?" she said. She had picked up a stick somewhere and was poking the dead twisted one with it.

"Are you sure you should be doing that?"

"Look, if it's gonna come to life and take a chunk out of me, I'd rather it did now than when my back was turned."

There was a certain logic to this position. The dead twisted one did not take a chunk out of her, despite several solid pokes with the stick. I think Foxy might have been slightly disappointed.

On the far side of the dead ones was a little space, and then more carvings. I remembered walking through them for a long way, but I wasn't sure how long it had been. I hadn't exactly been in my right mind, had I? I'd been singing "Oh, Susanna" and it had gotten a bit strange after that.

"This is farther than I got," said Foxy. "I guess we just keep walking, then."

So we walked through more carvings, some of them very large indeed, and anchored down in the ground somehow. I didn't remember those. Had it been some enchantment, some *wicked voor*, that the hickory was keeping away?

And then I saw the white stone. It gleamed in the dim light like a tooth. There was the grassy bowl around it and the ferns around the base and the carvings of . . . something.

We stopped at the top of the bowl. The stones around the rim leaned inward, toward the stone, and I wondered vaguely if it was acting on their brains the way it had acted on mine. . . .

Settle down. They're rocks. They don't have brains.

Although up here in this place, who the hell knows? Maybe they do. In the Green Book, isn't there a bit where the narrator wonders if her family all got turned to stones? Maybe these are all the people who got stuck up here, the moonshiners and the frat boys and whatnot.

I squeezed the hickory twig tightly between my fingers, but the thoughts didn't go away. Apparently that was just me being paranoid, not any kind of magic.

"Huh!" said Foxy, looking at the stone.

"Do you feel like you want to go touch it?" I asked hesitantly. "I wanted to, the first time I saw it. . . ."

"I do," she said slowly, "but I ain't going to. I can feel the wanting to, though. It's like a pretty boy you know is more trouble than he's worth." She folded her arms and glared at the stone, and I pitied any pretty boy who had caused her trouble in the past.

"This is the second time I'm seeing it," I said. "I think I'm supposed to be pregnant now."

"We'll get you a test when we get back home, hey?"

"It'd have to get past the IUD first." Weird and creepy as the white stone was, I had a hard time imagining it was a match for that. "What about you?"

"Hon, if I get knocked up, it won't be magic; it'll be a goddamn miracle." She craned her neck, looking around the stone. "What's on the other side?"

I shook my head. "This is as far as I got. I saw the stone and things got a little weird."

I glanced down at Bongo. He was watching the stone intently, the way he watched cars out the window sometimes— was it going to go past the house, or was it the UPS guy and thus his mortal enemy?

It was so quiet here. There was no wind to ripple the grass of the bald or move clouds in the heavy gray sky. I couldn't hear any insects calling, or frogs, or birds.

No woodpeckers.

"Let's go around," Foxy said finally.

We skirted the rim of the grass bowl. Bongo continued to watch the stone, his whole body taut, his ears straining forward.

On the far side, we looked back at the white stone and Foxy gave a single bray of laughter. Bongo yanked on the leash, startled, and then gave her a reproachful glance.

"Sorry, buddy," she said to him. "Well. That's a helluva thing, isn't it?"

I stared at Ambrose's white stone and almost wanted to laugh myself.

From this side, it was obvious. It was two beings, and they were, not to put too fine a point upon it, screwing like rabbits.

Well, it wasn't like it was a surprise. Ambrose's white stone was clearly kin to this one. I just hadn't been expecting it to be quite so . . . *vivid*.

They were carved in much the same style as the rest of the stones, deeply scored lines that moved too much when you saw them from the corner of your eye. The top one had great curving horns, like a ram, and he was pulling back the head of his partner by her own horns, which were long and twisting like an antelope's. Her throat seemed very thick, like a beast's neck, and her face protruded into a muzzle like a beast, but her body was mostly human, if oddly proportioned.

Speaking of proportions . . . well, he had nothing to worry about in that department.

"That one I'd put in the front yard," said Foxy cheerfully. "Just to see the mailman's face."

"Heh," I said weakly.

The longer I looked, the less funny it got. Which is odd, because frankly, sex is hilarious. But the carvings were so detailed and the moiré-pattern movement made the bodies undulate and seem to thrust together and I was starting to get dizzy looking at it and I remembered the dream where I pressed myself against the white stone. Was the female beast enjoying it? Her mouth was open in what could have been passion or agony.

My head ached. I could feel a pulse beating in my right eye and in my temples and between my legs. . . . Dear God, was I getting turned on by the carving?

"I gotta sit down," I said.

"Not right here," suggested Foxy, taking my arm. She

steered me away from the stone. Once I was no longer looking at it, it got easier. My pulse stopped beating in my ears or anywhere else.

"What the hell is that thing?" I asked after a few minutes of sitting on the grass with my back to the carving. "I know it's stupid, but I felt—I felt like—"

And then I blushed. Which was nuts. The entire situation was completely batshit loony, and here I was blushing because among the batshit loony things was a statue with a big honking dick on it.

"It's okay, hon. If I was a few years younger . . . well." She shook her head. "I'm old enough to know better, but it's still got a wallop, doesn't it?"

A wallop. Yes. That was as good a description as any.

Bongo sat down and scratched behind his ear. Apparently it didn't work on dogs or on males, or at least on males whose testicles were a distant, vet-related memory.

"I guess old Ambrose was onto something after all," I said.

"If he's expecting us to get preggers from looking at it, he's still gonna be pretty disappointed. Had those bits out years ago. Not that they were doing me a helluva lot of good anyway, but it'd be a bitch to get cancer in a bit I ain't using."

"I hear you," I said absently, petting Bongo. "I don't know. Do you think the girl—whoever she was—actually got pregnant looking at a statue?"

"Oh, who the hell knows. For all I know, it just got her thinking about it and she went and found some nice young fella to get her in the family way. From the way your granddaddy talked about Ambrose, he'd have found that a lot more shocking than looking at a statue." Foxy snorted. "Certain sort of man would prob'ly *prefer* it if sex was all looking at statues and no actual poking."

"It is very likely that she did," said a voice behind us. "And bore a child of it, or more than one."

Foxy and I both jerked upright. Bongo—valiant guard dog that he was—looked up and wagged his tail.

There was a woman standing there. She was very tall and very pale. Even her eyes were pale. Her irises were flecked with red, and her pupils were the faded gray color of the sky.

"I have borne seven," she said. "Five drew no breaths. Of the other two . . . but we will speak of that later."

Where had she come from? Why hadn't we heard her?

"Who're you?" said Foxy, her chin jutting out.

"My name is Anna," said the woman. She pronounced it with a long first syllable, *ahhh-nuh*. "I am one of the people of this place."

I saw motion out of the corner of my eye. It was the same twisting moiré-pattern as the stones, but when I turned my head, there was a man standing there. He was as tall as she was and I suppose he was handsome, but there was something odd about his skin. He did not speak, but took his place beside the woman. He was even paler than she was. Both of them had hair that was not so much white as completely colorless, like mist.

Anna folded her hands together. "You will come with me now," she said. It was not a request but a statement of fact.

Foxy tried to push back nevertheless. "What if we don't?"

The pale woman shook her head.

And then I heard it. The click of bones. The hollow rattle of stones knocking together.

Tok . . . Tok . . . Tok . . .

Bongo's wagging stopped, and a whine started up in his throat.

Shapes began to appear out of the gloom behind her, coming from behind the stones or from inside the earth itself. The air twisted and untwisted until my eyes watered, but I could still see them all too well.

Effigies. Dozens of them.

Not on the other side of a window. Not with walls between us.

Right here.

Right now.

Tok . . . Tok . . . Tok . . .

I sucked in my breath, and honestly did not know if I would ever draw another one.

"You have no choice," the woman said, as monsters of stone and bone surrounded her. "You have trespassed into deep places, and the only way out is deeper still."

18

I think that Bongo is the only reason I didn't have a nervous breakdown on the spot.

There are stories of people enduring horrors—escaping war zones, walking for hundreds of miles barefoot, that sort of thing—because they are being strong for their children. I am not saying it's the same thing at all. Bongo, as I've said before, is not my child; he's my dog.

Nevertheless, at that moment, he needed me. He was making that horrible fear-growl, his back was humped up, and his tail was between his legs. I dropped down next to him and put my arms around him to keep him from lunging at an effigy and getting probably killed. He was peeing in terror, which meant he peed on my knee, but you know, I was feeling a little loose-bladdered myself.

Foxy stood over me and gripped my shoulder. I could hear her breathing, harsh and quick behind me.

"We'll leave," I said. "I'm sorry we bothered you. We'll go away and not come back."

"You will come with me now," repeated Anna, ignoring me.

"My dog can't," I said. I didn't look at the effigies. If I didn't look at the monsters, they couldn't be real, but there were so many and they were moving and I kept seeing bits of them, even as I tried not to look—hooves and horns and rocks and branches like antlers and old rags stretched over frames that weren't remotely human—*don't look don't look if you don't look they can't see you*—

"Then you will be killed," said the man, speaking for the first time. His voice was thinner than I expected and had a quaver in it, like a very old man's.

"I'm not refusing," I said. Foxy's fingers tightened on my shoulder. "This is not me refusing. We'll go with you. But my dog's scared. I'll carry him." I was speaking very calmly and rationally. I remember that. If I could just keep everyone talking, they wouldn't let the things I wasn't looking at get my dog.

I said *I'll carry him* as if it were that easy. Bongo weighs sixty-odd pounds. I'm not strong enough to carry something that size very far. But I didn't know what else to say.

Anna stepped forward until she was only a few feet from Bongo and me. I looked up at her, and she was impossibly tall. I know I was kneeling on the ground, but before I'd thought she was six foot four, maybe a bit more. Now she looked seven feet tall—eight, ten—taller than any human I'd ever seen.

She did something with her left hand.

The air around her fingers made another moiré-distortion pattern that drifted toward Bongo.

"No!" I put out a hand to ward it off.

It felt like the barest breath of air on my skin as it passed. My hand went through it. The tiny hairs on the back of my fingers stood on end, but that was all.

"He will take no harm of it," said Anna. "It is a charm to calm beasts; that is all."

She made the gesture again. This time it was faster. The distorted air shimmered around Bongo's face like a heat haze on the road.

I felt his trembling ease against my chest. The growl died away into nothing. He gave a short, puzzled whine, as if he could not quite remember why he had been angry, and then he turned his head and licked my face.

She had just done . . . what? Magic? Was that magic?

Of course it was fucking magic. What are you, stupid? What did you think was happening? How did you think the effigy was walking around, if not magic?

How are all *of them walking around, if not magic?*

Well. Yes.

I did not much like the prospect of someone magicking my dog, but if it meant that nobody got killed and Bongo wasn't pissing himself in terror, that was what mattered, right? Hell, if I'd had sedatives, I'd have jammed them down his throat and probably taken one myself.

I stood up. My own legs were shaking. Foxy's hand on my shoulder squeezed harder.

"We will go now," said Anna.

"Foxy . . ."

"Looks like we don't have much choice," she said. "C'mon, hon."

Anna swept her arm in a slow, dramatic gesture, pointing farther down the hill. She was wearing gray cloth wrapped around her, some kind of robe or sari or toga, something with a lot of folds. The cloth hung down from her arm when she gestured, making her look like some kind of classical statue.

I focused very hard on her arm and not on the milling shapes just behind it. Sooner or later I was going to have to look at them, but if I did, I was going to become as frozen as poor Bongo had been. I had to not look.

Everybody yells at Orpheus and Lot's wife. Put yourself in their shoes for five minutes and you'd yell a lot less, I promise you.

I gathered up Bongo's leash. He walked next to me, tail and ears up, a dog on a walk that was a bit boring but which held the hope of being interesting. I could hear the effigies walking on the grass. Their feet clicked when they touched stone. My skin was going to crawl off my body soon.

I locked my eyes on Anna.

She began to walk in the direction she had pointed. Downslope, into the gloomy twilight. I could see the bare trees in serrated ranks around us. I was starting to think that the trees would never leaf out, that their nature was just to be empty branches and twisting trunks. Perhaps they were parasitic. There's a fair number of parasitic plants. Beechdrops. Dodder.

Indian paintbrush. My aunt would have a field day. Was I thinking about plants so that I wouldn't think about monsters? You
bet your ass I was.

I don't know how long we walked. The slope got steeper.
I divided my time between staring at my feet and staring at
Anna's back. Her colorless hair seemed very bright in the dark-
ness, like fog on a dark night.

I didn't dare look around, but I knew Foxy was behind me.
I could hear her breathing.

"I'm sorry I got you into this, Foxy," I said.

"Shit, hon, I shoulda known better than to let either of us
get into this."

Stones loomed out of the dimness. Three of them, arranged
like a doorway. It looked like a scaled-down Stonehenge.

I did not want to go through those stones.

Stupid thing to say, obviously. I didn't want to be anywhere near here. I didn't want to be following the holler people with their horrific pets crowding around behind me. But I
really didn't want to go through the doorway. It exuded a kind
of . . . not menace, exactly. *Remoteness.* Like I was about to
pass through an airlock into an alien planet. Maybe I could
break away and run now, if I tried, and probably the things
would kill me, but if I went through those stones, I would be
somewhere else and there was no getting back under my own
power.

Anna passed over the stone threshold. Nothing obvious
happened. She didn't vanish or waver or turn strange colors.

I turned my head and looked behind me.

There were at least a dozen effigies close behind us. They formed a loose semicircle behind Foxy, moving restlessly back and forth. The dim light gleamed on pale bone and sparked on bits of rusted wire.

The one nearest me was hunched up like a vulture, shorter than I was. Its head was a broad fan shape, made of twigs tied to . . . Was that a broken shovel blade?

It turned its head. The twigs were bent and crooked and the hollow places they framed gazed back at me like eyes. There were more than two. There may have been more than ten.

The rest of its body was draped in roadkill rags. I couldn't make out details, and I was glad I couldn't. Suddenly the deer effigy seemed almost tame by comparison.

It was too dark now to see the rest clearly. That was fine. I had an impression of ragged bodies, limbs made of bone, and branches wrapped in wire and cord, some of them vaguely human or animal shaped, some of them not remotely human at all.

The twisted ones. The ones the rocks are supposed to resemble, or things made to resemble the rocks.

I could hear them moving. Bone clicked and branches creaked and things sighed and sloughed and tapped. Something out there sounded, incongruously, like denim rubbing together between someone's thighs as they walked: *shhfff . . . shhffff . . . shhhffff . . .*

If I tried to run, they would be on me at once.

"Foxy . . ."

"I see 'em too, hon."

I nodded.

Sticks and stones . . . , I thought. *Sticks and stones may break my bones . . .*

I didn't bother with the second line. Who gave a damn about words now?

With one hand on Bongo's collar and one wrapped around the hickory beads, I stepped through the doorway into the voor-ish dome.

Nothing dramatic happened when I stepped over the threshold. There wasn't a flash of light or a crack of thunder. It was just a little easier to see suddenly, as if it was not quite so dim.

When I looked down, there was a path at my feet.

The grass had been worn away to packed earth. Yellow-orange clay, with tiny pebbles embedded in it. That part was still like the landscape around the house, anyway.

The bare trees parted around the path. Unlike the wicker tunnel, they grew tall and straight, but it was still a long and winding way down.

I took a quick glance behind me. Foxy was there. So was the tall, pale man.

So were the effigies.

The archway stood at the top of the path, as remote and unreachable as a star.

Bongo's tail was up, wagging vaguely as he trotted after Anna. I envied him.

White stones gleamed like fireflies in the dark, dotting

the edge of the path. They were carved in patterns that at first seemed unfamiliar. Then I realized that they were the same as the twisted ones, the designs folded and doubled back on themselves . . . but they weren't doing the painful eye-burning jitter. I could look at them out of the corner of my eye and they didn't look as if they were crawling away.

That should have been comforting. It wasn't.

Either something was happening with my eyes or . . . or . . .

Maybe that moiré pattern is what happens when an enchantment meets the real world. Like heat haze on the road. Now you're not in the real world, so it isn't distorting the air around it anymore.

Thanks, self. That was real helpful. A+ coping mechanism.

If the white stones were enchanted, then there had been one sitting at the edge of my grandmother's garden for quite a while. Although for all I knew, that particular stone was a signpost of sorts, a warning to the other holler people that my grandmother's presence was foul.

I wondered how Cotgrave had figured that out in the first place. Ambrose, maybe. Or maybe he'd just stopped seeing the things after he met her. He hadn't written it down. I wished I knew. Maybe I'd have been able to repel the damn things now.

Anna turned to follow a bend in the path. I saw her profile. It was impassive but not serene, a set face with secrets behind it.

What had the Green Book said about the Lady Cassap? That she was the tallest and whitest of them all? Which meant . . . what, exactly? That the author was weirdly racist? That Cassap was closely related to the holler people? Close enough to summon snakes and do magic with wax dolls, not close enough to get out of being burned alive?

I could believe that the woman in front of me could summon snakes. Frankly, snakes would have been an improvement. Snakes are generally more scared of humans than humans are of them.

It would be nice to be around something that was more scared of me than I was of it. The effigies sure weren't.

Anna turned again, following a set of switchbacks down the hillside.

Something was moving among the trees. I could catch glimpses of things shifting—rags, perhaps. Grasses. Not leaves, not in this leafless forest.

A low, throbbing sound filled the air, and I nearly jumped out of my skin.

"Easy," said Foxy behind. "Easy, hon. That one's a mourning dove."

"Oh God," I said faintly. I felt embarrassed, which was probably stupid because being terrified out of my wits was absolutely the most logical thing I could be at the moment. Still, who knew they had mourning doves in . . . what? Fairyland? Hell?

I followed Anna. I couldn't shake a sense that I knew her from somewhere, but I couldn't remember from where.

Well, I don't really have context, do I? I mean, if you're used to seeing someone while surrounded by monsters, you don't recognize them when they're just getting a scone at the coffee shop, do you?

I was pretty sure I did not know her from the coffee shop.

The switchbacks continued down the hill. I began to see

buildings through the bare trees below us. They were made of pale stone or clay, squared off, like something you'd see at Mesa Verde or in the desert around Mesopotamia.

There were strange growths off the side of the buildings that at first looked like more trees. We were directly above one when I finally realized that it wasn't a tree but some kind of odd, lumpy construction of mud and branches.

It looked wildly out of place against the square stone buildings.

"Some kind of nests, looks like," whispered Foxy.

Once she said the word *nest*, it snapped into focus. They looked like swallow nests on the side of a building, only grown to enormous size. I wondered what would hatch inside that kind of nest and then decided immediately that I did *not* want to know, I would be infinitely happier *not* knowing. There was absolutely no good that could come of knowing a thing like that.

People like Ambrose talk about forbidden knowledge. Nobody talks about knowledge that is just a dreadfully bad idea all around.

The white man moved up to walk beside Anna. He passed close enough that I could see that his skin had thousands of fine lines in it. They didn't look like wrinkles, but like cracks, the way some porcelain glazes crackle and break.

It occurred to me suddenly that he might be an effigy himself, a very old skin over . . . what? Tree branches and wire? Bones? A human skeleton full of hagstones?

Bongo twitched as my fingers jerked on his leash. He glanced up at me, as if wondering what my problem was.

"Sorry," I whispered to my dog.

We reached the final switchback. The base of the path led to a square, lit with that gray, indirect light. From above, with no trees to block my view, I could look down into the heart of a cold city.

It looked empty. The doors were black rectangles. There were no lights. There were only a few things scuttling between the buildings, and from the way they moved, I knew they were not even so human as Anna was.

Maybe the other people are asleep. Or they don't want to get close to us.

Hell, for all I know, it's like The War of the Worlds *and they're afraid of catching some disease from us.*

I wondered briefly if I should worry about catching some terrible disease from Anna, then glumly decided that I was probably not going to live long enough to worry about whether I was up on my current vaccines.

Anna herself strode forward, never slowing. Her entourage of clicking, sighing effigies bunched up around us, until I knew that they were as close to me as Foxy was. I could have reached out and touched one, if I were so inclined.

I would rather have gnawed my hand off at the wrist.

Look, I ordered myself, as we entered that quiet square. *Look. The horror movie gets less scary once the monster comes out of the shadows. Just look at them. See what you're up against.*

I turned my head and saw the ones that flanked me.

The fan-headed one I knew already. It hopped like a vulture when it walked. Some of the others, though . . . I forced myself to study them as if they were some of my aunt Kate's samples, something safely under a microscope slide.

Rag. Bone. Wire. Stone.

Other things, too, natural and unnatural. One had bullet casings tied in among its hagstones. One had the deep rib cage and narrow hips of a greyhound, the ribs stuffed with dead birds and old mouse nests. One was scaled in what looked like black leather, until I realized that it was made of bits of blown-out tires.

Sticks and stones may break my bones. Sticks and stones may break my bones. It ran through my head with the same maddening jump-rope rhythm as the litany of the twisted ones, until the words had no meaning and it was just a rhyme pounding in my blood.

There was an effigy that had dozens of thin mud pipes along its back. It took me a moment to realize that they were the nests of mud-dauber wasps, the little clay chimneys that get built every summer, all tied together like organ pipes.

Two paced beside me on my right, humped and headless, as if someone had built a body and then decided they'd gone far enough. Empty sleeves of some material—cloth or hide, it was impossible to tell—hung down where the necks should be.

Perhaps I stared for too long, because one of those dangling sleeves moved as if there was something inside, something turning to look back at me. I jerked my eyes away and fixed them on Bongo's back.

"Where do you think they're taking us?" I whispered to Foxy.

"Shit, hon, does it matter?"

"You will be taken to a holding place," said Anna, not looking back at us, "until your fate has been determined."

"But where are we *now*?" I asked, looking over the effigies at the strange, empty city. I still had not seen another human, or even one as human-shaped as the holler people. "Is this more of the hill with the rocks?"

"No. The place of stones is a threshold place," said Anna. "One can reach your world and this one from there. Thresholds are powerful. But it is not safe."

"Safe?" I sank my teeth into my lower lip.

Anna shrugged. "The white stone. The stone attracts . . . attention. The voorish dome over this place keeps it unnoticed. There are things that one might speak with, perhaps even invoke, but one does not wish to live beside them day after day."

The irony of this statement coming from a woman standing flanked by monstrous effigies built of bone and mud and wire was so great that I had to bite the inside of my cheek to keep myself from yelling at her or shaking her or doing any one of a number of things that would undoubtedly get me horribly slaughtered in short order.

"Your critters there based on them stones?" asked Foxy, speaking up for the first time.

The man with the cracked skin turned his head and looked at her. His pupils dilated wrong. I'd have thought he was on drugs, except for the bit where I was in a cold city on the far side of impossible and if anybody was on drugs I would probably ask them if they'd share.

"They are modeled on many things," he said. "But those are shapes of power."

Most of me was terrified. Almost all of me, in fact. But underneath, a tiny little voice was saying, *Isn't that fascinating?*

You're under the voorish dome. You're somewhere that hardly anyone else has been. Even Cotgrave never got this far into the hills.

Isn't that interesting?

I didn't know whether to embrace that voice or try to smother it. It was like standing on a cliff and hearing the little voice that tells you to jump. For all I know, once you jump off, that voice says, *Isn't this fascinating?* all the way down. *Listen to the wind rushing by your ears. Isn't that interesting? Look at how sharp the rocks are below you. Aren't you intrigued?*

Foxy put her hand on my shoulder again. We all kept walking.

———

I truly don't remember very much more about the walk through the city. I think it must have taken at least another ten or fifteen minutes, but it's mostly a blur. I stared at Bongo's ears. Out of the corner of my eye, I kept seeing dark openings into buildings. I wondered if there were other holler people inside, watching us from the darkness.

Once I looked up, because we stepped into a shadow, and I saw the branches of one of the nests stretching over the street, connecting the two houses. Something came squirming out of a gap in the branches, something with long flat limbs or half-furled wings, dragging itself claw over claw up the structure.

It looked soft, like clay, and the branches left deep bloodless gouges in its flesh.

I must have made a noise because Foxy stepped up beside me and grabbed my arm.

"It's all right," she said.

"No, it isn't."

"Fine, it ain't, but I'm an old lady and you're supposed to be keeping my spirits up."

I croaked a laugh. Anna looked back over her shoulder, which surprised me. She hadn't looked at me when she'd answered my questions before.

The laughter didn't sit well in that place, and I was sorry I'd done it immediately, but at least it got me out from under the shadow of the nest.

Nothing else made an imprint on my memory. Just the dark doorways and the tapping of the effigies and the bits of motion.

Finally, we got where we were going. The street had curved around to reach what looked like a slanted stone wall in the hillside. Another dark opening yawned from it, but this one had double doors in it, standing open. Anna walked through them without a trace of fear and Bongo followed her, and I realized that if I didn't hurry, an effigy was going to go next and I would be left following one's back into the dark. My stomach lurched, and I rushed through the doors.

Despite the width of the doors, the corridor narrowed until I could have touched both sides with my outstretched arms. It was dim inside, but not completely dark. The lighting came from what looked like oil lamps in recessed niches. I wondered vaguely what kind of oil they were burning. Did they have kerosene in hell? Fairy whales? How did it work?

If you're thinking that I was focusing on something inconsequential in order to not think about what was happening, you are absolutely correct.

Someone must get the oil and refill the lamps, whispered the little voice in the abyss.

The corridor sloped downward underfoot. There were no stairs. It just went on and on and on. Sometimes we would pass another corridor that joined with ours, or a doorway gaping like an open mouth. I lost count of how many questionable oil lamps we passed, how many times my shadow swelled on the wall opposite the niches.

And it was a long, long, long way. . . .

The only mercy was that there were no echoes. I expected echoes in a corridor like that, but my footsteps fell muffled, as if there was a softness to the stone. I heard the faint tap of Bongo's nails and Foxy's heels clicking behind me, and that was all.

Compared to what I *could* have heard echoing, the silence of the stone was very welcome.

When Anna suddenly turned right and went into one of the other corridors, I almost stumbled. If Bongo hadn't been leading the way, I might have kept going, half hypnotized, until I ended up God knows where under the earth.

But Bongo tugged on the leash and I jerked my head up, startled, and Foxy ran into my back. "Sorry," she muttered. I think she was probably in the same state I was.

The corridor did not slope here, but it did curve from side to side like a snake. I no longer had any idea what direction we were facing, whether we'd come all the way around in a circle and passed underneath the sloping corridor, or if we were still going mostly in a straight line.

What I did know was that the unrelieved stone of the walls began to change. First it was only a few small hatch marks around the edges of the niches. Then the hatch marks began to expand, overlapping and twisting until they became long carved lines that connected the niches together.

They weren't straight lines. They would double back on themselves, break apart, then rejoin.

We came to a doorway where the carved lines wrapped around the threshold, not quite touching it. Unlike the other openings, there was a door in this one.

Anna opened it and gestured for Foxy and Bongo and me to go inside.

The room was not large, smaller than Cotgrave's bedroom. It reminded me of a sauna, not because it was hot but because there were benches along both sides. They appeared to be carved out of the same stone as the walls. A niche stood at the far end, with another of the oil lamps in it.

I looked at Foxy. Foxy shrugged. I clicked my tongue at Bongo and walked forward.

"We will return," said Anna, standing in the doorway. Her voice was even more remote than it had been. It might have been a recording for all the warmth in it. "We must discuss your fate. You will wait here."

Foxy looked at our cell, then back at Anna. "Doesn't look like we've got a lot of choice, do we?"

Anna inclined her head. Under her elbow, I saw one of the humped, headless effigies moving back and forth.

Foxy stepped inside. Anna nodded and closed the door.

19

We looked at the door. We looked at each other. We looked at the door again.

Bongo sat down on the floor.

"What am I gonna do if he has to pee?" I muttered.

"There's a grate," said Foxy.

There was indeed a grate, on the floor beneath the niche. It had metal bars. Foxy and I stared at it.

"Think you could fit through?" she asked.

I eyed it dubiously. "Not unless they leave us here long enough to lose some weight. And I don't know if dropping into the sewer would be an improvement. Do you think they even have sewers here?"

"I guess even holler people gotta shit."

"Those bone and wire things walking around probably don't."

"I dunno. What happens when they eat someone?"

I grimaced. From her expression, Foxy wasn't too keen on the answer to that question herself.

We abandoned the grate and sat down, backs against the wall. Bongo laid down on the floor between us.

"Do you think it's the same stuff as that white stone?" I asked, poking the wall.

Foxy gave me a look. "You got a whatsit on you?"

"A whatsit?"

"An X-ray spectrometer."

Even Bongo looked up at that.

"I don't know what that is," I admitted. "*Do* I have one on me?"

"Seems unlikely. That's the thing we used over at the cement plant when I worked there, to figure out if a batch went bad. You give me one of those, I'll tell you anything you want to know about these rocks."

"Well, if I trip over one, I'll let you know. Maybe we could ask Anna if we could borrow one."

Foxy snorted.

We sat in the room in silence for a minute. Finally, I said, "I'm scared shitless."

"Yeah," said Foxy. She closed her eyes and leaned her head back against the wall. "Me too."

"I sort of expected to die," I said. This was an awkward thing to express, as if I was picking my way through the words like I'd picked my way through the hill with the twisted stones. "Or . . . hell, I don't know what else I expected. But not for there to be a place on the other side of everything, with people and . . ." I shook my head. "There's too much *more* of it. Like, if you went out after . . . I dunno, after the Loch Ness Monster or something, and then it turned out that it was a secret government lab breeding plesiosaurs to blow up submarines."

Foxy opened her eyes and tilted her head sideways, like Bongo did when I did something particularly baffling. "You'll have to explain that one a little better."

I waved my hands helplessly. "It's too big! There's too much there! I mean, if I say, 'There's weird stuff in the hills,' everybody nods and says, 'Yup, doesn't surprise me,' but then I say, 'And they've got a whole city back there made out of white rocks and bird nests and . . . and walking deer skulls and things made out of old shovels tied together!' and *then* it sounds crazy." I groaned. "Do you think this is what happens to people who get abducted by aliens?"

She raised an eyebrow. "Most of those people are nuts, hon."

"I know. But everybody's gonna think we're nuts too, if we try to tell anybody about this."

Foxy laughed. There wasn't much humor in it. "I don't know that that's gonna be a problem."

I sighed. "Yeah," I said. "I know." I slid down on the floor and rubbed Bongo's ears. He thumped his tail.

We sat there in the silent room for what felt like years. I suppose it was probably hours, although it might have been less. Bongo stretched out and went to sleep. Well, why not? He'd had a long, exciting day full of running and climbing and scary things and then somebody came along and enchanted him to make him feel better. I'd want a nap, too. It was a lot for one elderly coonhound.

It was a lot for one thirtysomething woman.

The stone walls muffled sound. We didn't hear our captors approach until the door began to open. Bongo raised his head from his paws and gave a brief whine.

It was Anna, flanked again by effigies. I couldn't make out which ones these were. The shadows were thick around them, and all I could see was the occasional gleam of wire.

Anna spoke to them over her shoulder. "I will tell the prisoners of their fate."

They tapped and clicked at her. She stepped inside and shut the door behind her.

Foxy and I stared at her. She stood before us, inhumanly tall, inhumanly pale, her eyes full of red gleams.

Then she took three steps forward and sank down to her knees.

"You have to help me get out of here," hissed Anna. *"Please."*

Foxy said, " . . . whut?"

This was maybe not the most intelligent response, but it summed up my thoughts pretty well.

"Please," said Anna in a low, urgent voice. Crouched on the floor, something seemed to change in her face. She was still pale, but not like a corpse, and her eyes were plain brown, no longer flecked with red.

Was that some kind of illusion? A glamour, like they used to call spells back in the day?

Or is this the illusion? Is she trying to look more human for us?

"They can't hear us in here, I don't think, not with the door closed," she said. "At least, I don't think they can, but it's hard to tell. They don't react to things like we do."

"Are you . . . uh . . . in trouble?" I asked, thinking that whatever trouble she was in, we were probably in much worse straits and, if anything, we should be asking *her* for help.

She pushed her hair back from her eyes. "Yes. It's bad. This isn't a good place."

"I'd noticed," I said.

She gave a short, humorless laugh. "You would have, I imagine. I don't even see it anymore. You get used to everything. Except sometimes the poppets do things that no one could get used to."

"The poppets?" I asked, although I was pretty sure I already knew. "The bone and stick things?"

She nodded. "Uriah says they used to be shaped more like people. But he's been here too long. Much longer than me, and I've been here for years—I don't know how many years. I know it's been a long time. It was winter of seventy-three."

Foxy and I looked at each other over her head. Anna looked to be, at most, in her early thirties, and only if she'd been really relentless about skin care and exercise.

"It's been a while," said Foxy kindly. "What happened to you? Wandered in here, did you?"

"Ugh." Anna put her face in her hands. "I was so stupid. We'd go out in the woods behind my cousin's place and smoke grass, try to raise our consciousness, you know? And then one day a woman showed up while I was high and I actually asked her if she was my spirit guide. Can you imagine?"

Whatever I was expecting from the holler people, it wasn't this.

"Uh," I said.

Foxy had no such qualms. "Hell, hon, I was tripping balls one night and asked a cop if he was my daddy. It happens."

Anna nodded. "She was the one before me. She brought me back here. Then she *left*, that bitch."

"You can't leave?" I asked.

"Not for good. The poppets will let me go out for a bit, but they watch me. If I try to leave, they . . ." She swallowed. Whatever she was going to say, she apparently thought better of it. "They bring me back," she said.

I pictured long twig fingers closing over my arms, a deer-bone effigy picking me up and carrying me back to the place of stones, and shuddered.

Something snapped suddenly into focus, now that she was no longer so tall and pale. "Wait!" I said. "You were in the woods! I saw you! You're the hiker!"

Anna nodded. "I've been watching you," she said. "To see if you could help me."

"But you didn't look like . . ." I waved my hands, trying to express *tall and pale and red-eyed* all at once.

"It's nothing," she said. She waved her hand and suddenly

her eyes shone the color of brake lights. I recoiled and then they were brown again. "A little magic. Like the charm on your dog. So that people don't have a freak-out."

Have a freak-out, I thought. *I can almost hear the seventies.*

"I used to come out and see Frederick." She shook her head sadly. "I don't think he understood what I was trying to tell him. He kept trying to warn me. I told him it was too late, but . . . well."

Frederick. She means Cotgrave. Oh. He mentioned a girl in the woods.

I hadn't connected the hiker to Cotgrave's girl in the woods, but how could I? There were a lot of people in Pondsboro. It's not like you expect any of them to be magically concealing the fact that they're seven feet tall and the color of ice.

"I think he was pretty far gone by the end," I said.

Anna nodded. "He couldn't help me," she said.

"*You* were the one who sent the note. And drew 'Kilroy was here' on it."

She petted Bongo. "Yes. He used to draw it. I didn't know if you knew him, but I thought you might recognize it."

I tried not to sound accusing, but I'm pretty sure I failed. "I came because of the note. Because you asked for help! And instead you captured me—us—and locked us up in here!"

"Well, I didn't expect you to just walk in! I thought if you'd found the place of stones, you must know something about how things worked!"

Foxy gave a short bark of laughter.

"No," I said. "My dog wandered into it one day and then things started to go really sideways."

Anna stopped petting Bongo and shoved her hair out of her eyes. "You're not one of them, then. One of us?"

"Uh . . . what?"

"Part hidden folk. They go out and get children on ordinary folk. My father was one. That's why they wanted me here. But you're not one, are you?"

I raised my eyebrows, thinking of my dad and the roughness in his lungs. "Jesus, no. My dad's an actuary."

I don't know why I added that last bit, except that it seemed like being an actuary was the diametric opposite of being a holler person.

"Unnngghhh." Anna looked as if she might scream. "But you have to be! *Frederick was one!*"

"He *what?*" I said.

"He was one of us. Generations back, but there was a little bit there. How can't you have it?"

I blinked at her stupidly. "He was my stepgrandfather. Mine died in his thirties."

Anna collapsed onto the stone bench. "This is *awful.*"

I was getting a little fed up with her assumptions. It was looking like this was at least partly her fault. "You could have asked! Or, you know, *not* captured us!"

She shook her head. "I tried to keep everyone else out but you. I thought *you* could help me."

Foxy lifted her head. "That's why it felt like the place was trying to keep me out."

"I *tried,*" Anna repeated, sounding almost petulant. "Once you were in the place of stones, the poppets were going to bring you back no matter what. I had to make it look good. They're already suspicious of me. At least, I think they are. Who knows what goes on in their heads?"

"Don't you?" asked Foxy mildly.

Anna gave a high, humorless laugh that made the hair rise on the back of my neck. Bongo jumped.

I slid down on the floor and hugged my dog, feeling a territorial urge to claim him as mine, not hers. The hickory beads around my neck got tangled up in his collar, and as I wrapped my fingers around them to pull them loose, I had a strange sense of double vision. Anna, still looking like a hippie, with human eyes and human skin . . . and then behind that, as if through a frosted glass, Anna with red eyes and skin whiter than any white woman on earth.

Which one is real?

I dropped the beads against my chest. The vision faded, even though the beads were still touching the back of my neck. Perhaps the hickory was only strong enough to show me the glamour if I was holding it tightly.

Anna hunched up one shoulder in a shrug, unaware of any of this. "Look, I need your help. I have to get out of here. It's been too long. I can't do what they want. It's not working. I used to at least get pregnant, but now that doesn't even work anymore."

If she'd sounded like a grieving mother, I think I would have tried to say something sympathetic, but she didn't. She sounded irritated. And I know people are complicated and grieve in their own ways and all that, and maybe it wasn't even grief anymore, but that was one more strange thing going on.

I'm not judging. This whole situation was beyond anything I understood.

"We'll help you get away if we can," I said, which was a stupid thing to say, given that we were locked in a stone cell and she had free run of the place. "But there's effi . . . poppets at the house, too. If they come after you, won't they just come to the house?"

"The house, maybe." Anna dipped her head. "But if I can get far enough away, they'll give up. I'm sure they'll give up. They *have* to give up."

I wasn't so sure, but I also wasn't going to argue with her. Her eyes were doing a very unsettling thing, where they flashed red, then remembered they were supposed to be brown, but then the red would start seeping through again.

"What about the others?" I asked. "The other holler people. Won't they try to stop you if you leave?"

"What?"

"The . . ." It occurred to me that she might not know what I meant by "holler people." "The hidden people. Like you and the old man."

Anna stared at me, then gave another high, unsettling laugh.

"There aren't any others," she said. "He and I are the only ones left."

"There aren't any others?" I repeated stupidly. "What? How is that possible? You've got a whole city here!"

Even as I said it, I remembered how silent the city had been as we'd walked through it, how the only movement had been the effigies. At the time I'd thought that perhaps the others were sleeping or watching us from the windows.

Perhaps the truth was that there was no one left to watch.

But if that was true, then where were the effigies coming from? Somebody was building them.

Was it Anna? Or the other man—Uriah? *Now, there's an old-fashioned name. I wonder how long he's been in here. . . .*

An old-fashioned name, like . . . like Ambrose, for that matter . . .

Ambrose destroyed the white stone, but there was another one here. Cotgrave knew about the holler people when he was in Wales, and the narrator in the Green Book talks about them, so there had to be more. . . .

"Are there other cities?" I asked. "In other places?"

Anna gave me a startled, appraising look. "I don't know," she said. "Uriah said something about that once, but he rambles. Nobody ever comes from them, if there are."

Something rattled against the door. Anna stiffened.

She rose to her feet. It looked for a moment as if she stood in a light that no one could see, as her skin bleached whiter and whiter and her eyes grew strange.

"I'll come back," she whispered. "The poppets will want to take you to the Building next. I'll try to put them off, but if I can't, be ready."

"The build—"

"*Later.*"

She opened the door. A wall of bone and rags and twigs stood behind it, moving restlessly.

Anna stepped outside, head held high.

"Your cooperation has been noted," she said. "We will speak again."

She shut the door behind her and was gone.

"Holy crap," said Foxy.

"This is getting weirder and weirder," I said. "What do you think is going on?"

"Not a damn clue," said Foxy. She jerked her chin toward the door. "Not real keen on her. I feel bad for her, but something stinks."

"Yeah . . . ," I said. I wanted to feel bad for Anna, who was clearly a victim of . . . something . . . but there was a wrongness to her that I couldn't put my finger on.

It reminded me of the narrator of the Green Book. That same feeling that I knew I was supposed to pity them, but I mistrusted them instead.

Well, Anna had hauled me into a situation I had no idea how to fix, and she hadn't apologized; she'd just seemed annoyed. I was probably justified in being a little annoyed myself.

There was just something . . . *off*.

Off, I thought bitterly. *Yes, you're surrounded by monsters, trapped underground, but something is off. And you're still brooding because you didn't think the narrator of the Green Book was likable enough.*

Bongo liked Anna, but that didn't mean much. She'd put a spell on him. And anyway, Bongo liked everyone except for the UPS guy, and maybe he'd like the UPS guy too if he could do magic.

I wished I knew what it was that was nagging at me. Then I'd know if I should pay attention to the feeling or ignore it.

Of course, how I was supposed to pick out a subtle wrongness when I was being held in a cell by stick effigies under an empty city that was somehow in the hills behind my dead grandmother's house . . . ? *Yeah, no, we're way past subtlety.*

She isn't acting right, though. The way the narrator in the Green Book didn't act quite right.

If you'd been held prisoner by effigies for decades, getting pregnant from a rock, how the hell would you act?

But why did she care that I wasn't one of the holler people? If I was going to help her escape, what did it matter?

"Do you think there's really no other holler people?"

Foxy shrugged. "Didn't see any. Of course, that doesn't mean anything. And you're right that maybe there's none here, but there's some somewhere else."

"Maybe the effigies are getting made somewhere else. In another city. Cotgrave must have seen one in Wales and then ran . . ." *Ran across the sea and moved into a house with one in the backyard. There's irony for you.*

Maybe he didn't have a choice. Maybe he couldn't get away from them.

"Do you think this is a trap?" I asked, my brain a whirl of thoughts—Cotgrave drawn to my grandmother, whom he clearly despised, Cotgrave drawn to the house, not leaving, even once it became clear that the holler people had found him . . . Cotgrave trapped, and now we were trapped . . .

Foxy raised a carefully drawn eyebrow. "If it's a trap, she already sprung it. She's got us in a jail cell. Why come in here and lie to us about it?"

I grunted.

After a minute I said, "If there's no holler people, who the hell is making the effigies? Or the poppets or whatever she called them?"

"Maybe that old guy," said Foxy. "He looks like the sort who'd stick a wasp nest on a pig's body and call it a day."

"Uriah," I said. "When was the last time you heard of somebody named Uriah?"

"Sunday school, I think. He was a Hittite or a Levite or a Sodomite or whatever." She considered this. "Well, maybe not a Sodomite."

"I'm not judging." I considered. "Do you think he could have made all of them?"

"If I was immortal and bored, I'd probably get up to a whole lotta mischief."

"You think he's immortal?"

"I think that Anna girl sure as hell doesn't look like she was a teenager in seventy-three."

I sighed. "What do you think she meant about getting pregnant?"

Foxy considered this. "Sounded a bit like somebody wanted her to have kids, but she couldn't anymore. Said something similar when she caught us, didn't she?"

I have borne seven. Five drew no breaths.

"Hell," Foxy said, "if I was stuck here with nobody but that old Uriah guy and a bunch of walking twig monsters, having babies, I'd want to get the hell outta Dodge myself."

I snorted. This exactly echoed my thoughts, and she wasn't wrong, but still . . . still . . .

Why trap us? Why call for help when we pretty clearly weren't competent to give it?

No, *it wasn't* us. *It was* me. *She tried to keep Foxy out, remember?*

Why were the effigies staring in my windows anyway?

We didn't have enough information, and that was all there was to it.

We sat in silence. Bongo went back to sleep.

"You still got those sandwiches?"

"How can you possibly want to eat at a time like this?"

"Look, being terrified makes me hungry."

I dug in my pack and pulled out the Tupperware container.

As soon as it was open, the smell of tuna and mayo hit me and I was suddenly ravenous.

"Told you," said Foxy smugly, as I shoved down two sandwiches.

Ten minutes later, I was so tired I started to wonder if the tuna salad had been drugged.

"Perfectly normal," said Foxy. "Look, we ran like hell and then we got marched through the streets scared out of our wits. The adrenaline's gotta wear off sometime." She stretched out on the stone bench, using her backpack as a pillow. "Also, neither of us got much sleep last night."

I groaned. It felt incredibly dumb and dangerous to fall asleep with monsters everywhere, but it wasn't like I was going to be able to chip my way out of the cell using the Tupperware container. "I know you're right," I said. "It just feels wrong. And Anna told us to be ready."

"It's easier to run away if you're well rested. And they didn't kill us on the spot when they found us, so that's got to be worth something."

"You think they've got something else planned?"

"Hon, for all I know they're gonna eat us and are trying to find the recipe book."

On that comforting thought, she closed her eyes and began to snore.

I climbed down and curled up around Bongo. He was a bit puzzled, but happy to be the little spoon. I put my face in his ruff and smelled unwashed dog, which shouldn't have been a comforting smell, but at the moment I'd take what I could get.

I wanted to panic. I could feel the panic all through my body, as if my skin were stretched over the top of it, but I couldn't.

My dog needed me and I couldn't break down until he was safe, and that was all there was to it.

20

I must have slept for a few hours. Long enough for one of the clasps on Bongo's collar to imprint itself on my cheek, anyway. I sat up because Foxy nudged me.

"Huh?"

Bongo whined.

Foxy nudged me again with her foot, practically a kick.

I started to protest, then saw her face. She wasn't looking at me.

I turned my head very slowly.

The door was open, and the doorway was full of effigies.

I crab walked backward on one hand and both feet, dragging Bongo with me. He didn't fight it. I felt the moment I hit the metal grate on the floor because my fingers separated and a bar slammed into the space between my ring and middle finger with all my weight behind it. It was excruciating. I barely noticed.

The effigies stared at us, eyeless.

They weren't moving. I could see one of the headless, humpbacked ones and the one with the mud-dauber nests on its back. There were others behind it, but I couldn't make out where one ended and the next began. They filled the doorway and the hall, as far back as I could see, a river of sticks and stones.

. . . and broken bones . . . sticks and stones . . . and I twisted myself around like the twisted ones . . .

My shoulder hit the wall behind me. I could feel the metal bars digging into the backs of my legs. Bongo put a paw in a gap and slipped, then recovered.

And the effigies just stood there, watching. Their shadows painted the ceiling of the corridor, unmoving.

Very far away, muffled by the strange stone, I heard tapping sounds.

Maybe that's the ones in the back saying, "What's going on? I can't see!"

I shoved my hand in my mouth to muffle whatever came out next. Hysterical laughter or screaming, I had no idea.

With my other arm, I dragged Bongo's head down against my chest, as if he were a small child and I was trying to keep him from seeing something terrible. He let me do it. Dogs never let you do that.

Dogs didn't belong here, under the voorish dome.

People didn't either.

I heard a click beside me. It wasn't a twig-and-bone click. It was the sound of a gun being cocked.

"Foxy . . . ?" I didn't turn my head.

"I got six bullets," she said. Her voice was absolutely flat, and she wasn't talking to me. "I doubt y'all are gonna let me reload, but the first six could be interesting."

I tore my eyes away from the doorway and saw that she had a gun leveled in front of her. It looked gigantic, but that didn't mean anything, since any gun looked gigantic, as far as I was concerned.

I wanted to ask her a question, like, *Where the hell did that come from?* or maybe *Why didn't you shoot somebody before we ended up in a prison cell?* but it didn't really seem like the time.

The effigies didn't move. They didn't retreat. They didn't advance. They didn't even seem to notice.

None of them had eyes as I understood it. They had hollows and sockets and empty places full of darkness.

I still couldn't shake the feeling that they were studying us.

Foxy's wrists were starting to shake with the strain of holding the pistol up, but she never moved.

And then finally, minutes or hours later—I couldn't begin to tell you—the effigies began to leave. I saw the shadows ripple on the walls as they walked away. Some of them didn't even bother to turn around. They just reversed their limbs and began to move in the opposite direction. The corridor filled with *tick-tick-tick* noises.

The mud-dauber effigy tilted its head at me. Its head was a couple of sticks tied together with twine, not even solid, just a vague V-shape that might have been a muzzle and more mud-dauber wasps coming out the back, all bundled together like a pan flute.

It reached out with its forelimbs and pulled the door shut.

Foxy exhaled all at once and let her arms drop. She did something arcane with the gun and put it back into her backpack.

"Foxy, where did *that* come from?"

"My grandmomma. She said if I was gonna date boys, I should always carry cab fare and a condom—"

"That is *not* a condom, Foxy!"

"—and if any of 'em gave me trouble, I was to whip that piece out and show 'im that mine was bigger 'n his."

I digested this for a moment. "Interesting woman, your grandmother."

"Yeah, she was somethin' else. Anyway, I've had it in my backpack the whole time."

"Why didn't you pull it out when we were on the hillside?"

She snorted. "And how many of them do you expect me to shoot? I ain't Annie Oakley, I can't line up ten of those things with one bullet." She frowned. "I admit, I did think a bit about taking that Anna woman hostage on the spot, but when people are throwing uncanny shit around, I ain't inclined to return fire. Seemed pretty likely that I'd just get myself killed and then you and your puppy'd be here all alone. Figured it'd be better to keep it for the last resort."

Bongo heard the word *puppy* and tugged his head out of my armpit, wagging his tail. I wish I had a tenth of the emotional resilience of a dog.

I exhaled slowly. "Well, I guess they know you've got it

now." I couldn't believe how prepared she was, particularly in contrast to how unprepared I was. "You ever think about joining the FBI or the CIA or something, Foxy?"

"I looked into it once, but apparently they want you to have finished high school."

"Shame."

"That's what the nice agent said. He was a sweet boy. Made me breakfast in the morning and everything."

I examined my left hand. The webbing between my fingers had turned an angry red, and there was a jarring ache through my hand. I squeezed various bones and nothing made me scream in agony, so it probably wasn't broken. Not that I could have done a damn thing about it if it were.

At least it was the left. I can type, hunt and peck style, with my right hand if I have to. You know, in case I had to do any copyediting while I was sitting in the holler people's prison.

"It's interestin'," said Foxy slowly.

I looked up.

"They came here without any of the holler people."

"Anna said there weren't any more," I said.

"Yeah. She *said*. I ain't saying she's a liar exactly, but she's been leaving some bits out."

"Well, we've had one five-minute conversation . . . ," I said, determined to be fair if it killed me. "Not that I think you're wrong."

"Yeah." She nodded. "But if she's not telling them what to do, who told the things to come stare at us?"

I blinked. I hadn't thought of it. The first effigy, the deer-skull one, had been staring in my window, and I'd come to think of it as just a thing they did.

"And why?" I said. "What were they looking for?"

Foxy shrugged.

"And the Building . . ." I could practically hear the capital letter when Anna had said it.

Foxy shrugged again.

I put my arms around Bongo again and wondered if we'd ever get answers, or if finding out the truth was going to be even worse.

"What time do you think it is?" I asked.

"How the hell should I know?" She jerked her chin toward the door. "Listen up. Something's going on out there."

I listened. Even through the muffling silence of the door, I could faintly hear an angry raised voice and clacking sounds.

It was coming closer.

I wrapped my arms around Bongo. He quieted a little, but I could still hear the whine down in his chest, at the bottom of every exhale.

A final angry shout. A clatter of bone and metal. The door opened.

Anna came through and shut it behind her. Her eyes were as red as tail lights. "Get up," she said.

"What's going on?" I gripped Bongo's collar tight.

"It's the poppets. They're going to take you to the Building."

I swallowed. "Why?"

"To get a look at you, I suppose."

"They've been coming to the house," I snapped. "Staring

at me through the windows. Haven't they had a good enough look already?"

She shook her head, her hair whipping in frustration. "Who knows why they do what they do?"

"But I thought your people made them!" I remembered the passages in the Green Book, the Lady Cassap making a poppet, the clay men that the narrator made. Surely they were the same things, or something like them.

Anna gave a short, grinding laugh. "What? I've never made one."

"That old guy, then," said Foxy. "Uriah."

"Him?" Scorn dripped from Anna's voice. "He can't do much more than stare and mumble. He's been here for centuries. One of the last of the real old bloods, for all the good it does him now. No, he's not making them."

"Then where do they come from?"

"It doesn't matter," she whispered furiously. "Listen to me! We have to go now." She looked over my head at Foxy. "Afterward, we have to run, do you understand? The Building's near the edge. And they always stay together for a little bit after, so there'll be fewer of them."

"After what?" I asked. She ignored me.

"I'll distract them," she said. "Be ready."

"After *what*?"

Finally she glanced at me. "Ugh, I don't have time! You'll see!" Eventually I nodded. So did Foxy.

"We hear you," said Foxy grimly.

Anna yanked the door open again.

A corridor full of clicking shadows looked in at us. Far back, I could see Uriah, surrounded by made monsters.

Anna never faltered. She lifted her chin, inhumanly tall and inhumanly pale, and walked forward. The poppets parted to let her pass.

"Well," said Foxy softly, rising to her feet, "I guess if we don't want them to drag us, we'd better follow her."

I expected to take the long corridor to the surface again, but we did not. Instead we turned and turned again, until I was thoroughly lost.

These corridors were better lit, which was . . . Well, I don't know if that was good or not. There were oil lamps every few yards, the niches alternating between the left and right side. Each splash of light illuminated carvings that rippled and swirled on the opposite wall.

Either the magic on Bongo was starting to wear off or there were too many effigies around us, because he began to turn his head and look at them, his forehead wrinkling. I could see him trying to think. Normally he doesn't devote that much mental energy to anything that doesn't involve food.

I was not having an easy time of it myself. It was light enough in the corridor that I could see them clearly. I don't know if that was more frightening than blurry, indistinct shapes in the dark or not. There also seemed to be more of them than before, or perhaps they were just walking more closely.

That's it. They're moving like they have somewhere to be.
The Building.

I tried to picture what it could be. Another of these gray

stone boxes? A gigantic factory, turning out twig-and-skull creatures on an assembly line?

"Quit pokin' me," Foxy growled to something behind her.
"I ain't moving any faster in these heels."

"How are you not having a complete breakdown?" I asked
her. I heard myself laugh as I asked it, which I hadn't intended
to do. Panic was starting to claw inside my chest, as if one of
the effigies had crawled in there and was trying to carve their
way out.

That's a lovely mental image. And so helpful right now.

Foxy snorted. "Was in some protests back in the day and the
cops came to bust it up. These days, if I ain't being teargassed, I
figure I'm doing okay. Keep walking, hon."

She gave me a little shove in the back. I hadn't even realized that I was slowing down.

"Plus I took half a Valium earlier," she added.

"And you didn't share?"

"Well, I figured one of us needed to be sober in case we
needed to drive."

"Not a lot of cars around here, Foxy."

She sniffed. "There's a thing over there, got a muffler for a
rib cage. Looks like somebody tried to make a greyhound, then
got bored halfway through."

"I don't think we can drive away on a muffler."

"Not by *itself*. But I mean, we get enough of these things
together, we might be able to build a car outta spare parts."

"Did you ever see that old show, *The A-Team*?"

"Pfff! Hon, I saw it when it *aired*."

"There's that episode where they get locked in a barn and turn a tractor into a tank that shoots cabbages."

"I yield to nobody in my love of Mr. T, but that one might've been a tad unrealistic." She considered this. "Although they lock us in with an arc welder and I might work something out."

Listening to Foxy's outrageous comments kept me walking. If Anna heard them, she gave no sign.

Our procession slowed gradually, until it seemed like we were moving at a crawl. I looked forward and saw that ahead of Anna, Uriah was walking very slowly, his hands on the backs of two effigies that flanked him. Somehow the sight of a human—or something human enough—willingly touching one of the things made my stomach churn.

I turned to the carvings on the walls to keep from looking at Uriah's monsters. These carvings did not look like mere ornamentation. There were figures that looked human, very tall, always facing the viewer, with a great curved shape over their head. The sky? A rainbow, rendered in gray rock? The voorish dome?

The next set of carvings had the same figures, with smaller ones at their feet, like children. They reminded me of Egyptian carvings, how the kids always looked like the adults, only half the size.

We passed a half dozen more carvings, all of them similar except that the human figures were doing different things with their hands. Maybe an art historian could have made sense of it. I had the feeling that there was a great deal of information there, if only I had the ability to decipher it. One had the figures holding a baby, which was actually proportioned more or less like a baby, which made me wonder if I'd been wrong about the small figures being children. Representation of a royal family? A ruling class, and the others were peasants? Had I discovered holler people feudalism?

One of them was definitely a burial. I remember that one clearly. The human figure was lying down, wrapped in some kind of shroud. Something stood at its head, like a human with a bird's head, or maybe some kind of mask. The small figures covered their faces, backs bent as if in terrible grief.

The one after that had only the small figures, no large ones. Children whose parents had died? A population with a dead king?

The next carving had the small figures holding up a baby, and then it went back to the same sets as before—big figure, small figure, domed sky.

"You seeing these, Foxy?"

"Yep."

"And?"

"Kinda reminds me of that stuff in pyramids. Or the others. The big winged bulls."

"Assyrian?"

"Don't you swear at me."

We left the corridors through another door set in the hillside and stepped into the dead city.

It had grown dark. That surprised me somehow. I'd thought we were beyond day and night here. Nevertheless, the clouded sky had darkened to the color of cold liver. The air was cold.

Lamps had been lit in the city, but strangely.

I don't know why, but you expect streetlights to be regular. All at the same height, more or less evenly spaced. You expect it so much that you don't even think about it—you look up and notice immediately when a streetlight is out, because part of you knows that there is supposed to be a light right there.

The lights were set up wrong. They looked like some kind of cloth lanterns, but they were tacked up haphazardly. One building would have three of them and then there would be a long stretch of darkness. Two would be at chest height and the next dozen would be on the second story.

I'd say that it was unsettling, but I was a long way past unsettled. The holler people were gone, Anna had said. Had the effigies done it? Did it have some esoteric significance, or had they just been given an order to put up lights from here to here, without any innate understanding of how lights even worked?

Isn't that interesting? whispered the little voice.

It didn't really matter anyway. The lantern cloth was torn and ragged and most of them gave off only a dim, firefly glow. One or two blazed bright as day, casting shadows behind the effigies that were almost as grotesque as the creatures themselves.

The panic was settling into a new phase. I felt distant and disassociated. I could hear all my thoughts coming from a long way off, echoing inside my head.

For some reason I thought of Skip describing the difference between his ups and downs. Could something as simple as panic have an up and a down form? One panic had felt like

I was going to run screaming into the city. This one felt like I might simply sit down and put my arms over my head and wait for an effigy to kill me.

Probably it was nothing like that. I wasn't bipolar. What the hell did I know about it?

One of the streets we passed down widened into a kind of courtyard with a carved stone in the center. It occurred to me, looking at it, that I had not seen anything like the carved stones since we entered the city. The one here was on a raised brick dais, as if it were a piece of sculpture.

The effigies slowed as we entered this courtyard, filing around the stone in a circle. Anna put out a hand and we stood to one side, waiting.

Tok . . . tok . . . tok . . .

Tap, tap, tap, tap.

Click . . . click . . .

They were making noises at the stone, turning their . . . heads, I guess, those that had heads . . . moving bits of themselves back and forth.

"Are they worshipping it?" I said. I sounded very calm. I was asking the question from very far away.

Anna shrugged.

The very old holler person, Uriah, looked over at me with filmed eyes and said, "They do courtesy to their makers."

"What does that mean?" asked Foxy.

Uriah blinked at her. His eyelids moved a little too slowly, like a lizard's. "It is . . . what we were . . ." He fell silent for a long moment, then added, "It was long ago."

"Why here and not up on the hill?" I asked.

Uriah blinked a few more times. "This one is *here*."

I wasn't sure if he understood me or thought he'd answered me or what.

The effigies were moving. If they were human, I'd say they would be swaying, but they weren't doing it like humans would. Parts of them would move and others would stay still. One of the effigies, the greyhound one, began to turn back on itself, crawling up and over its own hindquarters in an impossible corkscrew.

And I twisted myself around like the twisted ones. . . .

They're better at it than I was, I thought, and had the urge to laugh hysterically and then perhaps begin screaming.

The stone was one of the ones that I thought of as the dead ones. I stared at it. The lines didn't squirm like they had on the hill, but they still had a motion to them. It looked like a corpse wrapped in a shroud. After seeing the carved burial on the walls, I was pretty sure that I wasn't just making that up in my head. But as I kept staring, some of the carved lines seemed to resolve into a hand working its way loose from the wrappings. A shroud, or a binding?

A cocoon?

I reached my free hand up and gripped the line of hickory beads.

There was no strikingly obvious change, but the hand came into focus immediately. It looked like a human hand. I didn't know if that was good, bad, or just the way things were.

The effigies, with no signal that I could see, unwound from the circle and began to walk forward again.

I kept my eyes on the ground in front of me. I felt numb. The litany of the twisted ones kept chasing around in my head, tangled up with the corpse stone and the carving of all the little figures bent over with their hands over their faces.

"Oh hell," said Foxy, and I finally looked up.

One of the immense bird's nest constructions loomed at the end of the street. It was the largest one I'd seen. It had engulfed at least one building and was leaning over the nearby ones.

The entryway was lopsided and large enough to drive a car through.

Effigies stood in a straggling crowd around it, but they had left a long corridor clear.

"Come," said Anna, in her remote voice. "We are summoned into the Building."

21

I had to pick Bongo up and carry him. He would not walk into that doorway.

I wanted to walk into it even less, but no one was giving me a choice.

Be ready, Anna had said. Our escape lay on the other side of . . . whatever happened next.

Assuming she wasn't betraying us. Assuming that there *was* any way to betray us, since we couldn't get much more captive than we were. Assuming that she hadn't been lying, for some strange purpose of her own.

Assumption after assumption. But all I could do was go forward, not back.

I could not explain any of this to Bongo, so I picked him up in my arms. He whined miserably against my shoulder.

I felt as if I was betraying him. I also felt as if my back was going to give out, but surely I only needed to get him inside.

After that he'd probably be eager to leave under his own power.

I walked forward through the crowd of effigies. Twenty, at least. Maybe more. They blurred together at the edges. It felt like I was walking a gauntlet. Living junk turned its head and watched me, and everywhere I heard the soft, thoughtful clicking.

Please, I prayed, to any god that might be able to hear me in this place. *Please let my dog live.*

Anna had said we'd make a break for it after we came out of the Building. That implied we'd come out again, didn't it?

It's just a building. It's probably like a temple or something. We just need to go in and then we'll come out again.

Bongo can get away. He can outrun them, I bet. Foxy and I . . . Well, Foxy's got that gun. Surely she can take care of herself.

Which left me as the deadweight, but I expected that.

The doorway to the Building loomed in front of me. It wasn't a pitch-black opening. It was gray and layered, and I could see a little way inside. When I stepped over the threshold, my feet crackled on the surface below. It looked like . . . I didn't know, like something oddly familiar. Handmade paper, the kind you get with bits of leaf pressed into it or papier-mâché. Something like that.

The Building wasn't silent. At first I thought it was Bongo's trembling against my chest that made it seem to move, and then I realized that there was a thrumming sound, like distant machinery.

Machines? Here?

It didn't make any sense, but what did in this place?

Foxy stepped in behind me. "Better keep moving, hon," she said quietly. "There's a big one behind us, and I think it means business."

I didn't look over my shoulder. It wouldn't do me any good to look at it. Orpheus and Lot's wife might have been unable to resist looking back, but I was *done*.

Bongo's heartbeat raced against my chest.

"It's okay," I lied to him. "It's okay. I won't let anything happen to you."

The corridor was square at first. It seemed like the material had been layered over the interior of one of the stone buildings. Then it opened out into a room, rectangular but with the corners softened with drifts of the paper material.

The ceiling was full of twigs, like a mass of bird nests all woven together. It was hard to tell if the gigantic wicker structure on top had been built or had simply grown there. There were no leaves on the twigs, but maybe that didn't mean anything. There were no leaves on the trees around the voorish dome, either.

There was a second opening on the far side of the room. It was an irregular circle, and I had my doubts that it was part of the original stone building. The twigs ran down to meet it and the odd pulpy gray layers were built up around it.

I shifted Bongo against my hip, trying to see over him so that I didn't catch my footing, and suddenly I realized what the material reminded me of.

"Foxy?" I said softly.

"Yeah?"

"This is a paper wasp nest, isn't it?"

"Think so, hon. If the wasps were the size of horses."

This was not a comforting thought, but I had pretty much given up on comforting thoughts by this point.

Anna stood framed in the circular opening. She had halted. As I watched, she took a deep breath, lifted her head, and stepped forward.

We followed. Bongo had gone completely limp. I heaved him up so that his paws were on my shoulder and I could take more of his weight on my hip. If his heart hadn't been hammering against my collarbone, I would have worried that he was dead.

The circular tunnel sloped upward and was ribbed like a throat. That was another thought I wished I hadn't had. I wanted to slow down, but Foxy was right behind me, one hand on my backpack, and I knew something had to be right behind her.

It went around and around, like a spiral staircase. It wasn't as dark as it should have been. The paper let light through, maybe, or reflected it differently. The air was full of diffuse gray light, like the horizon just before dawn.

There were carvings on the walls here too.

I say carvings. Bas-relief made of paper? Sculpture? Something like that. Easier to carve than stone, I suppose. The same as inside the corridors, the tall figures, the small ones at their feet. Not all the small figures were human. Some of them looked like dogs or goats or maybe horses, some kind of four-legged animal, but scaled down. All of them walking up alongside us, in a great spiral, the large ones getting fewer and fewer, the small ones continuing on.

Ahead of us, the tunnel opened up.

Anna paused in the tunnel mouth. There was a light source in front of her, turning her into a black paper cutout. I didn't want to touch her but I was being pushed ahead, so I cleared my throat.

She stepped to one side and I came out, carrying my dog, into the heart of the Building.

———

You think really stupid things when you're horrified beyond belief. In this case, I thought: *Of course. Building. You think it's a noun, but it's also a verb.*

That's what was happening here.

Building.

The nest rose up on all sides, over a vast open space. We stood on the roof of the stone building and looked over the edge. The effigies had sheared down through what had once been a street, and the Building continued for an unknown distance below.

It didn't fall away into darkness, though. Darkness would have been an improvement.

The pit was filled with material, a mound of junk, of twigs and bone and discarded wire, skulls and pebbles, feathers and dead leaves. And it was alive.

The surface rippled like a pregnant animal's sides, heaving with contractions. Effigies picked their way across the mound like water bugs skating on the surface of a pond, tugging bits loose, binding them together. I watched two creatures like praying mantises with cow skulls for heads, working on a pile of clay that moved and squirmed under their claws, as they wrenched it into a shape I couldn't begin to fathom, then jabbed sticks into it, sticks and stones and broken bones, while it writhed in what looked like pain.

We'd wondered who made them, and suddenly it was obvious.

They were making themselves.

I thought of the white people in the Green Book, the holler people, making poppets to serve them. The holler people, having children with ordinary humans and the white stone, growing fewer and fewer as their blood grew thinner and thinner.

The human figures, surrounded by smaller ones. Not children, but their servants. Made things and the ones who made them.

And one day the holler people were gone, but their servants remained, and the servants began to replace themselves, over and over, the poppets building poppets of their own, growing farther and farther removed from any human hand, the small figures walking up the spiral, no longer human or animal, continuing on and on and on alone.

"Look up," said Foxy softly. "Or maybe don't."

I looked up.

Hundreds of effigies hung from the top of the nest, the way the deer-skull effigy had hung from the tree. They dangled on the ends of ropes like silent wind chimes.

Anna walked to the very edge of the roof. The two humped,

headless ones flanked her like an honor guard. She said, "I have brought the interlopers."

I didn't know what to expect next. For the mound to start talking? For it to open monstrous eyes and roll over and be an effigy made from the bones of giants? For the ground to open up and swallow us whole?

None of those things happened. If they had, I would probably have broken right there.

Instead the effigies behind us fanned out around us. More and more streamed through the doorway, the entire crowd that had been around the Building, a hall of wire and bone horrors. The ones working began to slow. The praying mantises paused in their assembly, holding the twitching, headless body of their child between them.

The ones hanging from the ceiling began to sway.

Clicking echoed from all around us. The praying mantises tapped their long twig fingers on their hollow skulls. Hagstones rattled in the rib cages of the hanging ones. The mud-dauber effigy stood closest to me and shuddered its body so that the mud tunnels chattered together like teeth.

I didn't ask what they were doing, because this, too, was blindingly obvious. They were talking.

Sticks and stones, sticks and stones, sticks and stones and talking bones . . .

A rattled discussion went on all around us, *click, click, click,* like the voices of monstrous insects, giant cicadas humming in the heat. Anna folded her arms in front of her and listened.

"What are they saying?" I croaked.

"The poppets are deciding whether to keep you," she said.

"They can't do that." My voice sounded very calm and conversational, as if I could convince Anna, and the effigies, that holding us prisoner was some kind of social faux pas.

"The alternative is to take you apart for materials."

Foxy swore.

The clicking grew louder and more agitated. The ones swaying from the ceiling began to clatter together, introducing discordant notes. A heated discussion? Did they have emotions? Did they get angry, happy, sad, frightened?

Did it matter?

"The newer ones say that you can perhaps be bred to make more masters," said Anna. "The old ones say that they must wait for better stock. Masters bred from your flesh will be weak, even with the white stone, as mine have become weak. The newer ones say that even those can be used for materials."

If I had not had Bongo in my arms, I might have panicked. Things were going a bit gray around the edges. They were talking about using me as a broodmare for . . . for however long someone lived under the voorish dome.

But I had Bongo. And I couldn't panic, because I had to take care of him, even if the flesh under discussion was trying to crawl off my body in sheer disgust.

"The dog and the old one will be made into bones," she continued. Her voice was flat and emotionless. "They will be given the task to guard you. It is"—her voice acquired some faint sheen of emotion, one I couldn't place—"an honor."

I looked at the two headless effigies beside her. It occurred to me that they walked beside her nearly every time I saw her, and I finally thought to wonder what had gone into their construction.

Or who.

I clutched Bongo against me. His eyes were closed and he was panting in the last extremes of distress.

"We will await your decision," said Anna to the crawling, clicking Building. She turned and stalked back the way we had come, no longer stately but angry, her face flushed, eyes glinting.

Is she mad that they're going to kill us?

I'd have liked to think that. I really would have. But she didn't look worried. She looked . . . thwarted.

Was she hoping for something else? Hoping they'd let us go? Hoping they'd let *her* go?

Oh.

I don't know why it took me so long to realize what she intended. My only defense is that the Building had been so shocking that I wasn't thinking clearly. But finally, finally, everything clicked together in my head.

Kilroy was here.

Then she left, that bitch.

You aren't one of us, are you?

Anna hadn't really called for help. She'd called for someone to take her place. And I had blundered in, thinking that somebody needed rescue and stupid enough to think that I might be the person to do the rescuing.

Me, lacking any blood of the holler people in my veins.

Because Cotgrave was my stepgrandfather, and that was an inelegant phrase and we'd all stopped using it and gone to other words, and maybe he'd been too confused at the end anyway to explain.

And now we were trapped in here with her.

She'd talked about running, but she'd been talking to Foxy. Foxy, whom she'd tried to keep out completely. Had she expected to trade me and be free? Had she assessed the situation and figured that it would be easier to get out with Foxy helping, that maybe the effigies wouldn't try to get her back if they had me instead?

I stared at her shoulders. If she could feel my eyes boring holes between her shoulder blades, she gave no sign.

She led the way down the spiral staircase, and I wanted to turn and run in the other direction, but that way lay the effigies and the Building and the creatures copying themselves in wood and bone, waiting for their masters to return.

So Foxy and I walked behind her. Uriah followed us, looking oddly lost without his escort.

The two headless ones were with us. The rest of the effigies were gathered around the edge of the roof, engaging in their wordless conversation, as they argued over whether to take us all apart into bones.

Anna had said that fewer of them would come with us after we went to the Building. This was certainly the least number I'd seen since we entered the voorish dome.

How long would it take for them to decide? Minutes? Hours? Years?

I didn't want to stick around to find out.

If we were going to escape, it had to be as soon as we left the Building. We might never get another chance.

I hoped Foxy was ready, too.

Don't be ridiculous. Foxy's probably way ahead of you. You're not the one who packed sandwiches and a handgun on this little jaunt.

The CIA had really missed out when they hadn't hired her. We'd probably be toppling governments on Mars by now.

We reached the square room. I set Bongo down because my back was going to give out. He was shaking badly, but he lunged for the end of the leash, pulling to get out of the Building.

"I'm with you, buddy," I muttered. "I want out of here too." I looked back at Foxy and jerked my head just a little, in the direction of the door.

She nodded, reached out, and grabbed Anna's wrist.

Anna looked briefly startled. Her brilliant red eyes flashed human brown and back again.

Foxy put her lips next to Anna's ear and hissed something.

Anna started to shake her head, but Foxy's grip on her wrist tightened. I could see polished nails digging into bone-white flesh.

Anna gave me a look that was pure rage and then seemed to deflate. She nodded once to Foxy.

Foxy released her.

"She won't do anything stupid now," she muttered, stepping in front of me. "Or I'll make her wish them things had kept her."

Apparently I wasn't the only one who had worked out Anna's plan to use me as a replacement.

Were we still going to run? Was she hoping that between the three of us, we could get far enough away that the effigies wouldn't find her? What was going on behind those red-brown eyes?

If I get far enough away, they'll give up. They have to give up.

Dear God, I hoped she was right about that.

I followed Foxy, following Anna. My stomach was churning with anticipation and terror. I could hear the tapping of the headless effigies following behind Foxy.

Would we run as soon as we got to the door? Outside the door? Down the street? Would Foxy give me a sign? Would I recognize the sign? Was *I* supposed to give her a sign?

The layered paper crunched under my feet as I crossed the threshold.

Anna had stopped a few feet from the opening. Bongo and I came out, and Foxy followed. I looked back over my shoulder and saw Uriah in the gloom, walking forward.

Without a word, without so much as a gesture, Anna reached down and picked up something lying at her feet.

It was a jagged piece of rebar. I wondered how long ago she'd placed it there, waiting for her moment.

She took three steps forward. Her skin was bone-white, and the moiré pattern blossomed around her like heat haze as she slammed the makeshift spear into Uriah's chest.

22

He fell backward. The blood was astonishingly bright on his white skin, and then he vanished into the gray shadows inside the Building.

My first thought was that it had been an accident.

This was incredibly stupid. I think I knew even at the time that it was stupid. But my brain just wasn't equipped to handle a murder happening in front of me. Therefore it couldn't have been a murder. Therefore it was an accident. Therefore we had to get help and call an ambulance and . . .

I took a step toward Uriah, and Foxy grabbed my arm.

My brain's frantic hamster-wheel running stopped. There were no ambulances in this place. There would be no help. Anna had murdered the other holler person in cold blood because it would make it easier to escape or he deserved it or she hated him for reasons of her own and it didn't matter because Foxy was dragging me now and Bongo was hauling on the end of the leash and we had to run.

So we ran.

Bongo had his back humped and his tail between his legs, but he still moved faster than any of us, choking as he strained against the collar. I couldn't run fast enough to keep him from doing it, but I did my best.

"It's all right," I gasped, as Foxy nearly stumbled trying to keep hold of me. "You can let go. I'm okay now."

"Good," she said. "Gave me a turn there. Hold on to your hickory."

I reached down the neck of my shirt and grabbed the string of wooden beads tighter.

In my head, I saw Uriah falling back, again and again. I hadn't known him. He was worse than a stranger. But it had been so fast, so irrevocable, I couldn't process it. I had to keep looking at the memory, over and over, trying to make it real.

Anna was a pale shape in front of us, running through the dark streets. She paused for us to catch up, her fierce eyes narrowing.

"Why?" I gasped. "Why kill him?"

She laughed. Her eyes flashed inhuman red. "To slow them down. They'll pay respects. They have to. It's why they exist. Now hurry!"

She took off again, dodging around a corner, and I ran, thinking of the small carved figures with their hands over their faces in grief. Would they mourn for Uriah? Would it buy us a little time?

Probably.

Probably not as much time as if the effigies had decided to take me in trade.

I don't trust her! I thought, and then I would have laughed at myself if I'd had enough breath, because it didn't matter if I trusted her or not, did it? I wasn't getting any better offers.

I had no idea where we were in the dead city, but I could see a line of trees ahead and above us. Was that the hillside we'd come down, from the place of white stones?

Hard to tell. We came such a long, long, long, long, long, long way, I thought bitterly.

Were we being pursued? I risked a glance over my shoulder, but the lights were too erratically placed. I didn't hear clicking, but surely the effigies couldn't be far behind.

I thought we might go back on the switchbacked path, but Anna made straight for the trees, scrambling up and over a low wall.

Bongo went over the wall like an antelope. I . . . didn't. It was only about shoulder height, but I had to leap and get my arms up on it, with my dog still yanking on the leash.

Adrenaline came to my rescue. I don't know that I could have done it if I hadn't been terrified and listening for pursuit. Also, Foxy got her shoulder under my ass and shoved.

"Didn't know we had that kind of relationship, Foxy," I panted.

"We live through this, hon, I'll even fart in front of you."

We were making jokes. We were making jokes while, in the back of my mind, a man fell down with a makeshift spear through his chest, blood on white skin. We were making jokes while unspeakable things chased us in the dark.

Maybe that's why we were making jokes.

I leaned down and caught her arm, hauling her up. My biceps screamed, but to hell with them.

Foxy teetered on the edge of the wall as one of her heels slipped, then got both feet up. I looked over her shoulder as I pulled and saw movement.

"Effigy!" I croaked.

Foxy swore, swung around, and drew her gun.

The two headless, four-legged ones that followed Anna came into view. I heard a hiss behind me as Anna saw them. "Will bullets stop them?" I asked.

"Let's find out," said Foxy, taking aim.

The gunshot woke echoes in the city like birds. Anna cried out, whether in surprise or grief, I couldn't tell.

The first bullet plunked into the body of the lead effigy. It staggered sideways, but kept coming. Its partner took the lead, the slack fabric of the neck beginning to sway back and forth, as if something inside was reaching through.

They reached the wall and stood on their hind legs.

The shot had knocked a hole out of the side of the first one. It leaked rags and sand and what looked like bits of pine needle and bark chips.

Foxy shot the second one in the shoulder, shattering the socket. It collapsed on that side, against the wall. The fabric began to move, more agitated, and I swore I heard something *snuffling* inside.

"Anna?" said Foxy, over her shoulder.

I looked up and saw, to my astonishment, that Anna's dead-white face was slicked with tears.

"Do it," she said, her voice shaking. "It's the only way."

Foxy emptied the clip into the effigies. She focused on the legs. They both fell, kicking feebly. The snuffling noises grew louder, and whatever was inside them began to jerk and twitch.

I didn't ask what it was. I had a horrible suspicion already.

Five drew no breaths . . . of the other two . . . but we will speak of that later.

We hadn't spoken of it after all. I hoped we never would.

Foxy slammed the empty gun back in her purse. "Come on," she said. "They'll have heard that."

We took off into the leafless forest.

The ground was dry and crackling underfoot. A whole army of effigies could have been after us and I wouldn't have been able to hear any of them over the sound of our footsteps and my own ragged breathing. Bongo was back to dragging me up the hillside.

The slope was steeper than it had looked on the endless switchbacks. There was no undergrowth, though, which helped. The trees were stark black in the gray, grim light.

Foxy began to fall behind. I didn't know whether to slow down or not. "Foxy?"

"I'm still here," she said.

"You want to take Bongo? He'll help pull you."

"I'm busy reloading, hon, and doing that while running is violating everything my granny ever taught me, but thanks."

And indeed, in a few minutes she caught back up again, and damn near started to outpace my dog and me.

I don't know how long we ran. Pain began to jab through my side with every step. How long would the effigies be arguing? Were they coming after us now? Were the things that hung from the ceiling even now detaching themselves, crawling over one another and down the walls, in a wave of clicking, rattling horror?

I looked over my shoulder and saw only darkness. Was it moving? I couldn't look long enough to tell. The footing was too uneven and Bongo wasn't slowing down.

"Anna?" I called. "Are we close?"

She turned her head to answer. I heard "Not much far—" and then something crashed through the trees to our left.

Bongo screamed. If you've never heard a dog scream before, you're lucky. It started like a bay but went high and terrible. He pulled up short, and I threw myself over him, desperate to get between my dog and whatever the crashing thing was.

Foxy yelled, "Get down!" but I was already down. It was probably for the best, because I heard a gunshot over my head and actually felt heat hit the back of my neck. I might have been imagining that, I don't know.

The muzzle flash illuminated the fan-headed effigy. I don't know how much damage the shot did. There wasn't enough light to tell. All I knew was that Foxy grabbed me by the collar and yanked me upright and Bongo was running again, nearly breaking my neck as his leash got tangled in my legs, but we straightened out somehow and Anna was shouting, and suddenly in front of us, a sight I'd never thought would be welcome, lay the edge of the trees and the beginning of the hill of white stones.

There was no moon in the sky, but the light on the hill was cold and blue and looked more like moonlight than it looked like anything else. The stones glowed white and the twisted carvings moved and wriggled and shifted in the corner of my eyes, as if they would come to life at any moment.

My side ached like someone had jammed a knife in it—
or a piece of rebar sharpened like a spear
—but the sight of the hill gave me a burst of energy.

We ran.

"The wicker tunnel," I gasped. "Back to the house."

What good being at the house was going to do me, I don't know, except that my truck was there. If I could get to the truck, I'd throw Foxy and Anna and Bongo in it and drive until we ran out of gas. Surely the effigies couldn't chase us that far, or if they did, I could get to other people. Other people seemed like a talisman.

I'd go to . . . to a mall or a Walmart or something. Surely unholy abominations wouldn't follow me to Walmart.

The white stone loomed before us. Even if I hadn't been wrapped in hickory beads, I doubt I'd have felt anything but disgust. We skidded around the edge of the depression and kept going.

"On your right," said Foxy, cool as a cucumber, and I looked over and saw a dark shape running alongside us. Flanking, not moving in. Foxy shot at it, missed, swore, and then managed to put another bullet in it. It fell down and rolled down the hillside. I didn't stay long enough to see if it got up again.

It was easier going now. The ground was less treacherous and easier to see. Unfortunately, I was also starting to hit the last of my strength. Even Bongo was slowing down, his panting turning into a wheeze.

Foxy had one hand on her chest, the other holding the gun by her side.

"Foxy!"

"Don't you worry," she panted. "I ain't dying yet."

"Anna, we have to rest!" I yelled.

She turned. She was the color of bone in the moonless moonlight, and her eyes glinted.

She didn't say a word, just pointed.

I looked over my shoulder and saw them.

A tide of effigies poured over the hillside toward us. I couldn't see where one left off and one began, only a wave of clicking sticks and bones, heaving like the sea.

Suddenly I wasn't tired anymore.

Bongo was surprised to find there was slack on the leash suddenly, but he didn't complain. I think at that moment, in sheer terror, I could have picked Foxy up and carried her.

We tore past the three stones lying on the ground. The litany of the twisted ones started up in my head, in time to my stride.

And I
twisted
myself
around
like the

twisted

ones

but it didn't quite match and my mind fell back on something else

sticks and stones

and broken bones

sticks and stones

and broken bones

and I heard another gunshot from somewhere and then the wicker tunnel was *right there* and I ran for it.

Anna skidded to a halt in front of it. I wanted to scream at her, to demand to know why she was stopping—she had to go *through*—and then I saw it.

The mud-dauber effigy stood in front of the tunnel mouth, blocking the way.

I stopped. I knew the tide of effigies was getting closer behind us, but all I could think of was Foxy and her gun.

It took far too long for Foxy to arrive, and her skin had an unhealthy gray tint, or maybe it was the un-moonlight. But she looked at the effigy and grunted and raised her pistol.

Anna was looking behind us, and I didn't dare look because I knew the tide of effigies was far too close and at any moment they were going to break over us like the sea.

The gunshots sounded like they came from a long way away, or maybe I was deaf from the previous shots. *Of course, I was supposed to wear ear protection*, I thought vaguely, which, going back to what I said earlier about thinking very insipid things when I'm in mortal terror.

The mud-dauber staggered sideways and fell down.

It wasn't dead. It grabbed for Bongo as he passed, and one of those long stick legs closed over my dog's haunch.

I shrieked in rage and stomped down on the sticks, hearing them crunch under my boot. The mud-dauber effigy made an almost mechanical buzzing noise, legs drawing up like a dying spider, but I stomped on it again, because *how dare it touch my dog?*

Foxy was already in the tunnel. Bongo was cowering at her feet. I turned to find Anna, to yell "Go!" and something grabbed me from behind.

The grip was inhumanly strong and spun me around. I looked down at my arms, expecting to see bone and twig, expecting to scream in horror.

I saw hands.

The tide of effigies broke around us, became a semicircle of staring, eyeless horrors, and Anna held me pinned in the mouth of the tunnel. Bongo's leash was still around my left wrist, and my arm twisted painfully backward as he tugged on it.

"Take her!" she shouted. "Let me go! I'm done, you hear me? I brought you a replacement. It's not my fault she isn't good enough. I can't do what you want anymore. *Now let me go!*"

Well. It's not like I hadn't guessed.

What a disappointment it must have been when I arrived, when it looked like the effigies had decided I wouldn't make a replacement after all.

"They won't take me," I said. "They won't. You know they won't."

"Shut up!" I could feel Anna's chest against my back, hear her breath rasping in and out. She was shaking violently.

The effigies, by contrast, stood like statues, unmoving. For a moment it seemed as if they were nothing but a mad artist's assemblage, nothing that had ever been or could ever be alive.

Then one, then another began to click.

Anna's shaking increased, until I was vibrating with it too.

The clicking spread throughout the crowd, a parliament of beetles rattling their shells together.

I felt something under my heel and realized I was standing on the mud-dauber's leg again, and half dead, blown apart, it was still opening and closing its twig fingers.

I recoiled, horrified. Anna's grip was slipping. I could feel her shaking her head.

"No . . . ," she whispered. "No, oh no . . ."

"I can't shoot her, hon," said Foxy softly. "Not without hitting you."

The clicking grew louder and louder. I watched an effigy in the foreground turn its head sideways and let it ratchet backward, ticking like a clock.

Bongo pulled on the leash again.

And I twisted myself around like the twisted ones. . . .

There is a trick that dog owners do with a leash. You've seen it done. Very likely you've done it yourself. It's a kind of pirouette, where the dog has wrapped the leash around you, and you spin to unwrap it. Otherwise the leash is around your legs and you're hobbled and likely to fall over.

Bongo's leash was behind Anna's legs. I sent him a silent

apology, yanked my left arm forward so that the leash pulled tight, and threw myself backward.

She shrieked and fell. I landed on top of her. Bongo yawped in outrage. Something popped inside my wrist.

The effigies took a step forward, clicking.

I rolled sideways, over my injured wrist. It hurt like blazes, but Anna had lost her grip on my arms. I started to crawl toward the tunnel, trying to drag the leash out from under her as I went.

Foxy grabbed my shoulders, hauling me into the tunnel. Bongo was yanking on the leash, and every tug felt like someone was hitting my wrist with a hammer.

Behind me, Anna began to scream.

I heard Foxy emptying her gun. The report deafened me. I crawled away, into the wicker tunnel, my head ringing and my wrist throbbing, trying to get to my knees so that I could pull the leash off my left wrist. Bongo barked furiously, which didn't help at all.

Then Foxy was picking me up and I somehow got the leash transferred and we staggered together down the tunnel. She said something, but I couldn't hear it over the ringing in my head.

A long time later, it seemed to me, I realized that Anna's screaming had stopped. I didn't know when it had stopped. Maybe when Foxy had fired her gun.

Leaning on each other like two drunks in a three-legged race, we stumbled toward the bottom of the tunnel. I knew it couldn't have been more than a few minutes, but it seemed to take an age of the earth. My lungs were raw from running, a pain that I welcomed because it had nothing to do with the pain in my wrist.

"Are they following us?" I asked.

"Don't know. Don't think so."

Bongo seemed to agree with her. He wasn't running, but shuffling along, nose to the ground, a tired dog ready to go home.

It occurred to me that it was a good thing he was a coonhound. A border collie would still be up on the hillside, trying to herd the effigies into the proper formation. Although a border collie might have been smart enough not to go up the hill in the first place, so it was probably a wash. . . .

"Why wouldn't they follow us?" I wondered out loud.

"Maybe we don't have anything they want."

No. No, I didn't have anything they wanted. My blood was all human and I was no replacement for Anna.

We reached the bottom of the tunnel. Our footing evened out. Bongo threaded through the opening and led us into the dark trees.

"Think we can get somebody to come back here and brick this thing up?" I asked.

I couldn't make out Foxy's face in the moonlight, but I felt her frown. "Not sure you can brick up a bunch of dead trees, but we can give it a go. Skip might know."

We were relying on Bongo now to get us home. It was dark and I had no idea where we were. I kept listening for the woodpecker knock of hagstones, but I didn't hear a thing.

Is it over?

Is it ever going to be over?

At last, far in the distance, I saw a light. I'd left the back porch light on.

It looked like a beacon. The real world. The normal world. Even if it was my grandmother's horrible hoarder house, it was just a dead woman with too much stuff. There were thousands of them in the real world, and it was a thing that real people dealt with.

I blinked back tears.

We hobbled around the side of the house. Bongo was starting to pull again. He wanted dinner. I wanted to fall down and not get up again for days. Years. Maybe ever.

I took a step up onto the porch.

And stopped.

The front door was open.

23

The screen was pushed back against the wall, and the inner door stood wide. The hallway was a square of darkness.

"Foxy," I said quietly, "tell me that Tomas and Skip came over to the house while we were gone."

"Don't know, hon." She reached into her purse and took out the gun.

"Have you got any more bullets?"

"No."

I pulled Bongo back from the porch.

"Let's go to my place," said Foxy. "Worse comes to worse, we can—"

I never did find out what we could do because I caught a flash of movement over her shoulder.

The deer effigy came around the front of the truck, skull gleaming white, running on all fours.

I grabbed Foxy with my injured wrist and practically threw

her into the house. I think I screamed something, probably "Shit!" or maybe I just screamed because my wrist throbbed with a deep, nauseating, yes-something-is-now-broken pain.

Bongo let out a low, awful growl and spun around, and I realized he was about to attack the damnable thing. I hauled him back by the collar and somehow we all fit inside the open doorway and I slammed the door in the effigy's face.

It was the screen door. It smashed into the wire mesh, tore it open, and I fell down over Bongo while it pawed through the opening, trying to get in.

Foxy grabbed the inner door and kicked me hard. I had a split second of hurt confusion, then realized she was rolling me out of the way.

The door hit the effigy with a sound like a baseball bat hitting a board, and then suddenly there was silence.

I curled around my wrist and my dog, making small, uhn-uhn-uhn noises of agony. I needed a doctor. I needed this to not be happening. I needed the world to go back to being a place I understood.

I was not going to get any of those things, so I let Foxy haul me to my feet.

We stood there for a moment, in an awkward half embrace. Her lips were bluish and I knew that was bad and I knew there was nothing I could do about it.

She pulled my jacket off me, which was confusing. When the sleeve went over my wrist, it was up there in the worst pains I've ever felt in my life. Then she started trying to put it back on me, which was even more confusing.

"What . . . ? What are you . . . ?"

"Zip up the jacket with your bad arm in front," she said. "It ain't a sling, but it's as good as we're gonna get in the next five minutes."

I let her work the zipper. With my arm tucked under my breasts, it didn't feel good, but at least I wasn't banging it around.

"What do we do?" I said.

"Wait until morning, I guess. Skip and Tomas'll come over to check on us."

I had no idea what time it was. I had no idea what *day* it was.

"We can call them," I said. "From the landline. If we just . . ."

I heard a clattering *tok-tok-tok* on the glass window and stiffened.

"It's at the window, isn't it?"

"Yep."

I turned.

The sofa still blocked most of the window, but I could see a narrow sliver of glass to one side, and the deer skull gazed at me eyelessly through it.

Tap . . . tap . . .

"You don't want me!" I screamed at the effigy. "You don't want me! I can't do what you want!"

It tilted its awful upside-down head. I would swear for an instant the damn thing looked confused.

How much individuality did they have? Had this one imprinted on me, as it hung in the tree, watching? Had it been separated from the others? Did it know that I wasn't able to make more of its masters?

I don't know why I stared so long. I'd seen enough of the effigies to last a lifetime. But there it was, one leg raised to tap against the glass. Its rib cage looked oddly human from here.

Maybe it was.

Dear God, what was it made out of?

Who was it made out of?

The two headless ones that had followed Anna around, had they been made from the bones of her children, as I suspected? And this one—I had thought of it as deer bones, but apart from the skull, I don't know a deer from a human.

Cotgrave had died in the woods, and the scavengers had gotten to him. Closed-casket funeral.

Had the scavengers been simple animals, or something more?

Who was in the effigy that looked in the window of Cotgrave's bedroom, who knocked on the front door of the house, trying to get in?

Trying to get *back* in?

"Of course . . . ," I whispered. "You don't smash the windows of your own house. You tap on the glass and wait for someone to let you back in."

Foxy gave me a worried look. "You lost me, hon."

"It's Cotgrave," I said. "That effigy. It's made of Cotgrave. It's got to be."

"Your granddaddy had a deer's head?"

"Okay, not just of Cotgrave." I shook my head. "But that's why it keeps trying to get in. It doesn't want us. It wants to come home."

"I hope you're not suggesting we open the door and let it in," said Foxy.

I shook my head. I wasn't quite that far gone.

But what would it do? a little voice whispered in my head. *Would it attack you? Was it even trying to attack you in the woods, or did it recognize its granddaughter and was trying to keep you from going up the hill? Maybe it would just go to Cotgrave's bedroom and curl up on the bed? Sit in his favorite chair and read the paper?*

I bit my knuckle to keep from breaking into hysterical laughter.

"Come on," said Foxy. "Just like last time. We just gotta wait until it goes away. Then we'll call Skip and Tomas and . . ."

Bongo began to growl again.

She made an exasperated sound. "Buddy, you're not helping."

Yeah, Bongo, just ignore the monster at the door. That monster is old news now. . . .

I reached down to put my hand on his head and realized that he wasn't facing the door.

He was facing down the hallway.

"Foxy," I said quietly.

She turned to me, and I pointed.

In the shadows of the hall, something moved.

I remembered suddenly the way that there had seemed to be two effigies chasing us in the tunnel.

I remembered the Building, and that the effigies could reproduce themselves.

I remembered these things much too late.

That movement was our only warning before an effigy erupted from my grandmother's doll room.

If it had been made entirely out of doll parts, I would probably have stood there and laughed, high-pitched and awful, while it took me apart. It would have been too much, too horrible, too movie-monster cliché. The killer doll. The china doll with the long fingernails and the murderous expression.

But the effigy was made out of many more things. Cotgrave's effigy had constructed it (Lovingly? Vengefully? Who knew?) out of the remnants of his dead wife's hoarding.

Maybe that was why I saw it so rarely. Maybe it wasn't hiding during the day. Maybe it was busy *working*.

The hoarding effigy was a papier-mâché of old newspapers, layered like the Building itself, furred with bits of cardboard boxes and old bottles of cleaner. There were doll parts, yes, dozens of them, little plastic limbs making up a rib cage built of bright pink severed legs, but they enclosed a jumble of wire coat hangers and broken plates.

The ancient typewriter had been broken apart, and the letters, with their metal shafts, made claws that gouged the floor and tore the carpet runner into long stringy threads.

I screamed. Foxy swore. Bongo's growl erupted into a high, awful bark, the sound of a dog desperately calling for help that he knows isn't going to come.

I hauled Bongo back by the collar, into the kitchen. We

couldn't go out the door, because the other effigy was there, and the back door was closed off, and I knew we were trapped like rats, I knew it, but I didn't know where else to go.

The hoarding effigy had no such concerns. If it hadn't skidded when it hit the linoleum, I imagine we would have died right there. But as soon as it reached the kitchen, its legs went sideways and it crashed into the counter and that bought us a small amount of time.

We went up the stairs. I only had one hand and I had to use it on Bongo, but he didn't object to running. Foxy was right behind me, knocking boxes loose and throwing them down onto the effigy. Her heart might be about to give out, but she wasn't going down alone.

At the top of the stairs, one door stood open. It was the room we'd watched the effigy from, approximately a thousand years ago. Some furniture, a man-high stack of old newspapers, and not much else. "Foxy! In here!"

We slammed the door shut behind us. I set my back against it while Foxy, having two good arms, grabbed a nightstand and started dragging it over.

The effigy hit the door with enough force to knock me forward an inch or two. I don't know if the metal claws made it hard to work doorknobs or if it didn't understand them, but it didn't seem to want to open the door so much as smash it down. I set my feet, trying to hold it until Foxy could get the furniture in place.

This effigy did not seem interested in scaring us. This one wanted us dead.

I thought of the gleeful malice that exuded from my grandmother's house and wasn't at all surprised. How could a creature made out of the essence of this place *not* want us all dead?

"This is bad," said Foxy.

"I *knew* it!" I said. "I thought I'd put doll parts in the truck and then there weren't any in the morning and I thought I was nuts, but I *wasn't*. It took them. Cotgrave's effigy took them."

"That's all very interesting," said Foxy, "but it's beating down the door, hon."

"Yes, I'd noticed."

The nightstand looked painfully fragile. I had enough space to brace the door with my good shoulder while she grabbed the other one. The doorframe rocked with the effigy's blows. I heard wood splintering an inch from my head.

Heeeere's Johnny! I thought. And then, *Oh God, if only I had an ax!*

"We've got to get out of here," I said. "This isn't going to hold."

"There's the window," said Foxy. "We can go out on the porch roof, but after that, we're running real thin on options."

Slam. Slam. Slam.

Sudden silence. I could hear claws clicking as the effigy stepped back from the door. What was it doing?

I heard it walking down the hall, into the next room. That one had been full of junk. A regular firetrap.

An idea crystalized into my head, as cold and clear as ice.

This house. This fucking awful house. Why had I fought

so hard for it? Let the monsters have it. The only thing I cared about was my friend and my dog.

Well, and my laptop, and that was still in the truck. Thank God.

If I did it wrong, we were going to die.

If I did nothing, we were still probably going to die.

"Foxy," I said quietly. "You have a lighter, don't you?"

"Yeah."

"Give it to me."

She didn't ask questions, just dug into her purse and handed it over. It was an old Zippo, weighty in my hand.

"You about to do what I think you're about to do, hon?"

"Burn this place to the ground, you mean?"

"Hey, it's your house. But I'd prefer to be outside before we do that."

"We'll jump down from the porch roof onto my truck."

Foxy gave me a dubious look.

Crack. The effigy hit the wall between us. Apparently it had decided that drywall was easier to get through than wood.

It was right. Metal flashed as its claws shredded through the wallboard. I didn't know how much space there was between studs or if there were pipes in the way, but I wasn't about to stick around to find out.

" . . . the truck, you say?" said Foxy.

"Get the window open," I said. I bent down, flicked the Zippo open—God bless stupid teenage me, who had spent hours learning to flip open my boyfriend's Zippo so that I could look cool—and lit the stack of newspapers on fire.

They caught with remarkable enthusiasm. I lit the carpet on fire just for good measure. The fire department could yell at me if we lived.

There was a monster coming in through the wall and I was in the top floor of a house, lighting it on fire, and what I felt was a sudden wild exhilaration.

Let it burn. Let this awful place and its secrets and its nightmares and the dead I hadn't asked for and the junk I never wanted burn.

The effigy got one of its arms through the wall and began tearing at the hole to widen it. I shoved the Zippo in my pocket.

Foxy kicked the window screen out. I heard the crackling of the newspapers and smelled burning. It was a very cheerful, campfire sort of smell, desperately incongruous given the circumstances.

I still don't know how we got Bongo through the window. I may have picked him up with one arm while Foxy pulled. But we got him out, and then I climbed out onto the porch roof after, praying he didn't take it in his head to run off the edge and break his neck and my other wrist in the process.

"Now the truck?" said Foxy.

"After the fire's caught," I said, looking over my shoulder. "I want that thing to burn, not be chasing us around the woods."

"Can't argue with that." She eyed the distance to the truck. "Think I can make it. Don't know how you'll convince the dog to do it, but we'll figure it out."

Presumably Cotgrave's effigy was still on the porch somewhere. It had been trying to get into the house. I just had to hope that it had gotten in, and the fire would take it out, too.

Houses are supposed to catch fire really fast. In all the movies it goes from a shorted-out Christmas-tree light to flames shooting out of the roof in like two minutes. And you'd think this house, made of ancient materials and packed to the rafters with tinder, would practically explode into flame.

We waited on the roof and it didn't happen.

I could still see the orange flicker on the walls and obviously something inside was on fire, but my hope that the whole place would turn into an inferno and take the effigy with it was starting to fade.

"Okay," I said. "Let's get to the truck—"

The hoarder effigy hit the open window like a freight train.

Its shoulders were too broad to get through. It turned and scrabbled at the windowsill, cracking the wood, slamming into it over and over. Bits of bone flew off. I watched one of the doll-leg ribs pop loose, then another, as it tried to drag itself through.

Something went *Fwooooosh!*

I don't know what caught, but suddenly the fire was no longer an orange glow but alive. It roared as if it was inhaling, and I heard glass shattering as the windows broke.

"Come on!" shouted Foxy. I could barely hear her over the fire, but when I turned, she was standing on top of my truck, Bongo in her arms. "Get the hell out of there!"

The effigy strained at the window. Another set of ribs broke off. Parts of its papery guts were spilling out onto the roof, and then a spark hit them and they, too, began to burn.

I ran for the corner of the porch roof.

Foxy and Bongo slid down into the bed of the truck and I vaulted the gap like an Olympic sprinter. I had been secretly afraid I'd come up short, and instead I nearly went over the other side. The roof rack stopped me. There was going to be an almighty dent in the roof, but who the hell cared anymore?

I flung myself into the bed, over the side, and opened the driver's side door. It seemed like an eternity while I dug for the keys—come on, Mouse, this is not the time to realize you've left them on the coffee table—but found them in the bottom of my pocket and slammed them into the ignition.

The truck started. My beautiful, faithful truck. I slammed it into reverse, glanced behind me out of habit, and then the burning effigy landed on the hood.

The truck hood dented under its weight. I didn't care about that—a truck without dents in it is probably a stupid truck anyway—but it was *touching* my *truck*.

I didn't even let *boyfriends* drive my truck.

Get it off get it off get it off this is mine this is mine you can't touch it it's on it it's on me *GET IT OFF!*

It glared at me eyelessly, its sides heaving as if were panting. The plastic doll legs had charred and melted. So had most of the bottles. One burned like a star—some kind of accelerant, God only knows what.

If it could get to me, I would burn, too.

If it could get to me, it would take me apart and then Cotgrave's effigy would come along and build me back up out of bones and all three of us would roam the woods together in a family, clicking and clacking with stones in our chest and ribs made of doll arms *and we could twist ourselves around like the twisted ones and lie down like the dead ones and . . .*

I slammed my foot on the accelerator.

Foxy and Bongo had thrown themselves flat in the truck bed. Maybe it didn't know they were there. Maybe it didn't care. I don't know. Maybe there was something of my grandmother in it, and there was no one she hated like her own flesh and blood.

I shot down the driveway in reverse while it clawed at the windshield with the typewriter keys, leaving huge scrapes in the paint and scratching the glass. It got a claw hooked under the windshield wipers and somehow it held on, even when the truck went off the driveway and hit the ditch and bounced hard. I had one hand to drive with and steering wasn't helping.

I threw the car into drive and plowed forward until I nearly hit the burning porch, then slammed on the brakes. I heard a yelp from the back, but I didn't dare stop to check on my passengers.

The effigy slid off the hood and rolled in the front yard, painted orange by the flames leaping from the roof. It didn't move.

I backed the truck away, leaving ruts in the yard, and then Cotgrave's effigy came down from the porch.

I gritted my teeth, ready to run it down if I had to . . . but I didn't.

It ignored the truck. It picked its way down the stairs, moving on four legs, down to the burning effigy. Then it curled itself up, like Bongo does when he goes to sleep, and lay down against the other one.

Cotgrave and his wife, I thought, watching the flames from the hoarder effigy lick across the deer hide. *Or Cotgrave and his house. Maybe it doesn't matter which.*

The roof fell in, and I pulled down the driveway and away from that terrible ruined house forever.

24

ell.

That is the end of the story, or at least of most of it. Once we were a few miles away, Foxy banged on the back window until I pulled over. Then she drove me to the ER and spun a story I can't even remember about squatters breaking into the house and a fire. My wrist was broken, but at least it was my left wrist, so I could still drive after they put it in the cast.

Officer Bob came out to take my statement. I told him I didn't know much. I hadn't seen anybody I could pick out of a lineup. It had been dark and Bongo was the only reason I woke up at all, and probably the only reason I hadn't died in the fire.

I don't know if he believed me, but he was kind about it, and that counted for a lot.

At some point Foxy left. Tomas came and got her. I think she must have called from the ER. I kept asking if she would be okay in the house, if the house was safe now, if anything would happen. There were other people around, so I couldn't say what I wanted to, just grabbed her sleeve and stared at her.

"It's all right," she said. "It's all right. They never wanted me. Ain't got the parts they need. I been there for years and nothing's ever happened."

A long time later I thought that maybe Anna might want revenge, but by then Foxy was long gone, and all I could do was beg Officer Bob to look in on them and make sure they were all right.

Pretty much as soon as they released me from the ER, I got in my truck and drove into town. Enid took one look at me and let me sleep in the back of the coffee shop for a couple of hours.

I told her there had been a fire but I honestly didn't remember much.

When I had about five hours of sleep in me, I drove to Pittsburgh. I stopped only at brightly lit places. Even those were too dim. I wanted the world to be lit up with halogens, with great blazes of artificial light. I wanted to see every corner of the world so I knew nothing could be hiding in it.

I tuned the radio to something loud and brassy and sang along with everything, whether I knew the words or not.

I got home and sat in the truck for probably an hour. Bongo was confused, but he'd gotten a cheeseburger at the last stop, so he was in a congenial mood.

The DJ came on to tell us what the last song had been, and I was puzzled for a moment that I wasn't being told about how my pledge would help support quality programming like this, and then I put my forehead on the steering wheel and cried hysterically for what felt like another hour.

Then I went inside and turned on every light in the house.

I never told my dad the truth. How could I? The official word was that I was asleep and somebody broke in, and Bongo woke me up. There was a struggle and my wrist got broken and a fire started somewhere in all the junk. Foxy was drinking out on the front porch and heard Bongo freaking out, so she came and managed to pull me out. I was still confused from being half asleep and it was dark. No, I don't know who'd break in. No, I didn't get a good look at anybody.

Dad apologized for how it had all gone down, and I told him there was no way he could have known. The doctor's got him pretty well medicated right now, trying to deal with the rattle in his lungs. I don't know how much longer he's got, and I'm not going to tear up what peace he's got trying to tell him the truth.

The insurance company didn't investigate the fire too hard. The place had obviously been a firetrap and we weren't asking for money to rebuild, just to have someone with a backhoe knock the whole place down and fill in the basement. Foxy says the stone's gone. I don't know if they did that, or if it was someone else. If it really was a signpost, maybe the effigies came and fetched it back, now that they didn't need it anymore.

I prefer to think it was the people with the backhoe.

The insurance company sent Dad what remained from

the settlement and he sent it to me. I looked at the check—six thousand dollars, a lot of money by my standards—and started crying. I needed the money and I couldn't keep it. Even the thought of cashing that check made me want to throw up. Anything I bought with that money would be tainted. If I tried to make a house payment with it, then my grandmother would own a little bit of my house. I couldn't do it.

I tried to send it to Foxy, and she refused. "I ain't gonna take money for arson, hon."

I tossed and turned for three nights before I finally got an idea and sent the whole damn thing to North Carolina Public Radio in memory of Freddy Cotgrave. I got the tax break, and maybe that's worth something.

Obviously the Green Book was never found. If it didn't burn, it's probably buried somewhere in the pile of rubble left from the house. I've got the manuscript, though. I didn't want that either, but Tomas had been reading it back at Foxy's place when the house burned.

They put it in an envelope and mailed it to me. It was a repeat of the insurance check—I cried. I wanted to throw up. I put it in the trash. I went back out and took it out of the trash.

I tried to put it in a drawer and it felt like there was a snake in the room. Every time I went into the back bedroom, I could feel it lurking there.

Eventually I rented a safe-deposit box. They're not that expensive, as it turns out. Now the bank can worry about it.

I suppose it goes without saying that I've pretty well lost my shit. My aunt wants me to see a therapist, but what am I going to tell them? There's no therapist in the world who will believe the truth, and I don't want to have to sit and lie to someone for sixty dollars an hour.

Hell, how do you tell someone, *I nearly spent the rest of my life giving birth to monsters in a city full of walking sticks and bones?* They'd have you on antipsychotics so fast that your head would spin, and that wouldn't help. I wish to God there was a medication that would make it all go away, but if there was, maybe I'd forget to watch for holler people. Maybe I wouldn't be so lucky next time.

It's better than it was. Bongo helps a lot. I can leave the house, and as long as I'm in my truck or someplace with people, I'm pretty okay. I put hickory twigs in all the windows, but that just looks like a weird decorating choice.

Do you know what I think about the most, though? It's not Cotgrave's effigy, lonely and wandering the woods near his dead wife's house until he had a chance to build her up again out of parts. It's not the stones or the voorish dome or the fact that there's got to be other cities out there like the one in Wales, maybe less dead, full of the holler people and their servants.

It's the linoleum in my grandmother's kitchen.

When the hoarder effigy reached the kitchen, it skidded. Its feet nearly went out from under it. That's probably the only reason we made it to the stairs.

Three whole lives, hinging on shitty seventies linoleum. If she'd left the original hardwood, we'd be dead. Everybody talks about how awful it is that people cover up the nice wood floors in houses, and it turned out to save my life.

I feel like the world must be full of things like that. Stupid minor things nobody pays attention to, and then one day you pick up the umbrella stand you've been meaning to throw out and beat the killer over the head with it, or you trip over the pizza boxes that you meant to throw out and the killer gets you instead.

Things like dog leashes or hickory beads.

I still carry the beads with me. If I leave them at home, I panic and have to go back. They've become a security blanket. As long as I've got them, I can probably see the holler people coming.

Foxy and I still talk. Well, text mostly. After our little jaunt, she allowed as how a cell phone might be useful to have around, and Tomas set her up with a cheap one. She likes texting. I think she'd communicate entirely in emojis and smiley faces if she could. Skip is fine. Tomas gets hassled sometimes by people who think that anybody like him must be from another country, but that's nothing new. Foxy went on a new heart medication after Skip badgered her into it. She says it makes her cranky, but I remember how blue her lips would get and I'm glad she's on it.

No effigies in the woods. No holler people. If they're still back there—and of course they're still back there—everything's very quiet.

"Why don't you move?" I asked her, one of the few times that we talked instead of texting.

"With what money?" asked Foxy. "Ain't nobody gonna buy this crappy piece of dirt out here, and my social security ain't gonna pay for a house anywhere else."

"I could help," I promised recklessly. Half the time my own mortgage was a struggle, but I'd bring all three of them up to Pittsburgh if I had to.

"Nah. It's fine, hon. No different from living by a dump or one of them toxic waste things. I keep my hickory and I don't go walking in the woods on that side."

A long silence. I heard the soft static of the line. Even after I got my phone fixed, Foxy's connection wasn't good.

I wondered if she was thinking about Anna too.

I should hate Anna for what she did. I know I should. She would have sold me for her own freedom without a second thought.

But I think of what it must have been like, walking the corridors of that dead city, seeing nothing but monsters around you. When she found out she was pregnant, was she hopeful? Did she think that maybe it would be more company than Uriah and the effigies? And what kind of monstrous midwife had attended her, what claws of bone and twig and wire reached out to catch her firstborn?

Was it easier, after she stopped being able to carry a child? *It doesn't work anymore. I can't do what they want.*

Did she just stop caring? Or was she still hoping, every time? Did she plead her case to the Building, to the things hanging from the ceiling? Did they have a long, rattling conference about her fate?

In the end, did the effigies drag her to the white stone anyway?

Sometimes at night I wake up thinking I'm her and that if I

turn my head I'll find out that I didn't get out of the dome after all. If I open my eyes there will be effigies around me, and the weight on my legs won't be Bongo but something made out of his bones.

It takes me a long time after that to turn on the light.

No, I don't hate Anna. If she hadn't called me, maybe I'd be able to sleep at night. Maybe I wouldn't think about monsters pressing against the walls of the world, effigies making more and more copies of themselves, waiting for their masters to come home.

Or until they overflow the hills and break through.

But I still can't hate her. Sometimes I even feel guilty. Here I am, trembling and quaking in the dark, at the mere possibility of taking her place. What right do I have to be so broken, when she carried on, year after year, decade after decade?

All those years in the dead city, and she survived. I couldn't have done that. Maybe that was the gift of her inhuman blood, that she didn't kill herself or curl into a ball and give up. The Lady Cassap, the narrator of the Green Book said, had been burned alive. *And I wondered whether she cared, after all the strange things she had done . . .*

Perhaps that's what set the holler people apart, not the white skin and the red eyes, but the ability to be burned alive and not care or to walk a dead city for decades and not go mad.

"Do you think she's still back there?" I asked. Trying not to think of Anna, alone, having murdered the last of her human company. Anna, not aging fast enough, part of the effigies' desperate, twisted breeding program to bring back their old masters.

"No," said Foxy slowly. "No, I think maybe she didn't make it."

After she hung up, I stared at the phone and remembered how Anna's screaming had stopped after Foxy had fired her last bullets.

And I knew that I was never going to ask, and thus Foxy was never going to have to lie to me about what had happened.

I hoped like hell that she was right.

AUTHOR'S NOTE

Astute readers will have noticed immediately that the Green Book is the diary from Arthur Machen's found manuscript story, "The White People." Published in 1904, this is one of the great classics of horror. (His novel *The Great God Pan* gets a lot more press, but for my money, "The White People" is far superior.)

Now, I love a good found manuscript story as much as the next person, but one plot contrivance that drives me up the wall is "we found the manuscript, and then we lost it, and now I am re-creating it as best I can." These "re-creations" often read like the narrator conveniently had a photographic memory, even under extreme duress, capable of casually re-creating a hundred pages, usually handwritten, without much effort.

In my own experience, that's just not how memory works. So when I was writing Cotgrave's version of the Green Book, I wrote down as much as I could remember of "The White People" without referring back to the original, including noting all the bits where I could not, for the life of me, remember what came next. Eventually, I would go back and clean things up, add in more references and more direct quotes, but I tried very hard to preserve the initial experience of trying to transcribe a memory of a rambling, dreamlike narrative.

Another thing that has always frustrated me about found manuscript stories is how uncritically they're read by the narrator. Not for truth, but for style. Half the writers and all the editors I know would spontaneously generate a red pen and begin making corrections immediately. So I couldn't resist giving Mouse the opportunity to make editorial comments of her own.

I am, for the most part, a reteller of fairy tales, but retelling pulp horror is really not so different. There is the same process of trying to find the bones of the story, of throwing in references for the reader to pick out and (hopefully) feel a sense of smugness at having gotten the joke. In this case, however, Machen left many things ambiguous. The whole question of what the white stone's carvings looked like is never mentioned, and a great many details go unresolved. What's a writer to do?

Well, Lovecraft, bless his heart (that is a *Southern* bless his heart, in case anyone is curious), wrote a letter about "The White People" to a contemporary explaining what was going on with the stone, that it was clearly two monstrous creatures copulating, and that witnessing this accidentally got the narrator pregnant. Which is certainly one explanation. Lovecraft assumed that the narrator, horrified, would have killed herself to end the pregnancy. I, being me, had a slightly different interpretation of how such things would actually go down, and with one thing and another, that interpretation became *The Twisted Ones*.

They say all books are in dialogue with other books, and I can't speak to whether that's true or not. I can say, though, that this novel is in dialogue with a letter written about a short story that was itself about a book . . . and even typing that sentence out makes my head hurt.

Many thanks to my editor, Navah Wolfe, for asking to see the manuscript based on nothing more than a joke on Twitter, to my long-suffering agent Helen Breitwieser, who patiently tries to sell whatever genre I've decided to write this week, to my husband, Kevin, and my goat-wielding cheerleader Andrea. I could probably write books without you guys, but they would not be nearly so good and nobody would read them, so thank you for keeping me from embarrassing myself in front of the readers.

ABOUT THE AUTHOR

T. Kingfisher is the award-winning author of multiple novels, including *Clockwork Boys* and *The Seventh Bride*. When not cooking up weird fiction, she wanders around the garden taking pictures of interesting bugs. She lives in North Carolina with her husband, hounds, chickens, and an extremely bossy cat. Find her online at redwombatstudio.com.